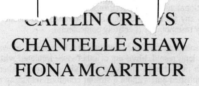

CAITLIN CREWS
CHANTELLE SHAW
FIONA McARTHUR

MILLS &
BOON

First Published in Great Britain 2017
By Mills & Boon, an imprint of HarperCollins*Publishers*
1 London Bridge Street, London, SE1 9GF

ONE NIGHT WITH THE PRINCE © 2017 Harlequin Books S. A.

A Royal Without Rules, *A Night In The Prince's Bed* and *The Prince Who Charmed Her* were first published in Great Britain by Harlequin (UK) Limited.

A Royal Without Rules © 2013 Caitlin Crews
A Night In The Prince's Bed © © 2014 Chantelle Shaw
The Prince Who Charmed Her © 2013 Fiona McArthur

ISBN: 978-0-263-92954-6

05-0317

Printed and bound in Spain
by CPI, Barcelona

A ROYAL
WITHOUT RULES

BY
CAITLIN CREWS

Caitlin Crews discovered her first romance novel at the age of twelve. It involved swashbuckling pirates, grand adventures, a heroine with rustling skirts and a mind of her own and a seriously mouthwatering and masterful hero. The book (the title of which remains lost in the mists of time) made a serious impression. Caitlin was immediately smitten with romances and romance heroes, to the detriment of her middle school social life. And so began her life-long love affair with romance novels, many of which she insists on keeping near her at all times.

Caitlin has made her home in places as far-flung as York, England and Atlanta, Georgia. She was raised near New York City and fell in love with London on her first visit when she was a teenager. She has backpacked in Zimbabwe, been on safari in Botswana and visited tiny villages in Namibia. She has, while visiting the place in question, declared her intention to live in Prague, Dublin, Paris, Athens, Nice, the Greek Islands, Rome, Venice and/or any of the Hawaiian islands. Writing about exotic places seems like the next best thing to moving there.

She currently lives in California, with her animator/comic book artist husband and their menagerie of ridiculous animals.

To Megan Haslam, who was so enthusiastic about this book even before I wrote it, and to Charlotte Ledger, who claimed Pato might have ruined her for all men.

Thanks for being such fantastic editors!

CHAPTER ONE

His Royal Highness Prince Patricio, the most debauched creature in the kingdom of Kitzinia—if not the entire world—and the bane of Adriana Righetti's existence, lay sprawled across his sumptuous, princely bed in his vast apartments in the Kitzinia Royal Palace, sound asleep despite the fact it was three minutes past noon.

And he was not, Adriana saw as she strode into the room, alone.

According to legend and the European tabloids, Pato, without the pressure of his older brother's responsibilities as heir apparent, and lacking the slightest shred of conscience or propriety, had not slept alone since puberty. Adriana had expected to find him wrapped around the trollop du jour—no doubt the same redhead he'd made such a spectacle of himself with at his brother's engagement celebration the night before.

Jackass.

But as she stared at the great bed before her, the frustration that had propelled her all the way through the palace shifted. She hadn't expected to find the redhead *and* a brunette, both women naked and draped over what was known as Kitzinia's royal treasure: Prince Pato's lean and golden torso, all smooth muscle and sculpted male beauty, cut off by a sheet riding scandalously low on his narrow hips.

Although *"scandalous"* in this context was, clearly, relative.

"No need to be so shy." Somehow, Adriana didn't react to the mocking gleam in Prince Pato's gaze when she looked up to find him watching her, his eyes sleepy and a crook to his wicked mouth. "There's always room for one more."

"I'm tempted." Her crisp tone was anything but. "But I'm afraid I must decline."

"This isn't a spectator sport."

Pato shifted the brunette off his chest with a consummate skill that spoke of long practice, and propped himself up on one elbow, not noticing or not caring that the sheet slipped lower as he moved. Adriana held her breath, but the sheet *just* preserved what little remained of his modesty. The redhead rolled away from him as Pato shoved his thick, too-long tawny hair back from his forehead, amusement gleaming in eyes Adriana knew perfectly well were hazel, yet looked like polished gold.

And then he smiled with challenge and command. "Climb in or get out."

Adriana eyed him in all his unapologetic, glorious flesh. Prince Pato, international manwhore and noted black sheep of the Kitzinia royal family, was the biggest waste of space alive. He stood for nothing save his own hedonism and selfishness, and she wanted to be anywhere in all the world but here.

Anywhere.

She'd spent the last three years as Crown Prince Lenz's personal assistant, a job she adored despite the fact it had often involved handling Pato's inevitable messes. This paternity suit, that jilted lover's vindictive appearance on television, this crashed sports car worth untold millions, that reckless and/or thoughtless act making embarrassing headlines… He was the thorn in his responsible older brother's side, and therefore dug deep and hard in hers.

And thanks to his inability to behave for one single day—even at his only brother's engagement party!—Pato was now *her* problem to handle in the two months leading up to Kitzinia's first royal wedding in a generation.

Adriana couldn't believe this was happening. She'd been demoted from working at the right hand of the future king to taking out the royal family's trash. After her years of loyalty, her hard work. Just when she'd started to kid herself that she really could begin to wash away the historic stain on the once proud Righetti name.

"Pato needs a keeper," Prince Lenz had said earlier this morning, having called Adriana into his private study upon her arrival at the palace. Adriana had ached for him and the burdens he had to shoulder. She would do anything he asked, anything at all; she only wished he'd asked for something else. Pato was the one part of palace life she couldn't abide. "There are only two months until the wedding and I can't have the papers filled with his usual exploits. Not when there's so much at stake."

What was at stake, Adriana knew full well, was Lenz's storybook marriage to the lovely Princess Lissette, which the world viewed as a fairy tale come to life—or would, if Pato could be contained for five minutes. Kitzinia was a tiny little country nestled high in the Alps, rich in world-renowned ski resorts and stunning mountain lakes bristling with castles and villas and all kinds of holiday-making splendor. Tourist economies like theirs thrived on fairy tales, not dissipated princes hell-bent on self-destruction in the glare of as many cameras as possible.

Two months in this hell, she thought now, still holding Pato's amused gaze. *Two months knee-deep in interchangeable women, sexual innuendo and his callous disregard for anything but his own pleasure.*

But Lenz wanted her to do this. Lenz, who had believed in her, overlooking her infamous surname when he'd hired her. Lenz, who she would have walked through fire for, had he wanted it. Lenz, who deserved better than his brother. Somehow, she would do this.

"I would sooner climb across a sea of broken glass on my hands and knees than into that circus carousel you call your bed," Adriana said, then smiled politely. "I mean that with all due respect, of course, Your Royal Highness."

Pato tilted back his head and laughed.

And Adriana was forced to admit—however grudgingly— that his laugh was impossibly compelling, like everything else about him. It wasn't fair. It never had been. If interiors matched exteriors, Lenz would be the Kitzinian prince who looked like this, with all that thick sun-and-chocolate hair that fell about Pato's lean face and hinted at his wildness, that sinful mouth, and the kind of bone structure that made artists and young girls weep. Lenz, not Pato, should have been the one who'd inherited their late mother's celebrated beauty. Those cheekbones, the gorgeous eyes and easy grace, the smile that caused riots, and the delighted laughter that lit whole rooms.

It simply wasn't fair.

Pato extricated himself from the pile of naked women on his bed and swung his long legs over the side, wrapping the sheet around his waist as he stood. As much to taunt her with the other women's nakedness as to conceal his own, Adriana thought, her eyes narrowing as he raised his arms high above his head and stretched. Long and lazy, like an arrogant cat. He grinned at her when she glared at him, and as he moved toward her she stiffened instinctively—and his grin only deepened.

"What is my brother's favorite lapdog doing in my bedroom this early in the day?" he asked, that low, husky voice of his no more than mildly curious. Still, his gaze raked over her and she felt a kind of clutching in her chest, a hitch in her breath. "Looking as pinch-faced and censorious as ever, I see."

"First of all," Adriana said, glancing pointedly at the delicate watch on her wrist and telling herself she wasn't *pinched* and didn't care that he thought so, "it's past noon. It's not early in the day by any definition."

"That depends entirely on what you did last night," he replied, unrepentant and amused, with a disconcerting lick of heat beneath. "I don't mean what *you* did, of course. I mean what *I* did, which I imagine was far more energetic than however it is you prepare yourself for another day of pointless subservience."

Adriana looked at him, then at the bed and its naked contents. Then back at him. She raised a disdainful eyebrow, and he laughed again, as if she delighted him. The last thing she wanted to do was delight him. If she had her way, she'd have nothing to do with him at all.

But this was not about her, she reminded herself. Fiercely.

"Second," she said, staring back at him repressively, which had no discernible effect, "it's past time for your companions to leave, no matter how energetic they may have been—and please, don't feel you need to share the details. I'm sure we'll read all about it in the papers, as usual." She aimed a chilly smile at him. "Will you do the honors or should I call the royal guard to remove them from the palace?"

"Are you offering to take their place?" Pato asked lazily.

He shifted, and despite herself, Adriana's gaze dropped to the expanse of his golden-brown chest, sun-kissed and finely honed, long and lean and—

For God's sake, she snapped at herself. *You've seen all this before, like everyone else with an internet connection.*

She'd even seen the pictures that were deemed too risqué for publication, which the palace had gnashed its collective teeth over and which, according to Lenz, had only made his shameless brother laugh. Which meant she'd seen every part of him. But she had never been this close, in person, to Prince Pato in his preferred state of undress.

It was…different. Much different.

When she forced her gaze upward, his expression was far too knowing.

"I like things my way in my bed," he said, his decadent mouth crooking into something too hot to be any kind of smile. "But don't worry. I'll make it worth your while if you follow my rules."

That crackled in the air, like a shower of sparks.

"I have no interest in your sexual résumé, thank you," Adriana snapped. She hadn't expected he'd be so *potent* up close. She'd assumed he'd repulse her—and he did, of course. Intellectually. "And in any case it's unnecessary, as it's been splashed on the cover of every tabloid magazine for years."

He shocked her completely by reaching over and tugging gently on the chic jacket she wore over her favorite pencil skirt. Once, twice, three times—and Adriana simply stood there, stunned. And let him.

By the time she recovered her wits, he'd dropped his hand, and she glanced down to see that he'd unbuttoned her jacket, so that the sides fell away and the silk of her thin pink camisole was the only thing standing between his heated gaze and her skin.

Adriana swallowed. Pato smiled.

"Rule number one," he said, his husky voice a low rumble that made her wildly beating heart pump even faster. Even harder. "You're overdressed. I prefer to see skin."

For a moment, there was nothing but blank noise in her head, and a dangerous heat thick and bright everywhere else.

But then she made herself breathe, forcing one breath and then the next, and cold, sweet reason returned with the flow of oxygen. This was Pato's game, wasn't it? This was what he did. And she wasn't here to play along.

"That won't work," she told him coolly, ignoring the urge to cover herself. That was undoubtedly what he thought she'd do, what he wanted her to do before she ran away, screaming, like all the previous staff members Lenz had assigned him over the years. She wasn't going to be one of them.

His golden eyes danced. "Won't it? Are you sure?"

"I'm not your brother's lapdog any longer." Adriana squared her shoulders and held his gaze, tilting her chin up. "Thanks to your appalling behavior last night, which managed to deeply offend your soon-to-be sister-in-law and her entire family—to say nothing of the entire diplomatic corps— I'm yours until your brother's wedding."

If anything, Pato's eyes were even more like gold then, liquid and scalding. As wicked as he was, and her whole body seemed to tighten from the inside out.

"Really." He looked at her as if he could eat her in one bite, and would. Possibly right then and there. "All mine?"

Adriana thought her heart might catapult from her chest, and she ignored the curl of heat low in her belly, as golden and liquid as his intent gaze. *This is what he does,* she reminded herself sternly. *He's* trying *to unnerve you.*

"Please calm yourself," she said with a dry amusement she wished she felt. "I'm your new assistant, secretary, aide. Babysitter. Keeper. I don't care what you call me. The job remains the same."

"I'm not in the market for a lapdog," Pato said in his lazy way, though Adriana thought something far more alert moved over his face for a scant second before it disappeared into the usual carelessness. "And if by some coincidence I was, I certainly wouldn't choose a little beige hen who's made a career out of scowling at me in prudish horror and ruffling her feathers in unspeakable outrage every time I breathe."

"Not when you breathe. Only when you act. Or open your mouth. Or—" Adriana inclined her head toward his naked torso, which took up far too much of her view, and shouldn't have affected her at all "—when you fling off your clothes at the slightest provocation, the way other people shake hands."

"Off you go." He made a dismissive, shooing sort of gesture with one hand, though his lips twitched. "Run back to my drearily good and noble brother and tell him I eat hens like you for breakfast."

"Then it's a pity you slept through breakfast, as usual," Adriana retorted. "I'm not going anywhere, Your Royal Highness. Call me whatever you like. You can't insult me."

"I insulted the easily offended Lissette and all of her family without even trying, or so you claim." His dark brows arched, invoking all manner of sins. Inviting her to commit them. "Imagine how offensive I could be if I put my mind to it and chose a target."

"I don't have to imagine that," Adriana assured him. "I'm the one who sorted out your last five scandals. This year."

"Various doctors I've never met have made extensive claims in any number of sleazy publications that I'm an adrenaline junkie," Pato continued, studying her, as if he knew perfectly well that the thing that curled low and tight inside her was brighter now, hotter. More dangerous. "I think that means I like a challenge. Shall we test that theory?"

"I'm not challenging you, Your Royal Highness." Adriana kept her expression perfectly smooth, and it was much harder than it should have been. "You can't insult me because, quite honestly, it doesn't matter what you think of me."

His lips quirked. "But I am a prince of the realm. Surely your role as subject and member of staff is to satisfy my every whim? I can think of several possibilities already."

How was he getting to her like this? It wasn't as if this was the first time they'd spoken, though it was certainly the longest and most unclothed interaction she'd had with the man. It was also the only extended conversation she'd ever had with him on her own. She'd never been the focus of all his attention before, she realized. She'd only been *near* it. That was the crucial difference, and it hummed in her like an electric current no matter how little she wanted it to. She shook her head at him.

"The only thing that matters is making sure you cease to be a liability to your brother for the next two months. My role is to make sure that happens." Adriana smiled again, reminding herself that she had dealt with far worse things than an oversexed black sheep prince. That she'd cut her teeth on far more unpleasant situations and had learned a long time ago to keep her cool. Why should this be any different? "And I should warn you, Your Royal Highness. I'm very good at my job."

"And still," he murmured, his head tilting slightly to one side, "all I hear is challenge piled upon challenge. I confess, it's like a siren song to me."

"Resist it," she suggested tartly.

He gave her a full smile then, and she had the strangest sense that he was profoundly dangerous, despite his seeming carelessness. That he was toying with her, stringing her along, for some twisted reason of his own. That he was something far more than disreputable, something far less easily dismissed. It was disconcerting—and, she told herself, highly unlikely.

"It isn't only your brother who wants me here, before you ask," Adriana said quickly, feeling suddenly as if she was out of her depth and desperate for a foothold. Any foothold. "Your father does, too. He made his wishes very clear to Lenz."

Adriana couldn't pinpoint what changed, precisely, as Pato didn't appear to move. But she felt the shift in him. She could sense it in the same way she knew, somehow, that he was far more predatory than he should have been, standing there naked with a sheet wrapped around his hips and his hair in disarray.

"Hauling out your biggest weapon already?" he asked quietly, and a chill sneaked down the length of her spine. "Does that mean I've found my way beneath your skin? Tactically speaking, you probably shouldn't have let me know that."

"I'm letting you know the situation," she replied, but she felt a prickle of apprehension. As if she'd underestimated him.

But that was impossible. This was Pato.

"Far be it from me to disobey my king," he said, a note she didn't recognize and couldn't interpret in his voice. It confused her—and worse, intrigued her, and that prickle filled out and became something more like a shiver as his eyes narrowed. "If he wishes to saddle me with the tedious morality police in the form of a Righetti, of all things, so be it. I adore irony."

Adriana laughed at that. Not because it was funny, but because she hadn't expected him to land that particular blow, and she should have. She was such a fool, she thought then, fighting back a wave of a very familiar, very old despair. She should have followed her brothers, her cousins, and left Kitzinia to live in happy anonymity abroad. Why did she imagine that she alone could shift the dark mark that hovered over her family, that branded them all, that no one in the kingdom ever forgot for an instant? Why did she still persist in believing there was anything she could do to change that?

But all she showed Pato was the calm smile she'd learned, over the years, was the best response. The only response.

"And here I would have said that you'd never have reason to learn the name of a little beige hen, no matter how long I've worked in the palace."

"I think you'll find that everybody knows your name,

Adriana," he said, watching her closely. "Blood will tell, they say. And yours…" He shrugged.

She didn't know why that felt like a punch. It was no more than the truth, and unlike most, he hadn't even been particularly rude while delivering it.

"Yes, Almado Righetti made a horrible choice a hundred years ago," she said evenly. She didn't blush or avert her eyes. She didn't cringe or cry. She'd outgrown all that before she'd left grammar school. It was that or collapse. Daily. "If you expect me to run away in tears simply because you've mentioned my family's history, I'm afraid you need to prepare yourself for disappointment."

Once again, that flash of something more, like a shadow across his gorgeous face, making those lush eyes seem clever. Aware. And once again, it was gone almost the moment Adriana saw it.

"I don't want or need a lapdog," he said, the steel in his tone not matching the easy way he stood, the tilt of his head, that hot gold gleam in his eyes.

"I don't work for you, Your Royal Highness," Adriana replied simply, and let her profound pleasure in that fact color her voice. "You are simply another task I must complete to Prince Lenz's satisfaction. And I will."

That strange undercurrent tugged at her again. She wished she could puzzle it out, but he only gazed at her, all his shockingly intense magnetism bright in the air between them. She had the stray thought that if he used his power for good, he could do anything. Anything at all.

But that was silly. Pato was a monument to wastefulness, nothing more. A royal pain in the ass. *Her* ass, now, and for the next two months.

"I don't recall any other martyrs in the Righetti family line," he drawled after a moment. "Your people run more to murderous traitors and conniving royal mistresses, yes?" A quirk of his dark brow. "I'm happy to discuss the latter, in case you wondered. I do so hate an empty bed."

"Evidently," Adriana agreed acidly, nodding toward the overflowing one behind him.

"Rule number two," he said, sinful and dark. "I'm a royal prince. It's always appropriate to kneel in my presence. You could start right now." He nodded at his feet, though his gaze burned. "Right here."

And for a helpless moment, she imagined doing exactly that, as if he'd conjured the image inside her head. Of her simply dropping to her knees before him, then pulling that sheet away and doing what he was clearly suggesting she do.... Adriana felt herself heat, then tremble deep inside, and he smiled. He knew.

God help her, but *he knew.*

When she heard one of his bedmates call his name from behind him, Adriana jumped on it as if it was a lifeline— and told herself she didn't care that he knew exactly how much he'd got to her. Or that the curve in his wicked mouth mocked her.

"It looks like you're needed," Adriana said, pure adrenaline keeping her voice as calm and unbothered as it should have been. She knew she couldn't show him any fear, or any hint that she might waver. He was like some kind of wild animal who would pounce at the slightest hint of either— she knew that with a deep certainty she had no interest at all in testing.

"I often am," he said, a world of sensual promise in his voice, and that calm light of too much experience in his gaze. "Shall I demonstrate why?"

She eyed the pouty redhead, who was finally sitting up in the bed, apparently as unconcerned with her nudity as Pato was.

Adriana hated him. She hated this. She didn't know or

want to know why he'd succeeded in getting to her—she wanted to do her job and then return to happily loathing him from afar.

"I suggest you get rid of them, put some clothes on and meet me in your private parlor," she said in a clipped voice. "We need to discuss how this is going to go."

"Oh, we will," Pato agreed huskily, a dark gleam in his gaze and a certain cast to his mouth that made something deep inside her quiver. "We can start with how little I like being told what to do."

"You can talk all you want," Adriana replied, that same kick of adrenaline making her bold. Or maybe it was something else—something more to do with that odd hunger that made her feel edgy and needy, and pulsed in her as he looked at her that way. "I'll listen. I might even nod supportively. But then, one way or another, you'll behave."

Pato rid himself of his companions with as little fuss as possible, showered, and then called his brother.

"All these years I thought it was true love," he said sardonically when Lenz answered. "The descendant of the kingdom's most famous traitor and the besotted future king in a doomed romance. Isn't that what they whisper in the corners of the palace? The gossip blogs?"

There was a brief silence, which he knew was Lenz clearing whatever room he was in. Pato was happy to wait. He didn't know why he felt so raw inside, as if he was angry. When he was never angry. When he had often been accused of being incapable of achieving the state of anger, so offensively blasé was he.

And yet. He thought of Adriana Righetti and her dark brown eyes, the way she'd spoken to him. He pressed one hand against the center of his chest. Hard.

"What are you talking about?" Lenz asked, after a muttered conversation and the sound of a door closing.

"Your latest discard," Pato said. He stood there for a moment in his dressing room, scowling at his own wardrobe. What the hell was the matter with him? He felt…tight. Restless. As if this wasn't all part of the plan. He hadn't expected her to be…*her*. "Thank you for the warning that this was happening today."

"Do you require warnings now?" Lenz sounded amused. "Has the Playboy Prince lost his magic touch?"

"I'm merely considering how best to proceed," Pato said, that raw thing in him seeming to tie itself into a knot, because he knew how he'd *like* to proceed. It was hot and raw inside him. Emphatic. "Yet all I find myself thinking about are those Righetti royal mistresses. She looks just like them. Tell me, brother, what other gifts has she inherited? Please tell me they're kinky."

"Stop!" Lenz bit out the sharp command, something Pato very rarely heard directed at him. "Have some respect. Adriana isn't like that. She never…"

But he didn't finish. And Pato blinked, everything in him going still. Too still. As if this mattered.

"Does that mean what I think that means?" he asked. It couldn't. He shouldn't care—but there was that raw thing in him, and he had to know. "Is it possible? Was Adriana Righetti, in fact, no more than your personal assistant?"

Lenz muttered a curse. "Is that so difficult to believe?"

"It defies all reason," Pato retorted. But he smiled, a deep satisfaction moving through him, and he thought of the way Adriana had looked at him, determination and awareness in her dark eyes. He felt it kick in him. Hard. "You kept her for three whole years. What exactly were you doing?"

"Working," Lenz said drily. "She happens to be a great deal more than a pretty face." He cleared his throat. "Speaking of which, the papers are having a grand time attempting to uncover the identity of your mystery woman."

"Which one?" Pato asked, still smiling.

Lenz sighed. "And still the public adores you. I can't think why."

"We all have our roles to play." He heard the restlessness in his voice then, the darkness. It was harder and harder to keep it at bay.

His older brother let out another sigh, this one tinged with bitterness, and Pato felt his own rise to the surface. Not that it was ever far away. Especially not now.

"I thought it would feel different at this point," Lenz said quietly. "I thought I would feel triumphant. Victorious. *Something.* Instead, I am nothing but an imposter."

Pato pulled on a pair of trousers and a shirt and roamed out of his dressing room, then around the great bedchamber, hardly seeing any of it. There was too much history, too much water under the bridge, and only some of it theirs. Chess pieces put in place and manipulated across the years. Choices and vows made and then kept. They were in the final stages of a very long game, with far too much at stake. Far too much to lose.

"Don't lose faith now," he said, his voice gruff. "It's almost done."

Lenz's laugh was harsh. "What does faith have to do with it? It's all lies and misdirection. Callous manipulation."

"If you don't have faith in this course of ours, Lenz," Pato said fiercely, the rawness in his brother's voice scraping inside him, "then all of this has been in vain. All of it, for all these years. And then what will we do?"

There was a muffled noise that suggested one of Lenz's aides had poked a head in.

"I must go," his brother said after another low conversation. "And this is about sacrifice, Pato, though never mine.

Don't think it doesn't keep me awake, wondering at my own vanity. If I was a good man, a good brother…"

He didn't finish. What would be the point? Pato rubbed a hand over his eyes.

"It's done," he said. "The choice is made. We are who are and there's no going back."

There was a long pause, and Pato knew exactly which demons danced there between them, taunting his brother, dark and vicious. They were his, too.

"Be as kind to Adriana as you can," Lenz said abruptly. "I like her."

"We are all of us pawns, brother," Pato reminded him softly.

"Be nice to her anyway."

"Is that a command?" The raw thing in him was growing, hot and hungry. And Lenz had never touched her.

"If it has to be." Lenz snorted. "Will it work?"

Pato laughed, though it was a darker sound than it should have been. He thought of all the moving parts of this game, all they'd done and all there was left to do before it was over. And then he thought of Adriana Righetti's sharp smile on her courtesan's mouth, then the dazed expression on her face when he'd told her to kneel. And the heat in him seemed to simmer, then become intent.

"It's never worked before," he told his brother. "But hope springs eternal, does it not?"

His certainly did.

He found Adriana waiting for him as promised in the relatively small reception room off the grandiose main foyer of his lavish palace apartment. It was filled with fussy antiques, commanding works of art and the gilt-edged glamor that was meant to proclaim his exalted status to all who entered. Pato much preferred the flat he kept in London, where he wasn't required to impart a history lesson every time a guest glanced at a chair.

She was every bit as beautiful as her famously promiscuous ancestors, Pato thought, standing in the doorway and studying her. More so. She stood at the windows that looked out over the cold, blue waters of the alpine lake surrounding the palace, impatient hands on her hips and her stiff back to the door, and there was nothing in the least bit beige about her. Or even henlike, come to that. She'd refastened her jacket, and he appreciated the line of it almost as much as he'd enjoyed ruining that line when he'd unbuttoned it earlier. It skimmed over the elegant shape of her body before flaring slightly at her hips, over the narrow sheath of the skirt she wore and the high heels that made her legs look long and lean and as if they'd fit nicely wrapped around his back.

And she had in her genetic arsenal the most celebrated temptresses in the history of the kingdom. How could he possibly resist?

Anticipation moved in him, hard and bright. He needed her with him to play out this part of the game—but he hadn't expected he'd enjoy himself. And now, he thought, he would. Oh, how he would.

There were so many ways to be nice, after all, and Pato knew every last one of them.

CHAPTER TWO

TEN DAYS LATER, Adriana stood in the middle of a glittering embassy ballroom, a serene smile pasted to her face, while inside, she itched to kill Pato. Preferably with her very own hands.

It was a feeling she was growing accustomed to the more time she spent in his presence—and the more he pulled his little stunts. Like tonight's disappearing act in the middle of a reception where he was supposed to be calmly discharging his royal duties.

Please, she scoffed inside her head, her gaze moving around the room for the fifth time, holding out hope that she'd somehow missed him before, that he'd somehow blended into a crowd for the first time in his life. *As if he has the slightest idea what the word* duty *means!*

"The prince stepped out to take an important phone call," she lied to the ambassador beside her, when she accepted, finally, what she already knew. Pato had vanished, which could only bode ill. She kept her smile in place. "Why don't I see if I can help expedite things?"

"If you would be so kind," the ambassador murmured in reply, but without the sly, knowing look that usually accompanied any discussion of Pato or his suspicious absences in polite company. Nor did he look around to see if any women were also missing. Adriana viewed that as a point in her favor.

She had kept the paparazzi's favorite prince scandal-free for ten whole days. That was something of a record, if she did say so herself. Her intention was to continue her winning streak—but that meant finding him. And fast.

Because Adriana couldn't kid herself. She hadn't *contained* Pato over the past ten days. He'd laughed at her when she'd told her she planned to try. She'd simply babysat him, making sure he was never out of her sight unless he was asleep. That had involved frustrating days with Pato forever in her personal space, always teasing her and testing her, then doing as he pleased, with Adriana as his annoyed escort. It had meant long nights unable to sleep as she waited for the inevitable phone call from the guards she'd placed at his door to keep Pato in and the parade of trollops out. All she really had going for her was her fierce determination to bend him to her will—his brother's will, she reminded herself sternly—whether he wanted to or not.

Naturally, he didn't want to do anything of the kind.

Though he was always laughing, always shallow and reckless and the life of the party, if not the party itself, Adriana had come to realize that Pato had a fearsome will of his own. Iron and steel, wholly unbendable, beneath that impossibly pretty face and all his trademark languor.

Tonight he'd simply slipped away from the embassy receiving line, showing Adriana that he'd been indulging her this whole time. Allowing her to *think* she was making some kind of progress when, in fact, he'd been in control from the start.

She could practically *see* his mocking smile, and it burned through her, making her flush hot with the force of her temper. She excused herself from the ambassador and his aides, then walked calmly across the ballroom floor as if she was headed nowhere more interesting than the powder room, nodding by rote to those she passed and not even paying attention to the usual swell of her loathed surname like a wake of whispers behind her as she went. She was too focused on Pato, damn him.

He would *not* be the reason she failed Lenz. *He would not.*

But Pato wasn't corrupting innocents in the library, or involved in something sordid in any of the receiving rooms. She checked all of them—including every last closet because, the man was capable of anything—then stood there fuming. Had he *left?* Was he even now gallivanting about the city, causing trouble in one of the slick nightclubs he favored, filled as they were with the bored and the rich? How would she explain that to Lenz when it was all over the tabloids in the morning? But that was when she heard a soft thump from above her. Adriana tilted her head back and studied at the ceiling. The only thing above her was the ambassador's residence....

Of course. That bastard.

Adriana climbed the stairs as fast as she could without running, and then smiled at the armed guard who stood sentry at the entrance to the residence. She waved her mobile at him.

"I'm Prince Pato's assistant," she said matter-of-factly. "And I have His Majesty the King on the line...?"

She let her voice trail away, and had to fight back the rush of fury that swirled in her when the guard nodded her in, confirming her suspicions. She'd wanted to be mistaken, she really had.

And now she wanted to kill him. She *would* kill him.

Once on the other side of the ornate entryway, Adriana could hear music—and above it, a peal of feminine laughter. Her teeth clenched together, making her jaw ache. She marched down the hallway, stopped outside the cracked door where the noise came from, and then had to take a moment to prepare herself.

You already found him in bed with two women, a brisk voice inside her pointed out. *You handled it.*

She tucked her clutch beneath her arm, and wished she was wearing something more like a suit of armor, and not a sparkly blue gown that tied behind her neck, flowed to her feet and left her arms bare. For some reason, it made her feel intensely vulnerable, a sensation that mixed with her galloping temper and left her feeling faintly ill.

He was sleeping *when you saw that,* another voice countered. *He is probably not sleeping now.*

God, she hated him. She hated that this was her life. Adriana steeled herself and pushed through the door.

The music was loud, electronic and hypnotic, filling the dimly lit room. Adriana saw the woman first. She was completely naked save for a tiny black thong, plus long dark hair spilling down to the small of her back, and she was dancing.

If that was the word for it. It was carnal. Seductive. She moved to the music as if it was part of her, sensual and dark, writhing and spinning in the space between the two low couches that took up most of the floor space of the cozy room.

Performing, Adriana realized after a stunned moment. She was performing.

Pato lounged on the far couch, his long legs thrust out in front of him and crossed at the ankle, his elegant suit jacket open over his magnificent chest, and his lean arms stretched out along the back of the seat. He was fully clothed, which both surprised and oddly disappointed Adriana, but he looked no less the perfect picture of sexual indolence even though his skin wasn't showing.

Her throat went dry. The woman bent over backward, her hips circling in open, lustful invitation, her arms in the air before her. The music was like a dark throb, moving inside Adriana like a demand, a caress.

She swallowed hard, and that was when she realized Pato was looking straight at her.

Her heart stopped. Then kicked, exploding into her ribs, making her stomach drop. But Adriana didn't—couldn't—move.

The moment stretched out between them, electric and fierce. There was only that arrogant golden stare of his, as if the woman before him didn't exist. As if the music was for Adriana alone—for him. She had the panicked thought that he'd *wanted* her to find him like this, that this was some kind of trap. That he knew, somehow, the riot inside of her, the confusion. The heat.

Adriana didn't know how long she stood there, frozen on the outside and that catastrophic fire within. But eventually—seconds later? years?—Pato lifted one hand, pointed a remote toward the entertainment center on the far wall and silenced the music. All without looking away from Adriana for an instant.

The sudden silence made her flinch. Pato's mouth curved in one corner, wicked and knowing.

"It's time to go, Your Royal Highness," Adriana said stiffly into the quiet. She was aware, on some level, that the other woman was speaking, scowling at her. But Adriana couldn't seem to hear a word she said. Couldn't seem to see anything but Pato.

"You could come sit down, Adriana." His dark brows rose in challenge as he patted the sofa cushion beside him, and she was certain he knew the very moment her nipples pulled taut in a reaction she didn't understand. He smiled. "Watch. Enjoy. Who knows what might happen?"

"Not a single thing you're imagining right now, I assure you," Adriana said, struggling to control her voice.

She forced her shoulders back, stood straighter. She would not let this man best her. She couldn't let herself feel these

things, whatever they were. She had too much to prove—
and too much too lose. Adriana jerked her gaze away from
him, ignoring his low chuckle, and frowned at the woman,
who still stood there wearing nothing but a black thong and
an attitude.

"Aren't you the ambassador's daughter?" she asked
sharply. "Should we call downstairs and ask your father what
he thinks about your innovative approach to foreign policy?"

The woman made an extremely rude and anatomically
challenging suggestion.

"No, thank you," Adriana replied coolly, unable, on some
level, to process the fact that she was having this conversation while gazing at this woman's bared breasts. Not the first
set of naked breasts she'd seen in Pato's company. She could
only pray it was the last. "But I'm sure that if you walked
into the ballroom dressed like this you'd have a few takers.
No doubt that would delight your father even further."

Pato laughed then, rising from the couch with that sinuous
masculine grace he didn't deserve, and straightened his suit
jacket with a practiced tug. He did not look at all ashamed,
or even caught out. He looked the way he always did: deeply
amused. Lazy and disreputable. Unfairly sexy. His darker-
than-blond hair was long enough to hint at a curl, and he
wore it so carelessly, as if fingers had just or were about to
run through it. That wicked mouth of his made him look like
a satyr, not a prince. And those golden eyes gleamed as he
held her gaze, connecting with a punch to all that confused
heat inside her. Making it bloom into an open flame.

"There is no need for threats, Adriana," he said, sardonic
and low, and she felt it everywhere. "Nothing would please
me more than to do your bidding."

The ambassador's daughter moved then, plastering herself to his long, lean body, rubbing her naked breasts against
his chest as she flung her arms around his neck, hooked one

leg over his hip and pressed her mouth to his. He didn't kiss her the way Adriana had once seen him kiss one of his paramours in an almost-hidden alcove in the palace—carnal and demanding and an obvious, smoking-hot prelude to what came next. This was not *that,* thank goodness. But he didn't exactly fight her off, either.

"Then by all means, let's have you do my bidding, Your Royal Highness," Adriana said icily, everything inside her seeming to fold in on itself, like a fist. "Whenever you can tear yourself away, of course."

Pato set the other woman aside with a practiced ease that reminded Adriana of the same dexterity he'd showed in his bed that other morning. It made that fist curl tighter. Harder. He murmured something Adriana couldn't hear, that made the ambassador's thonged daughter smile at him as if he'd licked her. And then he smoothed down his tie, buttoned his jacket and sauntered toward the doorway as if there wasn't a nearly naked woman panting behind him and a formal reception he was supposed to be attending below.

Adriana stepped back to let him move into the hallway, and took more pleasure than she should have in snapping the door shut behind him. Perhaps with slightly more force than necessary.

"Temper, temper," Pato murmured, eyeing her with laughter in that golden gaze. "And here I thought you'd be so proud of me."

"I doubt you thought anything of the kind." She'd never wanted to hit another human being so much in all her life. "I doubt you *think.* And why on earth would I be proud of this embarrassing display?"

He propped one shoulder against the closed door and waved a languid hand down the length of him, inviting her to take a long look. She declined. Mostly.

"Am I not clothed?" he asked, taunting her. Again. "'Keep

your clothes on, Your Royal Highness,' you said in that prissy way of yours in the car on the way over tonight. I am delighted, as ever, to obey."

"You wouldn't know how to *obey* if it was your job," she snapped at him. "Not that I imagine you know what one of those is, either."

"You make a good point," he said, and that was when it occurred to Adriana that they hadn't moved at all—that they were standing entirely too close in that doorway. His face shifted from pretty to predatory, and her head spun. "I'm better at giving the orders, it's true. Rule number three, Adriana. The faster you obey me, the harder and the longer you'll come. Consider it my personal guarantee."

She couldn't believe he'd said that. Her entire body seemed to ignite, then liquefy.

"Enough," she muttered, but she didn't fool him with her horrified tone, if that flash of amused satisfaction in his gaze meant anything. Desperation made her lash out. "You shouldn't share these sad rules of yours, Your Royal Highness. It only makes you that much more pathetic—the dissipated, aging bachelor, growing more pitiable by the moment, on a fast track to complete irrelevance."

"Yes," he agreed. He leaned closer, surrounding her, mesmerizing her. "That's exactly why you're breathing so fast, why your cheeks are so flushed. You pity me."

Adriana ducked around him and started down the hall, telling herself none of that had happened. None of it. No dancing girl, no strange awareness. No *rules* that made her belly feel tight and needy. And certainly not the look she'd just seen in his eyes, stamped hard on his face. But her heart clattered in her chest, it was as hard to breathe as he'd suggested, and she knew she was lying.

Worse, he was right beside her.

"You're welcome," Pato said after a moment, sounding

smug and irritatingly male. It made her pulse race, but she refused to look at him. She couldn't seem to stop herself from imagining what kind of orders he'd give…and she hated herself for wondering.

"I beg your pardon?" she asked icily, furious with herself.

"Someone needs to provide fodder for your fantasies, Adriana. I live to serve."

She stopped walking, her hand on the door that led out of the residence. When she looked at him, she ignored the impact of that hot golden gaze of his and smiled instead. Poisonously.

"My fantasies involve killing you," she told him. "I spend hours imagining burying you in the palace gardens beneath the thorniest rose bushes, so I'd never have to deal with you again." She paused, then added with exaggerated politeness, "Your Royal Highness."

Pato grinned widely, and leaned down close. Too close. Adriana was aware, suddenly and wildly, of all the skin she was showing, all of it *right there,* within his reach. All that bare flesh, so close to that satyr's mouth of his. That wicked mouth with a slight smear of crimson on it, a sordid little memento that did nothing to detract from his devastating appeal. Or from her insane response to him.

"I knew you fantasized about me," he murmured, his voice insinuating, delicious. Seductive. "I can see it on your face when you think it's not showing."

He ran his fingertip down the sparkling blue strap that rose from the bodice of her gown and fastened at the nape of her neck. That was all. That was enough. He touched nothing but the fabric, up and down and back again, lazy and slow and so very nearly innocuous.

And Adriana burned. And shivered. And hated herself.

"Someday," he whispered, his eyes ablaze, "I'll tell you what you do in my fantasies. They're often…complicated."

Adriana focused on that smear of lipstick on his perfect lips. She didn't understand any of this. She should be horrified, disgusted. She should find him categorically repulsive. Why didn't she? What was *wrong* with her?

But she was terrified that she already knew.

"That's certainly something to look forward to," she said, the deliberate insincerity in her voice like a slap, just as she'd intended, but he only grinned again. "In the meantime, you have lipstick all over your mouth." She kept her expression smooth as she stepped back, away from him. She snapped open her clutch, reached inside with a hand that was *not* shaking, and produced a tissue. "I know you like to trumpet your conquests to all and sundry but not, I beg you, tonight. Not the ambassador's daughter."

"They wouldn't think it was the ambassador's daughter who put her mouth all over me, Adriana." He held her with that golden stare for another ageless moment, so sure of himself. So sure of *her*. He took the tissue from her hand then, his fingers brushing over hers—leaving nothing behind but heat and confusion, neither of which she could afford. "Small minds prefer the simplest explanations. They'd assume it was you."

"You must have done *something*," Adriana's father said peevishly, and not for the first time. "I told you to ingratiate yourself, to be obliging, didn't I? I told you to be careful!"

"You did," Adriana agreed. She didn't look over at her mother, who was preparing breakfast at the stove. She didn't have to look; she could feel her mother's sympathy like a cool breeze through the room. She tried to rub away the tension in her temples, the churning confusion inside her. "But I didn't do anything, I promise. Lenz thinks this is a great opportunity for me."

There was a tense silence then, and Adriana blinked as she realized her mistake. Her stomach twisted.

"'*Lenz?*'" Her father's brows clapped together. "You're quite familiar with the crown prince and future king of Kitzinia, are you not? I don't need to tell you where that leads, Adriana. I don't need to remind you whose blood runs through your veins. The shame of it."

He didn't. He really didn't, as she was the one who lived it in ways he couldn't imagine, being male. But he always did, anyway. She could see that same old lecture building in him, making his whole body stiffen.

"Papa," she said gently, reaching over to cover his hands with hers. "I worked with him for three years. A certain amount of familiarity is to be expected."

"And yet he insults you like this, throwing you to his dog of a brother like refuse, straight back into the tabloids." Her father frowned at her, and a small chill tickled the back of her neck. "Perhaps his expectation was for rather more familiarity than you offered, have you thought of that?"

It wasn't the first time her father had managed to articulate her deepest fears. But this time it seemed to sting more. Adriana pulled her hands away.

"Eat, Emilio," her mother said then, slipping into her usual seat and raising her brows when Adriana's father only scowled at the cooked breakfast she set before him. "You hate it when your eggs get cold."

"It was never like that," Adriana said, pushed to defend herself—though she wasn't sure she was addressing her father as much as herself. "Lenz is a good man."

"He is a man," her father replied shortly, something she didn't like in his gaze. "A very powerful man. And you are a very beautiful woman with only a terrible history and a disgraced family name to protect you."

"Emilio, please," her mother interjected.

Her father looked at her for an uncomfortable moment, then dropped his gaze to his meal, his silence almost worse. Adriana excused herself, unable to imagine eating even a bite when her stomach was in knots.

She made her way through the ancient villa to her childhood bedroom. It would be easier to leave Kitzinia altogether, she knew. She'd sat up nights as a child, listening to her mother beg her father to emigrate, to live in a place where their surname need never cause any kind of reaction at all. But Emilio Righetti was too proud to abandon the country his ancestor had betrayed, and Adriana understood it, no matter how hard it was to bear sometimes, no matter how she wished she didn't. Because when it came right down to it, she was the same.

She shut the door to her bedroom behind her and sank down on the edge of her bed. She was so tired, though she didn't dare let herself sleep. She had to return to the palace. Had to face Pato again.

Adriana let her eyes drift shut, wishing herself far away from the villa she'd grown up in, surrounded by the remains of the once vast Righetti wealth. If she looked out her window, she could see the causeway the kingdom had built in the 1950s, linking the red-roofed, picturesque city that spread along the lakeside to the royal palace that sat proudly on its own island in the middle of the blue water, its towers and spires thrust high against the backdrop of the snowcapped Alps. The villa boasted one of the finest addresses in the old city, a clear indication that the Righettis had once been highly favored by many Kitzinian rulers.

Now the villa was a national landmark. A reminder. The birthplace and home of the man who had murdered his king, betrayed his country, nearly toppling the kingdom with his treachery. Because of him, all the rest of the Righetti family history was seen through a negative lens. There had been

other royal mistresses from other noble Kitzinian families—
but only the Righettis enjoyed the label of witches. Whores.

There was no escape from who she was, Adriana knew.
Not as long as she stayed here. And she didn't understand
what was happening to her now—what was happening *in*
her. What had ignited in her last night at that embassy party
under Pato's arrogant golden stare. What had stalked her
dreams all through the long night, erotic and wild, and still
thrummed beneath her skin when she woke...

That was a lie, she thought now, cupping a hand over the
nape of her neck as if she could ease the tension she felt.
Adriana knew exactly what was happening. She didn't *want*
to understand it, because she didn't want to admit it. Yet the
way her father had looked at her today, as if she was somehow visibly tainted by the family history, made it impossible
to keep lying to herself.

She'd heard it all her life. It had been flung at her in school
and was whispered behind her back even now. It wasn't
enough that she was assumed to be traitorous by blood, like
all her male relatives. She was the only female Righetti of
her generation, and more, was the very image of her famous
forebears—there were portraits in the Royal Gallery to prove
it. They were well-known and well-documented whores, all
the way down to Adriana's great-aunt, who had famously
beguiled one of the king's cousins into walking away from
his dukedom, disowned and disgraced.

And Adriana was just like them.

She knew exactly how tainted she really was, how very
much she lived down to her family's legacy. Because it wasn't
Lenz who had dreamed of something more familiar. It was
her.

Lenz was good and kind, and he'd believed in her. He'd
given her a chance. Adriana was the first Righetti to set foot
in the palace since her traitorous ancestor had been executed

there a hundred years ago, and Lenz had made that happen. He'd changed everything. He'd given her hope. And in return, Adriana had adored him, happy simply to be near him.

And yet she'd dreamed of Pato in ways she'd never dreamed of his brother. Wild and sensual. Explicit. Maybe it shouldn't surprise her that she couldn't get Pato out of her head, she thought now in a wave of misery. Maybe it was programmed into her very flesh, her bones, to want him. To want anything, anyone royal, moving from one prince to the next. To be exactly what she'd always been: a Righetti.

That was what they said in the tabloids, which had pounced on her switch from Lenz's office to Pato's with malicious glee, after three years of going a bit easier on her. *She's failed to snare Prince Lenz with her Righetti wiles—will the shameless Pato be easier to trap?*

Maybe this had all been inevitable from the start.

Her mobile phone chirped at her from the bedside table, snapping her eyes open. She reached for it and tensed when she saw the name that flashed on the screen. It felt like confirmation that she was cursed. But she picked it up, because Pato was her job. Her responsibility. It didn't matter what she felt.

It only mattered what she did, and she controlled that. Not him. Not the ghosts of her slutty ancestors. Not her own treacherous blood.

Stop being so melodramatic, she ordered herself, pulling in a deep breath. *Nothing is inevitable.*

"It's eight-fifteen in the morning," she said by way of a greeting, and she didn't bother to sweeten her tone. "Surely too early for your usual debauchery."

"Pack your bags," Pato said, sounding uncharacteristically alert despite the hour. "We're flying to London this afternoon. There's some charity thing I had no intention of attending, and now, apparently, must. My brother commands it."

Adriana blinked, and sorted through the possibilities in her head.

"Presumably you mean the Children's Foundation, of which you and your brother are major benefactors," she said crisply. "And their annual ball."

"Presumably," he agreed, that alertness blending into his more typical laziness, and prickling over her skin no matter how badly she didn't want to be affected. "I don't really care, I only follow orders. And Adriana?"

"Yes?" But she knew. She could hear it in his voice. She could imagine that smile in the corner of his mouth, that gleam in his eyes. She didn't have to see any of it—she felt it. Her eyes drifted shut again, and she hated herself anew.

"It's never too early for debauchery," he said in that low, stirring way that was only his. "I'd be delighted to prove that to you. You can make it back to the palace in what? Twenty minutes?"

"You need to stop," she retorted, not realizing she meant to speak, and then it sat there between them. Pato didn't reply, but she could *feel* him. That disconcerting power of his, that predatory beauty. She dropped her forehead into one hand, kept her eyes shut. "I'm not your toy. I don't expect you to make my job easy for me, but this is unacceptable." He still didn't speak, but she could feel the thrum of him inside her, the electricity. "Not every woman you meet wants to sleep with you."

He laughed, and she felt it slide through her like light, illuminating too many truths she'd prefer to hide away forever. Exposing her. Making that curl of heat glow again, low and hot, proving what a liar she was.

"Rule number four," he began.

"Would you like to know what you can do with your rules?" she demanded, desperate.

"Adriana," he chided her, though she could hear the thread

of laughter in his voice. Somehow, that made it worse. "I'm fairly certain I could legally have you beheaded for speaking to me in such an appalling fashion, given the medieval laws of our great kingdom. I am your prince and your employer, not one of your common little boyfriends. A modicum of respect, please."

She was too raw. Too unbalanced. It crossed her mind then that she might not survive him. Certainly not intact. That he might be the thing that finally broke her.

"I apologize, Your Royal Highness," she said, her voice much too close to a whisper. "I don't know what came over me."

"Rule number four," he said again, softly. And meanwhile her heart thudded so hard in her chest that she could feel the echo of it in her ears, her teeth. Her sex. "If you can't muster up the courage to say it to my face, I'm not going to take it seriously."

Because he knew, of course. That she was using this phone conversation to hide, because she doubted her own strength when he was standing in front of her. He'd watched it, hadn't he? Exploited it. He knew exactly how weak she was.

And now she did, too.

"London," she said, changing the subject, because she had to end this conversation right now. She had to find her balance again, or at least figure out how to fake it. "A charity ball. I'll pack appropriately, of course."

"Say it to my face, Adriana," he urged her, and she told herself she didn't recognize what she heard in his voice then. But her skin broke out in goose bumps, even her breasts felt heavy, and she knew better. She knew. "See what happens."

"I should be back in the palace within the hour, Your Royal Highness," she said politely, and hung up.

And then sat there on the edge of her bed, her head in her

hands, and wondered what the hell would become of her if she couldn't find a way to control this. To control *herself.*

Because she was terribly afraid that if she couldn't, Pato would.

CHAPTER THREE

THE CHARITY BALL in London was, of course, as tedious as every other charity ball Pato had ever attended. He smiled. He posed for obligatory photographs with Lenz and the chilly Lissette, as well as with any number of other people whose names he forgot almost before he heard them. He then contemplated impaling himself on the dramatic ice sculpture near the lavish buffet to see if that might enliven the evening in some small way.

"Restrain yourself," Adriana replied, in that stuffy voice that he found amused him far more than it should, when he announced his intentions. Pato angled a look at her.

She stood beside him as she had all evening, never more than three steps away, as if she'd put him on an invisible leash and was holding it tight. Her lovely face was smoothed to polite placidity, she knew exactly how to blend into the background whenever someone came to speak to him, and she held her mobile phone tight in one hand as if she planned to use it to subdue him if he made a break for it. She'd been nothing but irritatingly serene and unflappably professional since she'd returned to the palace with her packed bag this morning. And all this time, across the span of Europe and the whole of London, she'd managed to avoid looking at him directly.

Pato found her fascinating.

"Restraint?" he asked, noting the way her shoulders tensed

beneath the cap sleeves of the elegant black sheath she wore when he spoke. Every time he spoke. It made him want to press his mouth to her collarbone, to lick his way up the curve of her neck to the subdued sparkle of small diamonds at her ears. "I'm unfamiliar with the concept."

She smiled slightly, but kept her attention trained on the dance floor in front of them. "Truer words have never been spoken, Your Royal Highness."

He laughed. He liked it when she slapped at him, when her voice was something more than cool, smooth, bland. He liked when he could sense her temper, her frustration. He found that the more he told her how bored he was, the less bored he actually felt.

Pato knew he was on dangerous ground. He didn't care. He hadn't enjoyed himself so much in years.

A curvy brunette in a slinky dress slithered up to him then, her heavily kohled eyes sweeping over Adriana dismissively before she leaned in close and ran her hands over Pato's chest.

"Your Royal Highness," she purred, her lips painted a sultry red that matched the fingernails she ran along the length of his tie. "We meet again. I knew we would."

Pato smiled indulgently. He had no idea who she was. "And you were right."

Beside him, he felt Adriana bristle, and he enjoyed that immensely, so he picked up the brunette's hand and kissed it, making her lean even more heavily against him.

"Dance with me," she commanded him in a sultry voice.

Pato didn't feel like dancing and he wasn't particularly fond of commands, but he could feel Adriana's disapproval like a cold wind at his back, and so he smiled wider.

"I'm afraid I'm here with my own version of an electronic ankle bracelet," he said blithely, turning slightly. He indicated Adriana with a nod of his head, and was pleased to notice she flushed. At the attention? Or was that the sweet kick of her temper? And why did he want so badly to know? "It's like a walking house arrest."

The brunette blinked, looking from him to Adriana and then back.

"What did you do?" she asked, wide-eyed, no doubt plotting her call to the tabloids as she spoke.

"Haven't you heard?" Pato asked, his eyes on Adriana and the way her hand tensed around her mobile as she glared out at the crowd. "I've been very, very naughty. Again."

The brunette made some reply, but Pato watched Adriana, who dragged her gaze to his then as if it hurt her to do it. Even better, her meltingly brown eyes shot fire at him.

"There you are," he said quietly, with a satisfaction he didn't bother to hide. He smiled when her eyes narrowed. He tried to make his voice sound like a supplicant's, but what came out was more like lazy challenge. "Am I allowed to dance, Adriana? Is that permitted?"

"Stay where I can see you," she ordered him, all smooth command, as if she really did have him under her control. His smile deepened when she turned a cool gaze on the brunette. "Please don't force me to invoke Kitzinian law, ma'am. No leaving the ballroom. No public displays. Keep it clean and polite. Do you understand?"

The woman nodded, looking slightly dazed, and Pato laughed.

"My very own prison warden," he said, as if he approved. "I am duly chastened."

He pulled the brunette into his arms as he took to the floor, but he couldn't seem to take his eyes off Adriana, who stood where he'd left her, looking calm and unruffled. Serene. She even gazed at him across the swell of bodies, a kind of victory in her dark eyes. He felt it like a direct challenge.

When the interminable dance was finished, he murmured the appropriate things to the brunette, forgot her and then prowled back over to the assistant he'd never wanted in the first place. This time, she looked at him as he approached. More than that, she met his eyes boldly. He didn't know why that should affect him far more than the way the lush brunette had leaned against him throughout the dance, trying to entice him with her curves.

"You don't know who that woman is, do you?" Adriana asked when he reached her side, her tone mild. Polite. Pato knew better than to believe it.

"I haven't the faintest idea."

"But you slept with her." Something like panic flared in her dark gaze, intriguing him even as she blinked it away. The tips of her ears were red, he noticed, up there near her swept-back blond hair, and her eyes were too bright. "Didn't you?"

"Probably." He arched a brow at her. "Are you asking that in an official capacity, Adriana? Or are you jealous?"

"I'm merely curious," she said with a sniff, sounding as if she was discussing something as dry and uninteresting as his daily schedule. "I imagine, at this point, you can't walk across a single room in Europe without tripping over legions of former conquests."

"Well," he said. "I rarely trip."

"It must be difficult, at this point, to find someone you *haven't* already been intimate with." She smiled at him, that killer smile he'd seen before, sweet and deadly, which was supposed to be a weapon and instead delighted him. "Then again, it's not as if you can remember, anyway, can you?"

Pato stood there for a moment, that same jagged restlessness beating at him, making him want things he'd given up a long time ago. Making him hard and wild, and shoving him much too close to a line he couldn't allow himself to cross.

And still she smiled at him like that, as if she could handle this kind of battle, when he knew she was completely unaware of how much danger she was in.

"Ah," he said in the low voice he could see made her shiver, and then he smiled as if she was prey and he was already on her. In her. "I see." And he was closer than he should have been. He was much too close and he didn't care at all, because her eyes widened and were that intoxicating shade of the finest Swiss chocolate. "You're under the impression that you can shame me."

They stared at each other, while laughter and conversation and the music kicked around them. Her lovely face flushed red. He saw the flash of that same panic he'd seen before, as if she wasn't at all as controlled as she pretended, but she didn't look away. Brave, he thought. Or foolish.

Pato lost himself in her dark gaze then, electric and alive and focused on him as if nothing else existed. As if he was already buried deep inside her, and she was waiting for him to move.

That image didn't help matters at all. He blew out a breath.

"Come," he said shortly, annoyed with himself. He turned on his heel and started across the great ballroom, knowing she had no choice but to follow, to keep him on that absurd leash of hers. And she did.

"Where are you going?" she asked as she fell into step with him. He didn't think that hint of breathlessness in her voice was from walking, and it carved out something like a smile inside him.

"It's like we're chained together, Adriana." He couldn't seem to find his footing, and that was a catastrophe waiting to happen. And still, he didn't care about that the way he knew he should. "Think of the possibilities."

"No, thank you," she replied, predictably, and he indulged himself and wrapped his hand around her upper arm, feigning solicitousness as he moved her through the door that led out toward the gardens. She jumped when he touched her, electric shock and that darker kick beneath it. He knew because he felt it, too. Her skin was softer than satin, warm and smooth beneath his palm, she smelled faintly of jasmine, and he shouldn't have done it. Because now he knew.

Her eyes flew to his, and it punched through him hard, making him want to push her back against the nearest wall, lift her against him, lose himself completely in the burn of it. In her.

"Are you sure?" he asked, as they moved from the bright light of the ballroom into the soft, cool dark outside. He led her across the wide patio, skirting the small clumps of people who stood clustered around the bar tables that dotted it here and there. "Five minutes ago my sexual escapades were foremost on your mind. Don't tell me you've lost interest so quickly."

He looked down at her, and made no effort to contain the heat in him. The fire. He felt a tremor run through her, and God help him, he wanted her more than he'd wanted anything in years.

"I didn't realize you were so sensitive about your scandalous past, Your Royal Highness," she said, in a rendition of her usual cool he might have believed, had he not been looking into the wild heat in her gaze. "I'll take care not to mention it again."

"Somehow," he murmured, his grip on her arm tightening just enough to make her suck in a breath, just enough to torture himself, "I very much doubt that."

At some point, he was going to have to figure out why this woman got to him like this. But not tonight. Not now.

She pulled her arm from his grip as he steered her between two tables, as if concerned they couldn't make it through the narrow channel side by side. But she rubbed at the place he'd touched her as if he'd left behind a mark, and Pato smiled.

In the deepest, farthest shadows of the patio, he found an empty table, the candle in the center, which should have been glowing, unlit. But he didn't need candlelight to see her as she deliberately put the table between them, keeping as far out of his reach as she could. His eyes adjusted to the dark and he studied the flush on her cheeks, the hectic sparkle in her gaze.

And then he waited, leaning his elbows on the table and watching her. Her pretty eyes widened. She shifted from one foot to the other. He made her nervous, and he couldn't pretend he didn't like it.

"I wasn't trying to shame you," she said after long moments passed, just the two of them in a far, dark corner, all the nerves he could see on her face rich in her voice. And there was something else, he thought as he studied her. Something he couldn't quite identify.

"Of course you were."

"I didn't mean—"

"You did."

She looked stricken for a moment, then dropped her gaze to the tabletop, and he watched as she crossed her arms as if she thought she needed to hold herself together. Or protect herself.

"What are you ashamed of, Adriana?" he asked softly.

She flinched as if he'd slapped her, telling him a great deal more than he imagined she meant to do, but her expression was clear when she lifted her head. That mask again. She let out a breath and then she opened her mouth—

"Don't lie to me," he heard himself say, and worse, he could feel how important it was to him that she heed him. How absurdly, dangerously important. "Don't clean it up. Just tell me."

"I'm a Righetti, Your Royal Highness," she said after a moment, her dark eyes glittering in the shadows. "Shame runs like blood in our veins. It's who we are."

Pato didn't know how long they stood like that, held in that taut, near-painful moment. He didn't know how long he gazed at her, at the proud tilt of her chin and the faintest tremor in her lips, with that darkness in her eyes. He didn't know how she'd punched into him so completely that her hand might as well have ripped through his chest. That was what it felt like, and he didn't want that. He didn't want *this*. He couldn't.

"Adriana," he said finally, but his voice was no more than a rasp. And then he saw figures approaching from the corner of his eye, and he stopped, almost grateful for the intrusion into a moment that shouldn't have happened in the first place.

She dropped her gaze again, and hunched her shoulders slightly as she stood there, as if warding off whoever had come to stand at the table a small distance behind her. Pato didn't spare them a glance. He didn't look away from Adriana for even a moment, and the fact that was more dangerous than anything that had come before didn't escape him.

He wanted to touch her. He wanted to pull her against him, hold her, soothe her somehow, and he felt hollow inside because of it. Hollow and twisted, and stuck where he'd put himself, on the other side of an incidental table and an impossible divide, useless and corrupt and dismissable.

A fine bed he'd made, indeed.

And then she stiffened again, as if she'd been struck, and Pato frowned as he recognized the voices coming from behind her.

"Was that wise, do you think?" The cold, precise tones of Princess Lissette, her faint accent making the words seem even icier. She sounded as blonde and Nordic as she looked, Pato thought uncharitably. And as frigid.

"I'm not sure what wisdom has to do with it."

There was no mistaking his brother's voice, and the ruthlessly careful way he spoke while in public. The dutiful Crown Prince Lenz and his arranged-since-the-cradle bride stood at the next table, a candle bright between them, the warm glow doing nothing to ease their stiff, wary postures.

There were worse beds to lie in than his, Pato knew, eyeing his brother. *Poor bastard.*

"One must strive to be compassionate, of course," Lissette continued in the same measured way. "But even I know of her family's notoriety. Do you worry that it reflects badly on your judgment, your discernment, that you selected her to be your assistant when she is widely regarded as something of a pariah?"

Pato went still. Adriana seemed turned to stone, a statue, her eyes lowered as she bent slightly forward over her crossed arms.

"Look at me," he ordered her in an undertone, but she ignored him.

Behind her, an uncomfortable silence swelled. Pato saw his brother begin to frown, then remember himself and fight it back. His ice princess fiancée only gazed back at him calmly. Pato wanted to order them to stop talking, to point out that Adriana was *right here*—but he didn't trust that the princess would stop. Or that she wasn't already aware that Adriana stood at the next table. And he didn't want Adriana to be any more of a target. A dim alarm sounded in him then, questioning that unusual protective urge, but he shoved it aside.

"This will all go much smoother, I think," Lenz said finally, an edge to his voice, "if you do not speak of things you don't understand, Princess."

"I believe I understand perfectly," she replied with cool hauteur. "You took a traitor's daughter as your mistress and flaunted her in the face of Kitzinian society, for years. What is there to misunderstand?"

"Adriana Righetti was never my mistress," Lenz snapped, his tone scathing. Even derisive. "Credit me with slightly more intelligence than that, Lissette."

There were other voices then, calling out for the happy royal couple from some distance across the patio, and Pato watched in a quiet fury as his brother pasted on his usual public smile, offered his arm to his fiancée—who smiled back in the same way as she took it—before they glided away. He had the wholly uncharacteristic urge to smack their heads together.

Then he glanced back at Adriana, who still hadn't moved a muscle.

"Look at me," he said again, with an odd urgency he didn't understand.

She lifted her head then and the pain on her face stunned him into silence. He could see it in her dark eyes, slicked not with embarrassment but with a kind of grief.

For a moment he was lost. This wasn't the tough, impervious Adriana he'd grown accustomed to over the past days—unflappable, he'd assumed, thanks to growing up a beautiful Righetti girl in the sharp teeth of Kitzinian society. But then, suddenly, he understood.

And didn't care at all for how it made him feel.

"My God," he said flatly. "You're in love with him."

Adriana woke up in a rush and had no idea where she was.

She was on her stomach on an unfamiliar bed in a sunlit room she'd never seen before. She blinked, frowned, and realized as she did both that her head ached and that she'd neglected to remove her eye makeup the night before. What—

There was a slight movement behind her, a small shift against the mattress.

She was not alone in the bed.

Adriana froze. Then, very slowly, her heart pounding, she turned to look, somehow knowing what she would see even as she prayed she was mistaken.

Please not him. Please not him. Please—

Prince Pato lay sprawled out on his back, the sheets kicked off, naked save for a pair of tight navy blue briefs that clung to his narrow hips. The light from the skylights bathed him in shades of gold, and she couldn't quite take in that perfect, hard-packed flesh of his, so close beside her she could almost feel the heat he generated, and could see the rough shadow of his beard on his jaw. She couldn't make sense of all his fine masculine beauty, much less the picture of sheer abandon he made, sun-kissed and golden and stretched out so carelessly against the crisp white sheets.

She was in bed with Pato.

Her mouth was too dry; her eyes felt scraped and hollow. She felt fragile and broken, and had no idea how to pull herself together enough to handle this. Adriana was afraid she might be sick.

In a panic, she whipped her head around, yanked back the sheet and looked down at herself, not sure whether to be horrified or relieved to discover that while she wasn't naked, she wore only the matching cranberry hip-slung panties and bra she'd had on beneath her gown at the charity ball.

The ball. Adriana fought to keep breathing as images from the night before began to flood her head. Those strange, intense moments with Pato. His hand on her arm. The way he'd looked at her, as if he could see straight into her. Then Lenz's voice, so disgusted, so appalled.

She couldn't think about Lenz. She couldn't.

Had she really done this? Had she decided to become what she'd always been so proud she wasn't? With the one person in all the world best suited to debauch her—or anyone, come to that—completely? He did it by rote, no doubt. He could do it in his sleep. No wonder she couldn't recall it.

Adriana turned to look at him again, as if she might see her own actions tattooed on his smooth skin, and she jolted in shock.

Pato was awake. And watching her.

"Oh, my God," she whispered. She pulled the sheets up

to her neck, fought the urge to burst into tears, and stared at him in horror.

Pato's golden eyes were sleepy, his hair a thick, careless mess, and still he fairly oozed the same sensual menace he had the night before, when he'd been dressed so elegantly. He studied her for a long moment, and the great, wide bed felt like a tiny little cot, suddenly. Like a trap. Adriana's pulse beat at her, and she forgot about her headache.

"I hope you appreciate the sacrifice I made to your modesty," Pato said in that drawling way of his, as if he was too lazy to bother enunciating properly. He waved at the form-fitting briefs he wore. At that flat abdomen of his, the crisp dark hair that disappeared beneath the fabric. She jerked her eyes away, and his mouth curved. "I think you know very well I prefer to sleep naked."

Adriana felt dizzy, and part of her welcomed it. Encouraged it. It would be such a relief to simply faint dead away. To escape whatever morning-after this was. She lifted a hand to her head, only belatedly realizing that her hair had tumbled down from its chignon, and was hanging around her face in a wild mess that rivaled Pato's.

Somehow, that made it worse. It made her feel like the wanton slut she must have become last night. Was it possible to share a bed with Prince Pato and *not* be a wanton slut? Her chest felt tight.

He watched her as she pushed the mass of blond waves behind her shoulders, his golden gaze like a flame as it touched her. More images from the previous night flashed through her head then, as if the heat of his gaze triggered her memory, and she frowned at him.

"You got me drunk," she accused him.

Blaming him felt good. Clean. Far better to concentrate on that and not the images flickering in her head. Some dark-paneled pub, or possibly the kind of rich man's club a prince might frequent, thick with reds and woods and the shots of strong spirits Pato slid in front of her, one after the next, his golden gaze never leaving her face. His elegant hands brushing hers. That wicked mouth of his much too close.

"You got you drunk," he corrected, shifting over to his side and propping his head up on one hand as he continued to regard her with that lazy intent that made her belly fold in on itself. "Who was I to stand in your way?"

A dark street, laughter. *Her* laughter, and the wicked current of his voice beneath it. Her arm around Pato's waist and his lean, hard arm around her shoulders. Then being held high against his chest as he moved through some kind of lobby...

This was awful, Adriana thought then, her chest aching with the sobs, the screams, she refused to let out. This was beyond awful.

"My God." She said it again, despite the decided lack of any divine intervention this morning. She squeezed her eyes shut, bracing herself for the blow. Preparing herself, because she had to know. "Did you—? Did we—?"

There was nothing but silence. Adriana dared to open her eyes again, to find that Pato was staring at her in outrage.

She shuddered. "Does that mean we did?" she asked in a tiny voice.

"First of all," he said, in that low voice of his that curled around her like a caress, and she couldn't seem to shake it off, "I am not in the habit of taking advantage of drunk women who pretend to detest me when they are sober, no matter how much they beg."

His gaze was hard on hers, and Adriana felt caught in the heat, the command, that surely a wastrel like Pato shouldn't have at his disposal. Eventually, his mouth moved into a small, sexy grin that shouldn't have tugged at her like that, all fire and need in the core of her, then a shiver everywhere else. She couldn't seem to think, to move. To breathe. She could only stare back at him, her heart going wild, as if he was holding her captive in the palm of his hand.

"And second," he said silkily, "if we had, you wouldn't have to ask. You'd know."

"Oh," Adriana said faintly, not sure she was breathing. "Well. If you're sure…?"

Pato shook his head. "I'm sure."

She believed him. He was only *looking* at her now, all that gleaming attention of his focused on her. He wasn't even touching her, and she felt branded. Scalded. Changed. She had a perfect memory of his hand on her arm, the heat of it, the punch of it, the way everything inside her had wound deliciously tight. She believed him, and yet there was something inside her that almost wished—

Stop, she snapped at herself, off balance and scared and much too close to falling apart.

Adriana realized belatedly that far too much time had passed and she'd done nothing but stare at him, while he watched her and no doubt read every last thought that crossed her mind. He was lethal; she understood that now, in a way she hadn't before. He was lethal and she was in bed with him and somehow by the grace of God she hadn't succumbed to his darker nature or, worse, *hers*…

Adriana frowned. "Did you say I *begged?*"

Pato smiled.

"For what?" she asked in an appalled whisper. "Exactly?"

He smiled wider.

"This can't be happening." She was barely audible, even to her own ears, but she felt each word like a stone slamming through her. "Did I—" But even as she asked, she shut herself off. "No. I don't want to know."

"You begged very prettily," he told her then, that wild gleam in his eyes, which made her feel much too hot, too constricted, as if she might burst wide-open. "If it helps."

It helped confirm that she hated herself, Adriana thought, that old black wave of self-loathing rising in her and then drenching her, drowning her, in all the ways she'd let herself down. *Blood really will tell,* she thought bitterly. *You've been fooling yourself all these years, but in the end, you're no better than any of them. Righetti whores.*

She managed to take a breath, then another one.

And then, through her confusion, one thing became perfectly clear: it was time to accept who she was, once and for all. And that meant it was time to change her life.

"Thank you, Your Royal Highness," she said stiffly, not looking at him. "I'm sorry that I let myself get so out of control and that you had to deal with me. How incredibly unprofessional."

She scrambled to crawl out of the bed, away from him. This had to end. What was she was doing here, disgracing herself with a prince, when she could be living without the weight of all of this in some happy foreign land like her brothers? She'd been so desperate to prove herself—and now she'd proved only that she was exactly who everyone thought she was.

Enough, she thought grimly.

And there was what Lenz had said, the way he'd said it, but she didn't want to think about that. She didn't want to let it hurt her the way she suspected it would when she did.

It seemed to take an hour to reach the edge of the bed, and as she went to swing her feet to the ground, Pato simply reached out and hauled her back by the arm until she was on her side and facing him. No sheet this time to hide behind. Just far too much of her nearly naked body far too near his. Panic screamed through her, making her skin burst into flames.

"You can't just...*manhandle* people!" she exclaimed heatedly.

Pato shrugged, and the total lack of concern in the gesture reminded her forcefully that, black sheep or not, he was a royal prince. Pampered and indulged. Used to getting whatever he wanted. He wasn't required to concern himself with other people's feelings, particularly hers.

That should have disgusted her. It alarmed her that it didn't.

"I think we're a bit past worrying about professionalism," he said, his voice mild, though his eyes were intent on hers, and his mouth looked dangerous in a new way with his jaw unshaved and his thick hair so unruly.

And all of him *so close.*

"I need to leave," she replied evenly. "The palace, the royal family—I should have done it a long time ago." She started to pull away from him, but he only shifted position and smoothed his hand down to the indentation of her waist. He rested it there, almost idly, and she froze as if he was pressing her to the bed with brute force.

It would have been easier if he had been, she recognized on some level. It would have been unambiguous. But instead he was only touching her, *barely* touching her, and she couldn't seem to form the words to demand he let her go. She only trembled. Inside and out.

And he knew. His eyes gleamed, and he knew.

"At least let me get back under the sheet," she said desperately.

"Why?" He shrugged again, so lazy. So at ease. "You're showing less skin than you would if you were wearing a bikini."

"You've never seen me in a bikini," she managed to say. "It would be inappropriate."

His fingers traced the faintest pattern along the curve of her body, and she could no more help the shiver of goose bumps that rose on her skin than she could turn back time and avoid this scenario in the first place. He looked at the telltale prickle of flesh, his hand tightened at her waist and she let out a tiny, involuntary sound that made his golden gaze darken and focus on her, hot and hungry.

But when he spoke again, his voice was light.

"I hate to be indelicate, Adriana, but I've already seen all of this. You're about eight hours too late for modesty."

"It's time for me to leave," she said, desperate and determined in equal measure. "You never wanted an assistant in the first place, and I think it's high time I rethink my career prospects."

Pato only raised a dark brow.

"I have no business being at the palace," she said urgently. "The princess was right. If I'd had any idea that working for your brother would harm *his* reputation, I never would have taken the job in the first place. I would never want people to think less of him because of me. I would never want to compromise his reputation, or—"

"You can't possibly be this naive."

Something Adriana had never seen before moved over Pato's face. His hand tightened briefly, and then he released her and sat up in a smooth roll.

He shoved his hair back and pinned her with a glare when she scrambled away from him and to her knees on the far side of the bed, pulling the sheet back over her as she went. She had never seen him look like that. Brooding, dark. No hint of his famous laughter, his notorious smile.

"I'm being rational, not naive," she countered, unable to tear her eyes away from him when he looked like this, as if he was someone else. Someone ruthless and hard. Not like easy, careless Pato at all. "Your brother was the first person to believe in me, but it was wrong of me to take advantage of that."

Pato shook his head, rubbing at his jaw with one hand as if he was keeping words back manually.

"I abused his kindness," she continued, her unease growing. "His—"

"For God's sake, Adriana," Pato spat out. "He wasn't being *kind*. He was grooming you to be his mistress."

CHAPTER FOUR

FOR A LONG, breathless moment, Adriana could only stare at him, another piece of her world crumbling into dust in this bed, shattering in that relentless golden gaze.

"That's absurd." She felt turned inside out. "He would never do something like that."

"You know all about his previous assistants, I'm sure," Pato said, in that same blunt way, a hard gleam in his gaze and no hint of a curve on that mouth of his. "Did you never question why he cycled so many of them through that position? And why they all had such different sets of credentials? One an art historian, another a socialite? Lenz prefers his mistresses be accessible."

Adriana felt as if she'd slipped sideways into some alternate reality, where nothing made sense any longer. Lenz had wanted her, all this time, as she'd so often daydreamed he might—but not as his mistress. She'd never wanted *that*. And now she sat too close to naked in the morning sun with Pato, of all people, who looked like some harsher version of himself, and she was terrified that he might be right. Hadn't her father said the same thing only yesterday?

"He's a good man," she whispered, shaken.

"Yes," Pato said impatiently. "And yet he's still flesh and blood like all the rest of us."

She shook her head, and looked down at the bed. She'd

done this. She understood that, if nothing else. This was the Righetti curse. *This was her fault.* Her head felt heavy again, and it pounded, but she knew it wasn't a leftover from last night. It was the generations of Righettis running wild in her blood, and her silly notion she could be any different.

"Do people really think that I'm his mistress?" she asked, sounding like a stranger to her own ears. She was afraid to look at Pato then, but she made herself do it anyway. His eyes seemed darker than usual, and they glittered.

"Of course." There was an edge to his low voice then, a darker sheen to that intent way he looked at her. "You are a Righetti, he is a Kitzinian prince, and one thing we know about history, Adriana, is that it repeats itself until it kills us all."

Suddenly, the fact that she was practically naked with this man seemed obscene, disgusting. As if her flesh itself were evil, as if it had made her do this—her body ignoring her brain and acting of its own accord. She slid out of the bed and looked around wildly, her eyes falling on the nearest chair. She walked over and grabbed the oversize wrap that she'd worn against the cool London weather, dropped the sheet that made everything seem too sexual, and covered herself.

It didn't make her feel any better.

Adriana couldn't understand how she'd been so blind, so stupid. How she hadn't known that *of course* people would think the worst of her, no matter if the tabloids had eased off—out of respect for Lenz, she understood now in a miserable rush of insight. No one had cared that she was good at her job, that she'd never so much as touched the future king. Why had she imagined any of that would matter? *Because you wanted to pretend. Because you wanted to believe you could be someone else.*

But she was a Righetti. There was never any mistaking

that. She should have known it would poison everyone and everything she came into contact with. Even Lenz.

She turned then, and Pato still watched her, sitting there on his bed, a vision of indolent male beauty. Every inch of him royal, gorgeous and as utterly, deliberately corrupt as it was assumed she was. He'd chosen it. He was the Playboy Prince, scandalous and dissolute. But he was still a prince.

Adriana blinked. "So are you," she said slowly, as an idea took root inside her, and began to grow. "A Kitzinian prince, I mean."

Pato's mouth crooked. "To my father's everlasting dismay, yes."

It was so simple, Adriana thought then, staring at him as if she'd never seen him before. It could fix everything.

"Then we should make them all think that I'm *your* mistress," she said in a rush. She clutched the wrap tighter around her, drifting closer to the bed as she spoke. "The tabloids are halfway there already."

"I beg your pardon?"

"No one would be at all surprised to discover that *you* were sleeping with a Righetti," she continued excitedly, ignoring the odd, arrested look on his face. "Your brother is much too responsible to make that kind of mistake. But you live for mistakes. You're famous for them!"

"I'm not following you," he said, and she noticed then that his voice had gone low and hot, and not with the kind of heat she'd heard before.

"It wouldn't even take that much effort." She was warming to the topic as her mind raced ahead, picturing it. "One paparazzi picture and the whole world would be happy to believe that history was indeed repeating itself, but with a far more likely candidate than your brother."

Pato only looked at her for a long moment, and Adriana found herself remembering, suddenly, that he was second in line to the throne. One tragedy and he would be king. All of a sudden he looked as commanding, as regal, as a man in such a position should. Powerful beyond measure. Dangerous.

It was as if she hadn't seen him before. As if he'd been hiding, right there in plain sight, beneath the dissipated exterior. But how was that possible?

"It wouldn't be real, of course," she said quickly, confusion making her feel edgy. Or maybe that was him. "All we'd need was a few pictures and some good PR spin."

He laughed then, but it was a low, almost aggressive sound, and it made her whole body stiffen in reaction.

"You can't possibly be suggesting that we pretend you're sleeping with me to preserve my brother's reputation," he said softly, and Adriana didn't miss the fact that the tone he used was deadly. It made her stomach twist. "You are not actually standing here in my bedroom, wearing almost nothing, and proposing such a thing."

She searched his face, but he was a stranger, dark and hard.

"That's exactly what I'm proposing."

His jaw worked. His golden eyes flashed. "No."

She scowled at him. "Why not?"

"Do you really require a reason?" he demanded, and then he got to his feet, making everything that much more tense. "You'd be much better served making certain we both forget this absurd conversation ever happened."

That was when Adriana realized, in a kind of shock, that he was angry. Pato, who famously never got angry. Who was supposed to be carefree and easy in all things. Who had laughed off every sticky situation he'd ever been in.

But not this one. Not today. He was *angry*. And she had no idea why.

She watched him warily as he roamed around the foot of the bed, so close to naked, and now that temper she hadn't known he had spilling out around him like a black cloud.

But she couldn't stop. Not when she'd figured out a way to fix things. And what did he care, anyway? It wasn't as if *his* reputation was at stake.

"I don't understand," she said after a moment, trying to sound reasonable. Rational. "You've gone out of your way to link yourself to every woman with a bad reputation you've ever come across. Why not me? My bad reputation goes back centuries!"

"I actually did those things," he replied, that dark temper rich in his voice, in the narrow gaze he aimed at her. "I didn't pretend for the cameras. I don't apologize for who I am, but I also don't fake it."

Adriana blinked. "So your issue isn't the idea itself, then. It's that you need your debaucheries to be honest and truthful. Real."

The way he looked at her then made a low, dark pulse begin to drum in her, panic and heat and something else she'd never experienced before and couldn't name. It took everything she had not to bolt for the door and forget she'd ever started this.

"My reputation is my life's work," Pato said, and there was a certain harshness in his voice then, dark and grim and tired, that made something clutch hard in Adriana's chest. "It's not a cross I'm forced to bear. It's deliberate."

"Fine," she blurted out. She'd never felt so desperate. She only knew this had to happen, she had to have the opportunity to fix one thing her family name had ruined, just one thing—

"Fine?" he echoed, his golden eyes narrowing, focusing in on her in a way that should have made her fall over in a dead faint. Incinerate on the spot. Run.

Something.

But she met his gaze squarely instead.

"We don't have to fake it," Adriana said, very distinctly, so there could be no mistake. "I'll sleep with you."

All the air in the room evaporated into a shimmer of heat. Into the intensity of Pato's gaze, the electricity that arced between them, the tension bright and taut and very nearly painful.

He laughed, low and dark and wicked, and Adriana felt it like a touch, as if his strong, elegant hands were directly on her skin. It made her feel weak. It made her want to drop the wrap and press herself against him, to see if that might ease the heavy ache inside her, the pulse of it, the need.

But who was she kidding? She knew it would. And so did he.

"You have no idea what you're asking, Adriana," he scoffed. His mouth curved mockingly, knowingly, and that ache in her only grew sharper, more insistent. She suddenly wasn't at all sure what she was desperate for. But she couldn't look away. "You wouldn't know where to start."

Adriana couldn't stop the shivering, way down deep inside her.

Her bones felt like jelly and she didn't know what scared her more—that she might really follow through and throw herself at him, and God only knew what would become of her then, or that the terrible ache inside her might take her to the ground on its own, and then he'd know exactly how much he tormented her.

Though she suspected he already did.

Pato was coming toward her, that sun-kissed skin on careless display, the faint brush of dark hair across his hard pectoral muscles seeming to emphasize his fascinating, unapologetic maleness. And he watched her so intently as he moved, his golden eyes gleaming as if all the wickedness in the world was in him, dark and rich and his to use against her if he chose. All his.

She shouldn't find that at all intriguing. She shouldn't

wonder, now that she'd glimpsed a different side of this man, what else he hid behind his disreputable mask.

This is about Lenz, she reminded herself sharply. She refused to think about Pato's claim that her beloved crown prince had wanted her as his mistress all those years she'd believed they'd been working together in harmony. She couldn't let that matter. This was about saving the one thing she could save, the one thing her family name had blackened that she could actually wash clean.

She couldn't save herself, perhaps. But she could save Lenz's reputation.

"Your brother—" she began.

"Rule number five," Pato said smoothly, but with that alarming kick of dark fire beneath. "When attempting to negotiate your way into my bed, don't bring up my brother. Ever."

Adriana felt her pulse beating too hard inside her neck, her wrists. And lower, where it mixed with that ache in her, gave it bite. She forced herself to stand still as Pato roamed toward her. Forced herself to act as if he didn't, in fact, intimidate her—even when he stopped so close to her that she had to tilt her head back to look at him.

He crossed his arms over his chest, his eyes unreadable.

"Are we negotiating?" she asked, her voice so much smaller than it should have been. Telling him too much she shouldn't let him know.

"I don't take trembling virgins to my bed, Adriana," Pato said, with all that gold in his gaze and that curve to his lips, but still, that new hardness beneath. It almost made her miss what he'd said. Then it penetrated, and her body seemed to detonate into a long, red flush of humiliation—but he wasn't finished. "Particularly not trembling, terrified virgins who imagine themselves in love with my brother and view my bed as a sacrificial altar."

"I—" She'd never stammered in her life. She had to order herself to snap her mouth closed, to calm herself. Or at least to breathe. "I'm not terrified." His gaze never wavered, and yet she was sure it was consuming her where she stood. "And, of course, I'm certainly not a *virgin*."

His dark brows rose. "Convince me."

"How?" she demanded, bright red and humiliated. And trembling, just as he'd accused. He missed nothing. "Not that it would matter if I was or that it's any of your business, let me point out."

"But it is." He was merciless, his hard gaze hot. "You want in my bed? Then I want to know every last detail of your vast sexual experience. Convince me, Adriana. Consider it a job interview—your résumé. After all, you've read all about me in the tabloids. You said so yourself."

She told herself he couldn't possibly be asking that. *This couldn't possibly be happening.* But then, what part of this day so far was at all possible? She didn't drink to excess and wake up in men's beds. She didn't have extended conversations with royal Kitzinian princes in her underwear. And had she really told this man she would sleep with him?

So she took a deep breath and she told him what she thought he wanted to hear.

"I couldn't possibly count them all," she said primly, lifting her chin. "I stopped keeping track when I passed into triple digits."

He only shook his head at her.

"For all I know you and I have already slept together, in fact," she continued wildly. "Didn't you once tell an interviewer that you blacked out the better part of the last decade? Well, you're not alone. Who knows where I've been? You were probably there, too, making a spectacle of yourself."

"And somehow," Pato said mildly, "I remain unconvinced."

"Everybody knows I'm a whore," Adriana forced herself to

say, not wanting to admit how limited her sexual experience really was. She wasn't a virgin, true—but that was more or less a technicality, and deeply embarrassing to boot. "They've been calling me that since I was a child, before I even knew what the word meant. Why shouldn't I embrace it? You do."

"That doesn't answer the question, does it?" His gaze bored into her, not relenting at all. Not even the smallest bit. "You have not had sexual partners numbering in the triple digits, Adriana. I'd be very much surprised if you've had three in the whole of your life."

And then he simply stood there, staring down at her, somehow knowing these things that he shouldn't. It made her feel almost itchy, as if her skin had stopped fitting her properly. As if she was seconds away from exploding, humiliated and laid unacceptably bare.

"One." She bit out the admission, hating him, hating herself. And yet still as determined to go through with this as she was filled with that terrible, gnawing ache that she worried might consume her alive. *Do it for Lenz,* she ordered herself. "There was only one and it—"

He waited, his eyes intent and demanding on hers, and she couldn't do it. She couldn't tell this sleek, sensual, unapologetically carnal creature about that fumble in the dark, the shock of searing pain and then the unpleasant fullness that followed. That vulnerable, exposed feeling. She'd been seventeen. It had taken all of three unremarkable minutes in a bedroom at a party she shouldn't have gone to in the first place, and then he'd bragged to the whole school that the Righetti girl was as much of a whore as suspected.

"And?" Pato prompted her.

"It was mercifully brief."

"I feel seduced already," he said drily. "What a tempting picture you paint. How can I possibly resist the sacrificial near-virgin who wishes to prostrate herself in my bed for my brother's benefit? I've never been so aroused."

Each dry, sardonic word, delivered in that deliberately stinging way of his, made Adriana's fists tighten where she held the wrap around her. She felt that flush of heat that told her she was getting redder, broadcasting the fact he was getting to her. She felt that twist in her gut and still, that ache below. This was a disaster.

But you have to do it. You'll never be able to live with yourself if you don't. This might be the only opportunity you ever have to do something good with all this notoriety...

"Then teach me," she exclaimed, cutting him off before he could continue ripping her to shreds one sardonic word at a time.

For a moment, Pato only looked at her.

And then he closed the distance between them, reaching out to spear his hands into the wild tangle of her hair, making her go up slightly on her toes and brace her hands against the hot, hard planes of his chest or fall completely against him. Her wrap floated to the floor between them, and she forgot it as he held her face still, keeping her captive, a mere breath away from his beautiful mouth.

She heard a sharp, high sound, some kind of gasp, and realized only belatedly that she'd made it. The echo of it made her tremble, or perhaps that was the wildfire in his eyes.

"Teach me everything," she whispered, spurred on by some dark thing inside her she hardly recognized. But she saw the way his eyes flared, and the ache inside her bloomed in immediate response.

His mouth was so close to hers, his face dark and dangerous, that lethal fire in his gaze. And yet he only held her there, taut and breathless, while sensation after sensation shook through her. Towering flames in her throat, her breasts, her belly. That shocking brightness between her legs.

Her lips parted slightly, and she recognized it as the invitation it was. His gaze dropped to her mouth, hungry and hard, and she felt her nipples pull tight. Nothing existed but that pulse of heat that drummed in her, louder and wilder—

And then he dragged his gaze back to hers and let her go.

She caught herself before she staggered backward, but she was shaky, unbalanced, and for some reason felt as if she might burst into tears. She couldn't seem to form the words she needed, and his eyes darkened because, of course, he knew that, too. He'd done this to her deliberately.

"You can't handle me, Adriana," Pato growled. "Look at you. I've barely touched you and you're coming apart."

That dark thing inside of her roared through her, making her bold. Making her stark, raving mad. But she couldn't hold it in check. She couldn't stop.

She didn't *want* to stop, and she didn't want to think about why.

"It looks like you're the one who's coming apart, Your Royal Highness," she hissed. Taunting him. Poking at him, and she knew it. She wanted it—she wanted *him*—and the obvious truth of that was like another explosion, bathing her in a white-hot heat. Adriana had no choice then but to keep talking despite the way he looked at her. "Maybe your reputation is all lies and misdirection. Maybe the truth is *you* can't handle *me*."

When he laughed then, it was darker than what was inside her, darker and far wilder, and it connected to that ache in her, hard. So hard she stopped breathing.

And then he moved.

His arms came around her and his hands slid over her bottom with an easy command, as if he'd touched her a thousand times before and just as carnally, slipping directly into her panties and pausing to test her curves, her flesh, against the heat of his palms. She made a wild sort of sound, but as she did he hauled her to him and lifted her against him, pulling her legs around his waist even as her back hit the wall behind her.

The room seemed to spin around, but that was only Pato, pressing her to the wall of his chest and the wall at her back, molding his hips to hers, the hardest part of him flush against her. Skin. Heat. Fires within fires, and she was afraid she was already burned to a crisp. Everything hurt—but was eased by the heat of him, only to hurt again. And again.

She expected an explosion. A detonation. Something to match that searing blaze in his gaze, the drum of anticipation beneath her skin, that hunger between her legs that he was only making worse. Her eyes were glazed and wide, and she could feel him everywhere. That perfect, lean body pressed against her, into her, so powerful and male, holding her steady so far from the ground.

His hands moved over her skin, leaving trails of fire in his wake. He traced the curve of her breasts, teased the hard tips with his thumbs until she moaned. He moved his hips, rocking against her, making her breath come in desperate pants even as her core ignited into a glorious, molten ache that she never wanted to end, that she wasn't sure she'd survive.

Adriana couldn't think. She could only hold on to his broad, hard shoulders and surrender to the dark exultation that roared in her, that made her try to get closer to him, that made her think she might die if she couldn't taste him. That made her want things she'd only read about before. That made her want everything.

He leaned in close, so close that when his wicked mouth curved again, she felt it against her own lips, and it made her shake against him, the small moan escaping her before she could stop it.

"Let me see if I can handle this," he mocked her.

"I don't think you can," she heard herself say. "Or you already would have."

As if she was as wanton as he was, and as unashamed. As if she knew what she was demanding.

That smile of his deepened, torturing her. Delighting her.

And then, slowly and deliberately, with one hand on her bottom to move her against him in a sinuous rhythm that made her feel weak, the other at her jaw to hold her where he wanted her, Pato took his own sweet time and licked his way into her mouth.

Ruining her, Adriana thought while the world disappeared, forever.

He never should have tasted her.

That it was a terrible mistake was a certainty, but Adriana clung to him like honey, melting and hot, tasting like sugar and fire with her lithe body wrapped all around him. Pato couldn't stop himself. For a heady moment—his mouth angled over hers, tasting her again and again and again—he even forgot why he should.

This was supposed to be a lesson to her. A way to decidedly call her bluff, nothing more.

And yet he wanted to take her where they stood, pressed up against the wall, thrusting into the heat of her he could feel scalding him through the thin layers that barely separated them. She was so soft. So responsive.

Perfect.

But she didn't want *him,* no matter what her body shouted at him. No matter what he felt in his arms, what he tasted.

She met him even as he grew bolder, hotter, more demanding. She kissed him as if she'd forgotten who it was she truly wanted. She bloomed beneath his hands, incandescent and addicting. She twined her arms around his neck and writhed against him as if she was as desperate as he was, as if she wanted nothing more than Pato deep inside of her.

But she wanted Lenz. She was in love with Lenz. Pato had seen it.

It was that unpalatable fact that he couldn't make himself ignore, no matter how hard he was and no matter what he would have given, in that moment, to simply drive into her and ride them both into an oblivion where Lenz did not exist. Could never exist.

Where there was only this heat. This need. This delicious electricity, intense and greedy, that made him want to taste every part of her, make her scream out in pleasure while he did, and then take her until she sobbed his name.

His name, not his brother's.

But he couldn't stop. He didn't *want* to stop. What was this woman doing to him? He'd never acted with so little thought before. He'd never forgot to hide himself. He'd certainly never opened his mouth and let some part of the truth come out. It was as if he'd lost the control that had defined him since he was eighteen....

That couldn't happen. He couldn't let it.

He spun around, walking them back to the bed with Adriana still wrapped around him, and then he tortured himself by bringing them down on the mattress—catching himself on one arm so he didn't crush her, but letting himself revel in the feel of her beneath him the way he wanted her, even for a moment.

Pato had never put much stock in the kingdom's insistence that Righetti women were akin to witches, temptresses and jezebels without equal, but pulling himself away from Adriana, from all that soft, hot fire, was the hardest thing he could remember doing.

He didn't understand this. He didn't understand himself.

"I can handle it, Adriana," he told her. "I can handle you. But I won't."

He stood over her, telling himself it didn't matter that she sprawled there before him, her lips swollen from his, her breasts spilling from her bra and crying out for his hands, her silken limbs spread out before him like a dessert he hungered for as if he was a starving man. It didn't matter because it couldn't.

He smirked, knowing it would hit her like a slap. "But I appreciate the offer."

Her face blazed red as he'd thought it would, and she looked tense and unhappy as she pushed herself up to a sitting position. Her lovely blond hair fell in a sexy tangle around her pretty face, making her look as if he'd already had her. He wished he had, with an edge of desperation that should have alarmed him. But she sat before him, with all that lust and wild need still stamped on her face, and the only thing he felt was that pounding desire.

She inclined her head at the clear evidence that he wanted her, badly and unmistakably, then looked up to hold his gaze with hers, her chocolate eyes dark and still too hot.

"I can see how much you appreciate it, Your Royal Highness," she said softly, but with that kick beneath that he couldn't help but enjoy. He didn't understand why he liked her edginess. Why he liked how unafraid she was of him, even now.

He could still taste her. He was so hard for her it hurt, and he wasn't used to denying himself anything. Much less women. He couldn't remember the last time he'd tried. Pato had slept with any number of women who had assumed he'd be a conduit to his brother, who had cold-bloodedly used him for that purpose. It had never bothered Pato before.

He didn't know why it bothered him now—why that look on her face in the shadows last night kept flashing in his head. He only knew he wouldn't—couldn't—be this woman's path to his brother, no matter her reasons, no matter how convoluted it all was. He wanted her head to be full of him, and nothing else.

"We can't always have what we want," he said quietly. He meant it more than she knew.

"You can. You do." She frowned at him. "You've made a career out of it."

Pato shook his head. "You're not going to win this argument with me. No matter how sweetly you pout, or how naked you get. Not that I don't enjoy both."

She made a small sound of frustration, mixed, he could tell from the color in her cheeks, with that embarrassment that he found himself entirely too obsessed with. When was the last time he'd met a woman who still blushed?

"Is there any woman alive you *haven't* slept with?" she demanded. "Or is it only me?"

"It's only you," Pato assured her, not knowing why he was doing this. Not understanding what there was to gain from it. Surely it would be better simply to have her. That was the time-honored approach to situations like this. Chemistry never lasted. Sex was white-hot for only a small while, and then it burned itself out. The only thing denial ever did—or so he'd heard—was make the wanting worse.

But he had never wanted someone like this. And having tasted her, he very much doubted that sex would be a cure. More like his doom.

He didn't know where that thought came from, and yet it clawed into him.

"You didn't even know the word *no* until today!" she snapped at him.

"If I were you," he said in a low voice that he could see got to her when she shivered again, as if he'd run his fingers down the line of her elegant neck, "I'd quit now, before tempers are lost and consequences become far greater. I'd put on some clothes and remember myself. My place. Just a suggestion."

She pulled in a breath, and her hands balled into fists, and then she shook her head slightly as if she really was remembering herself.

"I told you I'd resign," she said after a moment. Her mouth firmed. "And I will. Today, in fact."

"No, you will not."

She *should* resign. He should see to it she was sacked, barred from the palace, kept away for her own good. She should take her melting brown eyes and that impossibly tempting body of hers, her irritating martyr's love for the undeserving Lenz, and leave Kitzinia far behind. She should protect herself from her family's history, from the endless, vicious rumor mill that comprised the highest levels of Kitzinian society, and was even nastier than usual when it came to her.

He wished he could protect her himself.

He was, Pato realized then, in terrible trouble. But this was a game, he reminded himself, and Adriana was a part of it. His strange, protective urges didn't matter—they couldn't. She wasn't going anywhere. He needed her to stay right where she was.

"You won't help me help your brother, and you won't let me leave," Adriana said, her voice as stiff as her body had become, her brown eyes rapidly cooling, which he told himself was better. "What *will* you let me do?"

"I suggest you do your job." It came out harsher than he'd intended, and he saw her blink, as if it hurt. He tried to force his usual laughter into his voice, that devil-may-care attitude he'd perfected, but he couldn't quite do it. "If you can. I can't promise I'll cooperate, but then, you knew that going in."

"I don't want—"

"I am Prince Patricio of Kitzinia and you are a Kitzinian

subject," he said, more himself in that moment than he'd allowed himself to be in years, and that, too, was trouble. Big trouble. It was too soon to be anything but Pato the Playboy, even here—and still, he couldn't stop. "You serve at my pleasure, Adriana. Yours is irrelevant."

For a breath, she seemed to freeze there before him. Then she averted her eyes in appropriate deference to his rank, and there was no particular triumph in winning that little skirmish, Pato found. Not when it made him feel empty. Adriana shot to her feet then and started for the door, her spine straight and every inch of her obviously, silently, furious. It hummed in the air between them. He knew it should offend his royal dignity, had he been possessed of any, but it only made him want to taste her again. Taste her temper. Let it take them both on a ride.

"Thank you, Your Royal Highness, for reminding me of my duty. And my place. I won't forget it again."

She spoke as she moved, her words perfectly polite if not *quite* as respectful as they should have been. There was that edge beneath it, that slap, that was all Adriana. It made him hunger for her all over again.

He reached out and snagged her elbow as she passed, pulling her against him, her back to his front, cursing himself as he did it but completely unable to stop.

"I won't forget this," he said, directly into her ear, all of her soft skin smooth and warm and delicious against his chest, his aching sex. "As you march around to my brother's tune and make your doomed attempts to keep me in line, I'll remember all of this." He let his gaze drift down over her body, satisfaction moving hard in him when her nipples hardened, when another flush worked over her sensitive skin, when her eyes eased closed and her breath went shallow. "I'll remember those freckles between your breasts, for example, three in a line. I'll wonder how they taste. I'll be thinking about the way you look right now, kissed and wild and desperate, when you're ordering me around in your conservative little business suits. It will always be there, hanging in the air between us like a fog."

She shook her head in confusion, and he could feel the fine, delicate tremors that shook in her, the staccato beat of her pulse, all that need and fire and loss. It raged just as brightly in him.

"Then why…?"

Pato leaned closer, spurred on by demons he didn't recognize, needs he didn't understand at all. But their teeth were in him. Deep. And he wanted them in her, too.

"*My* pleasure, Adriana," he told her fiercely, as if it was some kind of promise. A dark threat. He couldn't tell the difference any longer. "Not yours."

CHAPTER FIVE

ADRIANA EYED PATO across the aisle of his royal jet as it winged its way into the night from the glittering shores of Monaco back to Kitzinia, cutting inward across the top of Italy toward Switzerland, Liechtenstein and home.

He was still wearing the formal black tie he'd worn to debonair effect earlier this evening, causing the usual deafening screams when he'd walked the red carpet into the star-studded charity event. Now he murmured into his mobile phone while he lounged on the leather sofa that stretched along one side of the luxury aircraft's lounge area. It had been a long night for him, she thought without a shred of sympathy, as he'd not only had to say a few words at the banquet dinner, but had fended off, at last count, three Hollywood actresses, the lusty wife of a French politician, a determined countess, two socialites and one extremely overconfident caterer.

Left to his own devices, Adriana was well aware, Pato would have stayed in Monaco through the night as he had in years past, partying much too hard with all the celebrities who had flocked to the grand charity event there, and running the risk of either appearing drunk at his engagement with the Kitzinian Red Cross the following morning, or missing it entirely.

She'd insisted they leave tonight. He'd eventually acquiesced.

But Adriana didn't kid herself. She didn't know why he'd pretended to listen to her more often than not in the weeks since that humiliating morning in his London flat. She only knew she found it suspicious.

And that certainly wasn't to suggest he'd *behaved*.

"Your schedule is full this week," she'd told him one morning not long after they'd returned from London, standing stiffly in his office in the palace. Wearing nothing but a pair of battered jeans, he'd been kicked back in the huge, red leather chair behind his massive desk, with his feet propped up on the glossy surface, looking more like a male model than a royal prince.

"I'm bored to tears already," he'd said, his hands stacked behind his head and his golden gaze trained on her in a way that made her want to squirm. She'd somehow managed to refrain. "I think I'd prefer to spend the week in the Maldives."

"Because you require a holiday, no doubt, after all of your hard work doing…what, exactly?"

Pato's mouth had curved, and he'd stretched back even farther in his chair, making his magnificent chest move in ways that only called attention to all those lean, fine muscles packed beneath his sun-kissed skin.

Adriana had kept her eyes trained on his face. Barely.

"Oh, I work hard," he'd told her in that soft, suggestive way that she'd wished she found disgusting. But since London, she'd been unable to dampen the fires he'd lit inside her, and she'd felt the burn of it then. Bright and hot.

"Perhaps if you dressed appropriately," she'd said briskly, forcing a calm smile she didn't feel, and telling herself there was no fire, nothing to burn but her shameful folly, "you might find you had more appropriate feelings about your actual duties, as well."

He'd grinned. "Are my clothes what make me, then?" he'd

asked silkily. "Because I feel confident I'm never more my-self than when I'm wearing nothing at all. Don't you think?"

Adriana hadn't wanted to touch that, and so she'd listed off his week's worth of engagements while his eyes laughed at her. Charities and foundations. Various events to support and promote Kitzinian commerce and businesses. Tours of war memorials on the anniversary of one of the kingdom's most famous battles from the Great War. A visit to a city in the southern part of the country that had been devastated by a recent fire. Balls, dinners, speeches. The usual.

"Not one of those things sounds like any fun at all," Pato had said, still lounging there lazily, as if he'd already men-tally excused himself to the Maldives.

Adriana didn't understand what had happened to her—what she'd done. She shouldn't have responded to him like that in London. She shouldn't have lost her head, surrendered herself to him so easily. So completely. If he hadn't stopped, she knew with a deep sense of shame, she wouldn't have.

And every day she had to stand there before him, both of them perfectly aware of that fact.

It made her hate him all the more. Almost as much as she hated herself. She'd worked closely with Lenz for three years. They'd traveled all over the world together. She'd adored him, admired him. And not once had she so much as brushed his hand inappropriately. Never had she worried that she couldn't control herself.

But Pato had touched her and it had been like cracking open a Pandora's box. Need, dark and wild. Lust and *want* and that fire she'd never felt before in all her life. Proof, at last, that she was a Righetti in more than simply name.

It had to be that tainted blood in her that had made her act so out of character she'd assured herself every day since London. It had to be that infamous Righetti nature taking hold of her, just as the entire kingdom had predicted since her birth, and just as the tabloids claimed daily, speculating madly about her relationship with Pato.

Because it couldn't be him. It couldn't be.

"Yours is a life of great sacrifice and terrible, terrible burdens, Your Royal Highness," she'd said then, without bothering to hide her sarcastic tone. Forgetting herself the way she did too often around him. "However do you cope?"

For a moment their eyes had locked across the wide expanse of his desk, and the look in his—a quiet, supremely male satisfaction she didn't understand at all, though it made something in her shiver—caused her heart to pound. Erratic and hard.

"Does your lingerie match today, Adriana?" he'd asked softly. Deliberately. Taunting her with the memory of that London morning. "I liked it. Next time, I'll taste it before I take it off you."

Adriana had flinched, then felt herself flush hot and red. She'd remembered—she'd *felt*—his hands on her, slipping into her panties to mold the curves of her backside to his palms, caressing her breasts through her bra. The heat of her embarrassment had flamed into a different kind of warmth altogether, pooling everywhere he'd touched her in London, and then starting to ache anew. And she'd been certain that she'd turned the very same cranberry color as the lingerie she'd worn then as she'd stood there before him in that office.

Pato, of course, had smiled.

She'd opened her mouth to say something, anything. To blister him with the force of all the anger and humiliation and dark despair that swirled in her. To save herself from the truths she didn't want to face, truths that moved in her like blood, like need, like all the rest of the things she didn't want to accept.

"I told you how I feel about challenges," he'd said before she could speak, dropping his hands from behind his head and shifting in his chair, his gaze intense. "Disrespect me all you like, I don't mind. But you should bear in mind that, first, it will reflect on you should you be foolish enough to do it in public, not on me. And second, you won't like the way I retaliate. Do you understand me?"

She'd understood him all too well. Adriana had fled his office as if he'd been chasing her, when all that had actually followed her out into the gleaming hall was the sound of his laughter.

And her own deep and abiding shame at her weakness. But then, she carried that with her wherever she went.

Adriana shifted in her seat now, flipping the pages in her book as if she was reading fiercely and quickly, when in fact she hadn't been able to make sense of a single word since the plane had left the airport in Nice, France. Pato was still on his mobile phone, speaking in Italian to one of his vast collection of equally disreputable friends, his low voice and wicked laughter curling through her, into her, despite her best efforts to simply ignore him.

But she couldn't seem to do it.

Her body remembered London too well, even all these weeks later. It thrilled to the memories. They were *right there* beneath her skin, dancing in her veins, pulsing hot and wild in her core. All it took was his voice, a dark look, that smile, and her body thundered for more. More heat, more flame. More of that darkly addictive kiss. More of Pato, God help her. Adriana was terribly afraid that he'd flipped some kind of switch in her and ruined her forever.

And that wasn't the only thing he'd ruined.

"You are clearly a miracle worker," Lenz had said as the young royals had stood together outside a ballroom in the capital city one evening with their various attendants, waiting to make their formal entrance into a foundation's gala event. "There hasn't been a single scandal since you took Pato in hand."

Adriana had wanted nothing more than to bask in his praise. Lenz had always been, if not precisely comfortable to be around, at least easy to work for. He'd never been as dangerously beautiful as Pato, but Adriana had always found him attractive in his own, far less flashy way. The sandy hair, the kind blue eyes. He was shorter than his brother, more solid than lean, but he'd looked every inch the king he'd become. It was the way he held himself, the way he spoke. It was who he was, and Adriana had always adored him for it.

Ordinarily, she would have hung on his every word and only allowed herself to think about the way it made her ache for him when she was alone. But that night she'd been much too aware of Pato standing on the other side of the great doorway, with Princess Lissette. Adriana had been too conscious of that golden gaze of his, mocking her. Reminding her.

He was grooming you to be his mistress.

And when she'd looked at Lenz—*really* looked at him, searching for the *man* and not the Crown Prince of Kitzinia she'd always been so awed by—she'd seen an awareness in his gaze, something darker and richer and clearly not platonic.

There had been no mistaking it. No unseeing it. And no denying it.

"I'm afraid I can't take credit for it, Your Royal Highness," she'd said, feeling sick to her stomach. Deeply ashamed of herself and of him, too, though she hadn't wanted to admit that. She'd been so sure Lenz was different. She'd been so *certain*. She hadn't been able to meet his eyes again. "He's been nothing but cooperative."

"Pato? Cooperative? You must be speaking of a different brother."

Lenz had laughed and Adriana had smiled automatically. But she'd been unable to ignore how close he stood to her, how familiar he was when he spoke to her. Too close. Too familiar. Just as her father had warned, and she'd been too blind to see it. Blind and ignorant, and it made her feel sicker.

Worse, she'd been grimly certain that Pato could see every single thought that crossed her mind. And the Princess Lissette had been watching her as well, her cool gaze sharp, her icy words from the ball in London ringing in Adriana's head.

She is widely regarded as something of a pariah.

Adriana had been relieved when it had been time for the royal entrance. They'd all swept inside to the usual fanfare, the other attendants had disappeared to find their own seats and she'd been left behind in the hall, finally alone. Finally away from all those censorious, amused, *aware* eyes on her. Away from Lenz, who wasn't at all who she'd imagined him to be. Away from Pato, who was far more than she could handle, just as he'd warned her.

Adriana had stood there for a very long time, holding on to the wall as if letting go of it might tip her off the side of the earth and away into nothing.

"You seemed so uncomfortable with my brother last night," Pato had taunted her the very next day, his golden gaze hard on her. She'd been trapped in the back of a car with him en route to another event, and she'd felt too raw, too broken, to contend with the man she'd glimpsed in London, so relentless and powerful. She'd decided she preferred him shiftless and lazy, hip deep in scandal. It was easier. "Or perhaps it's only that I expected to see more chemistry between you, given that you wish to make such a great and noble sacrifice to save him."

His tone had been so dry. He was talking about *her life* as if he hadn't punched huge holes right through the center of it. Adriana had learned long ago how to act tough even if she wasn't, how to shrug off the cruel things people said and did to her—but it had been too much that day.

He'd taken everything that had ever meant something to her. Her belief in Lenz. Her position in the palace. Her self-respect. *Everything.* And finally, something had simply cracked.

"I understand this is all a joke to you," she'd said in a low voice, staring out the window at the red-roofed city, historic houses and church spires, the wide blue lake in the distance, the Alps towering over everything. "And why shouldn't it be? It doesn't matter what you do—the people adore you. There are never any consequences. You never have to pay a price. You have the option to slide through life as pampered and as shallow as you please."

"Yes," he'd replied, sounding lazy as usual, but when she'd glanced back at him his gaze was dark. She might have thought he looked troubled, had he been someone else. Her stomach had twisted into a hard knot. "I'm a terrible disappointment. Sometimes even to myself."

Adriana hadn't understood the tension that had flared between them then, the odd edginess that had filled the interior of the car, fragile and heavy at once. She hadn't *wanted* to understand it. But she'd been afraid she did. That Pandora's box might have been opened, and there wasn't a thing she could do to change it after the fact. But that didn't mean that she needed to rummage around inside it, picking up things best left where they were.

"Your brother was the first man who was ever kind to me," she'd said, her voice sounding oddly soft in the confines of the car. "It changed everything. It made me believe—" But she hadn't been able to say it, not to Pato, who couldn't possibly have understood what it had meant to her to feel safe, at last. Who would mock her, she'd been sure. "I would have been perfectly happy to keep on believing that. You didn't have to tell me otherwise."

"Adriana." He'd said her name like a caress, a note she'd

never heard before in his voice, and she'd held up a hand to stop him from saying anything further. There had been tears pricking at the back of her eyes and it had already been far too painful.

He would take everything. She knew he would. She'd always known, and it was that, she'd acknowledged then, that scared her most of all.

"You did it deliberately," she'd said quietly, and she'd forced herself to look at him. "Because you could. Because you thought it was *funny.*"

"Did you imagine he would love you back?" Pato had asked, an oddly gruff note in his voice then, his gleaming eyes unreadable, and it had hurt her almost more than she could bear. "Walk away from his betrothal, risk the throne he's prepared for all his life? Just as the Duke of Reinsmark did for your great-aunt Sandrine?"

"It wasn't about what Lenz would or wouldn't do," she'd whispered fiercely, fighting back the wild tilt and spin of her emotions, while Pato's words had dripped into her like poison, bitter and painful. "People protect those they care about. If you cared about anything in the world besides pleasuring yourself, you'd know that, and you wouldn't careen through your life destroy—"

He had reached over and silenced her with his finger on her lips, and she hadn't had time to analyze the way her heart slammed into her ribs, the way her whole body seemed to twist into a dark, sheer ripple of joy at even so small and furious a touch from him.

"Don't."

It had been a command, a low whisper, his voice a rough velvet, and that had hurt, too. The car had come to a stop, but Pato hadn't moved. He hadn't looked away from her, pinning her to her seat with too much darkness in his gaze and an expression she'd never seen before on his face, making him a different man all over again.

"You don't know what I care about," he'd told her in that low rasp. "And I never thought any of that was *funny.*"

She'd felt that touch on her mouth for days.

"Ci vediamo," Pato said into his mobile with a laugh now, ending his call.

Adriana snapped back into the present to find him looking at her from where he lounged there across the plane's small aisle. She felt as deeply disconcerted as if the scene in the car had only just happened, as if it hadn't been days ago, and she was afraid he could take one look at her and know exactly what she was thinking. He'd done it before.

If he could, tonight he chose to keep that to himself.

"Good book?" he asked mildly, as if he cared.

"It's enthralling," she replied at once. "I can't bear to put it down for even a second."

"You haven't looked at it in at least five minutes."

"I doubt you were paying that much attention," she said coolly. "Certainly not while making juvenile plans to wreak havoc across Italy with your highly questionable race car driving friends who, last I checked the gossip columns, think the modeling industry exists purely to supply them with arm candy."

He laughed as if she delighted him, and she felt it everywhere, like the touch of the sun. He moved in her like light, she thought in despair, even when he wasn't touching her. She was lost. If she was honest, she'd been lost from the start, when he'd stood there before her with such unapologetic arrogance, naked beneath a bedsheet, and laughed at the idea that she could make him behave.

She should have listened to him. She certainly shouldn't have listened to Lenz, whose motivations for sending her to Pato in the first place, she'd realized at some point while standing in that hallway after seeing him again, couldn't possibly be what she'd imagined them to be when she'd raced off to do his bidding. And she couldn't listen to the tumult inside her, the fire and the need, the chaos that Pato stirred in her without even seeming to try, because that way lay nothing but madness. She was sure of it.

Adriana didn't know what she was going to do.

"Keep looking at me like that," Pato said then, making her realize that she'd been staring at him for far too long—and that he was staring back, his eyes gleaming with a dark fire she recognized, "and I won't be responsible for what happens next."

Pato expected her to throw that back in his face. He expected that cutting tongue of hers, the sweet slap of that smile she used like a razor and sharpened so often and so comprehensively on his skin. He liked both far more than he should.

But her eyes only darkened as they clung to his, and a hectic flush spread over those elegant cheekbones he wanted to taste. He was uncomfortably hard within the next breath, the wild, encompassing need he'd been trying to tell himself he'd imagined, or embellished, slamming into him again, sinking its claws deep, making him burn hot, and *want*.

How could he want her this much?

It had been weeks since London, and his fascination with her should have ebbed by now, as his little fascinations usually did in much less time. And most of *those* women had not fancied themselves tragically in love with his brother. But Adriana was always with him, always right there within his reach, prickly and unimpressed and severe. He spent his days studying her lovely face and its many masks, reading her every gesture, poking at her himself when he grew tired of the distance she tried to put between them.

This woman was his doom. He understood that on a primal level, and yet couldn't do the very thing he needed to do to avert it. He couldn't let her walk away. That was part of the game—but he found he couldn't bear the thought of it.

And he didn't like to think about the implications of that.

"Careful, Adriana," he said quietly. Her chest rose and fell too fast and her hands clenched almost fitfully at the thick paperback she held. If he asked, she would claim she didn't want him and never had—but he could see the truth written all over her. He recognized what burned in her, no matter what she claimed. It made him harder, wilder. Closer to desperate than he'd been in years. "I'm in a dangerous mood tonight."

She blinked then, looking down into her lap and smoothing her hands over the abused book, and he had rendered himself so ridiculous when it came to this woman that he felt it like loss.

"I don't know how you can tell the difference between that and any of your other moods," she said in her usual sharp way, which Pato told himself was better than that lost, hungry stare that could only lead to complications he knew he should avoid. "They're all dangerous, sooner or later, aren't they? And we both know who'll have to clean up the mess."

"I expected applause when we boarded the plane," he told her, smiling when her gaze came back to his, her brows arched over those warm, wary eyes that made him forget about the hollow places inside him. "A grateful speech or two, perhaps even a few thankful tears."

"You board planes all the time," she pointed out, her expression smooth, and that decidedly disrespectful glint in her dark eyes that he enjoyed far too much. "I was unaware that you required encouragement to continue doing so. I'll be sure to make a note of that for future reference. Perhaps the Royal Guard can break from their regular duties protecting our beloved sovereign, and perform a salute."

"I want only your applause, Adriana," he told her silkily.

"After all, you're the one who insisted I become chaste and pure, and so I have. At your command."

"I'm sorry," she murmured, something that looked like a smirk flashing across her mouth before she wisely bit it back. "Did you describe yourself as 'chaste and pure'? In an airplane, of all places, where we are that much closer to lightning, should you be struck down where you sit?"

She was a problem. A terrible problem, the ruin of everything he'd worked for all these years, but Pato couldn't seem to keep himself from enjoying her. He couldn't seem to do anything but bask in her. Tart and quick and the most fun he'd had in ages. With that sweet, hot fire beneath that would burn them both.

"Shall I tell you what I got up to at this particular benefit last year?" he asked.

"Unnecessary," she assured him. "The video of your ill-conceived spa adventure is still available on the internet. Never has the phrase 'the royal jewels' been so widely and hideously abused."

He laughed, and spread out his hands in front of him as if in surrender—noting the way her eyes narrowed in suspicion, as if she knew exactly how unlikely it was he might ever truly surrender anything.

"And look at me now," he invited her. "Not a single lascivious actress in sight, no spa tub in a hotel room that was meant to be private, and I'm not even drunk. You should be proud, Adriana."

She shifted in her chair, crossing her legs, and then frowning at him when his gaze drifted to trace the elegant line of them from the hem of her demure skirt down to the delicate heels she wore.

"Your transformation has been astonishing," she said in repressive tones when he grinned back at her. "But you'll forgive me if I can't quite figure out your angle. I only know you must have one."

"I prefer curves to angles, actually," he said, and laughed again at her expression of polite yet clear distaste at the innuendo. "And it has to be said, I've always found lingerie a particularly persuasive argument."

Adriana let out a breath, as if he'd hit her. Something terribly sad moved over her face then, surprising him and piercing into him. She ran her hands down the length of her skirt, smoothing out nonexistent wrinkles, betraying her anxiety.

Pato knew he was a bastard—he'd gone out of his way to make sure he was—but this woman made him feel it. Keenly. She made him wish he was a different man. A better one. The sort of good one she deserved.

"Perhaps you've managed to convince me of the error of my ways," he said quietly, hating himself further because he wasn't that man. He couldn't be that man, no matter how much she made him wish otherwise. "Just because it hasn't been done before doesn't mean it's impossible."

Her dark eyes met his and made something twist in him, sharp and serrated.

"We both know I did nothing of the kind," she said, her voice soft and matter-of-fact. She let out a small breath. "All I managed to do was make myself one among your many conquests, indistinguishable from the rest of the horde."

"I don't know why you'd think yourself indistinguishable," he said, keeping his tone light.

He could have sworn what he saw flash in her dark eyes then was despair, but she swallowed it back and forced a smile that made his chest hurt.

"I should have realized," she said, and he wondered if she knew how bitter she sounded then, how broken. "You've always been a trophy collector, haven't you? And what a prize you won in London. You get to brag that the Righetti whore propositioned you and you—*you,* of all people—turned her down. My congratulations, Your Royal Highness. That's quite a coup."

For a long moment a black temper pulsed in him, and Pato didn't dare speak. He only studied her face. She was pale now, and sat too straight, too stiff. Her eyes were dark again in exactly the same way they'd been that morning in the car, when he'd felt pushed to confront her about Lenz, and was fairly certain she'd broken his heart. Had he had one to break.

Pato hated this. He was perilously close to hating himself. For the first time since he was eighteen, he wished that he could do exactly what he wanted without having to worry about anyone else. Without having to play these deep, endless games. Adriana sat there and looked at him as if he was exactly the depraved degenerate he'd gone to great lengths to ensure he really was, when she was the first woman he'd ever met that he wanted to think better of him. The irony wasn't lost on him.

It stung. *Congratulations, indeed,* he thought ruefully. This was what doom looked like as it happened, and he was doing nothing at all to prevent it.

"Adriana," he said, trying to keep his temper from his voice. Trying to make sense of his determination to protect her not only from the things he shouldn't allow himself to want from her, but from herself. "You and I both know you're no whore. Why do you torture yourself over the lies that strangers tell? They're only stories. They're not even about you."

"On the contrary," she said after a moment, her voice thick and uneven. "Some of us are defined by the stories strangers tell."

"You're the only one who can define yourself," he countered gently. "All they can do is tell another story, and who cares if they do?"

Emotion moved through her then, raw and powerful. He saw it on her face, in the way her eyes went damp, in the faint tremor of her lips. Her hands balled into fists in her lap and she moved restlessly in her seat, stamping both feet into the floor as if she needed the balance.

"Easy for you to say," she stated, a raw edge to her voice. "Not all of us can be as beloved as you are no matter what you do, forgiven our trespasses the moment we make them."

"Fondness is hardly the same thing as forgiveness."

Her dark eyes seared into him. "You cheerfully admit each and every one of your transgressions," she said. "There are videos, photographs, whole tabloids devoted to your bacchanals. But you are still the most popular young royal in all of Europe. No one cares how dirty you get. It doesn't cling to you. It doesn't matter."

"I prefer 'adventurous' to 'dirty,' I think," he said mildly, watching her closely, seeing nothing but shadows in her beautiful eyes. "Especially in that tone."

"Meanwhile," she said, as if he hadn't spoken, "I happen to be related to three women who slept with Kitzinian royalty over a hundred and fifty years ago, and one woman who ruined a duke more recently. I'm the most notorious slut in the kingdom, thanks to them." She pulled in a breath. "It isn't even *my* dirt, but I'm covered in it, head to toe, and I'll never be clean. Ever." Her eyes held his for a long moment, fierce and dark. "It isn't just another story strangers tell. It's my life."

Pato was aware that he needed to shut this down now, before he forgot himself. But instead, he shook his head and continued talking, as if he was someone else. Someone with the freedom to have dangerous conversations with a woman he found far too fascinating, as if both of them weren't pawns in a game only he knew they were playing.

"You must know that almost all of that is jealousy," he said, letting out a small laugh at the idea that she didn't. "You're a legend, Adriana, whether you earned it or not. Women are envious of the attention you get, simply because you have a notorious name and the temerity to be beautiful. Men simply want you."

She let out a frustrated noise, and snatched up her book again, that smooth mask of hers descending once more. But he could see right through it now.

"I don't want to discuss this," she said, more to the book than to him. "You can't possibly understand. There's not a day of your life you've been envious of anyone, because why should you be? And you certainly don't *want* me. You made that perfectly clear in London."

Pato didn't know he meant to move. He shouldn't have. But one moment he was on the couch and the next he was looming over her, swiveling her chair around and leaning over her, into her, planting his hands on the armrests and caging her between his arms. Risking everything, and he didn't care.

"I never said I didn't want you," he growled down at her.

Pato felt unhinged and unpredictable, capable of anything. Especially a mistake of this magnitude—but he couldn't seem to stop himself. Adriana still smelled of jasmine and her eyes were that rich, deep brown, and he didn't have it in him to fight off this madness any longer.

"Not that I want to revisit the most humiliating morning of my life," she said from between her teeth, "but you did. If not in words, then in actions. And don't misunderstand me, I'm grateful. I wasn't myself."

"The question on the table that morning was not whether or not I wanted you." He moved even closer, watching in satisfaction as her pretty eyes widened with a shock of awareness he felt like hands on his skin. "The question was whether or not I wanted to sleep with you knowing full well you planned to shut your eyes and imagine Lenz in my place. They're not quite the same thing."

She paled, then burst into that bright red blush that Pato found intoxicating. He liked her cheeks rosy, her cool exterior cracked and all her masks useless, the truth of her emotions laid bare before him.

"What does it matter?" Her voice was barely a whisper. "It didn't happen. Crisis averted. There's no need to talk about it now."

"I told you I wouldn't forget," he said, intent and hungry, "and I haven't. I remember the noises you made in the back of your throat when I kissed you, when you rubbed against me like silk, hot and—"

"Please!" Her voice was low. Uncertain. "Stop."

"What do *you* want, Adriana? That's tonight's question."

He leaned in closer, so he could hear the tiny hitch in her breath, and so he could find the pulse in her neck that was drumming madly, giving her away, and tease it with his tongue.

She whispered something that came out more a moan, and he smiled against the delicate column of her throat. Her skin smelled of his favorite flowers and her hair smelled of holidays in the sun, and he wanted to be deep inside her more than he wanted his next breath.

"And when I talk about *want,* I don't mean something tame," he said, a growl against the side of her neck, directly into her satiny skin, so he could feel her tremble against his lips. "I mean hunger. Undeniable, unquenchable hunger. Not because you're drunk. Not because you want to martyr yourself to your great unrequited love. *Hunger,* Adriana. What do you want? What are you hungry for?"

"Please…" she whispered, desperation thick in her voice. She was right there on the edge, right where he wanted her.

He could feel it. He felt it flood through him, dark and thrilling and scorchingly hot.

"I don't think you love him, Adriana," he told her then, and she let out a small sound of distress. "Not really. I know you're not hungry for him. Not like this."

She trembled. She shook. But she didn't argue.

"I asked you a question," he urged her, his mouth at her jaw. "If it helps, I already know the answer. All you have to do is admit it."

CHAPTER SIX

ADRIANA'S BREATH CAME out like a sigh. A release.

Like surrender, Pato thought, satisfaction moving through him like another kind of need, dark and demanding, like all the ways he wanted her.

"I thought it would help your brother's reputation," she said almost too softly, her eyes bright with heat. "I really did."

He nipped at her jaw, and she shivered.

"But I never would have suggested—" She broke off, bit her lip in agitation, then tried again. "I mean, I wouldn't have thought of it if I didn't—"

Pato waited, but she only pulled in a ragged breath, then another. She could hardly sit still. She was flushed hot, shining with the same need he felt pulling at him. Coming apart, right there in the chair, and he'd hardly touched her.

She was going to be the end of him. He knew it.

He couldn't wait.

"Say it," he ordered her. "If you didn't...?"

He felt her give in to it before he saw it, a shift in that tension that tightened the air between them. And then her shoulders lowered, she let out a long breath, and what stormed in him then felt like much, much more than simple victory.

"If I didn't want you," she admitted hoarsely.

Pato kissed her, hard and long and deep, his fingers spearing into her sleek chignon and sending pins scattering to the floor.

And she met him, the feel of her mouth beneath his again—at last—like a revelation.

He couldn't get enough of her taste. He angled his jaw for a better fit and it got hotter, wilder, and then he thought he might explode when he felt her hands running along his arms, trailing over his chest, making him wish he could remove all the layers of his formal clothes simply by wishing them away.

He wanted her mindless. Now. He wanted her falling apart in his arms, lost to this passion that might very well destroy them both. He wanted to claim her.

Pato broke away from the glory of her mouth and sank to his knees before her, making room for himself between her legs. She made a small, dazed sort of sound. He grinned at her, then simply pulled her hips toward him, pushing her skirt up toward her waist and out of his way as he positioned her at the edge of her seat.

He ran his palms up her smooth, satiny thighs, grinning wider as she bit back a moan. He sank his hands underneath her, grasping her perfect bottom and ducking lower, arranging her so that her legs fell over his shoulders and hung down his back. Then he tilted her hips toward him.

"Oh, my God," she whispered, slumped down in her chair with her skirt around her waist and that delectable flush heating her face, making her dark chocolate eyes melt and shine as they met his.

She was delicious and shivering and his. All his, at last.

God help them both.

"Hold on," Pato advised her, hardly recognizing his own voice, so stark with desire was it. So focused. "You'll need it."

He lifted her to him, smiling at the pretty scrap of blue lace that covered the sweet heat of her, and then he leaned forward to suck her into his mouth.

* * *

The shock of his mouth against the very center of her need took Adriana's breath, so that the scream she let out sounded only inside her, ricocheting like a bullet against glass and shattering whatever it touched.

The heat. The fire. The terrible, wonderful ache.

His wicked, talented mouth, so hot and demanding, pressed against the tiny layer of lace that separated them. His hard shoulders felt massive and the fabric of his jacket rough against the tender skin behind her knees. His clever hands gripped her and held her fast, and his impossibly beautiful face was between her thighs so that all she could see when she looked down was that thick, wild hair of his, sunshine and chocolate and that delicious bit too long, and her own hands fisted in the mass of it as if they'd gone there of their own accord.

She thought she'd died. She wanted to die. She didn't know how anyone could take this much pleasure, this much scalding heat, and live through it—

And then he made a low noise of male pleasure, shoved her thong out of his way and licked deep into her molten core.

Adriana burst into a firestorm of white-hot heat and exploded over the edge of the world, lost in a shower of shivering flames.

When she was herself again, or whatever was left of her, she couldn't seem to catch her breath. And Pato was laughing in dark masculine delight, right there against the heat of her core, making the pleasure curl in her all over again, sweeter and hotter than before.

"Again, I think," he murmured, each syllable humming into her and making her press against him before she knew she meant to move, greedy and mindless and adrift in need.

And he took her all over again.

He used his tongue and the scrape of his teeth. His mouth

learned her, possessed her, commanding and effortless. His jaw moved against the tender skin of her thighs, the faint rasp of his beard making the fire in her reach higher, burn hotter. The hands that held her to him caressed her, a low roll of sensation that made her shudder and writhe against him, into him, wanting nothing in the world but this. Him.

And that coiling thing inside her that he knew exactly how to wind tight. Then tighter. Then even tighter still.

Adriana felt the fire surge into something almost unbearable, her whole body stretched taut and breathless, heard his growl of approval and her own high, keening noise—

And then, again, she was nothing more than the fire and the need, shattering into a thousand bright, hot pieces against his wicked, wicked mouth, and then falling in flames all around him.

When Adriana opened her eyes this time, reality slammed into her like a hammer at her temples.

What had she done?

Pato had moved to lounge on the floor, his back against the couch opposite her, with his long legs stretched out and nearly tangled with hers. He wasn't smiling. Those golden eyes were trained on her, brooding and dark, and she didn't know how long she stared back at him, too shaken and dazed to do anything else.

But that hammer kept at its relentless pounding, and she forced her gaze from his, looking down at herself as if he'd taken her body from her and replaced it with someone else's. That was certainly what it felt like.

She thought she might cry. Adriana struggled to sit upright, tugging her skirt back down toward her knees, aware as she did so that she could still feel him. That mouth of his all over the core of her, his hands wrapped so tightly over her bottom. It felt as if every place he'd touched her was a separate drum, and each beat in her with its own dark pulse.

Then something else hit her, and she froze. She didn't have much practical experience, but Adriana recognized that what had happened had been…unequal. She swallowed nervously, sneaked a glance at him and then away.

"You didn't—" She was still in pieces and wasn't sure she'd ever manage to reassemble herself. Not the way she'd been before. Not now that he'd demonstrated exactly how much she'd been lying to herself. She cleared her throat. "I mean, if you'd like…"

"How tempting," Pato said drily when she couldn't finish the sentence, his gaze harder when she met it, a darker shade of gold she'd never seen before. "But I prefer screams of passion to insincere sacrifices, thank you. To say nothing of enthusiastic participants."

And the worst part, she realized, as her heart kicked at her and made her feel dizzy, was that she couldn't run from him the way she had that morning in London. She couldn't find a far-off corner of his luxurious penthouse and hide herself away until she wrestled her reactions under control. They were on a plane. There was no hiding from what she'd done this time. No rationalizations, no excuses. And she hadn't had anything to drink but water all night long.

The silence between them stretched and held, nothing but the sound of the jet's engines humming all around them, and Adriana didn't have the slightest idea what to do. She was aware of him in ways she suspected would haunt her long after this flight was over, ways she should have recognized and avoided weeks ago. Why had she thought she could handle this—handle him? Why had she been so unpardonably arrogant?

He'd been leading her here all along, she understood. And she'd let him, telling herself that what was happening to her wasn't happening at all. Telling herself stories about tainted blood and Pandora's box. Thinking she could fight it with snappy lines and some attitude.

She'd known she was scraped raw by this, by the things that had happened between them. What he'd done and what he'd said. The brutal honesty, the impossible need. But it was her own appalling weakness that shamed her deep into her bones. That made her wonder if she'd ever known herself at all.

"Why did you do that?" she asked, when the silence outside her head and the noise within was too much.

His dark brows edged higher. There was the faintest twitch of that mouth of his, which she now knew so intimately she could still feel the aftershocks.

"I wanted to know how you tasted," he said.

So simple. So matter-of-fact. So Pato.

A helpless kind of misery surged through her, tangled up with that fire he'd set in her that never died out, and she wished she hadn't asked. She kept her eyes on the floor, where his feet were much too close to hers, and wondered how she could find something so innocuous so threatening—and yet so strangely comforting at the same time.

"Was that your first?" he asked, with no particular inflection in his voice. "Or should I say, your first two?"

"My first...?" she echoed, confused.

And then his meaning hit her, humiliation close behind, and she felt the scalding heat of shame climb up her chest and stain her cheeks. She wanted to curl into a ball and disappear, but instead she sat up straight, as if posture alone could erase what had happened. What she'd done. What she'd let him do to her without a single protest, as if she'd been waiting her whole life to play the whore for him.

Weren't you? that voice spat at her, and she flinched.

"I apologize if I was deficient, Your Royal Highness." She

threw the words at him, in an agony of embarrassment. "I neglected to sleep with the requisite seven thousand people necessary to match your level of—"

"There was only the one, I know," he interrupted, his even tone at odds with the storm in his eyes and that unusually straight line of his mouth. No crook, no curve. Serious, for once, and it made it all that much worse. "And I imagine all five seconds of unskilled fumbling did not lead to any wild heights of passion on your part."

Adriana couldn't believe this conversation was happening. She couldn't believe any of this had happened. If she could have thrown herself out the plane's window right then and there, she would have. A nice, quiet plummet from a great height into the cold embrace of the Alps sounded like blessed relief.

But Pato was still looking at her. There was no escape.

"Of course it wasn't my first," she managed to say, but she couldn't look at him while she said it. She couldn't believe she was answering such a personal question—but then, he'd had his mouth between her legs. What was the point of pretending she had any boundaries? Any shame? "I might not have cut a swathe across the planet like some, but I didn't take a vow of celibacy."

"With a man," he clarified, and there was the slightest hint of amusement in his eyes then, the faintest spark. "A private grope beneath the covers, just you and your hand in the dark, isn't the same thing at all. Is it?"

Adriana didn't understand how she could have forgotten how much she hated him. She remembered now. It roared through her, battling the treacherous, traitorous embers of that fire he'd licked into a consuming blaze, filling her with the force of it, the cleansing power—

But it burned itself out just as quickly, leaving behind the emptiness. That great abyss she'd been skirting her whole life, and there was nothing holding her back from it anymore, was there? She had spent three years with Lenz, thinking her dedication proved she wasn't what her surname said she was. And hardly more than a month with Pato, demonstrating exactly why Righetti women were notorious.

She had betrayed herself and her family in every possible way.

And he was still simply looking at her, still sitting there before her as if sprawling on the floor made him less threatening, less diabolical. Less *him*.

Worse, as if he expected an answer.

"Adriana," he began evenly, almost kindly, and she couldn't take it.

She was horrified when tears filled her eyes, that hopelessness washing over her and leaving her cruelly exposed. She shook her head, lifting her hands and then dropping them back into her lap.

He had destroyed her. He'd taken her apart and she'd let him, and she didn't have any idea how she would survive this. She didn't know what to *do*. If she wasn't who she'd always thought she was, if she was instead who she'd always feared she might become, then she had nothing.

Nothing to hold on to anymore. Nothing to fight for. Nothing at all.

"What do you want from me?" she asked him, and she didn't sound like herself, so broken and small. She felt the tears spill over, the heat of them on her cheeks, and she was too far gone to care. Though her eyes blurred, she focused on him, dark and male and still. "Is this it—to make me become everything I hate? Everything I spent my whole life fighting against? Are you happy now?"

He didn't answer, and she couldn't see him any longer, anyway, so she stopped pretending and covered her face with her hands, letting the tears flow unchecked into her palms, her humiliation complete.

She didn't hear him move. But she felt his hands on her, lifting her into the air and then bringing her down on his lap. Holding her, she realized when it finally penetrated. Prince Pato was *holding* her. She tried to push away, but he only pulled her closer, sliding her across his legs so that her face was nestled into the crook of his neck. There was the lightest of touches, as if he'd pressed a kiss to her hair.

He was warm and strong and deliciously solid, and it was so tempting to pretend that they were different people. That this meant something. That he cared.

That she was the kind of woman someone might care for in the first place.

It was shocking how easy it was to tell herself lies, she thought then, despairing of herself—and so very, very sad about how eager she was to believe them. Even now, when she knew better.

"We don't always get to play the versions of ourselves we prefer," Pato said after a long while, when Adriana's tears had faded away, and yet he still held her.

He smoothed a gentle hand over her hair as he spoke, and Adriana found that she didn't have the strength to fight it off the way she should. She couldn't seem to protect herself any longer. Not from him. Not from any of this. She could feel the rumble of his voice in his chest, and had to shut her eyes against the odd flood of emotion that rocked through her.

Too much sensation. Too many wild emotions, too huge and too dangerous. *Too much.*

"I don't think you understand," she whispered.

"The army was the only place I ever felt like a normal person," he replied. Did she imagine that his arms held her closer, more carefully, as if she really was something precious to him? And when had she started wanting him to think so? "None of the men in my unit cared that I was a prince. They cared if I did my job. They treated me the same way they treated each other. It was a revelation." He traced the same path over her hair, making her shiver again. "And if I like Pato the Playboy Prince less than I liked Pato the Soldier, well. One doesn't cancel out the other. They're both me."

There was nothing but his arms around her and the solid heat of him warming her from the inside out. Making her feel as if everything was somehow new. Maybe because he was holding her this way, maybe because he'd told her something about him she hadn't already read in a tabloid. Maybe because she didn't have the slightest idea what to do with his gentleness. Adriana felt hushed, out of time. As if nothing that happened here could hurt her.

It wasn't true, she knew. It never was. But she couldn't seem to keep herself from wanting, much too badly, to believe that just this once, it could be.

"Yes," she said, finding it easier to talk to that strong neck of his, much easier when she couldn't see that challenging golden gaze. She could fool herself into believing she was safe. And that he was. "But none of the versions of you—even the most scandalous and attention-seeking—are called a whore with quite the same amount of venom they use when it's me." He sighed, and she closed her eyes against the smooth, hot skin of his throat. "You know it's true."

She felt him swallow. "What they call you reflects far more on them than on you," he said gruffly.

"Perhaps it did when I wasn't exactly what they called me. But I can't cling to that anymore, can I?"

She pushed herself away from him then, sitting up with her arms braced against his chest so she could search his face, and the way he frowned at her, as if he was truly concerned, made her foolish heart swell.

"You said it yourself," she continued. "Kitzinian princes

and Righetti women. History repeating itself, right here on this plane." His frown deepened and she felt his body tighten beneath her, but she kept going. "I held my head up no matter what they said because I knew they were wrong. But now…" She shrugged, that emptiness yawning inside her again, black and deep. "Blood will tell, you said, and you were right."

Pato's gaze was so intense, meeting hers, that it very nearly hurt.

"What happened between us does not make you a whore."

"I think you'll find that it does. By definition."

His eyes moved over her face, dark and brooding, almost as if she'd insulted him with that simple truth.

"But," he said, his tone almost careful, "you were happy enough to risk that definition when it was your suggestion, and when you thought it would benefit Lenz."

There was no reason that should hurt her. She didn't know why it did. *I don't think you love him,* he'd told her in that low, sure voice.

"That was different," she whispered, shaken. "That was a plan hatched in desperation. This was…"

She couldn't finish. Pato looked at her for a long moment, and then his eyes warmed again to the gold she knew, his mouth hinted at that wicked curve she'd tasted and felt pressed against her very core, and she didn't know if it was joy or fear that twisted inside her, coiling tight and making it difficult to breathe.

"Passion, Adriana," he said with soft intent. "This was passion."

She told herself she didn't feel that ring inside her like a bell. That there was no *click* of recognition, no sudden swell of understanding. She didn't know what he was talking about, she told herself desperately, but she was quite certain she shouldn't have anything to do with either passion or princes. There was only one place that would lead her, and on this end of history she very much doubted she'd end up with her portrait in the Royal Gallery. Like her great-aunt Sandrine, she'd be no more than a footnote in a history book, quietly despised.

"Passion is nothing but an excuse weak people use to justify their terrible behavior," she told him, frowning.

"You sound like a very grim and humorless cleric," Pato said mildly, his palms smoothing down her back to land at her hips. "Did my mouth feel like a justification to you? Did the way you came apart in my hands feel like an excuse? Or were you more alive in those moments than ever before?"

Adriana pushed at his chest then, desperate to get away from him, and she was all too aware that she was able to climb out of his lap and scramble to her feet at last only because he chose to let her go.

"It doesn't matter what it felt like." She wished her voice didn't still have that telltale rasp. She wished Pato hadn't made it sound as if this was something more than the usual games he played with every female who crossed his path. More than that, she wished there wasn't that part of her that wanted so badly to believe him. "I know what it makes me."

Pato shoved his hair back from his face with one hand and muttered something she was happy she didn't catch. She wanted to make a break for the bathroom and bar herself inside, but her legs were too shaky beneath her, and she sat down on the chair instead, as far away from him as she could get. Which wasn't far at all. Not nearly far enough to recover.

"My mother was a very fragile woman," he said after a long moment, surprising Adriana.

She blinked, not following him. "Your mother?"

Queen Matilda had been an icon before her death from cancer some fifteen years ago. She was still an icon all these years later, beloved the world over. Her grave was still piled high with flowers and trinkets, as mourners continued to make pilgrimages to pay their respects. She had been graceful, regal, feminine and lovely. Her smile had once been called "Kitzinian sunshine" by the rhapsodic British press, while at home she'd been known as the kingdom's greatest weapon.

She had been anything but *fragile*.

"She was so beautiful," Pato said, his voice dark, skating over Adriana's skin and making her wrap her arms around herself. "From the time she was a girl, that was the only thing she knew. How beautiful she was and what that would get her. A king, a throne, adoring subjects. But my father married a pretty face he could add to his collection of lovely things and then ignore, and my mother didn't know what to do when the constant attention she lived for was taken away from her."

Pato's eyes were troubled when they met hers, and Adriana caught her breath. That same celebrated beauty his mother had been so famous for was stamped all over him, though somehow, he made it deeply masculine. He was gilded and perfect, just as she had been before him, and Adriana would never have called him the least bit fragile, either. Until this moment, when he almost looked...

But she couldn't let herself think it. There was too much at stake and she couldn't trust herself. She didn't dare. What he felt wasn't her concern. It couldn't be.

He smiled then, but it wasn't his usual smile. This one felt like nails digging into her, sharp and deep, and she wanted to hold him the way he'd held her, as if she could make him feel safe for a moment, however fleeting.

You're such a fool.

"You don't have to tell me this," she said hurriedly, suddenly afraid of where this was going. What it would do to her if he showed her things she knew he shouldn't. "It's your family's private, personal business."

She wanted him too much. She'd proved it in unmistakable

terms, with her legs flung over his shoulders and her body laid open for his touch. Somewhere inside of her, where she was afraid to look because she didn't want to admit it, Adriana knew what that meant. She knew.

He gave half the world his body. She would survive that; his women always did. But if he gave her his secrets, she would never recover.

"So she did the only thing she knew how to do," Pato said, his gaze never leaving Adriana's, once again that different, harder version of himself, every inch of him powerful. Determined. *Bleak,* Adriana thought, and ached for him. "She found the attention she needed."

Adriana stared at him, not wanting to understand what he was saying. Not wanting to make the connection. He nodded, as if he could see the question she didn't want to ask right there on her face.

"There were always men," he said, confirming it, and Adriana hugged herself that much tighter. "They kept her happy. They made her smile, laugh, dance in the palace corridors and pick flowers in the gardens. They made her *herself.* And my father didn't care how many lovers she took as long as she was discreet. He might not have wanted her the way she thought he should, the way she needed to be wanted, but he wanted her happy."

Adriana found it hard to swallow. She could only stare at Pato in shock. And hurt for him in ways she didn't understand. He leaned forward then, keeping his eyes on hers, hard and demanding. She felt that power of his fill the space between them, pressing at her like a command.

"Was my mother a whore, Adriana?" he asked, his voice a quiet lash. "Is that the word you'd use to describe her?"

She felt too hot, then too cold. Paralyzed.

"I can't— You shouldn't—"

Pato only watched her, his mouth in that serious line, and

she felt the ruthlessness he hid behind his easy smiles and his laughter pressing into her from all sides and sinking deep into her belly. How had she ever imagined this man was *careless?*

"Of course not," she said at last, feeling outside herself. Desperate. As if what she said would keep her from shaking apart from the inside out. "She was the queen. But that doesn't mean—"

"It's a word people use when they need a weapon," he said, very distinctly, and that look in his eyes made Adriana feel naked. Intensely vulnerable. As if he could see all the ugliness she hid there, the encroaching darkness. "It's a means of control. It's a prison they herd you into because they think you need to be contained."

She shook her head, unable to speak, unable to handle what was happening inside her. Some kind of earthquake, rolling long and hard and destroying foundations she hadn't known she'd built in the first place.

"That's all well and good," she whispered, hardly aware of what she was saying, seeing only Pato and that look on his face, "but there's no one here but you and me and what happened between us, the way I just—"

"Don't do it," he warned her, cutting her off, his eyes flashing. "Don't make it ugly simply because it was intense. There was nothing ugly about it. You taste like a dream and your responsiveness is a gift, not a curse."

What moved in her then was so overwhelming she thought for a long, panicked moment that she might actually be sick, right there on the floor. She was too hot again, then freezing cold, and she might have thought she'd come down with a fever if she hadn't seen the way he looked at her. If she hadn't felt it deep inside her, making so many things she'd taken for granted crumble into dust.

But she couldn't bring herself to look away. She was falling apart—he was making sure she did—and she didn't *want* to look away.

"Don't use their weapons on yourself," he told her then, very distinctly, the royal command and that brooding darkness making her shiver as his gaze devoured her, changed her, demanded she listen to him. "Don't lock yourself in their prison. And don't let me hear you use that word to describe yourself again, Adriana. As far as I'm concerned, it's a declaration of war."

But Adriana knew that the war had started the moment she'd been sent to work with this man, and despite what she'd told herself all these weeks, despite what she'd so desperately wanted to believe, she'd already lost.

Pato couldn't sleep, and he could *always* sleep.

This was one more thing that had never happened to him before Adriana had walked into his life and turned it inside out. He'd entertained a number of very detailed ideas about how he'd enjoy making her pay for that as he sprawled there in his decidedly empty bed—none of them particularly conducive to rest.

Damn her.

It was her insistence that she was, in fact, all the things the jackals called her that had him acting so outside his own parameters, he knew. It was maddening. Pato had handled any number of women over the years who had used their supposed fragility as a tool to try to manipulate him. He could have piloted a yacht across the sea of tears that had been cried on or near him, all by women angling for his affection, his protection, his money or his name—whatever they thought they could get.

He'd never been the slightest bit moved.

Adriana, by contrast, wanted nothing from him save his good behavior. She was appalled that he'd touched her, kissed her, made her forget herself. She'd now offered herself to him twice while making it perfectly clear that doing so was an act of great sacrifice on her part. A terrible sacrifice she would lower herself to suffer through, *even after* he'd brought her to a screaming, sobbing climax more than once.

She was killing him.

No wonder he was wide-awake in the middle of the night and storming through his rooms in a fury. If he'd been possessed of the ego of a lesser man, she might very well have deflated it by now. He'd even altered his behavior to please her. He, Pato, Playboy Prince, tabloid sensation and scandal magnet, hadn't even glanced at another woman unless it was specifically to annoy Adriana, since he didn't seem to be able to do without the way she took him to task.

He was like a lovesick puppy. He was disgusted with himself.

And he would never be able to fly on that plane again without being haunted by her. Her taste, her silken legs draped over his back, her gorgeous cries. He cursed into the dark room, but it didn't help.

The list of things he shouldn't have done grew longer every day, but tasting the heat of her, making her shatter around him, *twice,* was at the very top. It wasn't only that he'd tasted her at last and it had knocked him sideways, or that it had taken every shred of willpower he possessed to keep himself from driving into her and making her his in every possible way right there and then, again and again until they both collapsed. It wasn't only that he'd been unable to stop thinking about the fact that he was more than likely the first man to pleasure her, which made a wholly uncharacteristic barbarian stir to life inside him and beat at his chest in primitive masculine triumph. That was all bad enough.

But it went much deeper than that, and Pato knew it.

He'd known it while they were still in the air. He'd known

it when he'd started telling her things he never spoke about, ever. He'd known it when the plane had finally landed and he'd sent her off in a separate car and had found himself standing on the tarmac, staring at her disappearing taillights and wanting things he couldn't have.

He'd known for some time, if he was honest, but tonight it had all come into sharp and unmistakable focus.

Pato didn't simply want her in his bed.

He *liked* her. She made him laugh, she challenged him and she wasn't the least bit in awe of him. From the very start, she'd treated him as if she expected him to be the educated, intelligent, capable man he was supposed to be rather than the airy dilettante he played so well. He wanted to teach her every last sensual trick he'd ever learned, and bathe them both in that scalding heat of hers. He wanted to prove to her that the passion that flared between them was rare and good. He wanted to take away the pressure of all that family history she wore about her neck like an albatross.

Worst of all, most damning and most dangerous, he wanted to be that better man she deserved.

"It isn't even my dirt, but I'm covered in it," she'd said tonight, breaking the heart he didn't have all over again, and he'd wanted nothing more than to be the one who showed her that she had never been anything but beautiful and clean, all the way through. Pato never should have let himself get lost in the fantasy that he might be that man. He wasn't. There was no possibility that he could be anything to her, and couldn't allow himself to forget that again.

Not until the game he and Lenz had played for all these years reached its conclusion. He couldn't break the faith his brother had placed in him all those years ago. He couldn't break the vow he'd made. He wouldn't.

And he'd never been even remotely tempted to do so before.

Pato found himself on one of his balconies that looked out over the water to the mainland beyond and the city nestled there on the lakeshore. His eyes drifted toward the sparkling lights of the old city, the ancient quarter that had sprawled over the highest hill since the first thatched cottages were built there in medieval times. It was filled with museums and grand old houses, narrow little lanes dating back centuries and so many of Kitzinia's blue-blooded nobles in their luxurious, historic villas. And he knew precisely where the Righetti villa stood on the finest street in the quarter, one of the kingdom's most famous and most visited landmarks.

But tonight he didn't think about his murdered ancestor or Almado Righetti's plot to turn the kingdom over to foreign enemies, all in service to long-ago wars. It was only the house where she lived, where he imagined her as wide-awake as he was, as haunted by him as he was by her. He didn't care what her surname was. He didn't care if this was history repeating itself. He certainly didn't care about the malicious gossip of others.

The ways he wanted her almost scared him. Almost.

And of all the things he couldn't have while this game played on, he understood that she was going to hurt the worst. She already did.

Pato slammed his fist against the thick stone balustrade. Hard. As if that might wake him up, restore him to himself. It did nothing but make his knuckles ache, and it didn't make him any less alone.

He hated this game, but he couldn't lose his focus. There was one week left until the wedding, and she'd served her purpose. He had to let her go.

CHAPTER SEVEN

ADRIANA WALKED INTO the palace the following morning on shaky legs, trying with all her might to feel completely unaffected by what had happened the night before. And if she couldn't quite feel it, to *appear* as if she did. Cool. Calm. Professional. Not riddled with anxiety, her body still humming with leftover desire.

"I wanted to know how you tasted," she could hear him say, as if he whispered it into her ear. Her skin prickled at the memory.

Nothing had changed, she assured herself, save her understanding of her own weakness and her ability to tell herself lies. And nothing *would* change, because this was Pato. Careless, promiscuous, thoughtless, undependable for the whole of his adult life, and proud of it besides. No depth, she reminded herself. No conscience and no shame. Those hints she'd seen of another man—that ruthless power, that dark focus, that devastating gentleness—weren't him.

They couldn't be him.

And the things he'd said, which she could still feel running through her like something electric…well. She'd lost herself in a sensual storm. She'd never experienced anything like it before and she'd decided it was entirely possible she'd made it all seem much more intense than it had been. Pato had made her sob and writhe and fall to pieces. He'd made her body sing for him as if she were no more than an instrument—and well he should. *Passion,* he'd called it, and he would know. Sex was his occupation, his art. He was a master.

He'd mastered her without even trying very hard.

It was no wonder she'd concocted some fantasy around that, she told herself as she made her way down the gleaming marble hall that led to Pato's office. He did things like this— like *her*—all the time. The number of women who fantasized about him was no doubt astronomical, and none of them hung about the palace, clinging to his ankles. Nor would she.

She would be perfectly serene, she chanted to herself as she let herself into his office. Efficient and competent. And she wouldn't verbally spar with him anymore, as he obviously viewed it as a form of flirtation, and she found it far too easy to slip into, putting herself at risk. Last night was a mistake, never to be repeated. No conversation was necessary, no embarrassing postmortem. It was done. She marched around the quietly opulent office, turning on lights and arranging the papers he wouldn't read on his desk. The two of them would simply…move forward.

Or so Adriana told herself, over and over, as she waited for him to appear.

He didn't come. She waited, she lectured herself more sternly, and still he failed to saunter in, disheveled and lazy and wearing something that violated every possible palace protocol, the way he usually did. When Adriana realized he was going to miss his engagement with the Kitzinian Red Cross—after what she'd gone through to get him back into the country, specifically to meet with them—she braced herself, smoothed her hands over the very conservative suit she'd chosen this morning, which was in no way protective armor, and set off through the palace to find him.

Pato's bed, she was relieved to find when she made it to his bedroom, was empty.

It was only then, while she stared at the rumpled sheets and the indentation in the pillows where his head must have been at some point last night, that Adriana admitted to herself that maybe she was a little *too* relieved. That maybe it had hurt to imagine that he could have carried on with his usual depravity after she'd left him last night.

You are nothing but another instrument, she reminded herself harshly, amazed at her capacity for self-delusion. *And he happens to be a remarkably talented musician—no doubt because he practices so very, very often.*

If only she could make that sink in. If only she could make that traitorous part of her, the part that insisted on wild fantasies and childish hope no matter how many times it was crushed out of her, believe it.

"You look disappointed," Pato drawled from the doorway behind her. Adriana whirled around to face him, her heart leaping out of her chest. "Shall I ring a few bored socialites and have them fill up the bed? Just think of all the sanctimonious lectures you could deliver."

He sounded the way he looked this morning: dangerous. Edgy. Dark and something like grim. Adriana's breath tangled in her throat.

Pato was draped against the doorjamb, looking as boneless as he did rough around his gorgeous edges. His eyes glittered, too dark to shine like gold today, and he hadn't bothered to shave. His hair stood about his head in a careless mess, and he was wearing an open, button-down shirt over those ancient jeans he preferred, she'd often thought, because they molded so tightly to his perfectly formed body. He looked moody and formidable, that ruthless power he usually concealed a black cloud around him today, making it impossible for Adriana to pretend she'd imagined it.

And the way he was looking at her made her heart stutter.

She'd been so sure that she was prepared to see him again. She wasn't.

Her whole body simply shuddered into a blazing, embarrassing heat at the sight of him. She felt as if she'd been lit on fire. Her nipples hardened as her breasts swelled against her bra. Her belly tightened, while her core melted into that hot, needy ache. Her skin prickled with awareness, and she could feel the dark heat of his gaze all the way through her, from the nape of her neck to the soles of her feet. Not ten minutes ago she'd vowed she wouldn't spar with him anymore, but she understood in a flash of insight that it was that or simply surrender to this wildness inside her—and she wasn't that far gone, surely. Not yet.

"I'm relieved, actually," she managed to say, making her voice as brisk as she could. "The last thing I wanted to do today was troll about your usual dens of iniquity, looking for you in the dregs of last night's parties, especially when you are expected to charm the Red Cross in less than hour."

He looked at her for a long moment, his beautiful face hard and his eyes dark, and yet she had the strangest notion that he was in some kind of pain. She had to grit her teeth to keep herself from doing something stupid, like trying to reach out to him. Like imagining that she of all people could see beneath his surface to the far more complicated man beneath.

Such hubris, a voice inside her hissed, *and we all know what comes after pride like yours. Like night follows day.*

"It's amazing," Pato said in a low voice, something in it raising the fine hairs on the back of her neck. "It's as if you never wrapped your legs around my neck and let me taste you. You may not remember it, Adriana, but I do."

Adriana went utterly still.

She should have anticipated this. She should have known. It had been the same when she was seventeen. She could still remember with perfect clarity the faces of all her schoolmates who'd gathered around to point and stare and laugh as she'd walked out of that party alone. Used and humiliated. She could still remember the name they'd called her snaking along with her like a shadow, following her, connected to her, the truth of her as far as they'd been concerned. Inevitable.

The Righetti whore.

Pato was only one person, not a crowd of cruel teenagers, and yet she recognized that this was worse. Much, much worse. She could feel it deep inside, in parts of her that pack of kids had never touched.

But she'd be damned if he'd see her cry again, Adriana thought then with a sharp flash of defiance. She'd rather he executed her alongside Almado Righetti's ghost in the old castle keep than show him one more tear.

"Is this the part where you call me a whore?" she asked, her stomach in a hard knot but her voice crisp. Her head high. "You're not doing it right. It works much better when mixed with public humiliation, so you can get the satisfaction of watching me walk a little gauntlet of shame. Would you like me to assemble a crowd? We can start over when they arrive."

Pato didn't move, but his eyes went completely black. Frigid and furious at once. Adriana crossed her arms over her chest and refused to cower or cringe. That deep defiance felt like strength, sweeping through her, making her stand tall. She would never bow her head in shame again. Never. Not even for a prince.

"If you want to call me names, feel free to do it to my face," she told him. "But I should warn you, I won't fall to pieces. I've survived far worse than you."

It shouldn't have been possible for his eyes to flash even darker, but they did, and she could feel the pulse of his temper rolling off him in waves. She told herself it didn't bother her in the least, because it shouldn't. It couldn't.

"You think you're ready to go to war with me, Adriana?"

he asked, that mild tone sounding alarms inside her, sending a little chill racing down her back. "I told you what would happen if you used that word again."

"Here's a news flash, Your Royal Highness," she snapped, ignoring the alarms, the chill, that look on his face. "I've been at war since the day I was born. I'm hardly afraid of one more battle, especially with a man best known for the revealing cut of his swimming costume and his ability to consume so much alcohol it ought to put him in a coma." She eyed him while a muscle she'd never seen before flared in his jaw. "Is that what today's little display of temper is all about? You're drunk?"

Pato straightened from the door, and her heart kicked at her in a sudden panic, not quite as tough as she was trying to appear. Adriana almost took an instinctive step back, but forced herself to stop. To stand still. He looked nothing less than predatory and the last thing she wanted to do was encourage him to give chase. Because he would, she knew on some primal level. In this mood he might do anything.

"No," he growled in a voice like gravel, when she'd almost forgotten she'd asked him a question. "I'm not drunk. Not even a little."

She didn't like the way he watched her then. Panic and awareness twisted inside her, sending out a shower of sparks, but Adriana didn't let herself back down. She wasn't going to break. Not this time. Not here.

"Perhaps you should consider getting drunk, then," she suggested icily. "It might improve your disposition."

She didn't see him move, and then he was right there in front of her, his hand on her jaw and his eyes so tortured, so dark, as he gazed down at her. Adriana didn't understand what was happening. The things he was saying, that dangerous tone of voice, his dark demeanor—but then she looked in his eyes and she wanted to cry. And not for herself.

"What's wrong?" she whispered.

Something she didn't understand flashed through those eyes. Then he bent his head and brushed his lips across hers. It was soft and light, hardly a kiss at all, and even so, Adriana felt it as if he'd wrapped both hands around her heart and squeezed tight. Her eyes closed of their own accord, and she felt the sweetness of it work through her, warming her, making her feel as if she glowed.

And then he let go of her, though he didn't step back, and when she looked at him he was that dark, edgy stranger again. His mouth was severe as he gazed at her, a grim line without the faintest possibility of any curve. Much less anything sweet.

"For the first time since you walked through the door and started ordering me around," he said quietly, "I feel like myself."

Adriana stared at him for a long moment. He looked back at her, that wicked mouth unrecognizable, those beautiful eyes so terribly dark and filled with things she didn't understand—but she understood this. He didn't need to call her names. He didn't need to stoop to the level of seventeen-year-olds. He was a royal prince. He could do it with a glance, a single sentence.

She had to stop imagining that anything would ever be different.

"If you want to be rid of me, Pato," she said, fighting to keep her voice cool and her head high, "you don't have to play these cruel little games. All you have to do is dismiss me, and you could have done that with a text. No unpleasant scene required."

He reached over and ran the back of one hand along her cheek, his knuckles slightly swollen, and Adriana fought to keep from jerking her head away. His touch was confusingly tender. It slid through her like honey. And it was at complete odds with everything he was saying.

"That's the first time you've used my name," he said, as if it shook him. And Adriana wanted to lean into him, to turn her head and kiss his hand, as if this was about affection.

But she knew better. This was another game. It couldn't be anything else—and she was finished playing. No matter what she thought she saw in his eyes then, as if using his name had been some kind of invocation. As if it had changed something.

"I'll take that as a yes, I'm dismissed," she said somehow, and take to step around him. The need to escape, to flee this place and him and never look back, was like a drumbeat inside her skin. "I'll leave my formal resignation letter on the desk in your office."

But he reached out and took her arm as he had once before in London, holding her against his side though they faced different directions.

"Adriana," he whispered, as if her name hurt him.

It hurt her.

But all this would pass. It would, it always did. All she had to do was walk out the door, and she'd never be allowed in his presence again. It wasn't as if she could work for Lenz again, not now. Her access to the palace would be revoked, and she'd never have to worry about her outsize reactions to Pato, her insatiable hunger for him. All that would fade away as if it had never happened, as if he'd never been anything more than a face on a glossy magazine. And she would move far away from Kitzinia, to a place where no one would recognize her name or her ancestors' faces in hers, and someday, she thought—*prayed*—she might even forget that she'd fallen in love with him without ever meaning to.

Everything inside her went still then. Quiet. The truth she'd been avoiding for much too long was like a hush, stealing through her, changing everything, making sure she would leave here, leave him, in tatters.

But then she supposed that, too, had always been inevitable. History had repeated itself, and he was right, it might kill her. But not where he could watch, she told herself fiercely. Not where he could see how far she'd fallen.

"Thank you, Your Royal Highness," she said, jerking her arm from his grasp, amazed that she sounded so calm. So controlled, as if her whole world hadn't shuddered to a halt and then altered forever. "This has been an educational experience. I particularly enjoyed your need to destroy the entire royal family, living and dead, in my esteem." She aimed a hard smile at him. "Rest assured, I now think as little of your family as you do of mine."

He met her gaze then, and what she saw on his face sliced into her, making her feel as if she might shake apart where she stood. Making her think she already had.

"Don't," he said, as he had in the car that day. That was all, and yet she felt it everywhere.

But his pain wasn't her problem, she told herself harshly. She couldn't let it matter.

"I didn't need to know any of that," she whispered fiercely. His secrets, that tempting glimpse of his inner self. As if any of it was real, or hers. She'd known it would lead nowhere good, and she was right. "And why would you risk telling me? I could walk out of here today and sell that story to the tabloids."

The way he looked at her didn't make any sense. It made her heart thud hard against her ribs. It made her eyes go blurry.

"You won't."

"You have no reason to think that. You don't know me. You don't even like me."

His smile was faint, like a ghost. "I trust you, Adriana."

It was sad how much she wished he did, despite everything. She was such a terrible, gullible fool. Such a deep and abiding disappointment to herself. Because he was still play-ing her. She knew it. She was one instrument among many, and he didn't know how to do anything else.

"Or," she said slowly, as the ugly truth of it penetrated even her thick skull, the misery crashing over her, into her, making her voice too thick, "you know perfectly well that the last person in the world anyone would believe when it came to accusations of promiscuity is me."

"Don't," he said again, his voice harsher.

And this time when he pulled her to him, he turned her so she came up hard against his chest, and then he held her face in his hands and kissed her. Ravenous and raw. Uncontrolled.

Dangerous.

And Adriana couldn't help herself. She kissed him back.

He slanted his head and she met him, kissing him with all the passion he'd showed her, all the love she hadn't wanted to admit she felt for him. The pain, the misery. Her foolish hopes. She held back nothing. She wrapped her arms around his neck and let him bend her backward, as if this was the happy ending to some kind of fairy tale instead of a sad good-bye at the close of a story even Adriana had known would end like this. Exactly like this, in dismissal and disgrace.

Pato kissed her again and again, as if he was as desperate, as torn, as she was. As if he felt what she did when she knew very well he didn't. He couldn't. He kissed her so thoroughly that she knew she would pretend he did, that it would be the fire she warmed herself near in all the lonely days to follow, and she kissed him back with the same ferocity so she could remember that, too.

But too soon he pulled away, still holding her face in his hands. He looked at her for a long moment, his eyes gleaming that darker gold that made her shiver deep inside, and then he stroked her cheeks with his thumbs, as if memorizing her.

Adriana didn't say a word. She couldn't. But she knew it was time to go, before she found she couldn't.

She pulled in a shuddering breath, and when she stepped back, Pato's gaze went stormy and his jaw flexed—but he dropped his hands and let her.

It was the hardest thing Adriana had ever had to do. It made her bones ache as if she was breaking them, but she did it. She wrenched herself away from him and turned toward the door.

And then stopped dead.

Because Lenz stood there, staring at them both in appalled disbelief.

Adriana made a small sound of distress, almost too low to hear, and Pato wanted nothing more than to put himself bodily between her and whatever attacked her—even if it was his brother. Even worse, if it was him.

But he couldn't. He certainly hadn't today. He didn't now, and he thought he loathed himself.

For a moment, they all stood there, frozen in place.

"Excuse me, Your Royal—" Adriana began, but Lenz interrupted her.

"I didn't give her to you so you could make her one of your bedmates, Pato." He threw the accusation into the room, his face a work of thunder. But Pato watched Adriana and the way she simply stood there, her spine achingly straight and her hands in fists at her sides. "What the hell are you thinking?"

Pato said nothing. He saw Adriana tremble slightly, and had to fight the need to pull her back against him, to protect her from this. He hated that she thought he was like those jackals who had hounded her all these years. He hated that she believed he thought so little of what had happened between them. He hated all of this.

And yet he had no choice, he reminded himself bitterly. It didn't matter that he had the taste of her in his mouth, that he would have held her there forever if she hadn't pulled away. He had to let her go.

"Enough," he snapped when Lenz opened his mouth again. Pato met his brother's eyes. Hard and unyielding. "This is not a conversation Adriana needs to take part in. Why don't you step aside and let her go?"

It appeared to dawn on Lenz that this was not a request. His eyes narrowed, but he walked stiffly into the room, leaving the exit clear.

Pato willed Adriana to look at him one last time—to let him study that beautiful face of hers once more—but he wasn't surprised that she didn't. The moment Lenz stopped moving, she left. She walked out of Pato's bedroom the way she'd walked into it, her head high and her back straight, and she didn't look back or break her stride.

And Pato stood there, listening to the sound of her heels against the polished floors until even that disappeared. And that was it. She was gone. He'd done his goddamned duty.

"You didn't have to sleep with her!" Lenz declared, sounding fierce and protective, which made Pato feel that much more hollow. "She deserves better than that!"

"By all means, brother, let's talk about what Adriana deserves," Pato murmured dangerously. "The crown prince installs her in the position usually allocated to his mistresses, and keeps her there for years. And then his dirty playboy brother takes his sordid turn. And we planned it that way, because we knew exactly what would happen if we brought the last Righetti girl into this game. Does she deserve any of that?"

Lenz stared at him. "What is she to you?" he asked after a long moment.

"She is nothing to me," Pato replied, his voice harsh. "Because *nothing* is the only thing I am allowed. *Nothing* is my stock in trade. I am useless, faithless, untrustworthy, and most of all, a great and continuing disgrace to my royal blood." He held Lenz's gaze for a taut breath. "Don't worry, brother. I know who I am."

Lenz looked pale then.

"Pato," he said carefully, as if he was afraid of what Pato's response might be. "We are finally in the endgame. We've worked too hard to get here. Didn't you tell me this yourself only weeks ago?"

Pato scraped his hands over his face as if that could change the growing hollowness inside him. As if anything could.

"I know what I promised." But he didn't look at Lenz. He felt unbalanced, half-drunk, and he knew it was Adriana. She'd crippled him, and she thought he didn't care. It was almost funny. "I have no intention of breaking my vow. I haven't yet, have I?"

Lenz stared at him, lifting one hand to stroke his mouth, clearly mulling over the right approach to a thorny problem he hadn't seen coming. Pato almost laughed then. This was why Lenz would make the perfect king. He could detach, step back, consider all outcomes. Pato, by contrast, couldn't seem to do anything but seethe and rage. Especially today.

"We picked Adriana because of her name, yes," Lenz said after several moments passed, his voice carefully diplomatic once again. "But she's special. I know it. I—"

Pato laughed then, a rusty blade of a sound that stopped his brother flat.

"We're not going to stand about like pimpled schoolboys and compare notes," he said in a tone that brooked no argument. "We'll be the only people in this petty kingdom who do not find it necessary to pick over her body like so many carrion crows."

For a moment, that simply hung there. Then Lenz blinked.

"Oh," he said in a curious voice, a new light in his eyes as he looked at Pato. "I didn't realize."

"She's out of this," Pato said, ignoring that. "She isn't coming back."

Lenz studied him. "Is that wise?" he asked quietly. "Can we afford a deviation from the plan at this point? The wedding—"

"Is in a week, I know." Pato couldn't hide the bleakness that washed over him then. He didn't try. "And she's out of this. She's free. If she deserves anything, it's that."

Lenz's brows rose, but he only nodded. "Fair enough."

Pato smiled then, though it was too sharp, and he understood that he was not himself. That he might never be himself again. That Adriana was gone and he was emptier than he'd been before, and he wasn't sure he could live with it the way he knew he must. But he smiled anyway.

"How is the king's health?" he asked, because Lenz was right. This was the end of this game, and he'd agreed years ago to play it. There was no changing that now, even if he'd changed the plan.

"The same," Lenz said. He didn't smile. He only looked tired. "The ministers are beginning to press him. It might happen sooner than we thought."

Pato nodded. It was exactly as they'd planned. It turned out they were good at this, this dance of high-stakes deception and royal intrigue.

He sickened himself.

"Then I suppose we play on," he said wearily.

Lenz's gaze was sad. "We always do."

Adriana walked through her family's villa slowly, taking the time to really look around her as she did. She couldn't remember the last time she'd paid attention to all the familiar things in front of her, which she'd somehow stopped seeing over the years. The graceful rooms, the antique furniture. The art still on the walls and the places where art had been removed and sold in the leaner years. All the *things* that made up a Kitzinian pedigree, a certain station in Kitzinian society, even a tarnished one. Collections of china in carved wood cabinets. Beautiful rugs, hand-tiled floors, mosaics lining the fountain in the center courtyard. Coats of arms, priceless statues and pieces of pottery handed down across centuries.

And in the small parlor in the farthest corner of the villa, the one no one talked about and never visited by accident, were the trio of portraits. The faces of the women whose choices hundreds of years ago had sentenced Adriana to infamy in the present.

"What they call you reflects far more on them than on you," Pato had said. She couldn't get his words out of her head.

Her father might hate their family history, Adriana thought as she stood in the musty room, but he still felt called upon to preserve it. And so the portraits hung on the walls of the villa instead of being packed away in the attic or burned in the back gardens. This was his duty to the Righetti legacy, however shameful he found it.

Adriana pulled open the heavy drapes to let the light in, and then stared up at the three great temptresses of old Kitzinia sitting there so prettily in their frames. The Righetti whores, lined up in chronological order. The harlots Carolina, Maria and Francesca.

And, of course, Adriana herself, though she, like her great-aunt Sandrine, could not expect to be rendered in oils and hung in museums. Times had changed.

She couldn't help the small laugh that escaped her. *She* didn't feel much like a notorious whore in the comfortable jeans and soft magenta sweater she'd tugged on when she'd arrived home from the palace. She studied the faces of the women before her, seeing herself in the shape of Carolina's brow, the color of Maria's hair and the curve of Francesca's lips. None of them looked particularly like slinking sexpots, either. They simply looked like young women somewhere around Adriana's age, all smiling, all bright-eyed, all pretty.

Don't lock yourself in their prison, Pato had said.

Maybe, Adriana thought, staring at the portraits but remembering the way he'd held her when she cried, they'd simply fallen in love.

She sat down heavily in the nearest chair, her own heart beating hard in her chest as if she'd run up a hill. How had that possibility never occurred to her before? Why had she always believed that she was descended from a line of women who were, for all intents and purposes, callous prostitutes?

Maybe they were in love.

It rang in her like a revolution.

The Righetti family had always kept their own copies of these portraits, and Adriana remembered being herded into this room by her grandmother after church on Sundays, as her aunts had been before her. Her grandmother had droned on about purity and morals, while Adriana had stood there feeling increasingly cross that her brothers were allowed to entertain themselves elsewhere.

The lecture had been repeated with increasing frequency throughout her adolescence, which was when Adriana had discovered the truth about her grandfather's younger sister, the lovely old woman with sparkling eyes who lived in France and whose name was only ever spoken in distaste. And Adriana had internalized every word of her grandmother's lecture. She'd accepted the fact that she was dirty, tainted. Ruined before she began. She'd never questioned a word of it.

"Don't use their weapons on yourself," Pato had said so fiercely, as if it had angered him to hear her talk about herself like that. As if the casual way she hated herself, her easy ac-

ceptance of the idea that she was the dirty thing others called her, was what was upsetting.

Not her. Not her name. Not what had happened between them.

And she realized then, as she sat in the presence of the women who'd supposedly ruined her, that she couldn't do it anymore. That well of ugliness she'd spent her whole life drawing from simply wasn't there in her gut the way it always had been. In its place, she thought in some astonishment, was that defiance she'd called on at the palace—that strength she hadn't known she had.

She looked at the Righetti women, at their mysterious smiles and the sparkle in their eyes, and she knew something else, too. These women hadn't been ashamed. They hadn't torn themselves apart in penance for their sins. Adriana knew for a fact that each and every one of them had died of old age, in their beds. These were not meek, placating women. They'd been the favorite lovers of kings and princes in times when that meant they'd wielded great power and political influence. They'd made their own rules.

And so, by God, would Adriana.

At some point she realized that tears were flowing down her cheeks. Was this joy? Heartbreak? Despair? How could she keep track of the wild emotions that clamored inside of her? Adriana knew only that she loved him. She loved Pato, and she wasn't ashamed of it, either. She didn't know how she would tell her father what had happened, or what she'd do next, but she couldn't hate herself for this.

She *wouldn't* hate herself for this.

Adriana had thought for a moment that she might have a heart attack when she'd turned to see Lenz standing there in Pato's doorway, when she'd seen that shocked look on his face. But seeing him there, standing next to his brother, had made everything very clear. *"I don't think you love him,"* Pato had told her, and he was right. Lenz had been kind to her, no matter what his ulterior motives, and she'd been so desperate to prove to him that she wasn't *that kind* of Righetti. She'd mistaken her gratitude for something more.

But Pato had changed her, she realized now, gazing at that trinity of women before her as she wiped at her cheeks. What had happened on that plane had altered everything. He had wanted her, and he'd encouraged her to want him back. He hadn't used her; if anything, she'd used him. Twice. And the things he'd said to her had knocked down walls inside her she'd never known were there.

It didn't matter what came after that. It didn't matter if he regretted opening up to her the way he had. It didn't matter that he'd rejected her today, or that it had hurt her terribly.

It didn't even matter if she never saw him again, though that possibility broke her heart. He'd given her a gift she could never repay, she understood now. She wasn't sure she ever would have got there on her own. He'd showed her how.

He'd set her free.

Later, Adriana sat on the wide sill at her open bedroom windows, looking out at the stretch of the kingdom below her, gleaming in the crisp afternoon light.

She watched the ferries cutting through the crystal blue lake toward the cities on the far shore, racing the pleasure boats with their white sails taut in the breeze. She let her eyes trace the graceful lines of the palace, the gentle bow of the causeway that connected it to the mainland, and the towering Alps all around. There was nothing keeping her here besides sentiment. She could go back to university, collect another degree. She could travel abroad the way she'd always meant to do. There was no reason she had to stay here. None at all.

And even so, even now, she found it hard to imagine leaving.

Adriana heard the motorcycle long before she saw it. It was brash and loud, shouting its way through the streets of the old city. Louder and louder it roared, until it whipped around the corner at the end of the lane, charged down her street in an obnoxious cloud of noise and then stopped directly below her windows.

Her heart slammed against her chest.

Pato tilted back his head and glanced up, pulling off his helmet and piercing her with a long, hard look. Adriana couldn't seem to move. His expression was serious, unsmiling, and he paused there, one foot on the ground, handling the sleek black machine beneath him with an easy, unconscious grace.

And his eyes gleamed gold for all that they were grave.

She didn't know how long they stared at each other. The whole city could have gathered around, jeering and pointing, and it wouldn't have registered. There was only Pato. Here, beneath her window. *Here.*

And then he smiled, and she felt it everywhere, like that hungry mouth of his, demanding and hot. *So hot.* She felt herself flush red.

Pato crooked his finger at her, arrogant and sure. He looked anything but careless. He was impossibly powerful, decidedly male, every inch of him a prince though he wore jeans and a black T-shirt that made love to his lean and chiseled body, and held that lethally beautiful machine between his legs.

Adriana scowled at him, because she wanted to melt, and saw his eyes heat in response. He crooked his finger again, with even more lazy command this time, and she shook her head.

"You dismissed me for a reason, or so I assume," she said, in a reasonable attempt at her usual brisk tone, as if she didn't care that he was here. That he'd come when she'd thought she'd never see him again. "You can't change your mind back and forth on a whim and expect—"

"Adriana," he said, and the sound of her name in his mouth like that, so quiet and so serious in the narrow, cobblestone street, made her fall silent. Pato didn't smile or laugh; he didn't show her that grin of his, though his golden gaze was bright. "Come here."

CHAPTER EIGHT

ADRIANA STEPPED INTO the street, pulling the door to the villa shut behind her, and felt Pato's eyes on her long before she turned to face him. His golden gaze seared into her, brighter than the afternoon around them, making her heart pick up speed.

"That machine is much too loud," she told him, the stern tone surprising her even as she used it. His mouth curved in the corner. "It's noise pollution and you are a—"

"Get on the bike." His voice was as commanding as that crook of his finger had been, and that gleam in his gaze had gone hotter, more challenging.

"I no longer serve you, Your Royal Highness," she said primly, though her heart was beating too fast, too hard, and she could see the way he studied the color on her cheeks in that lazy way of his. "At your pleasure or otherwise."

He still didn't smile, though the gleam in his eyes suggested it, and then he reached out and hooked his fingers in the waistband of her jeans. Her skin ignited at his touch, making her forget what she'd been saying. The burn of it went deep when he tugged her close, so close her head fell back and all she could see was him.

"I was cruel," Pato said, his voice dark. "Chastising me won't change that, though perhaps it makes you feel better. But you can admit you want me anyway." His gaze was steady. He wasn't toying with her. He knew. "There's no shame in it."

Adriana went white, then red. Shock. Embarrassment. Fury.

"I don't know what makes you think—"

Her breath left her in a rush when his fingers moved gently over the soft skin just beneath her waistband, teasing her. Tormenting her. Making whatever she was about to say a lie.

"Adriana." His voice was pure velvet now, wrapped around steel. "Get on the bike." He held out a helmet.

And she'd known she would, since the moment he'd appeared outside her windows, hadn't she? Why had she pretended otherwise? It wasn't as if Pato was fooled. It wasn't as if she'd fooled herself.

But there was admitting she loved him in the privacy of her own head, and then there was proving it beyond any doubt—announcing it out loud. And she was fairly certain that climbing up on the back of that motorcycle mere hours after he'd ripped out her heart, sacked her and undone three years of attempted rehabilitation to the Righetti reputation by kissing her like that in front of his brother constituted shouting it at the top of her lungs. *To* him.

She either loved him or she was a masochistic fool, Adriana thought then. Perhaps both.

But she donned the helmet and got on the bike.

Pato headed away from the palace, out of the city and up into the foothills.

Adriana clung to his back, luxuriating in the feel of all his corded, lean strength so close to her and the wind rushing around them. She was pressed into him, her arms wrapped around his waist, her breasts against his back, her legs on either side of his astride the motorcycle he operated as if it was an extension of himself. She felt surrounded by him, connected to him, a part of him.

It was either heaven or hell, she wasn't sure which. But she wanted it to never end.

Eventually he turned off the main roads and followed smaller, less-traveled ones around the far side of the lake, winding his way to a small cottage nestled in a hollow, looking out over a secluded cove. Adriana climbed off the motorcycle when he brought it to a roaring stop, her legs shaky beneath her. Her body felt too big suddenly, as if she'd outgrown her skin. As if it hurt to sever herself from him. She pulled off her helmet and handed it over, feeling somewhat shy. Overwhelmed.

Pato's gaze met hers as he removed his helmet. His mouth moved into a small curve, and she flushed. Again. She felt restless. Hectic and hot, and the way he looked at her didn't help. There might not be shame in wanting him, but there was too much need, and all of it too obvious now that she'd admitted it. Now that she'd stopped pretending.

And all she could seem to do was ache.

Adriana turned to look at the water instead, breathing in the peaceful, fragrant air. Pine and sun, summer flowers and the deep, quiet woods. It was still in ways the city never was. She watched the water lap gently at the rocks at the bottom of the sloping yard, blue and clear and pretty.

It made the odd tension inside her ease. Shift. Turn into something else entirely. They could have been worlds away from the city, the palace, she thought. They could have been anyone, anywhere. Anonymous and free.

"What is this place?" she asked, her voice sounding strange in the quiet, odd in her own mouth.

"It's my best kept secret." Pato stepped away from the motorcycle and shoved his thick hair back from his forehead. The movement made his T-shirt pull tight over that marvelous torso of his, and Adriana's mouth went dry. The gleam in his gaze when she met it again told her he could tell. "I come here to be alone."

She couldn't let herself think about that too closely. She wanted it to mean much, much more than it did.

"More secrets," she murmured instead. His gaze seemed to burn hotter the longer he looked at her, more intense. She tried to shake off the strangeness, the shakiness. All that want and need, and no barriers to contain them. It made her feel off-kilter. Vulnerable. *Alive.* "Private stories, secret cottages. Who knew the overexposed prince had so much to hide? Or that you were capable of hiding anything in the first place?"

He moved closer, and she felt that sizzling current leap between them and then work its way through her, lighting her up the way it always did. The way *he* always did. Fire upon fire, a chain reaction, sweeping over her unchecked until she was molten all the way through. As needy and as desperate as if he was already touching her. As if this morning had never happened.

But it had, and Adriana understood, even through the sweet ache of all that fire between them, that it would again. He wasn't hers. He could never be hers.

And yet she'd come with him, anyway. She'd barely hesitated.

Maybe, like the Righetti women who came before her, it was time she loved what she had for as long as she had it, instead of mourning what she might have had, were she braver. Pato had told her this was passion, this thing that flared between them. She wanted to explore it. She wanted to know what he meant. She wanted *him.*

It didn't feel like surrender to admit that. There was no shame. It felt like a hard-won victory.

"You weren't what I expected," Pato said, as if the words were pulled from him, urgent and dark. Serious. "I've been hiding in plain sight for fifteen years and no one's ever seen me, any hint of me at all, until—"

Adriana turned to him and put her hand over his mouth, that beautiful mouth of his she'd felt devouring her very core, wicked and insinuating and warm to the touch. She felt his lips against her palm now, and the familiar punch of heat that roared through her and connected with that pulsing fire low in her belly.

She didn't want his secrets. Secrets came at too high a price, and she knew she'd pay a hefty one already. She wanted *him.* She wanted to throw herself in this fire at last, and who cared what burned?

"Don't," she whispered, and smiled at him. His gaze was dark on hers for a breath, and another. Then his lips curved against her palm.

Adriana pushed up on her toes, pressed her body flush against his *at last,* and took his mouth with hers. Claiming him here, now. While she could.

Pato met her instantly. He buried one hand in her hair and hauled her against him, and this time she was ready for him. She wrapped herself around him, shameless and abandoned, and let herself glory in it. He let out a sound that was halfway between a laugh and a curse, and then he was sweeping her up into his arms and heading toward the cottage.

"But—" she protested, though she went quiet when he looked down at her, his golden eyes hot and wild, making her shiver in anticipation as she hooked an arm around his hard shoulders.

"Rule number six," he growled, leaning down to nip at her nose. "Don't ever put on a sex show in the yard. Unless it's planned." He shifted her against his chest, holding her with one arm while he worked the door of the cottage with his free hand. "And if it's planned, there should be paparazzi at the ready, not horrified tourists out for a bit of pleasure boating."

Adriana frowned at him as he ducked into the cottage, barely taking notice of the place as he kicked the door closed behind him and carried her inside. She saw high beams and white walls, cozy furniture in bold colors. But she was far more interested in what he'd said.

"Exactly how many 'sex shows' have you participated in?" she demanded. "Planned or unplanned?"

"I don't think you really want me to answer that," he replied, laughter gleaming in those eyes of his now, mixing with all the fire and coiling inside her, tighter and tighter.

"More than five?" she asked, pushing it. Poking at him. *Flirting,* she understood now. She'd been flirting all this time. From the moment he'd opened his eyes and offered her a space in his crowded bed. "Ten? I imagine there would have to be quite a few to justify the making of rules and regulations."

Pato only laughed, and set her down on her feet slowly, letting her body slide down the length of his. Adriana melted against him, almost unable to stand on her own when he let go of her. She swayed slightly, and she didn't care that he could see how he affected her. She wanted him to see it.

"A gentleman doesn't count such things," he said, with a wicked quirk of his mouth. "That would be indelicate."

"Happily, you are no gentleman," she pointed out. "A prince, yes. But never a gentleman."

"Lucky you," he murmured, and then slid his hands under the hem of her whisper-soft sweater, directly onto the bare skin beneath.

Adriana's breath left her in a rush. Pato moved one hand around to the small of her back, and left the other where it was, big and delicious on her abdomen. Then he simply held her there, as if basking in the feel of her skin against his palms, her body between in his grasp.

"Listen to me," he said, and it took her a moment to pull

herself out of her feverish little haze and focus on him again. When she did, his expression was serious. "I can't seem to resist you. But I don't think you're a whore, Adriana. I never did."

She felt gloriously free with his hands on her, with that fire burning so bright in her. With need lighting her up, making her pulse and glow.

"I don't care."

Pato shook his head impatiently. "I care. There are things you need to understand, things that are bigger than—"

"Later," she interrupted.

He frowned at her. So she reached down and grabbed the hem of her sweater herself, then pulled it up and off. She met his gaze as she tossed it aside, smiling slightly at the instant flash of heat there, and the way his hands tightened on her skin, as if he wasn't so controlled himself.

"Pato," she whispered. "I don't want to talk anymore."

He looked torn for a split second. Then that mouth of his curved into pure, male wickedness, and she knew the fire won. She felt it burn ever higher inside her, the flames licking all over her skin.

Pato stepped away from her and then reached back with one arm to tug that tight black T-shirt off his chest, throwing it on the floor near her sweater. This time, she could touch. Taste. This time she could lose herself in the sheer masculine perfection of that lean torso. She couldn't wait.

"Keep your eyes on me," he ordered when she reached for him, his golden gaze amused as it seared into her. "And no touching until I say otherwise."

The air inside the cottage seemed too tight, too hot. How could she keep from touching him? And why—? Pato only smiled.

"Surely," she managed to say, "the *point* is to touch. I feel certain that one of your ninety thousand supermodel lovers must have taught you that in all these years of your celebrated promiscuity."

"If there were ninety thousand supermodels," he said, grinning lazily at her, "they couldn't all be super, could they? I do have standards."

He laughed when she rolled her eyes. But when he looked at her, everything got gold and hot and desperate, and that ache in her bloomed into an open flame.

"The point," he murmured in that silken voice of his, making that flame reach higher and higher, "is to want this so badly you think you might die from it."

"Pato…"

She didn't know she'd said his name again until she saw the way his eyes darkened, then tracked over her body, resting on her breasts and the lilac bra she wore. She felt heavy. Desperate for his touch. Any touch at all.

"I want to know if you match again. I want you to show me." Slowly, so slowly, he lifted his gaze back to hers, and what she saw there made her pulse heat. "And then I want you naked, and if I do it myself I'll be inside you before I get those jeans over your hips and then we'll be done and Adriana?" She stared at him, so wild with heat she thought she might explode. Or die. Or both. His smile was dark and dangerous and she felt it in her toes. "We want this to last a little while."

Her throat was dry. Her heart was pounding. The things she wanted whirled inside her, making her skin pull tight as if she might burst out of it.

"But what if I want to undress you?" she asked. Because she did. Almost more than she could bear. Because if she never had him again, she wanted to have this. As much of him as she could.

He touched her then, and she shuddered at the sheer joy of it. He ran his hand over her cheek, into her hair, and then held her there. Simply held her, and it made the need inside her turn into a white-hot surge of lightning.

"I told you this a long time ago," he said in that same darkly thrilling tone. "But I meant it. I like things my way."

He leaned closer then and brushed his mouth over hers, making goose bumps rise all over her body. She whispered a soft curse and Pato laughed against her mouth.

"And so will you," he promised.

She believed him.

He released her, then raised a dark, imperious brow.

Adriana hurriedly kicked off her shoes, grinning when he did the same. Then she unbuttoned her jeans and peeled them down her legs, feeling awkward until she saw the way he watched her, as if every millimeter of skin she revealed was a revelation.

And then she stood there before him, once again in nothing but her bra and panties. In matching lilac-colored lace.

Pato's smile had a dangerous edge to it. It worked its way into her pulse, making her shift restlessly from foot to foot. He stripped off his own jeans with a minimum of fuss, leaving him in nothing but another pair of those tight briefs that made him look edible.

And she wanted to taste him so badly it began to hurt.

Need made her clumsy. She forgot to be shy. She forgot she was inexperienced. She forgot everything but the man watching her, his gaze getting harder and more intense by the second.

Adriana unhooked her bra. When she pulled it away from her breasts, her nipples were already taut, and she heard Pato let out a sigh. Then she bent and tugged off her panties, and she heard him mutter something beneath his breath. And when she straightened she was naked, and he was looking at her as if she was something holy.

She felt beautiful. She felt like the temptress, the wanton

she'd always been called, and when he looked at her like that, she was glad. Bold women lived in her blood, she knew that now, and watching the way his eyes moved over her, bathing her in golden fire, she finally felt as bold as they were. As free as he'd made her.

He took off his briefs, studied her for another long moment, as if committing the sight of her to memory, and then crooked his finger once more, that wicked smile taking over his mouth.

Adriana walked to him immediately, too desperate to mind his high-handedness. She sighed happily when his hands went to her waist, then smoothed down to her hips—and then he pulled her to him, tumbling them both down on the sofa and arranging her over his lap so she sat astride him.

"Be still," he told her when she squirmed against him, and it very nearly hurt her to stop, but she did it. Her heart beat so hard she could feel it in her temples.

For a moment, he only stared up at her.

She felt his hard thighs beneath her, and the hardest part of him pressed against her, making her hotter, wilder. Needier by the second. She saw the blazing heat in his eyes, the dark passion, and thought she could drown in that alone. He waited. He watched.

"Do you feel like you might die?" he asked, his voice a low whisper, teasing at her skin, moving through her body and making her tremble.

"I think I already did," she confessed.

His mouth curved. And then he leaned forward and sucked her nipple into his mouth without the slightest hesitation, all of that wet heat against the tender peak, and she was lost.

Pato didn't ask, she discovered quickly. He took.

He used his mouth and his tongue against the weight of her breasts, used the hint of his teeth, until Adriana writhed against him, the intense sensations somehow arrowing straight to her core.

She explored that glorious torso of his, sun-kissed and hot beneath her hands, her mouth. And all the while she rocked against his hard, proud length, rubbing all of her heat against him helplessly. Wantonly. And he encouraged it, a big hand against the small of her back to hold her against him, keeping her right where he wanted her.

The more she moved the closer he held her, driving her higher and higher, keeping them close but not yet joined, making her whimper with need. Making her die, she thought, over and over and over again.

And then, when she was out of her mind, he kissed her.

Again and again, taking her mouth and making it his, making *her* his, with that devastating mastery that made her feel deliciously weak, made her shake and rock into him and forget her own name. And then at last he was lifting her, arranging her, reaching between them to test her heat with his fingers.

Once. Then again. Then he grinned at her, wicked and knowing, and did something else, a glorious twist of his clever hand—

Adriana shattered around him, a clenching, rolling burst of fire and light.

But Pato wasn't done.

He laughed, she thought, and then the smooth, hot length of him was pressing against her entrance. He wrapped his hands around her hips, held her fast between them, then thrust deep inside.

And she shattered again, instantly, the second explosion building from the first and tearing her into a million brilliant pieces. It went on and on. She gasped and she sobbed and then, when she started to breathe again, he flipped them around on the sofa, so she was lying on her back and he was cradled between her thighs.

"My turn," he whispered, grinning down at her, his eyes lazy and dark, and focused on her as if nothing else existed but this. Her. The two of them together, finally.

At last, Adriana thought.

And then he began to move.

She was exquisite. *Perfect.* Soft and trembling all around him, clinging to him, wild for him, hot cream and soft silk and *his*.

Finally his, and who cared about the consequences.

Pato set a slow, steady pace, watching her as he took her, watching every shimmer of ecstasy, every hint of joy, that crossed her expressive face. Her hips met his with each thrust, moving in a sinuous rhythm that nearly made him lose his mind. And his control.

Slowly, carefully, he built up the fire in her all over again, leaning down to worship her perfect breasts, her lush mouth. He pulled her knees up to cradle his hips, tasted the salt and sweet of her elegant neck. And then, when he couldn't take any more, he reached between them to find the core of her, and pressed there, rocking against her, into her, until she stiffened against him once more.

Then, at last, he let himself go.

And this time, when she shot over the edge he followed her, listening to her scream out his name as they fell.

It's not enough, he thought then, even as he held her to him, their hearts thundering in concert. *It will never be enough.*

And afterward, he let her crawl over him and drive him wild with her sweet kisses, her delighted exploration of his body. He had her again in the shower, losing himself in the heat and the steam and the slick perfection of her skin beneath his hands. He picked her up and pressed her against the glass, her head tipped back and her mouth open in a kind of silent scream as he rode them both straight back into the heart of that shattering fire.

He wouldn't let her dry herself. Succumbing to an urge he chose not to examine, he did it himself, drying every millimeter of her lovely skin with a soft towel, kissing those three distracting freckles below her breasts, then squeezing the water from her hair. He combed through it slowly, holding her captive between his legs as he sat on the bed in the adjoining bedroom. He noted the colors that sifted through his fingers, testing the heavy silk in his hands.

When he was finished he turned her around, and lost himself for a while in the heaven of her lush, hot mouth, its perfect fit against his, that taste of her that flooded into him and made him crazy, and the sheer poetry of her warm, naked curves beneath his hands.

Pato didn't know how he was going to do what he had to do. He shouldn't have indulged himself. He shouldn't have let her distract him. And yet he didn't regret a single moment of it.

Finally, he set her away from him, as hard again as if he'd never had her, and tempted almost past endurance by the soft invitation on her face, the flush he could see everywhere, from her cheeks to the rosy tips of her breasts.

He had never wanted anything more than this woman. He understood he never would.

And then he wrapped her in a cashmere throw that matched her beautiful eyes, sat her back on the sofa in the living room, where the bed didn't tempt him, and broke the only vow he'd ever made.

"My mother died when I was eighteen," he told her, because he didn't know how else to begin.

Adriana's blond hair was still damp and hung around her face in dark waves, making her look younger than she was. Innocent, despite all the ways he'd touched her, tasted her.

He didn't know why that pulled at him, why it made his chest feel tight.

"I know," she said, sitting with her feet tucked beneath her and the cashmere throw wrapped all around her. She looked delicate. *Perfect,* he thought again, and he couldn't have her. Why couldn't he keep that in mind? "I remember."

"Lenz was twenty-five." Pato shoved his hands in the pockets of the jeans he'd yanked back on when they left the bedroom. He roamed the cottage's small living space restlessly as he talked. "He had completed his military service and had taken his place at the king's side. He'd trained his whole life for it, as befits the heir to the throne." Adriana's gaze tracked Pato as he moved, and he smiled slightly. "I was the spare, and had far fewer expectations placed on me. I'd just started university. I paid some attention to my studies, but I was more interested in the girls."

"Shocking," Adriana said drily, but she was smiling.

"I didn't have to be serious," Pato said darkly. "That was Lenz's job. His duty. I always got to be the favorite, the happy disaster, but he was meant to be king."

For a moment, Pato only gazed at her. He'd let her walk out of the palace today thinking he'd turned on her like all the others, like the people who had called her names and made her feel dirty. He'd seen the look on her face, the crushed betrayal she'd tried to hide, and he'd done it anyway.

He couldn't stand it. He couldn't live with it.

And there was only one way to apologize: he had to explain. His life. His choices. Why he couldn't have her no matter how much he wanted her. She'd cried in his arms and he'd meant what he'd said to her, and he didn't have it in him to let her down. Not Adriana. Not this time. The whole world could think he was waste of space, as pointless as he was promiscuous, but he'd found he couldn't handle it if she did, too. He simply couldn't bear it.

"Pato." She was frowning again, deeper this time, and she stood then, the throw draping around her like a cape. "You don't have to tell me anything. You don't have to do this, whatever this is."

"I do," he said, surprised to hear how rough his voice was. "I need you to understand."

He didn't tell her why. He wasn't entirely sure he knew.

She shook her head, smiling slightly. "I don't expect anything from you," she said. "I know who you are and I know who I am. I'm at peace with it."

He blinked, then scowled at her. "What?"

"I love you," she said, so softly he almost thought he'd imagined it. But she was gazing at him, those melting brown eyes warm and glowing, and he knew she'd said it. That she meant it. "And that has nothing to do with what happens here, or after we leave. You don't owe me anything." She held up a hand when he started to talk. "I don't expect or need you to say it back."

Pato stared at her until she grew visibly uncomfortable under the weight of it. Until her sweet expression started to creep back toward a frown.

"The only thing less attractive than watching you attempt to martyr yourself for my brother in my bed," he growled, his temper kicking in as he spoke, like a black band tight around his chest, his gut, "is watching you martyr yourself for me so soon after I've been inside you, listening to you scream out my name." She sucked in an appalled breath, but he didn't stop, couldn't stop, and he stalked toward her until he stood within arm's reach. "I have no desire whatsoever to be quietly and distantly loved by some selfless, bloodless saint locked away in her self-imposed nunnery, prostrating herself daily to whatever it is she thinks she can't have or doesn't deserve. No hairshirt, no mortification of the flesh. No, thank you."

That telltale tide of red swept over her, but this time, he

thought, it wasn't so simple as embarrassment. Her eyes narrowed and she drew herself up, pulling the throw tighter around her as if it could protect her from him.

"What an ugly thing to say," she breathed, and he had the impression she was afraid to truly voice the words—as if she thought she might start yelling if she did. He wished she would. "Even for you."

He crossed his arms over his chest and glared at her.

"You want to love me, Adriana?" he demanded, his voice rough and hot and impatient, welling up from that place inside he'd thought he'd excised long ago, that heart it seemed only she could reach. He'd be damned if he'd let her hide. Not if *he* couldn't. He angled himself closer. "Then love me. Make it hurt. Make it jealous and possessive and painful. Make demands. Make it real or don't bother."

CHAPTER NINE

THERE WERE STAINS of red high on Adriana's cheeks, a dazed look on her pretty face, and Pato gave in to his driving need to be closer to her. Closer, always closer, no matter how irritated he might be with her and her proclamation of so-called love, as tepid as whatever she'd imagined she felt for Lenz.

Pato reached over and sat her down on the sofa, then gripped the back of it, pinning her there with an arm on either side of her. Caging her. Putting his face too close to hers. He couldn't read the way she looked at him then, didn't understand the darkness in her gaze, that sheen that suggested emotions she'd prefer to conceal from him.

"I know all about hiding, Adriana," he said quietly, though he could still hear that edge in his voice. He could feel it inside him. "I can see it when it's right in front of me."

"I don't know why you want to tell me anything." There was a raggedness in her voice, and he could see it in her face. "I don't know why you hunted me down at the villa, why you brought me here. It would have been easier to simply let me go this morning. Isn't that why you did it?"

"You know why." He wanted to touch her. Taste that lovely mouth. Take her again and again until neither of them could speak. But he didn't. He couldn't. "I can't have you, Adriana, but it's not because I don't want you."

She didn't say a word, but she was breathing high and hard,

as if climbing a steep hill. He could see that same darkness in her eyes, deeper now. Her confusion. He pushed away from the sofa but continued to stand over her, looking down at this woman who might, in fact, be the death of him. She'd already ruined him; that much was certain.

"My mother left behind some personal papers," he said then. It was time to finish this, before he forgot why he wanted that, too. "She left them to my father, which seemed an odd choice, given his profound disinterest in her personal affairs while she was alive. But eventually, he read them. And discovered that Lenz was not, in fact, his biological son."

It was Pato's greatest secret, it wasn't only *his* secret, and she could use it to topple his brother's kingdom if she chose. And there it lay, huge and ugly between them, taking up all the air in the cottage.

Adriana made a small, shocked noise, and covered her mouth with her hands. Pato let her simply stare at him, let all the implications sink in. For long moments she seemed frozen. But eventually, she blinked.

"Did Lenz know?" she asked in a whisper.

"We were both called before the king." Pato could hear the grimness in his voice. He'd never told this story before—he'd never imagined he would tell it to anyone. It certainly wasn't part of the plan. "He informed us that a great crime had been perpetrated against the throne of Kitzinia, and that it must be rectified. That was how Lenz found out."

Adriana's eyes closed, as if that was too horrible to imagine. Pato had been there, and he felt much the same. He and Lenz had been ordered before the king, commanded to appear, even though Pato had been in England and Lenz in South Africa at the time. Pato remembered how baffled they'd been, jet-lagged and even somewhat concerned about their father. Until the nasty, furious way he had delivered the news, as if Lenz had engineered his paternity himself for the sole purpose of deception.

"You have no brother from this day forward," the king had intoned into the stunned, sick silence, glaring at Pato as if Lenz had disappeared into thin air. "You are my heir, and your mother's bastard is nothing to you."

"But," Pato had begun, his head spinning. "Father—"

"I have one son," the king had snarled. "One heir to this throne, Patricio, and God have mercy on this kingdom, but it's you."

Pato had never cared much for his father before that day. He'd always been a distant, disapproving presence who had rarely lowered himself to interact much with his second son, which had always suited Pato well enough, as he'd seen what it was like for Lenz to have all that critical attention focused on him. But after that day, Pato had loathed him.

"My father cannot bear scandal," he said now. "He is obsessed with even the slightest speck of dirt anywhere near his spotless reputation. And I had recently landed myself in the tabloids for the first time with an extremely inappropriate British pop star. The king was not pleased about it when I was merely the ornamental second son, or so I heard through the usual channels, but when it turned out I was his heir, he went apoplectic."

Adriana was still sitting there, so straight and shocked, her eyes still wide. "Did he plan to simply toss Lenz out on the street?"

"He did." Pato moved to the nearby armchair and lowered himself into it. "He thought he'd wait until my pop star scandal faded, exile Lenz from Kitzinia and force me to take on the duties of a crown prince in a sober and serious manner that would indicate my brush with the tabloids was no more than a regrettable, youthful indiscretion, never to be repeated."

Adriana only stared at him, shaking her head slightly as if she couldn't take it in. Or perhaps she was attempting to imagine him in the role of dutiful crown prince—a stretch for anyone, he was well aware. Even him.

"Lenz's exile was to be presented as an abdication well before he was to take the throne." Pato smiled slightly. Darkly. "But I never let the scandal die down. From that day forward, I made it my job to be an embarrassment. To make it abundantly clear that I was and am unfit for any kind of throne."

"Pato." She shifted then, moving forward in her seat as if she wanted to reach over and touch him. Her hands moved, but then she held them together in her lap. "You know I admire your brother. But if you're the heir to the throne...?" She searched his face. "Isn't it your birthright?"

"You sound like Lenz," Pato said roughly. He had to get up again then, had to move, and found himself staring out the windows that looked down to the peaceful water. "I never envied Lenz his position. I never wished for his responsibilities. And when they were handed to me, I didn't want them. Can you imagine if it was announced I was supposed to be king? The people would take up arms and riot in the streets."

"They might object to the Playboy Prince, yes," Adriana said after a long moment. "You've made sure of that. But that's not who you are."

His breath left him. He ignored the ache in his chest.

"My choice was a throne or a brother," he said quietly. He turned to face her. "I chose my brother. And I don't regret it."

"Pato..." she whispered, and the look in her eyes nearly undid him.

"Since then," he said gruffly, pushing forward because he couldn't stay in this moment, couldn't let himself explore the way she gazed at him, "my father has had to pretend to keep Lenz in his good graces, because his pride won't allow him to explain the situation to his ministers. Especially when, as you say, I've made certain the alternative is so unacceptable."

For a moment there was nothing in the room but the sound of his own pounding heart.

"You're a good man, Pato," Adriana said then. There was a scratchy undertone to her voice that made him think she was holding back tears. For him. And he thought it might undo him. "And a very good brother."

Pato looked at her, then away, before he forgot what he could and couldn't have. Before he forgot he'd chosen to be a hollow man, with an empty life. Before he was tempted to believe her.

"My father is also unwell," he said instead, bitterly. "It is, ironically enough, his heart."

Adriana was worried about her own.

She hardly knew where to look, what to think. Nothing he was telling her could possibly be true—and yet it all made a horrible sense. It explained the chilliness she'd always sensed between Lenz and the king. It explained Lenz's extraordinary patience with Pato's messy escapades. More, it explained how Pato could do all the scandalous things he'd done and yet also be the man who'd held her on the plane, then quietly rid her of a lifetime of shame. It explained everything.

He stood there at the window so calmly, half-naked as ever, all sun-kissed skin and masculine grace, talking with such seeming nonchalance about things that would over-throw their government. He had given up a throne. He loved his brother more than he wanted what was his by birthright. He had deliberately crafted his own mythology to serve his own ends and to force his father, the king, into doing what he wanted him to do. He'd even hinted at this once before, in London, when he'd said his reputation was his life's work.

He was truly remarkable, she thought then. And he was hers.

It didn't matter for how long. It didn't matter if he couldn't have her, as he'd said. It didn't matter if all she ever had of him was the distance and the unrequited love that he'd mocked. He'd given her his secrets. He'd stepped out of hiding and shown her who he really was, because he believed she deserved to know. Because he hadn't wanted to let her leave him the way she had this morning, thinking the worst of him.

He would rather have her know the dangerous truth than have her think he didn't care.

That he cared, that he must or he would never have shared any of this with her, that he really must trust her, dawned inside her like the sun.

He was hers.

"His health is deteriorating, he is not a candidate for surgery and he is an unacceptable risk to the kingdom," Pato was saying. "He should have stepped down already. He will have no choice when Lenz marries Lissette, as she was betrothed at birth to the heir to the Kitzinian throne." Pato shrugged at Adriana's quizzical look. "If Lenz marries her, it is an assertion that he is, in fact, that heir. There can be no going back unless my father wants an international incident that could well become a war. He will have no choice but to face the inevitable." Pato's mouth moved into a curve that was far darker than usual. "He has grown more desperate by the day for another option."

"You," Adriana said.

"Me," Pato agreed, "even though I've gone to great lengths to keep myself out of the running." He sighed, and then leveled a look at her that made something twist in her stomach, made a sense of foreboding trickle down her back. "He had convinced himself that the kingdom would excuse me as a young man sowing his oats, who could in time settle down, as men do. But now he believes I am skulking about with one of Lenz's cast-off mistresses, which he finds truly distasteful. Worse, he is superstitious enough to believe that Righetti women possess some kind of witchcraft, and that I am weak enough to be under your spell."

Adriana couldn't breathe, as if he'd slammed that straight into her gut. But she couldn't look away from him, either.

"Bewitched by a woman descended from traitors and temptresses," Pato said softly, his golden eyes darker, more intense. "Crafted by the ages to be my downfall."

"You want him to think that," she managed to say, despite feeling as if the room were drawing tight on all sides. "That's why you decided to behave these last weeks. You wanted him to think I was influencing you."

"Yes."

His gaze was dark. Demanding. Without apology, and Adriana felt so brittle, suddenly. So close to breaking, and that wave of misery she'd thought she was rid of waited there for her, she knew. In the next breath. Or the one following. And it would crash over her and take her to her knees if she let it.

But she still couldn't look away from him.

"Was it all a game?" she whispered, that familiar emptiness opening again inside her, reminding her how easy it was to be sucked back in. "Was any of it real?"

"You know that it was both." His gaze bored into her, challenging her. "Almost from the very beginning."

She shook her head, aware that it felt too full, too fragile. That she did. There was too much noise in her ears and that dark pit in her stomach, and all she wanted was to get to her feet and run—but she couldn't seem to move.

"I don't know that."

"You do."

He pushed away from the wall and came toward her then, imposing and beautiful, and she knew the truth about him now. She knew his indolence was an act, that the powerful, ruthless man she'd glimpsed was who Pato was. Now she couldn't pretend she didn't see it. She couldn't pretend he was lazy, pointless, careless—any of the things he'd pretended he was. He'd manipulated her every step of the way and would no doubt do it again. He'd given up a throne for this. What was one woman next to that? She was nothing but collateral damage.

And still, she didn't move. Still, her heart ached for him. No matter what this meant for her, what it said about the last years of her life.

"This is why you have to leave the palace, Adriana," he said, that dark urgency in his voice and stamped across his face. "You deserve better than these games. No one comes out of them without being compromised. No one wins."

She struggled with the tears that pricked suddenly at the back of her eyes, and then he was right there, sinking down in front of her to kneel on the floor and take her face between his hands.

"I don't want to let you go," he whispered fiercely. "But I will. Somehow, I will. I promise."

The same old voices snaked through her then, crawling out of that darkness inside her to whisper the same old poison. *He wanted the Righetti whore and he got her, didn't he?* She'd been a means to an end for him, a tool. *Another instrument.* Something he could use and then toss aside. *"Remember who you are, Adriana,"* her father had said when she'd first got the job at the palace. *"Remember that your disgrace is already assumed—they only seek confirmation."* She was nothing but her surname, her face, her family's everlasting shame, another headline in another tabloid paper. Temptresses and a traitor, marking her as surely as if she wore their sins tattooed across her cheeks.

But Pato had trusted her. He'd come for her when he could have simply let her leave, none the wiser. He'd brought her here, and she'd been the one to insist they give in to the wild passion between them, not Pato. He'd wanted to talk and she hadn't let him. And now he'd told her everything, and yes, it hurt. But he'd told her a story that could rock the whole kingdom, and he wanted to set her free. Again.

And all *she* wanted to do, all she could think to do, was run away and hide—which was just what she'd done when she was seventeen. It was what she always did.

No wonder he'd mocked her declaration of love, she thought then, a different kind of shame winding through her. It wasn't love at all. It was safe and removed. It was loving the idea of him, not loving the man. The complicated, dangerous man, who wasn't safe at all and had never pretended otherwise—he only made her feel that she might be safe when she was with him.

Make it hurt, he'd challenged her, scowling at her, refusing to accept her half measures. *Make it real or don't bother.*

And this was her chance to step out of hiding, just as he'd done. She wanted to be bold. She wanted to feel *alive.* For once in her life, she wanted to use her infamous name and her notoriety instead of sitting back and letting others use it against her.

Not as a sacrifice. Pato deserved better than that. He deserved a gift.

"It sounds like I'm an excellent weapon," she said. She wrapped her hands around his wrists, tilted her face to his and lost herself in all that dark gold. "Why don't you use me? I'm sure your father isn't the only one who assumes that I'm your mistress as well as Lenz's. Why not make it public and damn yourself in his eyes forever?"

"I'm not going to use you that way, Adriana." Pato's voice was harsh. "I didn't accept the offer when it was for Lenz, and I won't do it now. You are not a whore. You do not wield dark magic that turns unsuspecting men into your slaves. You're better than this fairy-tale villain they've made you, that I've helped them make you, and I refuse to take part in it any longer. I won't."

She couldn't help herself then. She leaned in and kissed him, feeling the electric charge that shuddered through him, then sizzled in her, making what she'd intended to be sweet turn into something else entirely. When she pulled away, his eyes were still dark, but gleamed gold.

"I'm genetically predisposed to be the mistress of a Kitzinian prince," she told him, and smiled at him. She could do this. In truth, she already had. "And I'm already notorious. You may not want to accept your birthright, Pato, but I do."

He looked at her for what felt like a very long time. His hands still cupped her cheeks, and she was sure he could see through her, all the way down to the deepest part of her soul.

"I won't let you sacrifice yourself for this kingdom," he said finally, his gaze more gold than grim, though his mouth remained serious. "It has never done anything for you but make your life a misery."

"It's no sacrifice," she said, her hands tightening around his wrists. "I don't want to martyr myself, I want to help."

Another long moment, taut and electric, and then he shook his head.

"We have a week until the wedding." Pato stood, drawing her to her feet and into his arms. As he gazed down at her, his mouth began to curve into that wicked quirk she recognized. "Lenz will marry his ice princess, the poor bastard. The spectacle will bring in hordes of tourists, just as my parents' wedding did a generation ago. My father will finally cede the throne, and will spend the rest of his miserable life faced with the knowledge that the son he raised and then rejected is his king. And life will carry on, Adriana, without a single mention of the Righetti family, traitors and temptresses, or you."

"But—"

"I promise," he whispered against her mouth.

And then he kissed her, igniting fire and need and that searing joy, and she decided there were far better things to do with the man she loved than argue.

For now.

Adriana woke the morning before the royal wedding with a smile on her face. She turned off her alarm and settled back against her pillow, smiling at the light pouring in through her windows as if the sun shone only for her. As if it was simply another gift Pato had given her.

They hadn't spoken again of his letting her go.

Pato was not considered a legendary lover by accident, she'd learned. His reputed skills were no tabloid exaggeration. He'd had her twice more before they'd left the cottage that day, reducing her to a sobbing, writhing mess again and again, until she was deliciously limp, content simply to cling to him on the drive back into the city, thinking not of thrones and notoriety but him. Only him.

"Come to the palace tomorrow," he'd told her, letting her off on a deserted corner some distance from her family's villa, out of the circle of light thrown by the nearest streetlamp, safe from prying eyes and gossiping tongues.

"You sacked me," she'd reminded him primly. He'd grinned at her, sitting on that lethal-looking motorcycle and holding fast to one of her hands.

"I changed my mind. I do that." His wicked brows rose. "It is my great royal privilege."

"I'm not sure I want the job," she'd teased. "My employer is embarrassing and often inappropriately dressed. And the hours are terrible."

He'd tugged her to him then, kissing her as slowly and as thoroughly as if he hadn't done so already that day, too many times to count. He kissed her until she was boneless against him, and only then did he let her go.

"Don't be late," he'd said, his eyes gleaming in the dark. "And I do hope you can behave yourself. I can't have my assistant throwing herself at me at every opportunity. I take my position as the royal ornament and national disaster very seriously."

He'd roared off, splitting the night with the noise his motorcycle made, and Adriana had fairly danced all the way back to the villa.

And then, the following morning, he'd sauntered into his office wearing nothing but a pair of dark trousers low on his narrow hips. He'd shut the door behind him and had her over his desk before he'd even said good-morning. She'd had to bite her own hand to make sure she stayed quiet while Pato moved inside her, whispering dark and thrilling things in her ear, pushing them both straight over the edge.

He'd started as he meant to go on, Adriana thought now, rolling out of her bed and padding into her bath. They'd followed his usual schedule, packed this week with extra wedding requirements. The difference was, every time they were alone they'd been unable to keep their hands off each other. The car, his office, even a blazingly hot encounter all of three steps away from a corporate luncheon. He'd simply glanced into what was probably a coatroom, pulled her inside and braced her against a chair that sat near the far wall.

"Hang on," he'd murmured, leaning over her back and wrapping his hands around her hips. And then he'd thrust into her, hot and hard and devastatingly talented, and she'd stopped caring about the speech he'd been meant to give. She'd cared about nothing at all but the wild blaze between them and the way they both burned in it, together.

Adriana left her bedroom then, twisting her hair up into a knot as she walked through the villa in search of her morning coffee. She felt lighter than she had in years. She smiled down the hallways toward that closed-off parlor, and took her time descending the grand stairs.

Last night Pato had been called upon to entertain visiting dignitaries and royals from across Europe, all in town for the wedding. When the long evening was over and they were alone in his car, he'd pulled Adriana to him. He'd tucked her beneath his arm, arranged her legs over his lap and rested his chin on the top of her head. Then he'd simply held her. When his driver started up the hill toward the Righetti villa, he'd hit the intercom and told him to simply keep driving.

They'd driven for a long time, circling around and around the city. Pato had played with her hair idly. She'd closed her eyes and let herself enjoy the luxury of time to bask in him. He'd held her close against his heart while the city bled light and noise all around them.

Inside the car, it had been quiet. Soft. Perfect. And Adriana had never felt more cherished. More loved.

She didn't notice the strained silence in the kitchen until she was pouring herself a cup of coffee. She turned to find her father staring at her, an arrested expression on his face she'd never seen before. Even her mother looked pale, one hand clutching at her heart as if it were broken, her eyes cast down toward the table.

"What's happened?" Adriana asked, terrified. She left her coffee on the counter and took a step toward the table, looking back and forth between her parents. Was it one of her brothers? "Has there been an accident?"

Her mother only shook her head as if she couldn't bear to speak, squeezing her eyes shut, and Adriana went cold.

"You know what you've done," her father stated in a hard voice. "And now, Adriana, so does the world."

It took her a moment to understand what he was saying— and that he really was speaking to her with all that chilly animosity. And when she did understand it, she shook her head in confusion.

"I don't know what you mean," she said.

"I blame myself." Her father pushed back his chair and climbed to his feet, looking far older than he had the day before. Adriana felt a deep pang of fear. Then he stood there for a moment, his hard gaze raking over her as if she was something dirty.

And she knew, then.

That familiar, panicked cold bloomed deep inside her, spreading out and turning black, ripping open that same old wound and letting the emptiness back in.

He knew about Pato.

"Papa," she said softly, reaching out a hand toward him, but he recoiled. Her throat constricted when she tried to swallow, and she slowly dropped her arm back to her side.

"I knew you were too beautiful," he told her in that terrible voice, and Adriana felt it like a knife, sinking deep into her belly. "I knew it would ruin us. Beauty like that is only the surface, Adriana, and everything beneath it is corrupt. Sinful. Twisted. I saw it myself in Sandrine, in her contempt for propriety. It runs in this family like a disease. I knew it was in you since the day you were born a girl."

She felt unsteady on her feet, as if he'd actually cut her open. Perhaps it would have been better—less painful—if he had. And she was too aware of her mother's continued silence in place of her usual unspoken support, weighing on Adriana like an indictment.

"There's no Righetti family disease," she said when she could speak. It was hard to keep her voice calm, her gaze steady as she faced her father. "There never was. We're only people, Papa, and we all make our own choices."

His lip curled, and he stared at her as if he'd never seen her before now. As if she'd worn a mask her whole life, until today, and what he saw beneath it disgusted him. It made her feel sick.

"Tell me he forced you. Coerced you. Tell me, daughter, that you did not betray your family's trust in you willingly. That you did not follow in the footsteps of all the whores who sullied the Righetti name before you and take *Prince Pato*—" he spat out the name as if it was the foulest of curses "—as your lover. Tell me you are not so stupid as to open your legs for that degenerate. *Tell me.*"

Adriana didn't understand how this was happening. Her head pounded and her heart felt like lead in her chest, and she didn't know what to do, how to make this better. How to explain what it was like to be free of her chains to the man who'd helped fashion them, because he wore so many of his own.

"He's not a degenerate," she whispered, and it was a mistake.

Her father let out a kind of roar—enraged and humiliated and broken. It made her mother jerk in her chair. It made Adriana want to cry. But instead, she wrapped her arms around her middle and watched him, waiting for his eyes to meet hers again.

When they did, she thought the look in them might leave marks.

"You don't understand," she said quickly, desperately.

"I cannot bear to look at you." He sounded deeply, irreversibly disgusted. It made her eyes fill with tears. "All I see are his fingerprints, sullying you. Ruining you. Making you nothing more than one more Righetti whore, like all the rest." He shook his head. "You have proved to the world that we are tainted. Dirty. You have destroyed us all over again, Adriana, and for what? The chance to be one more conquest in an endless line? The opportunity to warm a bed that has never gone cold? How could you?"

She shook, but she didn't move, not even when he turned and slammed out of the room, the silence he left behind heavy and loud, pressing into her, making her want to slide into a ball on the floor. But she didn't do it. She forced herself to look at her mother instead.

"Mama—" she began, but her mother shook her head hard, her lips pressed together in a tight line.

"You knew better," she said in a harsh whisper. "From the time you were small, you knew better than this. Righettis can't put a single foot wrong. Righettis must be above reproach—especially a girl who looks like you, as if you stepped out of one of those paintings. I took you to meet Sandrine myself—living out her days in a foreign country with a man who should have been a duke, cast out from her home forever. *You knew better.*"

It was such an unexpected slap that Adriana took a step back from the table, as if her mother really had hit her.

"I never did anything to be ashamed of," she blurted out, something reckless moving in her then, impossible to contain, as if she'd waited all her life for this conversation. "And yet the first thing you taught me was shame. Why do we punish ourselves before anyone else does?" Her voice cracked. "Why did you?"

But that made it worse. Her mother stood then, straight and sorrowful, both hands at her heart and her eyes like nails, staring at Adriana as if she was a stranger.

"You've made your bed, Adriana," she said coldly. "We'll all have to lie in it, won't we? I certainly hope it was worth it. Sandrine always thought so, but then, she died alone and far away, in a cloud of disgrace. And so will you."

Her mother didn't slam the door when she left. She simply walked away and didn't look back, which was worse. Worse than a slap.

And Adriana stood there in all that silence, awful and simmering and ugly, and tried to keep herself from falling apart.

She looked around desperately, as if a solution might rise up from the tiled floor, and that was when she saw the paper spread out in the middle of the wooden table as if her parents had pored over it together.

The paper.

For a moment she couldn't bring herself to look, because she could imagine what she'd see. She'd been imagining it, in one form or another, since she was a girl. She'd had nightmares about it more than once. She stared at the paper as if it were a serpent coiled up in the middle of the kitchen, fangs extended.

But in the end, she couldn't help herself.

Playboy Pato Succumbs to Witchy Righetti's Spell! Well known for her notorious wiles, Adriana Righetti—very much an heir to her family's storied charms—has made a shocking play for the kingdom's favorite bachelor—

She couldn't do it, she told herself, squeezing her eyes shut, her hand at her throat as if her pulse might leap out from beneath her skin.

But there was more. She had to look.

There was the helpful sidebar that ran down all the infamous members of the Righetti family, complete with pictures and a few snide lines detailing their sins. Carolina, shameless mistress to Crown Prince and later King Philip. Maria, rumored to have slept with all three royal princes and some assorted cousins with dukedoms in an effort to trade upward, until she reached Eduardo, the future king. Francesca, lifelong consort of Prince Vidal. Sandrine, who'd disrupted the Reinsmark dukedom. And Almado the traitor, who had assassinated King Oktav. And somehow it managed to suggest, without ever doing so directly, that Adriana herself had been mistress to all those Kitzinian royals before going on to personally betray the country, before taking her position in the palace and turning her attention to the easily seduced and obviously beguiled Pato.

And then there were the pictures.

They'd been taken the day before yesterday, she saw at once. She reached out to run a shaky finger over the series of photos before her, smudging the newspaper ink. She'd thought they were alone. Pato had spent the morning at an event, and they had been waiting in the antechamber of the hall for his driver to pull around. She'd been *certain* they were alone.

And that was why she hadn't protested when he'd turned to her with that wild and hungry look in his eyes. Why she'd leaned into him when he'd taken her mouth in a lush promise of a kiss. It had been devastating and quick, a mere appetizer to what he'd do once they climbed into the car, he'd informed her with that gleam of gold in his eyes. And he'd kept his word.

It had been a single kiss. Hot and private. *Theirs.*

But the pictures looked openly carnal. The very number of photographs made it seem they'd kissed for a long time, so focused on each other that they were reckless, careless. The paper tutted about the locale and the fact that neither of them had apparently noticed or cared that they'd been in public—"par for the course for Pato, but can Adriana's history make her anything but a terrible influence on the kingdom's bad boy?"

She had no idea how long she stood there in the kitchen, all alone with the newspaper and its malicious recounting and reshaping of her life into nasty little innuendos and silly nicknames. At first she didn't know what snapped her out of it—but then she heard the banging at the door, harsh and loud. And the shouting.

Her stomach sank to her feet. Paparazzi.

She should have expected them. She'd dealt with them a thousand times before—but never when *she* was the target. Adriana took a deep breath, and then pulled all the curtains shut without letting them get a glimpse of her, took the landline telephone off its hook, making it as difficult as possible for the cockroaches swarming in her street to get what they were after.

She didn't seek out her parents. They would expect an apology—an apology Adriana doubted they would accept. And she might feel sick to her stomach, she might feel battered and attacked, exposed and alone, but she wasn't sorry.

When she finally climbed back up to her room, her mobile was lit up with messages. Reporters. Supposed "friends" she hadn't spoken to in years. Her few actual friends, quietly wondering how she was. More reporters. And then the clipped and frigid tones of the king's private secretary, a man Adriana had seen from afar but had certainly never met, informing her that her services to the royal household were no longer required.

She was cut off. Dismissed. The Righetti contamination had been officially removed from the palace.

It was not until dusk began to creep through the streets that Adriana admitted to herself that she'd expected Pato to appear again—to race to the villa and save her, somehow, from this public disgrace. Make it better, even if this public stoning via newspaper was exactly what she'd volunteered for. Twice.

Because it turned out that being called a whore her whole life had not, in fact, prepared her for what it was like to see it printed in the newspapers and all across the internet, not as speculation this time, but fact. It hadn't prepared her for that scene in the kitchen with her parents. It hadn't prepared her at all.

And when she'd wanted to do this, she understood as she sat there, barricaded in her childhood bedroom, she'd thought only about how Lenz or Pato might benefit from this kind of media attention. She hadn't thought about her family at all, and the guilt of that grew heavier as the day wore on. This wasn't only about her. It never had been. This was her family's nightmare, and she'd made it real.

Pato had been right. She'd been so busy rushing to martyr herself that she hadn't stopped to consider precisely what that might entail. Or just how many people it would hurt besides her.

Eventually, she had to accept the fact that Pato wasn't coming.

And with it, a wave of other things she didn't want to think about. Such as how ruthless he really was, how manipulative. He'd told her so himself. How he'd promised this wouldn't happen, and yet it had. And what his silence today suggested that meant.

She couldn't cry. She could hardly move. It simply hurt too much.

Late that night, Adriana found herself in the parlor with the other harlots. She curled up in the chair below their portraits and stared at them until her eyes went blurry.

This was inevitable from the start, she told herself. *You walked right into it anyway, talking about love and imagining you were better than your past.*

Adriana had no one to blame for this but herself.

CHAPTER TEN

ADRIANA WOKE WITH a start, her heart pounding.

For a moment she didn't know where she was, but even as she uncurled herself from the chair she found herself in, she remembered, and a glance at the wall before her, and the three portraits hanging there, confirmed it.

Adriana stretched out the kink in her neck, the events of the previous day flooding back to her, one after the next, as she stood. Her father's face. Her mother's harsh words. The newspapers, the paparazzi. Pato's obvious betrayal. She shut her eyes against it, as if that might make it all vanish.

Last night she hadn't been able to cry. This morning, she refused to let herself indulge the urge. If the women hanging on the wall could smile, she told herself, then so could she.

She squared her shoulders, told herself she was ready to face the next battle—and that was when she heard the shouting. *Her father.*

Adriana threw open the door and stepped into the hall, moving toward the angry sound. Her stomach twisted into a hard knot as she tried to imagine what could be worse than yesterday's newspaper spread, which hadn't sent him into this kind of temper—

"You've done enough damage—you can want nothing more! Will you take the house down, brick by brick? Demand our blood from the stones?" Her father sounded upset and furious in a way that scared her, it was so much worse than yesterday. She picked up her speed. "How many of your sick, twisted little games—"

Adriana reached the stair, looked down and froze solid.

Pato stood there in the lower hall.

She didn't know what poured through her then, so intense it was like an acute flash of pain, and she couldn't tear her eyes away from him.

Pato wore the ceremonial military regalia that tradition dictated served as formal wear to a grand state occasion like his brother's wedding, a dark navy uniform accented in deep scarlet at the cuffs, the neck, and in lines down each leg, then liberally adorned with golden epaulets and brocades that trumpeted his rank. He'd even tamed his hair from its usual wildness, making him look utterly, heartbreakingly respectable. He stood tall and forbidding, staring at Adriana's father impassively, a trio of guards arranged behind him.

He looked every inch the royal prince he was. Like the king he could have been. He looked dangerously beautiful and completely inaccessible, and it ripped at her heart.

Adriana sucked in a breath, and his gaze snapped to hers, finding her there on the landing.

His gaze was the darkest she'd ever seen it, hard and intense, and she didn't know how long they stood there, eyes locked together. Her father was blocking the stairs, his voice louder by the second, and yet while Pato looked at her like that, she hardly heard him.

Pato jerked his gaze away abruptly, leaving Adriana feeling simultaneously relieved and bereft.

"No more," he said curtly, cutting into her father's diatribe with a tone of sheer command. He seemed taller, more formidable, and yet he didn't change expression as he stared at her father. "You forget yourself."

The air in the villa went taut. Thin. Adriana's father fell silent. Pato waited.

One breath. Another.

"Step aside," Pato ordered, his voice even, but there was no mistaking the crack of power in it. The expectation of obedience. The guards behind him stood straighter. "I won't ask again."

Adriana's father moved out of his way, and even as he did, Pato brushed past him, taking the steps with a controlled ferocity that made something inside Adriana turn over and start to heat. She couldn't seem to look away from him as he bore down on her, or even catch her breath, and then he was there. Prince Patricio of Kitzinia, in all his stately splendor, looking at her with the same hard intensity as before, nothing the least bit gold in his gaze.

"You brought guards?" she asked. Of all the things she might have said to him.

"I dislike the paparazzi blocking my movements," he said in that same even tone. Then his head tilted slightly. Regally. "Is there a private room?"

It was another command, demanding instant compliance.

Adriana didn't hesitate any more than her father had. She waved her hand down the hall she'd come from, and Pato inclined his head, indicating she should precede him.

She did—but not without looking back.

Her father stood in the lower hall, watching her with the same tortured expression he'd worn yesterday, and the guilt swept through her again, almost choking her. She opened her mouth, as if there was something she could say to take away his horror at what was his worst nightmare come to life, right before his eyes.

But Pato's hand was on the small of her back, urging her ahead of him. There was nothing she could say to make this better. Her father wouldn't forgive her, and on some level, she didn't blame him. She'd known better than to do this, and she'd done it anyway.

Adriana couldn't stand Pato touching her—it was too much to bear, and her body only wanted him the way it always did—so she broke away as she led him back into the parlor, moving all the way across the room before facing him, her back to the far wall.

Pato stepped inside, closed the door behind him, and his gaze cut immediately to the trio of paintings on the wall. He went still, his mouth flattening into a grim line.

It took him a long time to look at her again, but when he did, Adriana had recovered herself. Maybe it was the women on the wall, reminding her that she could do this, whatever this was. It took a lot of strength to survive being as hated as they'd been—as she was. She remembered that Sandrine's eyes had sparkled merrily when she'd met her, that the older woman had looked anything but cowed.

Adriana could survive these final, painful scenes with Pato. *She could.*

"I would have preferred to sacrifice myself, I think," she said coolly, pulling the familiar defense around her gratefully. She crossed her arms and ignored that flash in his gaze. "Rather than wake up yesterday to find myself burned to a crisp on your little pyre with no warning whatsoever. Call me controlling if you must."

He eyed her from across the room in a way that unnerved her, but she refused to back down.

"You believe I did this?" he asked mildly. But she knew him too well to be fooled by that tone.

"I don't know why you didn't ask for assistance," she continued, as if this was any other conversation she'd ever had with him. As if it was easy to pretend there was no emotion beneath this, no dark whirling thing that threatened to suck her under. "I've been handling your paparazzi encounters for a long time, Pato. At the very least, I might have suggested a better nickname for myself than 'Witchy Righetti.'"

Again, he gave her a long look, and it occurred to her belatedly that he was fighting for calm and control as much as she was. It made her heart kick in a kind of panic.

"I promised you I wouldn't use you that way," he reminded her, almost politely. As if he thought she might have forgotten.

And it was too much. He was here, and the way he was dressed made the difference in their situations painfully clear to her. He would walk away from this a prince. She would crawl away from this the disgraced daughter of a despised family, personally responsible for this new helping of shame and recrimination heaped on her family's name.

She used the only weapon she had.

"You also promised your brother that you wouldn't reveal his secret, I assume," she said, very distinctly, and told herself she was pleased when she saw something dark and raw in his gaze. "And yet you did. Why would I think you'd keep a relatively small promise to someone like me?"

A muscle worked in his jaw. His hands curled into fists. And he looked at her as if she'd torn him wide-open.

Adriana told herself she was glad. He wasn't here to save her. He couldn't undo what she'd done to her family. But if she could make him feel a little bit of what she did, all the better—even if that look on his face clawed into her, shredding her from within.

He laughed, but it was short. Bitter.

"This, then, is what you mean when you say you love me," he said quietly, his dark eyes pinning her to the wall behind her. "Is it better this way, Adriana? If you succeed in running me off—if you take that knife and bury it deep enough, twist it hard enough—will that get you what you want?"

He was moving toward her—one step, then another—dark and furious and something more than that. Something that made him look as destroyed as she felt, and there was nothing good about that at all.

"I don't want—" she began, but he laughed again, and this time, it made her shudder.

"I think you do," he said, low and intense. Damning her where she stood. "I think you want to hole up in this mausoleum and paint your own portrait to hang on that wall." He pointed at the trinity of pictures, but he didn't take his eyes off her. "That's what Righettis have been doing in this place for the last hundred years, wafting through the kingdom like ghosts, subjecting themselves to whatever punishment is thrown their way—"

"You don't have any idea what you're talking about!" she cried, aware that she was shouting. But there was something hard and itchy and hot inside her, and she had to get it out or it would kill her, she knew. "It's not as if you have any idea what it's like to be the most reviled family in the kingdom. And why would you? It wasn't *your* ancestor who murdered the king!" She swept her hand toward the portraits. "Or slept with several branches of the royal family tree!"

His eyes blazed at her, and she realized only belatedly that he'd come much too close to her, as if he'd stalked her without her noticing.

"Do you imagine that my family took control of the throne of Kitzinia because we asked nicely?" he demanded, sounding as incredulous as he did angry. "Is that how you remember the history of Europe? Because to my recollection, every kingdom that ever was came about in blood and treachery." He shook his head, and then somehow his hands were on her upper arms and he was even closer, and she knew she should push him away. She knew she should extricate herself—but she couldn't seem to move. "Your family isn't the only one in the kingdom with blood on its hands, Adriana.

But it is certainly the only one I can think of that's created a cult out of its guilt!"

She hung there, unable to breathe, unable to think, suspended between his hands as surely as she was caught in that dark, ferocious glare he kept trained on her.

"What do mean by that?" she asked in a whisper, and then shivered when he pulled her so close to him that his lips almost touched her as he spoke.

"You didn't kill any Kitzinian kings," he snapped. "And last I checked, the only prince you've slept with is me. Stop accepting the blame for history you can't change." Something flashed in his gaze then, and she felt the echo deep inside her, deep and threatening, as if might tear her in two. "For God's sake," he growled at her. "*You* are not a painting on the wall, Adriana. You don't have to shoulder this. *Fight back*."

Pato let go of her and stepped away.

He couldn't remember the last time he'd lost his temper. Not like this, so that it hummed in him still. And certainly not with that rough edge of need running through it, making him want nothing more than to continue this conversation while naked and deep inside her.

Even after she'd thrown what he'd told her in his face, he wanted her, with the same desperation as before. More, perhaps. He didn't know whether to laugh at that or simply despair of himself.

Adriana was breathing hard, and looking very little like the brazen harlot he'd read so much about yesterday. He could see the smudges of exhaustion beneath her beautiful eyes, the vulnerable cast to her sweet mouth, the flush in her cheeks that failed to disguise the paleness of her face. He let his gaze fall over her, from the blond waves in a messy knot on the back of her head, to a face scrubbed free of cosmetics, to the loose cotton clothes she wore that might very well be her pajamas. And her bare feet.

For some reason, the fact that he could see her toes made his chest hurt.

"I didn't plant that story," he told her then, biting out the words he shouldn't have to say. She raised a hand to her mouth as if she thought she might cry, then lowered it again, as if she was still trying to put on a front for him. He hated it. "It was Lissette."

"What?" Adriana shook her head. "Why?"

"Lenz told her the truth." Adriana's eyes flew to his, shocked. "He felt she deserved to make an informed decision about whether or not to marry him. She, in turn, felt that my father couldn't be trusted not to pull a last-minute stunt at the wedding, so she decided to make it clear that he was without options."

Adriana swallowed. "Lenz must be happy that she wants him anyway."

"That, or she very much wants to be queen of Kitzinia," Pato retorted. His voice lowered. "But I'm certainly pleased to learn that your opinion of me is as poor today as it ever was. And why is that, do you suppose?"

She blinked, and when she looked at him again, there was an anguish in her eyes that tore at him.

"You've been working toward this for a very long time," she said in a hushed tone. "You've given up so much. I thought that if you needed to do it, you would. And I'd volunteered, hadn't I?" He only watched her, until she shifted uncomfortably, her expression pure misery. "It seemed like the kind of thing you'd do."

"Why?" he asked quietly, though his voice was like a blade. He could see it cut at her. "What makes me so untrustworthy, Adriana?"

"I never said that," she whispered, but she was trembling.

"I know why," he told her. "And so do you. At the end of the day, I'm nothing more than a whore myself, and in my case, a real one. And who could possibly trust a whore?"

She flinched, and then she simply collapsed. Her hands flew up to cover her face and she bent over her knees, and for a simmering moment, Pato thought she was sick. But then he saw the sobs shake her body, silent and racking.

Pato couldn't stay away from her, not when she was falling apart right in front of him. Not when he'd pushed her there himself.

He moved toward her, but she held up a hand to ward him off, and straightened, tears streaming down her face. He considered that for a brief moment and then he simply took hold of her hand and pulled her into his arms.

"Listen to me," he said, his voice raw. "I can't give you what you deserve. I can't give you anything except tabloid gossip and innuendo, and I hate that. *I hate it.*" He shifted her against him, taking her chin in his hand and gently bringing her eyes to his, those melting chocolate eyes, wet and hurt and still the most beautiful he'd ever seen. "But you have to know that I love you, Adriana. I love you and I would never deliberately hurt you. You can trust that, if nothing else. I swear it."

"Pato..." she said, as if his name was a prayer.

"I can't fix this," he told her, the same fury that had ignited in him when he'd seen the papers yesterday surging in him again. That same dark, encompassing rage that had nearly taken him apart. "I can't protect you the way I should. The only thing I can do is let you go." She was shaking her head and he slid his hand from her chin to her soft cheek, holding her there. "You deserve better."

He watched her struggle to take a breath, and she didn't seem to care that her face was wet with tears. She frowned at him.

"And what will you do while I'm out there somewhere, finding whatever it is I deserve?" she asked. She shook her head again, decisively. "Martyr yourself?"

"It's not the same thing."

"It's exactly the same thing," she retorted.

"I don't have a choice," he exclaimed. "This doesn't end simply because Lenz marries today. I told you. Thrones are won by treachery. My father will be a threat until he's dead— or until Lenz produces his own heir. Pato the Playboy isn't going anywhere."

Adriana watched him for a moment, then angled herself back to wipe at her eyes. His hand dropped away, and he missed touching her immediately, so much his fingers twitched.

"The Princess Lissette strikes me as highly motivated," she said, a hint of that dryness in her voice that he adored, that he knew would haunt him forever. "I give her ten months, maybe a year, before she kicks off the next generation."

"You have to live better than this," he told her softly. "Please."

Adriana looked at him for a long time. He thought she might simply agree, and it would kill him, but he would let her leave him. He had no choice. But then she sighed.

"I thought you told me love was meant to hurt if it mattered," she said, her gaze on his, hard and warm at the same time. "And who's the martyr now? If you order me out of the country, does that mean you can wallow on your own crucifix?"

That dug beneath his skin, straight on into the center of him, making it hard to breathe for a moment. He said her name softly—a warning, or his own version of a prayer? He wasn't sure he could tell.

"Make it real or don't bother calling it love, Pato," she declared, slicing into him with his own words. Daring him.

"It *already* hurts. It's *already* painful. What's another year of the same?"

"You don't know what you're saying."

"I'm the one they picked apart the most in those papers," she reminded him, her eyes gleaming wet again. "I know exactly what I'm saying."

"This has been *one day* of tabloid coverage," he pointed out, determined to make her see reason. "Are you really prepared for the endless onslaught? Day after day after day, until sometimes you wonder if the story they're telling is the truth and you're the lie?"

She moved to him then and put her hands on his chest, leaning into him, making him want nothing more than to hold her close and keep her there forever.

"I have to think that it's better if there's someone else around to tell you which is which," she whispered. "And yesterday was a bad day in the tabloids, but it wasn't the first. I've been a favorite target since I turned sixteen."

Pato couldn't help himself. She was the only one who'd ever seen him, who'd looked straight through all the masks he wore and found him. And she thought he was a good man.

He wanted that. He wanted her. He wanted *this,* however he could have it.

"If you don't go now, Adriana," he warned her, even as he pulled her closer, "I will never let you try again. I will order you to stay with me, and it will ruin you. You will be the most infamous of all the Righettis, worse even than your great-aunt and her disgraced duke. The papers will never let it go. The people will be worse."

She shrugged, but her eyes were tight on his. "Let them say what they want. They do anyway."

"Your friends and family will think you've turned to the dark side," he said, his tone serious, though he could feel his mouth begin to curve, and saw an instant answering spark in her warm gaze. "They will despair of you. They will stage interventions, cut you off, sell secrets and lies to the tabloids and claim you brought it upon yourself."

"I think I love you most of all when you're romantic," she teased, and he could see the smile she tried to hide, even as he soaked in the words he'd wanted to hear again, ever since he'd thrown them back in her face at the cottage. "When you paint me such beautiful pictures of our future. Be still my heart."

But he wasn't done.

"It will be hard and lonely," he promised her. "But when it's done, my brother will sit on that throne, his heir will be hale and hearty and *his,* and I will make you a princess." Pato moved his hands to her head, smoothed back her pretty hair, then tilted her face up. "I will marry you in the great cathedral and make every single one of these Kitzinian hypocrites bow down before you. Our babies will be fat and happy, and know as little as possible of palace life. None of this intrigue. None of these games. And I will make you happy or die trying, I promise you."

"I love you, Pato," she told him, fierce and sure, the truth of it a wild light in her gaze. There was nothing tepid or lukewarm about it, and it burned into him like fire. "I'm not going to give you up." Her mouth curved. "And that means your famous debauchery starts and ends with me. No ambassador's daughters. No nameless former lovers. No *energetic* threesomes."

He grinned. "You think you can handle me all by yourself?"

"Try me," she whispered. "I know how much you like a challenge."

He took her mouth then, hot and hard, making them both shudder. And when he pulled back again, her eyes were shining, and he knew. She was his, at last.

His. For good.

When he let her go again she was smiling, until she glanced at the portraits on the wall and a shadow moved over her face.

"I have to think that someday my family will forgive me for this," she said quietly. "It will hurt them worst of all."

He kissed her again, bringing her attention back to him.

"I suspect they'll find a way to work past the shame," he said, amused, "when their daughter is a princess and the Righetti lands and fortunes are restored to their former glory by an eternally grateful monarch. I suspect they will discover that, secretly, they supported you all along."

Her smile then was like the sun, warm and bright, lighting up all the dark places inside him. Filling in the hollows. He would do the same for her, he vowed. He would take away the darkness. He would bathe her in light until she had no shadows left to haunt her.

He would spend the rest of his life chasing them away, one by one. She was right—he loved a challenge.

"I've never been scandalous *on purpose,*" she said then, as if the idea thrilled her.

Pato laughed. "I've never been anything else. You'll catch on. We can practice at my brother's wedding. I believe we're already late."

"It shouldn't be too hard," she told him, in that way of hers that made him want to lock the door and indulge himself in the perfect taste of her, especially when she looked at him as if she saw nothing but forever in his gaze. Then she smiled. "Rule number seven. I'm a Righetti. Scandal is in my blood."

* * * * *

A NIGHT IN THE
PRINCE'S BED

BY
CHANTELLE SHAW

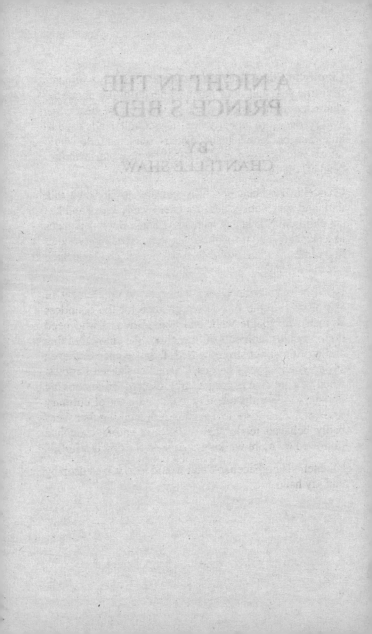

Chantelle Shaw lives on the Kent coast, five minutes from the sea, and does much of her thinking about the characters in her books while walking on the beach. An avid reader from an early age, her schoolfriends used to hide their books when she visited—but Chantelle would retreat into her own world and still writes stories in her head all the time.

Chantelle has been blissfully married to her own tall, dark and very patient hero for over twenty years and has six children. She began to read Mills & Boon romances as a teenager, and throughout the years of being a stay-at-home mum to her brood found romantic fiction helped her to stay sane!

Her aim is to write books that provide an element of escapism, fun and of course romance for the countless women who juggle work and home-life and who need their precious moments of 'me' time. She enjoys reading and writing about strong-willed, feisty women and even stronger-willed sexy heroes. Chantelle is at her happiest when writing. She is particularly inspired while cooking dinner, which unfortunately results in a lot of culinary disasters! She also loves gardening, taking her very badly behaved terrier for walks and eating chocolate (followed by more walking. . .at least the dog is slim!).

Chantelle is on Facebook and would love you to drop by and say hello.

CHAPTER ONE

He was here. Again.

Mina had told herself that she would not look for him, but as she stepped out from the wings her eyes darted to the audience thronged in the standing area in front of the stage, and her heart gave a jolt when she saw him.

The unique design of Shakespeare's Globe on London's South Bank meant that the actors on stage could see the individual faces of the audience. The theatre was a modern reconstruction of the famous Elizabethan playhouse, an amphitheatre with an open roof, above which the sky was now turning to indigo as dusk gathered. To try to recreate the atmosphere of the original theatre, minimal lighting was used, and without the glare of footlights Mina could clearly see the man's chiselled features; his razor-edged cheekbones and resolute jaw shaded with stubble that exacerbated his raw masculinity.

His mouth was unsmiling, almost stern, yet his lips held a sensual promise that Mina found intriguing. From the stage she could not make out the colour of his eyes, but she noted the lighter streaks in his dark blond hair. He was wearing the same black leather jacket he had worn on the three previous evenings, and he was so devastatingly sexy that Mina could not tear her eyes from him.

She was curious about why he was in the audience

again. It was true that Joshua Hart's directorial debut of William Shakespeare's iconic love story *Romeo and Juliet* had received rave reviews, but why would anyone choose to stand for two and a half hours to watch the same play for three evenings in a row? Maybe he couldn't afford a seat in one of the galleries, she mused. Tickets for the standing area—known as the yard—were inexpensive and popular, providing the best view of the stage and offering a unique sense of intimacy between the audience and the actors.

Mina tried to look away from him, but her head turned in his direction of its own accord, as if she were a puppet and he had pulled one of her strings. He was staring at her, and the intensity of his gaze stole her breath. Everything faded—the audience and the members of the cast on stage with her—and she was only aware of him.

On the periphery of her consciousness Mina became aware of the lengthening silence. She sensed the growing tension of the actors around her and realised that they were waiting for her to speak. Her mind went blank. She stared at the audience and sickening fear churned in her stomach as she registered the hundreds of pairs of eyes staring back at her.

Oh, God! Stage-fright was an actor's worst nightmare. Her tongue was stuck to the roof of her mouth and sweat beaded on her brow. Instinctively she raised her hands to her ears to check that her hearing aids were in place.

'*Focus,* Mina!' A fierce whisper from one of the other actors dragged her from the brink of panic. Her brain clicked into gear and, snatching a breath, she delivered her first line.

'"How now, who calls?"'

Kat Nichols, who was playing the role of Nurse, let out an audible sigh of relief.

"'Your mother.'"

"'Madam, I am here. What is your will?'"

The actress playing Lady Capulet stepped forward to speak her lines, and the conversation between Lady Capulet and the Nurse allowed Mina a few seconds to compose herself. Her hesitation had been brief and she prayed that the audience had been unaware of her lapse in concentration. But Joshua would not have missed it. The play's director was standing in the wings and even without glancing at him Mina sensed his irritation. Joshua Hart demanded perfection from every member of the cast, but especially from his daughter.

Mina knew she had ignored one of acting's golden rules when she had broken the 'fourth wall'—the imaginary wall between the actors on stage and the audience. For a few moments she had stepped out of character of the teenage Juliet and given the audience a glimpse of her true self—Mina Hart, a twenty-five year-old partially deaf actress.

It was unlikely that anyone in the audience was aware of her hearing impairment. Few people outside the circle of her family and close friends knew that as a result of contracting meningitis when she was eight she had been left with serious hearing loss. The digital hearing aids she wore were small enough to fit discreetly inside her ears and were hidden by her long hair. The latest designed aids enabled her to have a telephone conversation and listen to music. Sometimes she could almost forget how lonely and cut off she had felt as a deaf child who had struggled to cope in a world that overnight had become silent.

Although Mina had complete confidence in her hearing aids, old habits remained. She was an expert at lip-reading and from instinct rather than necessity she watched Lady Capulet's lips move as she spoke.

"'Tell me, daughter Juliet, how stands your dispositions to be married?'"

The exquisite poetry of Shakespeare's prose was music to Mina's ears and touched her soul. Reality slipped away. She was not an actress, she *was* Juliet, a maid of not yet fourteen who was expected to marry a man of her parents' choosing, a girl on the brink of womanhood who was not free to fall in love, unaware that by the end of the night she would have lost her heart irrevocably to Romeo.

Speaking in a clear voice, Juliet replied to her mother.

"'It is an honour that I dream not of.'"

The play continued without further hitches, but in one corner of her mind Mina was aware that the man in the audience didn't take his eyes off her.

Shakespeare's tale of star-crossed lovers was drawing to its tragic conclusion. After standing for more than two hours, Prince Aksel Thoresen's legs were beginning to ache, but he barely registered the discomfort. His eyes were riveted on the stage, as Juliet, kneeling by her dead husband Romeo, picked up a dagger and plunged the blade into her heart.

A collective sigh from the audience rippled around the theatre like a mournful breeze. Everyone knew how the ill-fated love story ended, but as Juliet's lifeless form slumped across the body of her lover Aksel felt a sudden constriction in his throat. All the members of the cast were skilled actors, but Mina Hart, who played Juliet, was outstanding. Her vivid and emotive portrayal of a young woman falling in love was electrifying.

Aksel's decision to visit Shakespeare's Globe three nights ago had been at the end of another frustrating day of discussions between the governing council of Storvhal and British government ministers. Storvhal was a principality stretching above Norway and Russia in the Arctic Circle. The country had been governed by the Thoresen royal dynasty for eight hundred years, and Aksel, as monarch and head of state, had supreme authority over his elected council of government. It was a position of great privilege and responsibility that he had shouldered since the death of his father, Prince Geir. He had never admitted to anyone that sometimes the role that had been his destiny from birth felt like a burden.

His visit to London had been to discuss proposals for a new trade agreement between Britain and Storvhal, but negotiations had been hampered by endless red tape. A trip to the theatre had seemed a good way to unwind, away from the rounds of diplomatic talks. He had certainly not expected that he would develop a fascination with the play's leading actress.

The play ended, and as the actors walked onto the stage and bowed to the audience Aksel could not tear his eyes from Mina. This was the last evening that the play would be performed at the Globe. It was also his last night in London. Having finally secured a trade agreement with the UK, tomorrow he was returning to Storvhal and his royal duties, which, as his grandmother constantly reminded him, meant that he must choose a suitable bride to be his princess and produce an heir.

'It is your duty to ensure the continuation of the Thoresen royal dynasty,' Princess Eldrun had insisted in a surprisingly fierce voice for a woman of ninety who had recently been seriously ill with pneumonia. 'It is my greatest wish to see you married before I die.'

Emotional blackmail from anyone else would have left Aksel unmoved. From childhood it had been impressed on him that duty and responsibility took precedence over his personal feelings. Only once had he allowed his heart to rule his head. He had been in his twenties when he had fallen in love with a beautiful Russian model, but the discovery that Karena had betrayed him was only one of the reasons why he had built an impenetrable wall around his emotions.

His grandmother was the single chink in his armour. Princess Eldrun had helped her husband, Prince Fredrik, to rule Storvhal for fifty years and Aksel had immense respect for her. When she had fallen ill and the doctors had warned him to prepare for the worst he had realised just how much he valued her wise counsel. But even for his grandmother's sake Aksel was not going to rush into marriage. He would choose a bride when he was ready, but it would not be a love match. Being Prince of Storvhal allowed Aksel many privileges but falling in love was not one of them, just as it had not been for his Viking ancestors.

Perhaps it was the knowledge that his grandmother's health was failing that had caused his uncharacteristic emotional response to the tragedy of *Romeo and Juliet*, he brooded. Today was the twelfth anniversary of when his father had been killed in a helicopter crash in Monaco— the playground of the rich and famous where Prince Geir had spent most of his time—to the dismay of the Storvhalian people. In contrast to his father Aksel had devoted himself to affairs of state and slowly won back support for the monarchy, but his popularity came with a price.

In Storvhal he could rarely escape the limelight. The media watched him closely, determined to report any sign of him becoming a party-loving playboy as his father had been. There would be no opportunities for him to go out alone as he had been able to do in London. If he went to the theatre he would have to sit in the royal box, in full view of everyone in the auditorium. He would not be able to stand unrecognised in a crowd and be moved almost to tears by the greatest love story ever told.

He stared at Mina Hart. The cast wore Renaissance costumes and she was dressed in a simple white gown made of gauzy material that skimmed her slender figure. Her long auburn hair framed her heart-shaped face and she looked innocent yet sensual. Aksel felt his body tauten with desire. For a moment he allowed himself to imagine what might happen if he were free to pursue her. But the inescapable truth was that his life was bound by duty. For the past three evenings he had escaped to a fantasy world, but now he must step back to reality.

This was the last time he would see Mina. He studied her face as if he could imprint her features on his memory, and felt a curious ache in his chest as he murmured beneath his breath, 'Goodbye, sweet Juliet.'

'Are you coming for a drink?' Kat Nichols asked as she followed Mina out of the theatre. 'Everyone's meeting up at the Riverside Arms to celebrate the play's successful run.'

Mina had planned to go straight home after the evening performance but she changed her mind when Kat gave a persuasive smile. 'Okay, I'll come for one drink. It's strange to think that we won't be appearing at the Globe any more.'

'But maybe we'll be appearing on Broadway soon.' Kat gave Mina a sideways glance as they walked the short distance to the pub. 'Everyone knows that your father has been in negotiations to take the production to New York. Has he said anything to you about what's going to happen?'

Mina shook her head. 'I know everyone thinks Joshua confides in me because I'm his daughter, but he doesn't treat me any differently from the rest of the cast. I had to audition three times for the role of Juliet. Dad doesn't give me any special favours.'

If anything, her father was tougher on her than other members of the cast, Mina thought ruefully. Joshua Hart was himself a brilliant actor, and a demanding perfectionist. He was not the easiest man to get on with, and Mina's relationship with him had been strained since the events that had happened while she had been filming in America had led Joshua to accuse her of bringing the Hart name into disrepute.

Kat was not deterred. 'Just imagine if we do appear on Broadway! It would be a fantastic career opportunity. You never know, we might even get spotted by a top film director and whisked off to LA.'

'Take it from me, LA isn't so wonderful,' Mina said drily.

Kat gave her a close look. 'I've heard rumours, but what did actually happen when you went to America to make a film?'

Mina hesitated. She had become good friends with Kat, but even so she could not bear to talk about the darkest period of her life. Her memories of the film director Dexter Price were still painful two years after their relationship had ended in a storm of newspaper headlines. She couldn't believe she had been such a gullible fool to have fallen in love with Dex, but she had been alone in LA for her first major film role—young, naïve, and desperately insecure about her hearing impairment. The American film industry demanded perfection, and she had felt acutely conscious of her disability.

She had been grateful for Dexter's reassurance, and within a short time she had fallen for his blend of sophistication and easy charm. Looking back, Mina wondered if one reason why she had been drawn to Dex was because he had reminded her of her father. Both were powerful men who were highly regarded in the acting world, and Dex had given her the support she had always craved from Joshua Hart. When Mina had found out that Dex had lied to her it was not only his betrayal that had left her heartbroken, but the fact that once again her father had failed to support her when she had needed him.

'Mina?'

Kat's voice jolted Mina from her thoughts. She gave her friend an apologetic smile as they reached the pub and she opened the door. 'I'll tell you about it another time.'

The pub was busy and fortunately the din of voices was too loud for Kat to pursue the subject. Mina spotted some of the play's cast sitting at a nearby table. 'I'll get the first round,' she told Kat. 'Save me a seat.'

As she fought her way to the bar Mina decided she would have one drink and then leave. The noisy pub made her feel disorientated and she longed for the peace and quiet of her flat. She suspected that there were a few journalists amongst the crowd. Rumours that Joshua Hart's production of *Romeo and Juliet* might go to New York were circulating, and for the past week the paparazzi had been hanging about the theatre hoping for a scoop.

Mina squeezed through the crowd of people gathered in front of the bar and tried to catch the barman's eye. 'Excuse me!'

The barman walked straight past her and she wondered if he hadn't heard her. The loud background noise inside the pub made it difficult for her to hear her own voice and so regulate how loud or softly she spoke. Moments later the same thing happened again when another barman ignored her and went to serve someone else. It was situations like this that made her conscious of her hearing impairment. Her hearing aids worked incredibly well, but as the bar staff continued to take no notice of her she felt a resurgence of her old insecurities about her deafness. She felt invisible, even though she could see herself in the mirror behind the bar.

As she watched her reflection a figure appeared at her shoulder. Mina tensed as she met his gaze in the mirror and her heart slammed against her ribs as she recognised him. It was *him*—the man who had been in the audience—and close up he was even more gorgeous than she'd thought when she had seen him from the stage.

His eyes were a brilliant topaz-blue, glittering like gemstones beneath his well-defined brows that were a shade darker than his streaked blond hair. When Mina had seen him at the theatre the firm line of his mouth had looked forbidding, but as she watched him in the mirror he gave her a smoulderingly sexy smile that made her catch her breath.

'Perhaps I can be of assistance?'

The gravelly huskiness of his voice caused the tiny hairs on the back of Mina's neck to stand on end. She could not place his accent. Slowly she turned to face him, conscious that her pulse was racing.

'One advantage of my height is that I can usually attract the attention of bar staff,' he murmured. 'Can I buy you a drink?'

His stunning looks and sheer magnetism ensured that he would *never* be ignored. Mina flushed when she realised that she was staring at him. 'Actually, I'm trying to order drinks for my friends…but thanks for the offer.'

Her voice trailed off as her eyes locked with his. She could feel the vibration of her blood pounding in her ears as she studied his lean, handsome face. He was ruggedly male and utterly beautiful. Was this how Juliet had felt when she had first set eyes on Romeo? Mina wondered. In her character study of the role of Juliet she had tried to imagine how it felt to be a teenage girl who had fallen desperately in love at first sight with a young man. It had been more difficult than Mina had expected to step into Juliet's shoes. Could you really feel such intense emotion for someone you had just met, before you had got to know them?

Her common sense had rejected the idea. The story of *Romeo and Juliet* was just a fantasy. But now, in a heartbeat, Mina understood that it was possible to feel an overwhelming connection with a stranger. Even more startling was her certainty that the man felt it too. His eyes narrowed on her face and his body tensed like a jungle cat watching its prey.

Someone pushed past her on their way to the bar and knocked her against the stranger. Her breasts brushed his chest and an electrical current shot through her. Every nerve ending tingled and her nipples instantly hardened and throbbed. For a few seconds she felt dizzy as the heat of his body and the spicy scent of his aftershave hijacked her senses and filled her with a fierce yearning that pooled hot and molten in the pit of her stomach.

With a little gasp she jerked away from him. He was watching her intently, as if he could read her mind. In a desperate attempt to return to normality, she blurted out, 'You were at the theatre tonight. I saw you. Did you enjoy the play?'

His bright blue eyes burned into her. '*You* were— astonishing.'

He spoke in a low, intense voice, and Mina was startled to see colour flare briefly along his sharp cheekbones. She had the impression that he had intended to make a casual response to her question but the words had escaped his lips before he could prevent them.

Thinking about his lips was fatal. Her eyes focused on the sensual curve of his mouth and her breath caught in her throat.

'You came last night, too…and the night before that,' she said huskily.

'I couldn't keep away.' He stared deeply into her eyes, trapping her with his sensual magic so that Mina could not look away from him. Weakness washed over her and butterflies fluttered in her stomach. She swayed towards him, unable to control her body's response to the invisible lure of male pheromones and sizzling sexual chemistry.

A bemused expression crossed the man's face and he shook his head as if he was trying to snap back to reality. He pulled a hand through his dark blond hair, raking it back from his brow.

'Tell me what your friends want to drink and I'll place your order.'

Friends? The spell broke and Mina glanced around the busy pub. Somehow she gathered her thoughts and reeled off a list of drinks. The stranger had no trouble catching the attention of the bar staff and minutes later Mina paid for the round and wondered how she was going to carry a tray of drinks across the crowded room.

Once again the stranger came to her rescue and picked up the tray. 'I'll carry this. Show me where your friends are sitting.'

Kat's eyes widened when she spotted Mina approaching the table followed by a tall, fair-haired man who resembled a Viking. The stranger put the tray of drinks down on the table and Mina wondered if she should invite him to join her and her friends. She wished Kat would stop staring at him.

'Thanks for your help. I'm Mina, by the way.' Worried that she might not hear him in the noisy pub, she watched his mouth closely so that she could read his lips.

Amusement flashed in his blue eyes. 'I know. Your name was on the theatre programme.' He held out his hand. 'I'm Aksel.'

'That's not an English name,' Mina murmured, trying not to think about the firm grip of his fingers as she placed her hand in his. The touch of his skin on hers sent a tingling sensation up her arm and she felt strangely reluctant to withdraw her hand again.

He hesitated fractionally before replying, 'You're right. I am from Storvhal.'

'That's near Russia, isn't it—in the Arctic Circle?'

His brows lifted. 'I'm impressed. Storvhal is a very small country and most people haven't a clue where it is.'

'I'm addicted to playing general knowledge quizzes,' Mina admitted. 'The location of Storvhal often comes up.'

God, did that make her sound like a boring nerd who spent a lot of time on her own? People often assumed that actors led exciting and glamorous lives, but that was far from the truth, Mina thought wryly. There had been plenty of times when she'd been between acting roles and had to take cleaning jobs or stack shelves in a supermarket. Most actors, unless they made it big in the American film industry, struggled to earn a good living. But Mina was not driven by money and had been drawn to the stage because acting was in her blood.

The Harts were a renowned theatrical family, headed by Joshua Hart, who was regarded as the greatest Shakespearean actor of the past thirty years. Mina had wanted to be an actress since she was a small child and she had refused to allow her hearing loss to destroy her dream.

But the dream had turned sour in LA. Making a film there had been an eye-opener and she had hated the celebrity culture, the gossip and backbiting. The events in LA had had a profound effect on her and when she had returned to England she had re-evaluated what she wanted to do with her life, and she had recently qualified as a drama therapist.

One thing she was certain of was that she never wanted her private life to be splashed across the front pages of the tabloids ever again. It still made her shudder when she remembered the humiliation of reading explicit and inaccurate details about her relationship with Dexter Price in the newspapers. The paparazzi did not seem to care about reporting the truth, and Mina had been a target of their ruthless desire for scandal. She had developed a deep mistrust of the press—and in particular of the man she had just spotted entering the pub.

She froze when she recognised him. Steve Garratt was the journalist who had exposed her affair with Dexter. Garratt had written a scurrilous article in which he had accused Mina of sleeping with the film director to further her career while Dexter's wife had been undergoing treatment for cancer. Most of the article had been untrue. Mina had never been to bed with Dex—although she had been in love with him, and ready to take the next step in their relationship, before she had discovered that he was married. But no one had been interested in her side of the story, certainly not Steve Garratt.

What was Garratt doing here in the UK? It was unlikely to be a coincidence that he had turned up at the same time as rumours were rife that Joshua Hart's production of *Romeo and Juliet* might be performed on Broadway. Garratt was after a story and Mina's heart sank when the journalist looked over in her direction and gave her a cocky smile of recognition.

As he began to thread his way across the pub she felt a surge of panic. She could not bear the embarrassment of the journalist talking about the LA scandal in front of her friends from the theatre company. The story had been mostly forgotten after two years, and she had hoped it would remain dead and buried.

She glanced at the good-looking man who had introduced himself as Aksel. They were strangers, she reminded herself. The curious connection she felt with him must be a figment of her imagination.

'Well, it was nice to meet you,' she murmured. 'Thanks for your help.'

Aksel realised he was being dismissed. It was a novel experience for a prince and in different circumstances he might have been amused, but inexplicably he felt a rush of jealousy when he noticed that Mina was staring at a man who had just entered the pub. Was the man her boyfriend? It was of no interest to him, he reminded himself. He was regretting his decision to follow Mina into the pub, and her obvious interest in the man who was now approaching them was a signal to Aksel that it was time he left.

'You're welcome.' His eyes met hers, and for a split second he felt a crazy urge to grab hold of her hand and whisk her away from the crowded pub to somewhere they could be alone.

What the hell had got into him tonight? he asked himself irritably. His behaviour was completely out of character and he must end his ridiculous fascination with Mina Hart right now. 'Enjoy the rest of your evening,' he bade her curtly, and strode out of the pub without glancing back at her.

* * *

'Mina Hart, what a pleasant surprise!' Steve Garratt drawled. He smelled of stale cigarette smoke and Mina wrinkled her nose as he leaned too close to her.

'I find nothing pleasant about meeting you,' she said coldly. 'And I doubt you're surprised to see me. You're here for a reason, and I can guess what it is.'

The journalist grinned to reveal nicotine-stained teeth. It was warm inside the pub and his florid face was turning pinker. 'A little bird told me you'll soon be making your Broadway debut.'

'Who told you that?' Mina asked sharply. She glanced at his shifty expression and realised that he was hoping to goad her into giving him information.

'Come on, sweetheart. Everyone wants to know if your father will be directing *Romeo and Juliet* in New York. He must have told you whether it's going to happen. All the hacks are hoping to break the story. Give me an exclusive and I'll make sure you get good reviews if you do open on Broadway.'

'Joshua hasn't told me anything, but even if he had confided in me I wouldn't tell you. You're a weasel, Garratt. You nose around in people's private lives looking for scandal and if none exist you make up lies—like you did to me.' Mina broke off, breathing hard as she struggled to control her temper.

The journalist gave a cynical laugh. 'Am I supposed to feel sorry for you? Don't give me that bull about journalists respecting celebrities' private lives. Actors need publicity. You don't really believe that a film starring an unknown English actress would have been a box-office success on its own merits, do you? People went to see *Girl in the Mirror* because they were curious about the bimbo who screwed Dexter Price.'

Steve Garratt's mocking words made Mina's stomach churn. The pub felt claustrophobic and she was suddenly desperate for some fresh air. She pushed past the journalist, unable to bear being in his company for another second. 'You disgust me,' she told him bitterly.

Kat was chatting with the other members of the cast and Mina did not interrupt them. They would guess she had gone home, she told herself as she made her way across the crowded pub towards the door. Outside, it was dark. The October nights were drawing in and Mina's lightweight jacket did not offer much protection against the chilly wind. Head bowed, she walked briskly along the pavement that ran alongside the river. The reflection of the street lights made golden orbs on the black water, but soon she turned off the well-lit main road down a narrow alleyway that provided the quickest route to the tube station.

Her footsteps echoed loudly in the enclosed space. It wasn't late, but there was no one around, except for a gang of youths who were loitering at the other end of the alleyway. From the sound of their raucous voices Mina guessed they had been drinking. She thought about turning back and going the long route to the station, but she was tired and, having grown up in central London, she considered herself fairly streetwise. Keeping her head down, she continued walking, but as she drew nearer to the gang she noticed they were passing something between them and guessed it was a joint.

Her warning instincts flared. Something about the youths' body language told her that they were waiting for her to walk to the far end of the alley. She stopped abruptly and turned round, but as she hurriedly retraced her steps the gang followed her.

'Hey, pretty woman, why don't you want to walk this way?' one of them called out.

Another youth laughed. 'There's a film called *Pretty Woman*, about a slag who makes a living on the streets.' The owner of the voice, a skinhead with a tattoo on his neck, caught up with Mina and stood in front of her so that she was forced to stop walking. 'Is that what you do—sell your body? How much do you charge?' As the gang crowded around Mina the skinhead laughed. 'Do you do a discount for group sex?'

Mina swallowed, trying not to show that she was scared. 'Look, I don't want any trouble.' She took a step forwards and froze when the skinhead gripped her arm. 'Let go of me,' she demanded, sounding more confident than she felt.

'What if I don't want to let go of you?' the skinhead taunted. 'What are you going to do about it?' He slid his hand inside Mina's jacket and she felt a surge of fear and revulsion when he tugged her shirt buttons open. The situation was rapidly spiralling out of control. The youths were drunk, or high—probably both—and on a cold autumn night it was unlikely that anyone was around to help her.

'You'd better let me go. I'm meeting someone, and if I don't show up they'll start looking for me,' she improvised, thinking as she spoke that her friends at the pub would assume she had gone home.

The skinhead must have sensed that she was bluffing. 'So, where's your friend?'

'Here,' said a soft, menacing voice.

Mina's gaze shot to the end of the alleyway that she had entered a few minutes earlier and her heart did a somersault in her chest. The light from the street lamp behind him made his blond hair look like a halo. Surely no angel could be so devastatingly sexy, but to Mina, scared out of her wits, he was her guardian angel, her saviour.

The skinhead, surprised by the interruption, had loosed his grip on her arm, and Mina wrenched herself free.

'Aksel,' she said on a half-sob, and ran towards him.

CHAPTER TWO

'IT'S ALL RIGHT, Mina, you're safe,' Aksel murmured. He felt the tremors that shook her slender frame. When she had raced down the alleyway he had instinctively opened his arms and she had flown into them. He stroked her auburn hair, one part of his brain marvelling at how silky it felt. At the same time he eyed the gang of youths and felt a cold knot of rage in the pit of his stomach when the skinhead who had been terrorising Mina stepped forwards.

'Can't you count, mate? There's six of us and only one of you,' the gang leader said with a show of bravado.

'True, but I am worth more than the six of you combined,' Aksel drawled in an icy tone that cut through the air like tempered steel. He never lost his temper. A lifetime of controlling his emotions had taught him that anger was far more effective served ice-cold and deadly. 'I'm willing to take you all on.' He flicked his gaze over the gang members. 'But one at a time is fair, man to man—if you've got the guts of real men.'

He gently put Mina to one side and gave her a reassuring smile when her eyes widened in fear as she realised what he intended to do.

'Aksel...you can't fight them all,' she whispered.

He ignored her and strolled towards the skinhead

youth. 'If you're the leader of this pack of sewer rats I guess you'll want to go first.'

The skinhead had to tilt his head to look Aksel in the face, and doubt flickered in his eyes when he realised that his adversary was not only tall but powerfully built. Realising that he was in serious danger of losing face, he spat out a string of crude profanities as he backed up the alleyway. The other youths followed him and Aksel watched them until they reached the far end of the alley and disappeared.

'You have got to be nuts!' Mina sagged against the wall. Reaction to the knowledge that Aksel had saved her from being mugged or worse was setting in and her legs felt wobbly. 'They could have been carrying a weapon. You could have been hurt.'

She stared at him and felt weak for another reason as she studied his chiselled features and dark blond hair that had fallen forwards onto his brow. He raked it back with his hand and gave her a disarming smile that stole her breath.

'I could have handled them.' He frowned as Mina moved and the edges of her jacket parted to reveal her partially open shirt. 'That punk had no right to lay a finger on you. Did he hurt you?' Aksel felt a resurgence of the scalding anger that had gripped him when he had seen the skinhead gang leader seize hold of Mina. A lifetime of practice had made him adept at controlling his emotions, but when he had seen her scared face as the gang of youths crowded round her he had been filled with a murderous rage.

'No, I'm fine. *Oh...*' Mina coloured hotly as she glanced down and saw that her shirt was half open, exposing her lacy bra and the upper slopes of her breasts. She fumbled to refasten the buttons with trembling fingers. Nausea swept over her as her vivid imagination pictured what the gang of youths might have done to her if Aksel had not shown up.

'Thank you for coming to my rescue—again,' she said shakily, remembering how he had helped her order drinks at the bar earlier. The memory of how she had thrown herself into his arms when he had appeared in the alley brought another stain of colour to her cheeks. 'By the way, I'm sorry I behaved like an idiot and hugged you.'

His lips twitched. 'No problem. Feel free to hug me any time you like.'

'Oh,' Mina said again on a whispery breath that did not sound like her normal voice. But nothing about this evening was normal, and it was not surprising she felt breathless when Aksel was looking at her in a way that made her think he was remembering those few moments when he had caught her in his arms and held her so close to him that her breasts had been squashed against his chest.

Keen to move on from that embarrassing moment, she quickly changed the subject. 'What are you doing here?'

Aksel had been asking himself the same question since he had left the Globe Theatre after the performance. His car had been waiting for him, but as his chauffeur had opened the door he'd felt a surge of rebellion against the constrictions of his life. He knew that back at his hotel his council members who had accompanied him from Storvhal would be waiting to discuss the new trade deal. But Aksel's mind had been full of the Shakespearean tragedy that had stirred his soul, and the prospect of spending the rest of the evening discussing politics had seemed unendurable.

No doubt Harald Petersen, his elderly chief advisor and close friend of his grandmother, would be critical of the fact that he had dismissed his driver and bodyguard.

'I am sure I don't need to remind you that Storvhal's wealth and political importance in the world are growing, and there is an increased risk to your personal safety, sir,' Harald had said when Aksel had argued against the necessity of being accompanied by a bodyguard while he was in London.

'I think it's unlikely that I'd be recognised anywhere other than in my own country,' Aksel had pointed out. 'I've always kept a low media profile at home and abroad.' Unlike his father, whose dubious business dealings and playboy lifestyle had often made headlines around the world.

After he had sent his driver away, Aksel had strolled beside the river when he had spotted Mina entering a pub, and without stopping to question what he was doing he had followed her inside. His immediate thought when he had met her at the bar was that, close up, she was even more beautiful than he'd thought when he had seen her on stage. He'd looked into her deep green eyes and felt as if he were drowning.

'When you left the pub, I assumed I would never see you again.' Her soft voice pulled Aksel back to the alleyway.

'I was about to get into a taxi when I saw you come out of the pub. I watched you turn down this alleyway and decided to follow you. A badly lit alley doesn't seem a good place to walk on your own at night.'

Mina gave him a rueful glance. 'I'm on my way home and this is the quickest way to the station.'

'Why didn't you stay with your friends?' Aksel hesitated. 'You looked over at a man who walked into the pub and I thought he must be someone you knew.'

Aksel must be referring to Steve Garratt. Supressing a shudder, Mina shook her head. 'He was no one—just…a guy.' She swallowed, thinking that the only reason she had left the pub and started to walk to the station alone at night was because she'd wanted to get away from the journalist she despised.

She had a flashback to the terrifying moment when the gang of youths had surrounded her, and the colour drained from her face.

'Are you all right?' Aksel looked at her intently. 'You're in shock. Do you feel faint?'

Mina was not going to admit that she felt close to tears. 'I probably feel wobbly because I'm hungry. I'm always too nervous to eat before a performance,' she explained ruefully. 'That's why I was going home to get something to eat.'

His sensual smile evoked a coiling sensation in the pit of Mina's stomach.

'I have an idea. Why don't you have dinner with me? My hotel isn't far from here, and it has an excellent restaurant. I'm sure you won't feel like cooking a meal when you get home,' he said persuasively.

'I…I couldn't impose on you any further.' For a crazy moment she wanted to accept Aksel's invitation. It would be madness, she told herself. He was a stranger she had met in a pub and she knew nothing about him other than that he came from a country most people had never heard of. She looked at him curiously. 'Are you on holiday in England?'

'A business trip—I'm flying home tomorrow.'

She crushed her ridiculous feeling of disappointment. 'What line of business are you in?'

Was it her imagination, or did an awkward expression flit across his face before he replied? 'I work as an advisor for my country's government. My visit to London was with a delegation to discuss trade policies with Britain.'

Mina could not hide her surprise. With his streaked blond hair and leather jacket he looked more like a rock star than a government advisor. 'It sounds interesting,' she murmured.

His laughter echoed through the alleyway; a warm, mellow sound that melted Mina's insides. 'I would have expected an actress to be more convincing at pretending that my job sounds fascinating,' he said softly. 'Can I persuade you to have dinner with me if I promise I won't bore you with details about trade policies?'

As she met his glinting, bright blue gaze Mina thought it would be impossible for Aksel to bore her. Her common sense told her to walk back out to the main street and hail a taxi to take her home. She would be mad to go to dinner with a stranger, even if he was the sexiest man she had ever laid eyes on. She had followed her heart in LA but her experience with Dexter Price had left her wary and mistrustful, not just of other men but of her own judgement.

'I'm not dressed for dinner at a restaurant.' She made another attempt to ignore the voice of temptation that was telling her to throw caution to the wind and go with Aksel. Besides, it was the truth. Her cotton gypsy skirt and cheesecloth shirt were very boho chic, according to Kat, but not a suitable outfit to wear to dinner.

'You look fine to me,' Aksel assured her in his seductive, gravelly voice. 'There's just one thing. You've done your buttons up in the wrong order.'

He moved closer, and Mina caught her breath as he lifted his hands and fastened her shirt buttons properly. He smelled of sandalwood cologne, mingled with a clean, fresh fragrance of soap and another barely discernible scent that was intensely male and caused Mina's stomach muscles to tighten.

As if he sensed her indecision, Aksel gave her another of his sexy smiles that set Mina's pulse racing. 'I understand the hotel restaurant serves a rich chocolate mousse that is utterly decadent. What do you say to us both sampling it this evening?'

His gravelly voice was electrifying, or maybe it was the expression in his eyes as he'd put a subtle emphasis on the word decadent. They both knew he hadn't been thinking about chocolate dessert as he'd said it, and Mina was unable to control the tiny tremor that ran through her.

He frowned. 'You're cold. Here...' Before she could protest he slipped off his leather jacket and draped it around her shoulders. The silk lining was warm from his body and Mina felt a wild, wanton heat steal through her veins. He caught hold of her hand and led her back to the entrance of the alleyway, but then he stopped and glanced down at her, his expression enigmatic.

'I have a taxi waiting. I'll ask the driver to take us to my hotel, or take you home. It's your choice.'

It was crunch time, Mina realised. She sensed that if she chose to go home Aksel would not argue. It would be sensible to refuse his offer of dinner, but a spark of rebellion flared inside her. Since she had returned from LA she had built a shell around herself and stayed firmly inside her comfort zone, afraid to try new experiences. But what harm could there be in agreeing to have dinner with Aksel, who had rescued her from the youths and behaved like a perfect gentleman? Was she going to run a mile from every handsome man she met and allow what had happened with Dexter Price to affect her for the rest of her life?

She hoped he could not tell that butterflies were dancing in her stomach. 'All right, you win. You've seduced me with talk of chocolate mousse, and I'd like to come back to your hotel.'

The moment the words left her lips she realised how suggestive they sounded and colour rushed into her cheeks. 'To have dinner, I meant,' she added quickly. Oh, God, why had she said seduced? She didn't want him to guess that she wished he would kiss her, she thought numbly as her eyes locked with his.

He gave a husky laugh and lowered his head towards her so that his warm breath whispered across her lips. 'I know you meant dinner,' he assured her. His smile was wolfish as he said softly, 'Seduction will come later.'

And then Aksel did what he had wanted to do since he had first set eyes on Juliet three nights ago, what he had ached to do since he had drowned in Mina's deep green gaze when he had met her in the pub. He cupped her face in his hands and brushed his mouth over hers, once, twice, until she parted her lips beneath his.

Mina dissolved instantly when Aksel slanted his mouth over hers. She had fantasised about him kissing her since she had first noticed him in the audience three nights ago, and now fantasy and reality merged in a fire-storm of passion. Her heart pounded as he pulled her hard against him. His body was all powerful muscle and sinew but the heat of his skin through his shirt made her melt into him as he deepened the kiss and it became ach-ingly sensual.

'Oh,' she whispered helplessly as he probed his tongue between her lips. Her little gasp gave Aksel the access he desired, and he slid his hand beneath Mina's hair to cup her nape while he crushed her mouth beneath his. The sweet eagerness of her response drew a ragged groan from him. He could have kissed her for ever, but one part of his brain reminded him that he was a prince and he was breaking every rule of protocol by kissing a woman he barely knew in a public alleyway.

Reluctantly he lifted his mouth from hers. 'Will you come with me, Mina?'

Mina stared into Aksel's eyes that glittered as brightly as the stars she could see winking in the black strip of sky above the alleyway. Her common sense warned her to refuse, but on a deeper instinctive level she knew she would be safe with him. She nodded mutely and followed him out of the alley to the main road where a taxi was waiting.

She couldn't stop looking at him, drinking in the chiselled masculine beauty of his face and his sensual mouth that had wreaked havoc on hers. And he could not stop looking at her. They were both blind to everything around them, and as they climbed into the taxi neither of them noticed the man who had just emerged from the pub and watched them from the shadows before he got into his car and followed the taxi at a discreet distance.

Some time soon his common sense was going to return, Aksel assured himself as he gave the taxi driver the name of his hotel and leaned back against the seat. He glanced at Mina and was shocked by how out of control she made him feel. He wanted to kiss her again. Hell, he wanted to do a lot more than kiss her, he acknowledged derisively. His body throbbed with desire, and only the knowledge that the taxi driver was watching them in the rear-view mirror stopped him from drawing her into his arms and running his hands over the soft contours of her body that she had pressed against him when they had kissed in the alleyway.

The taxi driver's curiosity reminded Aksel that he had not thought things through when he had invited Mina to dinner. Journalists from Storvhal had accompanied the trade delegation to London and they would jump at the chance to report that the prince had entertained a beautiful actress at his hotel. It was the kind of story his enemies would seize on to fuel rumours that he was turning into a playboy like his father had been.

Scandal had followed Prince Geir like a bad smell, Aksel remembered grimly. During his reign there had even been a move by some of the population to overthrow the monarchy. The protest groups had grown quiet since Aksel had become Prince of Storvhal, but he was conscious of the necessity to conduct his private life with absolute discretion.

While he was debating what to do, his phone rang and presented him with a solution to the problem. Aksel knew that his personal assistant was completely trustworthy, and he instructed Benedict to arrange a private dinner for him and a guest.

Mina did not recognise the language Aksel was speaking when he answered his phone, but she guessed it was Storvhalian. It was a more guttural sound than Italian, which she had learned to speak a little when she had spent a month in Sicily with her sister Darcey.

Listening to Aksel talking in an unfamiliar language reminded Mina that she knew nothing about him other than that he worked as some kind of advisor for his government. She had also discovered that he was an amazing kisser, which suggested he'd had plenty of practice at kissing women, she thought ruefully. She glanced at his chiselled profile and acknowledged that with his stunning looks he was likely to be very sexually experienced. Maybe he had a girlfriend in Storvhal. She stiffened as another thought struck her. Maybe he had a wife.

He finished his phone conversation and must have

mistaken the reason for her tension because he said softly, 'Forgive my rudeness. I am used to speaking to my PA in my own language.'

'It's late to be talking to a member of your staff.' Mina hesitated. 'I wondered if it was a girlfriend who called you...or your wife.'

His brows lifted. 'I'm not married. Do you think I would have asked you to dinner—hell, do you think I would have kissed you if I was in a relationship?'

Mina held her ground. 'Some men would.'

'I'm not one of them.'

The quiet implacability of his tone convinced her. Perhaps she was a fool to trust him, but Mina sensed that Aksel had a strong code of honour. He had a curious, almost regal air about him that made her wonder if his role in the Storvhalian government was more important that he had led her to believe. Perhaps he was actually a member of the government rather than an advisor.

But would a government minister have kissed her with such fierce passion? Why not? she mused. Not all politicians were crusty old men. Aksel was an incredibly handsome, sexy, *unmarried* man who was free to kiss her, just as she was free to kiss him. Heat flooded through her as she recalled the firm pressure of his lips on hers, the hunger that had exploded in her belly when he had pushed his tongue into her mouth.

'You spoke as if you have personal experience of the type of man who would cheat on his wife.'

Mina shrugged. 'I was just making a general comment.' She sensed from the assessing look Aksel gave her that he wasn't convinced, but to her relief he did not pursue the subject as the taxi came to a halt outside one of London's most exclusive hotels.

'You didn't say you were staying at The Erskine,' she

muttered, panic creeping into her voice as she watched a doorman dressed in a top hat and tailcoat usher a group of people into the hotel. The men were in tuxedos and the women were all wearing evening gowns. Mina glanced doubtfully at her gypsy skirt and flat ballet pumps. 'I'm definitely not wearing the right clothes for a place like this.'

'I'd forgotten that there's a charity function being held at the hotel this evening.' Aksel frowned as a flashbulb went off and he saw a pack of press photographers outside the hotel, telescopic lenses extended to snap pictures of celebrities attending the event. The last thing he wanted was to be photographed entering the hotel with a beautiful and very noticeable actress. It was the kind of thing that would trigger frantic speculation about his love-life back in Storvhal. He leaned forwards and spoke to the taxi driver, and seconds later the car pulled away from the kerb.

'There's another entrance we can use,' he told Mina. 'I've arranged for us to have dinner privately,' he explained as she slipped his leather jacket from her shoulders and handed it back to him. 'I'm not dressed for a black-tie event either.'

As the taxi turned down a narrow side street Mina checked her phone and read a text message from Kat, reminding her that Joshua Hart had asked the cast to meet at the Globe Theatre at nine a.m. the following day. After quickly texting a reply, she scrambled out of the taxi after Aksel. She stumbled on the uneven pavement and he shot an arm around her waist to steady her. The contact with his body made her catch her breath, and her pulse accelerated when he pulled her close. Keeping his arm around her, Aksel escorted her through an unremarkable-looking door into the hotel. Neither of them noticed the car that had pulled up behind the taxi.

Although they had entered the hotel via a back entrance, they still had to walk across the lobby: an oasis of marble and gold-leaf décor, which this evening was filled with sophisticated guests attending the charity function. Mina felt like a street urchin in her casual clothes and was glad that Aksel whisked her over to the lifts, away from the haughty glances of the reception staff.

As the doors closed she was intensely aware of him in the confined space and her heart lurched when he reached out a hand and brushed her hair back from her face. She tensed. Her hearing aids were tiny but they were fitted into the outer shell of her ears and were visible to someone standing close to her. There seemed no point telling him about her hearing loss when she would not see him again after this evening. He had already told her that he was returning to Storvhal tomorrow. She did not understand why he had asked her to have dinner with him, or why she had agreed, and she suddenly felt out of her depth. What on earth was she doing in a luxurious five-star hotel with a man she did not know?

'What's wrong?' he asked softly. 'If you've changed your mind about dinner I can arrange for you to be taken home.' He paused, and his husky voice sent a shiver across Mina's skin. 'But I hope you'll stay.'

She could feel her blood pounding in her ears, echoing her erratic heartbeat. It terrified her that he had such a devastating effect on her. 'It's ridiculous for two strangers to have dinner,' she blurted out. 'I don't know anything about you.'

'You know that I am a fan of Shakespeare—and chocolate mousse.' His blue eyes glinted as bright as diamonds. 'And I have discovered that you have an incredible talent for acting, and kissing.'

Her breath caught in her throat. 'You shouldn't say that,' she whispered.

'Do you want me to say you're bad at kissing?' His lips twitched with amusement but the expression in his eyes was serious. 'I can't lie, angel, you are amazing, and all I can think of is how much I want to kiss you again.'

Mina did not know if she was relieved or disappointed when the lift stopped and the doors slid smoothly apart. As she followed Aksel along a carpeted corridor the voice of caution inside her head told her to race back to the lift. Her eyes widened when he opened a set of double doors into an exquisitely decorated room where a polished dining table set with silver cutlery and candles reflected the ornate chandelier suspended above it. Vases of oriental lilies placed around the room filled the air with their sweet perfume, and the lamps were dimmed to create an ambiance that was unsettlingly intimate.

Aksel strolled over to the bar and picked up a bottle of champagne from an ice bucket. He popped the cork with a deftness that suggested he was no stranger to champagne, filled two tall flutes and handed one to Mina.

'We'll have a drink while we look at the menu.'

Mina watched his throat move as he swallowed a mouthful of champagne. His dark blond hair had fallen forwards onto his brow again and she longed to run her fingers through it. Conscious that she was staring at him, she took a gulp of her drink and belatedly realised that champagne on an empty stomach was not a good idea. The bubbles hit the back of her throat and seemed to instantly enter her bloodstream, making her head spin.

'Come and sit down.' Aksel draped his jacket over the arm of a sofa and sat down, patting the empty space beside him. He hooked his ankle over his thigh and stretched one arm along the back of the sofa, causing his black silk shirt to strain across his broad chest. He looked indolent and so dangerously sexy that the thought of joining him on the sofa made Mina's heart hammer.

'Um…I'd like to use the bathroom before we eat.'

'The first door on your left along the corridor,' he advised.

Get a grip, Mina told herself sternly a few moments later as she stared at her flushed face in the bathroom mirror. She looked different, more alive, as if a lightbulb had been switched on inside her. Even her hair seemed to crackle with electricity, and her eyes looked enormous, the pupils dilated, reflecting the wild excitement that she could not control. She traced her tongue over her lips, remembering how the firm pressure of Aksel's mouth had forced them apart when he had kissed her.

She held her wrists under the cold tap, hoping to lower her temperature that seemed in danger of boiling over. Maybe if she took her jacket off she would cool down— but the sight of her pebble-hard nipples jutting provocatively beneath her thin shirt put paid to that idea. The jacket would have to stay on. It was better to look hot than desperate!

Oh, hell! Tempting though it was to hide in the bathroom, she had to go out and face him. You're an actress, she reminded herself. You can play cool and collected if you pretend he's in the audience and don't make eye contact with him.

Taking a deep breath, she returned to the dining room and to avoid looking at Aksel she picked up her glass and finished her champagne. He was standing by the window, but turned when she came in and walked towards her.

'I'd love to know what thoughts are going on behind

those mysterious deep green eyes,' he murmured as she swept her long eyelashes down.

'Actually, I was wondering why someone who can afford to stay at a five-star hotel would choose to buy the cheapest ticket at the theatre and stand for a two-hour performance, not just once, but on three evenings. But I suppose,' Mina voiced her thoughts, 'as you are in London on a business trip, your employer would pay for your hotel. You must be very good at your job for your government to put you up at The Erskine.'

Aksel hesitated. Although Mina had heard of Storvhal, she clearly had no idea of his identity, and he did not feel obliged to reveal that he was the ruling monarch of the principality. For one night he wanted to forget his royal responsibilities.

'It's true that my accommodation was arranged for me,' he murmured. 'The first evening when I visited the Globe the only tickets available were for the yard in front of the stage. I probably could have booked a seat in the gallery on the second and third night, but I'll admit I chose to stand so that I had a clear view of you.'

His voice roughened. 'The first time I saw you walk onto the stage you blew me away.'

Mina felt as if the air had been sucked out of her lungs. She understood what he meant because she had felt exactly the same when she had seen him in the audience: utterly blown away by his raw sexuality. Her eyes flew to his face, and the primitive hunger in his gaze mirrored the inexplicable, inescapable need that was flowing like a wild river through her body.

'Aksel...' She had meant it to sound like a remonstration but his name left her lips on a breathy whisper, an invitation, a plea.

'Angel.' He moved towards her, or maybe she moved

first. Mina did not know how she came to be in his arms,
only that they felt like bands of steel around her as he
pulled her into the hard, warm strength of his body and
bent his head to capture her mouth in a kiss that set her
on fire.

CHAPTER THREE

MINA REMEMBERED HOW she had run into Aksel's arms when she had fled from the youths in the alleyway. Her instincts had told her she would be safe with him, and she felt that same sense of security now, as if—ridiculous as it seemed—she belonged with him.

He kissed her with increasing passion until she trembled with the intensity of need he was arousing in her. When he eventually lifted his mouth from hers she pressed her lips to his cheek. The blond stubble on his jaw scraped against her skin, heightening her awareness of his raw masculinity. She arched her neck as he traced his lips down her throat, but when he smoothed her hair back behind her ear she quickly turned her head so that he did not see her hearing aids.

He moved his hands over her body, shaping her shoulders, tracing the length of her spine and finally cupping her bottom. She gasped when he jerked her against his pelvis and she felt the unmistakable hard ridge of his arousal. Perhaps she should have felt shocked, or pulled away from him, but she had no control over the molten warmth of her own desire.

'You have no idea how many times in the last three days I have imagined doing this—holding you, kissing you—' Aksel's voice lowered to a husky growl '—making love to you.'

Mina's heart turned over at the thought of where this was leading. Was she really contemplating making love with a man she had only spoken to for the first time a few hours ago? It was madness—and yet hadn't she thought of him constantly since she had spotted him in the audience three nights ago? She had tried to tell herself that she had become too absorbed in the role of Juliet, and had been looking for a real-life Romeo. Fantasising about the blond man in the audience had been just that—a fantasy. But being here with Aksel was real, and so was the urgent, all-consuming desire that was making her heart pound in her chest.

A tiny shred of her sanity still remained and she said almost desperately, 'I don't *do* things like this. I don't go back to strangers' hotels…' She broke off helplessly as he gave her a crooked smile.

'Will you believe that this is a new experience for me too, angel?' Aksel raked his hair back from his brow with an unsteady hand. The restrictions of being a prince meant that he had rarely had the opportunity, and never the inclination, to pick up a woman in a bar. He assured himself that he'd had no ulterior motive when he had invited Mina to his hotel other than that he wanted to get to know her a little better. But the minute they had been alone and he had looked into her deep green eyes his usual restraint had been swept away by a storm surge of desire, and now the situation was rapidly getting out of hand.

'I've never felt like this before,' he admitted rawly. 'I have never wanted any woman as desperately as I want you.'

They were supposed to be having dinner, Aksel reminded himself. Perhaps if they sat down at the table and studied the menu the madness that was making him behave so out of character would pass.

'Are you hungry?'

Aksel spoke in such a low tone that Mina struggled to hear him, but as she watched his lips shape the question she remembered that she had not eaten anything since breakfast. She felt light-headed, probably from the effects of the champagne, she acknowledged ruefully. But hunger seemed to heighten her other senses and evoked a different physical need inside her. Just the thought of Aksel making love to her made her gut twist with desire.

'Yes, I'm hungry,' she replied in a husky, sensual voice that did not sound like her own.

'Do you want to order some food?'

She hesitated for a heartbeat. 'It's not food I want,' she whispered.

He said something in his own language. Mina did not understand the words but the glitter in his eyes was unmistakable as he hauled her against him and brought his mouth down on hers in a kiss that plundered her soul. She did not protest when he lifted her into his arms and strode through a door at the far end of the dining room. With her hands linked at his nape and her face pressed against his throat she was barely aware of her surroundings until he set her on her feet and she saw that they were in a huge bedroom dominated by an enormous bed.

It occurred to her vaguely that he must have a very good job for his country's government to have arranged for him to stay in such a luxurious room. But then he placed his mouth over hers once more and she instantly succumbed to the sensual mastery of his kiss. She was barely aware of him removing her jacket or unbuttoning her shirt and sliding it off her shoulders. Her sheer white bra decorated with tiny lace flowers pushed her breasts high and her dark pink nipples tilted provocatively beneath the semi-transparent material.

Aksel made a harsh sound in his throat as he lifted his hand and traced a finger lightly over her breasts. 'You are even more beautiful than I imagined. You take my breath away.'

Mina's heart gave a jolt as he reached behind her and undid her bra, but she made no attempt to stop him. Not even his ragged groan pierced the mist of unreality that had descended over her, and she gave a little shiver of excitement as her bra cups fell away and her breasts spilled into his palms. She lifted her eyes to his face and saw dull colour streak along his high cheekbones. His reaction to her, the feral glitter in his eyes, made her feel intensely aware of her femininity and her sexual allure. After what had happened with Dexter she had deliberately kept her body hidden beneath shapeless clothes, unwilling to risk attracting any man's attention. But the past and all its humiliating horror seemed far away.

Her sense of unreality deepened. It seemed incredible that her fantasies about the man in the audience were coming true. She had imagined him kissing her, undressing her, and now, as Aksel unzipped her skirt and it fluttered to the floor, Mina allowed herself to sink deeper into the dream.

'Sweet Juliet,' he murmured as he bent his head and closed his lips around the tight bud of her nipple. The sensation was so exquisite that she cried out and arched her body like a slender bow, offering him her breasts and gasping with pleasure when he suckled her nipples in turn until they were swollen and tender.

She wanted to touch him as he was touching her and tore open his shirt buttons, parting the edges of his black silk shirt to reveal his golden tanned body. His skin gleamed like satin stretched taut over the defined ridges of his abdominal muscles. Dark blond hairs covered his chest and arrowed down over his flat stomach. Mina traced the fuzzy path with her fingers, but hesitated when she reached the waistband of his trousers as a voice of caution inside her head reminded her that her last sexual experience had been three years ago with a boyfriend she had dated for over a year.

Her heart-rate slowed and thudded painfully beneath her ribs. She must be crazy to think of having sex with a stranger. Aksel had proved that she could trust him when he had rescued her from the youths in the alleyway, and she was certain that if she called a halt now he would accept her decision. The sensible thing to do would be to tell him that she had changed her mind, but as she stared at his sculpted face with its slashing cheekbones and sensual mouth she could not formulate the words. The fire in his ice-blue eyes melted her resolve to walk away from him, and desire pooled hotly between her thighs when he stroked the bare strip of skin above the lace band of her hold-up stockings.

He held her gaze as he eased her panties aside and ran a finger up and down her moist opening until he felt her relax, allowing him to gently part her and slide deep into her silken heat.

'Beautiful,' he murmured when he discovered how aroused she was. He kissed her again with a blatant sensuality that drugged her senses so that she was barely aware of him removing the rest of her underwear before stripping out of his own clothes. He moved away from her for a moment, and she drew a shaky breath as she watched him take a protective sheath from the bedside drawer and slide it over his erection.

'I'm sure you agree that we don't want to take any risks,' he murmured.

Mina nodded mutely, shocked to realise that she was so caught up in the heat of sexual excitement she had not given a thought to contraception. Luckily Aksel was thinking clearly, but the fact that he was prepared for sex emphasised that his level of experience was far greater than hers. Doubt crept into her mind and she hoped he would not find her disappointing.

Her thoughts were distracted as he drew her into his arms once more. His powerful, muscular body reminded Mina of a golden-haired Norse god, but although he looked as formidable as a Viking warrior his hands were gentle as he cupped her bottom and lifted her against him.

She caught her breath when she felt the solid length of his erection jab into her belly.

'Wrap your legs around me,' he bade her tautly.

Trembling with anticipation, she gripped his shoulders for support and locked her ankles behind his back. Carefully he guided his thick shaft between her thighs and Mina buried her face against his neck to muffle her soft moan as he possessed her with a devastating powerful thrust. Her internal muscles stretched as he filled her. He withdrew slowly and then drove into her again, each thrust harder than the last so that her excitement swiftly mounted to fever pitch.

His shoulder muscles rippled beneath her hands as he supported her, making her aware of his immense strength. The sensation of him moving inside her was amazing, incredible, and indescribably beautiful. The world was spinning faster and faster, drawing her into a vortex of pleasure that grew more intense as he increased his pace. It was all happening too quickly. She gasped, feeling overwhelmed by Aksel's urgent passion and her equally urgent response to him.

'Angel, I'm sorry, I can't wait,' he groaned. He tightened his grip on her bottom and thrust so deeply into her that Mina wondered how much more she could take before her body shattered. She looked into his brilliant blue eyes and saw her need reflected in his burning gaze. His expression was almost tortured and she sensed he was fighting for control. He tipped his head back so that the veins on his neck stood out, and at the moment he exploded inside her Mina felt the first powerful ripples of her orgasm radiate out from her central core, and she gave a keening cry as she fell with him into ecstasy.

It was a long time before the world settled back on its axis, but eventually reality returned, bringing with it a tidal wave of guilt.

'I…I should go,' Mina whispered. She could taste tears at the back of her throat and forced herself to swallow them. There would be time for recriminations later, but her immediate aim was to slide off the bed where Aksel had laid her a few moments ago, and get dressed with as much dignity as possible—given the circumstances.

She stifled the urge to laugh hysterically as she considered the circumstances. It wasn't every night that she had wild and abandoned sex with a stranger—or any kind of sex, for that matter. A little moan of pain and shame rose in her throat and she bit down hard on her lip as she forced herself to look at the blond Viking sprawled beside her. Now that they were lying down she could admire the full glory of his naked body, the long legs and lean hips, the powerful abdominal muscles and broad chest.

Her eyes jerked to the one area of his body that she had avoided looking at. Even half aroused he was—

magnificent. Her stomach squirmed as she remembered how big he had felt when he had slowly filled her. Oh, God, what had she been thinking? Pretty much the same thoughts that were in her head now, Mina acknowledged with a choked sound of self-disgust.

She sat up and told herself it was ridiculous to feel shy that he was looking at her bare breasts when—let's face it—he'd done a lot more than simply look.

'Hey—angel?' Aksel propped himself up on one elbow and frowned when Mina quickly turned away from him. His gut clenched as he glimpsed a betraying shimmer in her eyes. *She was crying!* The idea that he had caused her to cry filled him with guilt. He had acted like a barbarian, he thought disgustedly. It was no excuse that for the first time in his life his iron self-restraint had been breached by her achingly sweet response to him. 'What's wrong?' he asked softly. 'Where are you going?'

Were there rules for this sort of occasion? If so, Mina did not know the rules. 'I thought I'd go home…now that…now that we've…' She watched his frown deepen and hoped he wasn't going to suggest they had dinner. The idea of sitting in that plush dining room while they were served by waiters who could probably guess what they'd had for an appetiser sent a shudder through her.

She tensed as he cupped her jaw and tilted her face to him.

'I didn't mean to make you cry, angel,' he said roughly. 'I'm sorry—I was too fast—too impatient…'

'*No*—' Mina did not want him to take the blame. He had nothing to blame himself for. 'It's not your fault—it's mine. It's just that I've never in my life gone to bed with a complete stranger…' her voice wobbled '…and I'm embarrassed.'

He did not seem to have listened to her, and doubt and remorse darkened his eyes. 'Angel...I should have—'

She shook her head, desperate to reassure him. 'You did everything right. It was...perfect.' She swallowed, thinking of those moments when she had come apart in his arms. Nothing had prepared her for the physical or emotional intensity of her orgasm. She had connected with him on a deeply fundamental level—as if they were each two halves of a whole—and even now she could not forget that feeling. 'It was beautiful,' she said huskily.

'For me too.' Aksel was surprised to find it was the truth. He leaned forwards and brushed his mouth over hers, felt the soft tremble of her lips and gently pulled her down so her head lay on his chest, and he stroked her hair. She reminded him of a young colt, nervous and unsure, ready to run away at any moment. Certainly she was not like the sophisticated women who occasionally shared his bed. Not at the palace, of course. Royal protocol demanded that only his wife could sleep with him in the prince's bedchamber. But he owned a private house a few kilometres out of Storvhal's capital city, Jonja, where he took his lovers, and also a cabin in the mountains where he took no one.

Making love with Mina had been unlike anything he'd ever experienced with other women. But he had known it would be. He'd known when he'd watched Juliet on stage and had been captivated by her sweet innocence mixed with exquisite sensuality that she would fulfil all his fantasies.

'I'm glad it was as good for you as it was for me,' he murmured. He rolled over, pinning her beneath him, and smiled when he heard her indrawn breath as he pushed his swelling, hardening shaft between her unresisting thighs. 'Something so good should be repeated, do you agree, angel?'

* * *

Life, Aksel mused, had a habit of throwing up problems when you least expected them. He rolled onto his side and studied his current problem. Mina's long auburn hair streamed across the pillows like a river of silk and her dark eyelashes lay on her cheeks in stark contrast to her creamy complexion. The sunlight filtering through the blinds revealed a sprinkling of tiny golden freckles on her nose. She looked curiously innocent and yet incredibly sexy as she moved and the sheet slipped down to expose one milky-pale breast tipped with a rose-pink nipple.

Aksel felt himself harden and he almost gave in to the delicious throb of desire that flooded through him. Only the realisation that if it was light outside then it could not be very early forced him to abandon the idea of drawing Mina into his arms. The clock showed that it was seven a.m. His private jet was scheduled to fly him and the members of the trade delegation back to Storvhal at eight-thirty, and he had a series of meetings booked for the afternoon before he was due to host a dinner party at the palace this evening.

Cursing beneath his breath, he sprang out of bed before he succumbed to the temptation of Mina's delectable body. Striding into the en-suite bathroom, he acknowledged that he had thrown his personal rule book out of the window when he had spent the night with her at his hotel. She was hardly the first woman he'd had sex with. He was thirty-five and did not live the life of a monk. But he chose his lovers from the tight-knit group of Storvhal's aristocracy. The women he met socially understood the need for discretion and ensured that details of the prince's private affairs never came to the attention of the media.

Falling asleep with Mina in his arms in a haze of sated exhaustion had compounded his folly, Aksel thought ruefully as he stood beneath an ice-cold shower. Meeting her had thrown up all kinds of problems, starting with the fact that she did not know who he was. Maybe that was why making love with her had been so amazing. Last night he had been able to forget for a few hours that he was a prince. He had just been a man blown away by his desire for a beautiful young woman who had captivated him since he had seen her in the role of Juliet.

But now the fantasy was over and he must focus on his royal duties. Frowning, Aksel reached for a towel embroidered with the monogram of the hotel. He knew he should feel grateful that he lived a life of great privilege, but he had learned during the twelve years that he had been monarch that personal freedom was the greatest privilege of all, and this morning more than at any other time in his life he was acutely aware that it was a luxury denied to him.

Mina breathed a sigh of relief as she peeped from beneath her lashes and watched Aksel walk into the bathroom. The sight of his broad back and taut buttocks evoked a melting sensation in the pit of her stomach. It was not only his golden hair and skin that reminded her of a Norse god. Last night he had demonstrated his formidable strength and energy—not to mention inventiveness, she thought, flushing hotly as memories of the various ways he had made love to her crowded her mind.

When she'd woken a few minutes ago and felt his erection nudge her thigh, her pulse had quickened with anticipation. But she'd pretended to be asleep when she had realised that the batteries in her hearing aids had died.

She had no idea how he would react if she revealed that she was partially deaf. They might have enjoyed a night of wild and totally amazing sex, but Aksel was still a stranger she had met in a pub, and in the cold light of day Mina felt a growing sense of shame at her wantonness. Her behaviour had been completely out of character, but Aksel did not know that.

She did not have a clue what the protocol was when you woke up in a man's hotel bedroom. What was she supposed to say to him? Thanks very much for the best sex I've ever had? She bit her lip. Okay, she'd behaved like an idiot and she felt vulnerable and out of her depth. It was imperative that she took control of the situation, and her first priority was to change the batteries in her hearing aids.

Conscious that Aksel might emerge from the bathroom at any moment, Mina did not waste time collecting up her clothes that were scattered across the floor, and instead wrapped a silk sheet from the bed around her before going to look for her handbag. Last night she had been too engrossed in Aksel to take much notice of her surroundings, but now she realised that this must be the hotel's penthouse suite. The door from the bedroom led into a luxurious sitting room, and beyond that was the dining room.

Her bare feet sank into the thick-pile carpet. She could only guess how much it would cost to stay in the lavish suite, and she wondered exactly what job Aksel did for his government.

In the dining room, the curtains had been opened and the table was set out for breakfast. The aroma of coffee and freshly baked rolls was enticing and Mina realised she was starving. Her handbag was on the chair where she had left it, and luckily the spare batteries she always carried with her were charged. It took a couple of seconds to replace the batteries in her hearing aids. She felt less vulnerable when she could hear again and her urgency to sneak out of Aksel's suite was replaced with a more acute need to allay her hunger pangs.

She was halfway through eating a roll spread with honey when she sensed that she was no longer alone. Glancing over her shoulder, she saw Aksel watching her from the doorway.

'You look like you're enjoying that,' he murmured.

It was ridiculous to feel embarrassed, Mina told herself. But she was conscious that she was naked beneath the sheet and that her nipples—still swollen from Aksel's ministrations last night—were clearly visible jutting beneath the silk. Colour flared on her cheeks as she remembered how he had kissed every inch of her body and suckled her breasts before he'd moved lower and pushed her legs apart to bestow the most intimate kiss of all.

Her appetite disappeared and she put the roll down on a plate. 'I hope you don't mind. I was hungry.'

'I'm not surprised,' he drawled, his eyes glinting. 'I ordered breakfast for you. After all, it's my fault you missed dinner last night.'

He couldn't take all the blame. It wasn't as if he'd forced her to stay with him, Mina thought guiltily. Her heart thudded as he walked towards her. Last night he had looked like a rock star in his leather jacket, but this morning he was dressed in a superbly tailored grey suit, white silk shirt and an ice-blue tie that matched the colour of his eyes. He was a suave and sophisticated stranger, and Mina clutched the sheet tighter round her. 'I should get dressed,' she mumbled.

'I wish you could stay as you are.' His voice thickened as he cupped her bare shoulders and pulled her towards him. 'Making love to you last night was amazing, and I wish the night could have lasted for ever.'

Mina's heart leapt as he dipped his head and kissed

her. She'd had no idea how Aksel would react after their night of passion, and had mentally prepared for him to state that it had been a mistake. The tenderness in his kiss was unexpected and utterly beguiling. She closed her eyes and melted against him, and the world disappeared as she was swept away by his sensual mastery.

It was a long time before he lifted his mouth from hers. 'You taste of honey,' he said huskily. With obvious reluctance he dropped his hands from her. 'My car is waiting to take me to the airport, but of course I'll take you home first.'

Her heart plummeted as his words catapulted her back to reality. 'You're flying back to Storvhal today, aren't you?'

'I have to, I'm afraid.' Aksel glanced at his watch and his jaw clenched. There was no time now to explain to Mina who he was. He could never escape the responsibilities that came with being a ruling monarch, but he was unwilling to accept that he would never see her again. However, inviting her to Storvhal would be fraught with difficulties.

'What about you? Do you have any plans now that the production of *Romeo and Juliet* has finished its run at the Globe?'

Perhaps later today she would hear if the play was going to Broadway, but Mina saw no point in mentioning it, or that she had an interview arranged for a position as a drama therapist with a health-care trust. She was by no means certain to get the job, and even if she were to be offered it there was still the problem of telling her father that she wanted to pull out of the play.

She shrugged. 'I don't have anything planned for the next couple of weeks. In the acting profession it's known as resting,' she said drily.

'I have to go to Paris at the end of next week. I was thinking about staying on for a couple of days to do some sightseeing.' Aksel paused and looked deeply into Mina's eyes. 'Would you like to meet up and spend the weekend with me?'

He wanted to meet her in Paris—the city of lovers! She strove to sound cool, despite the fact that her heart was racing because he wanted to see her again. 'That could be fun.'

A flame flickered in his blue eyes. 'I can guarantee it.' Unable to resist the lure of her soft mouth, Aksel bent his head, but at that moment his phone rang and he stifled a frustrated sigh when he saw that the call was from his PA. 'Excuse me, I need to take this,' he murmured.

Mina hurried back to the master bedroom. The tangled sheets on the bed were an embarrassing reminder of the passionate night she had spent with Aksel, but she felt better for knowing that it hadn't been a one-night stand. In the en-suite bathroom she bundled her hair into a shower cap and took a quick shower. It would be a mistake to read too much into his invitation to Paris, but the fact that he wanted to spend a weekend with her surely meant that he wanted to get to know her better—and not only in the bedroom.

A lifetime of practice allowed Aksel to greet Mina with an easy smile that disguised his tense mood when she walked back into the room. Her skirt looked even more crumpled after it had spent the night screwed up on the floor, and her long auburn hair fell in silky disarray around her shoulders, but her rather bohemian style was not foremost in his mind as he ushered her into the lift.

'The car is waiting round the back of the hotel,' he told her. He wondered what his PA's terse message meant. 'A situation has arisen' could mean anything. He hoped to God the trade deal hadn't fallen through.

Leading Mina to the rear of the lobby, he opened the door through which they had entered the hotel the previous night. A gust of wind whipped up the steps and lifted the hem of her skirt to reveal her slim thighs and lace stocking tops.

'*Oh…*' She frantically tried to push the lightweight material down. Another gust of wind almost knocked her off her feet and Aksel slid his arm around her waist to clamp her to his side as they walked out of the hotel.

'*Mina—over here!*' a voice called, and a flashbulb flared in the grey street. As Aksel turned his head towards the light the voice called again, '*Prince Aksel— fantastic!* Mina—you're a star. I asked you to give me a scoop, and this is gonna hit the headlines and make me rich!'

'What the hell…?' Cursing, Aksel glanced down at Mina's white face before shooting a furious glare at the man standing on the opposite pavement, holding a long-lens camera.

'Sir…' The chauffeur drew the car up against the kerb and jumped out, but the rear door had already been opened from inside by Aksel's PA.

'Quickly, sir…'

Aksel hardly needed to be told. He bundled Mina into the car before sliding in next to her, and the chauffeur slammed the door. As the car pulled away Aksel ran a hand through his hair and glared at the bespectacled young man sitting opposite him. 'Would you like to tell me what in hell's name is going on, Ben?'

CHAPTER FOUR

AKSEL'S PA, BENEDICT LINDBURG, grimaced. 'The paparazzi are swarming at the front of the hotel. I hoped you would be able to leave through the back door without being spotted.'

Glancing over his shoulder, Aksel could still see the florid-faced press photographer focusing his camera on the back of the car. 'I recognise him,' he said slowly. He looked at Mina, who was huddled into her jacket. 'That man came into the pub last night, and you looked at him as though you knew him.' His eyes narrowed on the twin spots of colour that flared on her white face. 'You told me he was no one in particular.'

He frowned as a curious, almost hunted expression flitted across Mina's face. 'Angel, who was that man? Do you have a problem?'

'With respect, sir, *you* have a problem,' Benedict Lindburg said quietly, handing Aksel a newspaper.

It took him a matter of seconds to skim the front page and he cursed savagely. 'What are the chances of us keeping this story contained?' he asked his PA.

'None,' was the short reply. 'The photo of you and Miss Hart entering the hotel through a back door last night has already been picked up by the media in Storvhal and is headline news. The pictures taken a few moments ago will doubtless already be posted on social media sites.'

Aksel's jaw clenched. 'Damn the paparazzi to hell.'

'I don't understand,' Mina said shakily. She had been shocked into silence when she had seen the journalist Steve Garratt as she and Aksel had emerged from the hotel, but she was puzzled by Aksel's reaction. 'What story? Why does it matter if we were seen going into the hotel last night?'

She recalled her suspicion that Aksel had an important role working for his country's government. Steve Garratt's words pushed into her head. The journalist had called out *Prince Aksel*. She stared at the newspaper photo of her and Aksel entering the hotel with their arms around each other. Above the picture the headline proclaimed *The Prince and the Showgirl!*

Mina turned stunned eyes on Aksel's hard-boned profile, trying frantically to recall any information she had read about Storvhal. The country was a principality—rather like Monaco was—an independent state with close connections to Norway, ruled by a monarch.

Realisation hit her like an ice-cold shower. 'You're a *prince*?' she choked.

'Prince Aksel the Second is head of the Royal House of Thoresen and Supreme Ruler of Storvhal,' the young man with the glasses said in a clipped tone. His expression behind his lenses was disapproving as he studied Mina's crumpled clothes.

She flushed, and asked tightly, 'And you are?'

'Benedict Lindburg, His Highness's personal assistant.'

His Highness! Mina bit her lip and stared at Aksel, wondering if she would wake up in a minute. If last night had seemed unreal, the events unfolding this morning were unbelievable. 'Why didn't you tell me?'

He gave her an odd, intent look. 'So you maintain that you did not know my identity when we met in the pub?'

'Of course I didn't.' Her voice faltered as she watched a muscle flicker in his jaw. There was no hint of his sexy, crooked smile on his mouth. His lips were set in a stern line and his face looked as though it had been sculpted from marble. 'Aksel...' she said uncertainly.

'Someone must have tipped off the press last night and told them that we would be entering the hotel through the back door.'

Aksel's voice was expressionless but inside his head his thoughts ran riot. Nothing made sense. No one had known that he had invited Mina to his hotel—except for Mina herself, his brain pointed out. He tensed as his mind violently rejected the possibility that he had made the most spectacular misjudgement of his life. But a memory slid like a snake into his mind and spewed poison.

'You sent a text message to someone as the taxi drew up outside the hotel,' he reminded her.

Mina's eyes flashed at his accusatory tone. 'I sent a message to my friend Kat to confirm that I would be at a cast meeting at the theatre this morning. I'll show you the damn text if you don't believe me,' she said hotly. Her eyes met Aksel's and she felt chilled by the cold speculation in his gaze.

His PA broke the tense silence. 'Is the meeting to discuss the announcement made in the press this morning that the Joshua Hart Theatre company will be performing *Romeo and Juliet* on Broadway?'

Mina blinked. 'There's been an announcement? I haven't spoken to my father but I have heard he has been in negotiations to take the play to New York.'

'The news about the play has received extra prominence in the media, due no doubt to speculation about your relationship with Prince Aksel,' Benedict Lindburg said stiffly.

Aksel swore beneath his breath. Since he had become ruler of Storvhal he had never lowered his guard, never slipped up—until he had looked into a pair of deep green eyes and lost his head. Shame seared him. Perhaps he was as weak as his father after all. If he was labelled a playboy prince by the press in Storvhal it could cause irreparable damage to his reputation and even to the monarchy.

He stared at Mina and despised himself for wanting to kiss her tremulous mouth. 'The journalist who was waiting for us this morning—he knew your name, and he said he'd asked you to give him a scoop,' Aksel said grimly. 'He *was* the same man who was in the pub.' He recalled the strange expression on Mina's face when she had seen the man the previous evening, and the truth hit him like a blow to his stomach. 'The journalist is a friend of yours, and you tipped him off that I'd invited you to my hotel last night.'

'I didn't!'

Her beautiful eyes widened. A man could drown in those deep green pools, Aksel thought. Hell, he could feel himself floundering, wanting to believe the shocked outrage in her voice. Only a gifted actress could feign such innocence. Mina had played Juliet so convincingly, taunted a voice in Aksel's head. She made a living out of pretence and playing make-believe.

Rage burned inside him, but beneath his anger was a savage feeling of betrayal that despite her denial Mina *must* have spoken to the press. He was aware of the same hollow sensation in his gut that he had felt as a young man, when he had learned that his mother had betrayed him.

When Aksel had found out that Karena did not really love him, he had been hurt. But far worse had been the discovery that his mother had encouraged the Russian model to seduce him, promising her a life of fame, fortune and luxury. After Prince Geir's death, Irina had had strong financial reasons for wanting to maintain a link between Russia and Storvhal, and she had believed it would be beneficial for her if her son married a Russian woman. But when her plan had been revealed, Aksel had realised just how cold and calculating his mother was, and how little she cared about him.

Helvete! If his own mother could betray him, why was he surprised that a woman he had picked up in a bar had done the same? he derided himself. Bitter experience had taught him never to trust any woman and he was furious with himself for being taken in by Mina's air of innocence.

Mina could tell from Aksel's cold expression that he did not believe her. 'I *didn't* know you are a prince,' she repeated. 'Even if I had, why would I have tipped off a journalist?'

'To create publicity for your father's theatre company,' Benedict Lindburg suggested smoothly.

'Keep out of this.' Mina rounded on the PA fiercely. 'You don't know anything about me.'

'As a matter of fact I know everything about you.' The PA handed a folder to Aksel with an apologetic shrug. 'The photo of you and Miss Hart was posted on social media sites shortly after it was taken last night. As soon as I was alerted to it I ran a security check on Miss Hart. My report includes details of Miss Hart's acting career in England and also in the United States.'

The colour drained from Mina's face as she stared at the folder in Aksel's hand. Without doubt his PA had unearthed the story about her relationship—her alleged white-hot affair—with the film director Dexter Price, which some of the media had labelled a publicity stunt to promote the film she had starred in. She had done nothing wrong, Mina reminded herself. She had not deserved to be vilified by the press, but what chance was there of Aksel believing her side of the story when she looked as guilty as hell of tipping off the journalist Steve Garratt.

She looked into Aksel's eyes and felt chilled to the bone. The Viking lover with the sexy smile had turned into a stranger. He had always been a stranger, she reminded herself. Just because he had made love to her as though she were the most precious person on the planet did not prove anything other than that he was very good at sex.

Shame swept through her as she remembered how she had responded to him in bed. She did not know what had come over her. And him a *prince*! She froze when Aksel opened the folder and sought his gaze, her eyes unconsciously pleading. If only they could go back to last night, to the private, magical world they had created.

'Aksel…' she whispered.

For a heartbeat she thought he was going to listen to her. Something flared in his eyes, and he stared at her mouth as if he wanted to kiss her. But then his jaw hardened and he deliberately turned away and looked down at the open file.

Mina could not bear to sit beside him while he read about the most humiliating episode in her life. The traffic was crawling around Marble Arch, and the car came to a standstill. The only thought in Mina's head was to run from Aksel—something she should have done last night, she acknowledged grimly. She must have been out of her mind to have slept with a stranger.

Before he realised her intention she opened the car door and scrambled out into the midst of four lanes of traffic.

Aksel sprang forwards and tried to grab hold of her. 'Don't be an idiot!' he yelled. 'You'll be killed!' His heart was in his mouth as he watched her weave through the cars, taxis and buses. Moments later he glimpsed Mina's long auburn hair as she disappeared down the steps leading to the underground station. Slowly he sank back in his seat, fighting a fierce urge to chase after her.

Benedict pulled the car door shut. The PA was startled when he thought he glimpsed emotion in the Prince of Storvhal's eyes. 'Sir…I'm sorry,' he said hesitantly.

The hot flood of rage inside Aksel had solidified into a cold, hard knot. It was bad enough that Mina had made a fool of him, and worse that his stupidity had been witnessed by a member of his staff.

His jaw tightened. He had certainly been a fool to have thought—even fleetingly—that making love with Mina had been somehow special. She'd had a few clever tricks—that was all. Like the way she had focused her big green eyes intently on his mouth. She'd made him feel as if he were the only man in the world for her.

He glanced at his PA and raised an eyebrow. 'I don't require your sympathy, Ben,' he drawled. 'I simply want you to get on with your job. Have you confirmed my meeting with the Danish Prime Minister yet?'

He must have been imagining things, Benedict told himself. The Ice Prince's face was as emotionless as always. Suitably chastened, the PA murmured, 'I'll do it right away, sir.'

* * *

Mina could hear her father's raised voice from the other end of the corridor.

'*Get out of my sight,*' Joshua Hart roared. 'I will not put up with guttersnipes from the tabloid press harassing me with tittle-tattle and nonsense.'

Forewarned that journalists must be in her father's office, Mina darted into a broom cupboard moments before two men clutching cameras and recording equipment shot past.

It was no surprise that the other members of the play's cast seemed to be keeping out of the director's way. Joshua in a temper reminded Mina of an angry bear, and she took a deep breath before she peeped cautiously around his office door.

'Oh, it's you.' He greeted her with a scowl. 'I hope you haven't brought any more damn journalists with you.'

'No.' Mina was pretty sure she had managed to slip through a side door of the Globe without being seen by the journalists milling about outside the theatre. She gave him a hesitant smile. 'It's great news about the play going to New York.'

Her father snorted. 'I tried to phone you last night to tell you the news first, before I announced it to the rest of the cast, but you didn't answer. I suppose you were with this chap of yours.' He glared at Mina from beneath his bushy eyebrows. 'It's all over the papers that you are dating a prince.'

Mina's heart sank when she saw copies of several of the morning's newspapers on her father's desk. The photograph on the front page showed her and Aksel entering his hotel through a back door, and it was clear from their body language that they had been on their way to bed.

'I'm not dating him,' she said quickly, but her father did not appear to have heard her.

'I would have thought you'd had enough publicity when you got involved with that film director in America. Heaven knows, you're an adult and you can lead your life how you want,' Joshua exploded. 'But having your love-life plastered across the newspapers is not the sort of publicity I want for the Hart family or my theatre company. Have you thought that this could have a detrimental effect when the play opens on Broadway?'

According to Dexter Price there was no such thing as bad publicity, Mina thought darkly. 'In what way do you mean detrimental?' she asked her father.

'We're performing Shakespeare on Broadway,' Joshua snapped. 'I don't want the production to turn into a soap opera because Juliet is sleeping with a European aristocrat. You know how fascinated the Americans are by that sort of thing.'

Mina bit her lip as she stared at her father's furious face. She had hoped for his support but she should have known that he would be more concerned about the play than her. Joshua had been an unpredictable parent while she was growing up, and Mina and her brother and sisters had learned to deal with his mood swings and artistic temperament.

'I assure you I didn't ask for the publicity,' she said stiffly. 'I won't be seeing Aks…the prince…again so you need not worry that I'll attract adverse press coverage.'

It was obvious from the way Aksel had been so quick to believe the worst of her that he'd never had any intention of meeting her in Paris. He was a prince, for heaven's sake, and she had been a one-night stand. She swallowed the sudden lump in her throat, remembering how he had kissed her with such beguiling tenderness at the hotel that morning. He had made her think that he genuinely did want to see her again. She grimaced. His performance had been worthy of an award for best actor.

'Your mother's worried about you,' Joshua muttered. 'You'd better phone her.' He sat down at his desk. 'I've told the cast to assemble on the stage and I'll be along to discuss the New York project when I've made a couple of calls.'

Kat Nichols was the first person Mina saw when she walked through the theatre.

'Mina! I couldn't believe it when I saw the newspapers. Who would have guessed that the blond hunk from the pub is a *prince*?'

Not me, unfortunately, Mina thought ruefully.

Kat looked at her closely. 'Are you okay? Some of the papers have dragged up a story about you and a film director in LA.' She could not hide her curiosity. 'What did exactly happen between you and Dexter Price?'

Mina bit her lip. Now that the newspapers had reprinted the lies about her, she might as well tell Kat the truth.

'I'd been picked for a lead role in what was touted as the next big blockbuster film,' she said heavily. 'During filming I formed a close relationship with Dexter. I naïvely believed that he wanted to keep our friendship quiet to protect me from gossip. He never took me to popular bars or restaurants where we might be seen together. But a journalist got wind that something was going on and managed to take some damning photos of us.'

She grimaced. 'I only ever kissed Dex, but pictures of us were splashed across the newspapers and appeared to prove that we were having a sordid affair. It turned out that Dex was married—although he had told me he was divorced. Not only that, but his wife had been diagnosed with breast cancer.'

'Oh, God, how awful for her, and for you,' Kat murmured.

'The press labelled me a heartless marriage-wrecker,' Mina said flatly as she relived the nightmare that had unfolded in LA. 'Dex lied to me. I hadn't known he had a wife, let alone that she was seriously ill. I felt so guilty that she had been hurt, but Dex didn't care. He actually said that the publicity about our relationship would be good for the film.'

'What a bastard,' Kat said fiercely.

'I wanted to come home straight away, but I had to finish the film. Too many people would have been affected if I'd pulled out. Luckily there were only two more weeks of filming left but I was hounded by the paparazzi until I left LA.'

'Some journalists have been at the theatre this morning, trying to get members of the cast to talk about you. But no one has,' Kat added quickly.

'No one knows much about me,' Mina said drily. Although she got on well with most of the other cast members, she guarded her privacy. She felt sick knowing that everyone would be gossiping about her personal life, and her temper simmered because once again she had unwittingly become headline news. If Aksel had told her that he was the Prince of Storvhal she would never have agreed to go to his hotel. Her bitter experience with Dex had taught her to steer clear of people who were in the public eye.

She went with Kat to join the other actors, who were gathered on the stage. The buzz of conversation faded and there was an awkward silence until Laurence Adams, who played Mercutio, said brightly, 'That was a great

PR stunt, Mina. The story about your relationship with a prince who is supposedly one of Europe's most eligible bachelors has gone global on the same day that it was announced that our production of *Romeo and Juliet* is going to Broadway. With all the media interest I reckon we'll be a sell-out in New York.'

No way, Mina silently vowed, would she allow any of the cast to know how humiliated she felt. When she had been growing up, being the only deaf child in a mainstream school had taught Mina to develop a tough shell and hide her feelings of insecurity and hurt when she was teased for being 'different'. Acting had become a means of survival, and now she utilised all her theatrical skills to brazen out the embarrassing situation.

Lifting her chin, she said airily, 'Yeah, I'm thrilled that I was pictured with a prince. Apparently the story is on all the American news networks and everyone in New York will know that the play will be opening there soon. I'm sure you're right and we'll perform to a full house every night.'

Several of the cast cheered, but beside her Kat stiffened and muttered warningly, 'Mina—he's here!'

Mina's heart missed a beat. She turned her head to tell Kat that she did not find the joke funny, but the words froze on her lips as she looked up at the gallery and saw a golden-haired Viking staring down at the stage.

Aksel's stern face could have been carved from granite, and even from a distance Mina felt chilled by his icy stare. He did not say a word, but as she replayed her statement in her head, her frustration boiled over.

'I…I didn't mean what I said,' she called up to him.

His silence was crushing. He stared at her for a few more seconds before he swung round and the sound of his footsteps as he strode from the gallery reverberated around the theatre.

'I swear, I didn't know you are a damn prince,' Mina shouted after him. But he did not turn his head and moments later he had disappeared.

He had walked out without giving her a chance to explain! Who was this cold man who had replaced her caring lover of the night before? The fiasco of the damning photograph in the newspaper was *his* fault. His royal status made him a target for the paparazzi. Her stomach lurched as she realised that Steve Garratt must have recognised Aksel in the pub the previous evening. The journalist must have seen her get into the taxi with Aksel and followed them to the hotel. Garratt had certainly got the scoop he'd wanted, she thought bitterly.

She choked back an angry sob. Aksel had refused to listen to her—just as her father so often did not listen. When she had first lost her hearing, Mina had also lost her confidence to speak. Years of speech therapy had helped her to find her voice again, and thanks to her hearing aids she was able to disguise her hearing impairment. But deep inside her there still lingered the insecure little girl who had felt trapped and alone in a silent world. Being deprived of one of her senses made her feel invisible and insignificant.

Damn Aksel for ignoring her, she thought furiously as she ran through the theatre. She would make him listen to her!

But when she reached the exit there was no sign of him and the only people outside the theatre were some journalists. The sound of a car's engine drew her attention to the road, and her heart sank when she saw the sleek black limousine that had collected her and Aksel from the hotel earlier pull away from the kerb.

The journalists spotted her and crowded around the door. 'Miss Hart—are you in a relationship with Prince Aksel of Storvhal?'

'Are you hoping that the prince will visit you while you are performing in New York?'

Kat rushed up as Mina slammed the door shut to block out the journalists' questions.

'Joshua is in a furious temper,' Kat told her breathlessly. 'He's demanding to know why you invited the prince here to the theatre.'

Mina groaned. She could not cope with her father when he was in one of his unreasonable moods. But in fairness she could understand why he was angry with her. The announcement that he would be directing his theatre company's production of *Romeo and Juliet* on Broadway should have been a highlight of Joshua's career, but Mina had unwittingly stolen his thunder. The press were more interested in her relationship with a prince than in the play.

'I have to get away from here,' she muttered.

'My car is parked round the back. We might be able to slip out without being seen. But, Mina…' Kat hesitated, looking concerned. 'I drove past your flat on my way here this morning and saw press photographers outside.'

'I'm not going home,' Mina said grimly. 'Will you give me a lift to the airport?'

Benedict Lindburg, sitting in the front of the limousine with the driver, took one look at Aksel's face as he climbed into the rear of the car and wisely did not say a word.

At least his PA knew when to keep his opinion to himself, Aksel thought darkly as he hit a button to activate the privacy screen that separated him from the occupants in the front of the car. It was unlikely that his chief advisor would show the same diplomacy. He grimaced as his phone rang and Harald Petersen's name flashed on the caller display.

'It's a personal matter,' Aksel explained curtly, in answer to his advisor's query about why the royal flight from London to Storvhal had been delayed.

There was a tiny hesitation before Harald said smoothly, 'I understand that you have cancelled all your meetings for this afternoon. If you have a problem, sir, I hope that I can be of assistance.'

The problem—as Harald damn well knew—was the photograph and the headline *'The Prince and the Show-girl'* that had made the front page of the newspapers in England and Storvhal, and no doubt the rest of the world. But the real problem was *him*, Aksel thought grimly. He cursed the crazy impulse that had caused him to instruct his driver to turn the car around when they had been on the way to the airport, and take him to the Globe Theatre. But his conscience had been nagging. He had remembered the charity function that had been held at the Erskine hotel last night, and the members of the press who had been gathered outside to take pictures of the celebrity guests. It was possible that the paparazzi had been covering other entrances to the hotel, and Aksel had realised that he might have been wrong when he had accused Mina of tipping off a journalist that they would enter via a back door.

The article in the newspaper about her affair with a married film director in LA was damning, but when he'd read the sordid details Aksel had struggled to equate the heartless bimbo described in the paper with the woman who had responded with such sweet eagerness when he had made love to her. There had been a curious innocence to Mina that had touched something inside him. But now he knew it had been an act. Overhearing her at the theatre had ripped the blinkers from his eyes, and the realisation that she was as calculating and mercenary as his mother and Karena filled him with icy rage.

'The photograph in the newspapers of you and the English actress could have repercussions in Storvhal,' Harald Petersen murmured. 'I fear that people will be reminded of your father's playboy image, and it is imperative we think of a damage-limitation strategy. Perhaps you could issue a statement to deny that you are involved with Miss Hart—although that will be less believable now that there is a second photograph of you leaving the hotel with her.' Harald gave a pained sigh. 'I assume you will not be seeing her again. I'm afraid the Storvhalian people will not approve of you having an affair with her, and I am sure I do not need to remind you that your duty to your country must come before any other consideration.'

Aksel's jaw clenched and he tightened his grip on his phone until his knuckles whitened. 'You're right—you don't need to remind me of my duty,' he said harshly. *'Helvete!* You, above all people, Harald, know the sacrifice I made to ensure the stability of the country when Storvhal was on the brink of civil unrest. Only you, amongst my staff, know that Karena gave me an illegitimate child. My son is dead, and for eight years I have kept Finn's brief existence a secret because I understood that I must focus on ruling Storvhal and try to repair the damage my father caused to the monarchy.'

His tone became steely as he fought to disguise the rawness of his emotions. 'Do not throw duty in my face, Harald. I swore when I was crowned that I would fulfil the expectations that the people of Storvhal have of their prince, but I have paid a personal price that will haunt me for ever.'

Aksel ended the call and his head fell back against the leather car seat. He could feel his heart jerking painfully beneath his ribs as he replayed his conversation with his chief advisor in his mind. How *could* Harald have implied that he needed to be reminded of his duty to his country? He had given Storvhal everything. He had spent more than a decade paying for his father's sins, and had striven to be a perfect prince, even though it meant that he'd had to bury his grief for his son deep inside him.

The baby had been born in Russia and tragically had only lived for a few weeks. Losing Finn had ripped Aksel's heart out. Every time his grandmother spoke of the need for him to have an heir Aksel pictured his baby boy and felt a familiar ache in his chest. But his grandmother had no idea how he felt. No one in his life, apart from his chief advisor, knew about Finn.

His thoughts turned again to Mina and for some inexplicable reason the ache inside him intensified. His mouth twisted cynically. He'd had sex with her, but of course she had not touched him on an emotional level, he assured himself. Aksel had buried his heart with his baby son, and the Ice Prince—the name that he knew his staff called him behind his back—was incapable of feeling anything.

CHAPTER FIVE

NOTHING HAD PREPARED Mina for the bone-biting cold as she walked through the doors of Storvhal's international airport into a land of snow and ice.

'Are you sure you want to do this?' Kat had asked when she had dropped Mina off at Heathrow. 'Where on earth is Storvhal, anyway?'

'It's an island that stretches across the northern border of Norway and Russia.'

Kat had eyed Mina's thin cotton skirt and jacket doubtfully. 'Well, in that case you'd better borrow my coat.'

Mina had baulked at the idea of wearing her friend's purple leopard-print coat with a hood trimmed with pink marabou feathers but she hadn't had the heart to refuse. Now she was less concerned about Kat's eccentric taste in fashion, and was simply grateful that the eye-catching coat provided some protection against the freezing temperature, as did the fur-lined boots and gloves she had bought in the airport shop along with a few other essentials. But the coat and boots would not keep her warm for long when a sign on the airport wall displayed a temperature of minus six degrees.

The fact that it was dark at three o'clock in the afternoon was another shock. But she was in the Arctic Circle, Mina reminded herself. According to the tourist guide she had picked up, Storvhal would soon be in polar night—meaning that there would be no daylight at all from the end of October until February.

She did not plan to be in Storvhal for long—although admittedly her exact plans were sketchy. She had been furious with Aksel when she had flown from England, and determined to defend herself against his accusation that she had tipped off the journalist and was therefore responsible for the photograph of them in the papers. But now that she had arrived in his icy, alien country she was starting to question her sanity.

Her sister often teased her for being impulsive. Mina felt a sudden pang of longing to be in Sicily, at the castle Torre d'Aquila with Darcey and Salvatore. Her brother-in-law had made her feel so welcome when she had visited in the summer. It was wonderful that Darcey was so happy and in love. Mina could not help but feel a little envious that her sister was adored by her handsome husband. If she ever got married she hoped she would share a love as strong as theirs.

A blast of icy wind prompted Mina to walk towards a taxi parked outside the airport terminal. To her relief the driver spoke good English and he nodded when she asked him to take her to the royal palace, which was mentioned in the tourist guide.

'The palace is open to the public during the week. You should be in time for the last tour of the day,' he told her. 'It's very spectacular. It was built in the twelfth century by a Viking warrior who was the first prince of Storvhal. If you look at the newspaper,' the driver continued, 'you will see that our current prince has made the headlines today.'

Mina glanced at the newspaper on the seat beside her and her heart sank. The paper must be a later edition than the one she had seen earlier, and the photo on the front page was of her and Aksel emerging from the hotel that morning. The wind had whipped her skirt up to her thighs, and her tangled hair looked as if she had just got out of bed. Aksel had his arm around her and wore the satisfied expression of a man who had enjoyed a night of hot sex.

Oh, God! Mina cringed. The taxi driver glanced at her in his rear-view mirror and she was thankful that her face was hidden by the hood of her coat.

'According to the press reports, the prince is having an affair with an English actress. I feel sorry for him,' the driver continued. 'The people of Storvhal take great interest in Prince Aksel's private life. I guess they are afraid that he will turn out like his late father.'

'What was wrong with his father?' Mina was curious to learn any information about Aksel.

'Prince Geir was not a good monarch. People called him the playboy prince because he was more interested in partying with beautiful women on his yacht in Monaco than ruling the country.' The driver shrugged. 'It did not help his popularity when he married a Russian woman. Historically, Storvhalians have mistrusted Russia. Prince Geir was accused of making secret business deals with Russian companies and increasing his personal wealth by selling off Storvhal's natural resources.

'Since Prince Aksel has ruled Storvhal he has avoided any hint of scandal and has restored support for the monarchy,' the driver explained. 'He won't be pleased to have his personal life made public—and I'm sure the princess will be upset.'

Mina's heart lurched sickeningly. 'The *princess*...do you mean Prince Aksel is married?'

The memory of learning that Dexter had a wife and

was not divorced as he had told her was still raw in Mina's mind. Aksel had insisted that he was not married, but he could have lied. She shuddered to think that she might have been a gullible fool for a second time.

The driver did not appear to notice the sudden sharpness in her voice. 'Oh, no, I meant Princess Eldrun—Prince Aksel's grandmother. She ruled Storvhal with her husband, Prince Fredrik, for many years. When he died and Prince Geir inherited the throne the princess did not hide her disappointment that her son was a poor monarch. Geir was killed in a helicopter crash on his way to visit one of his many mistresses. It is common knowledge that Princess Eldrun hopes her grandson will choose a Storvhalian bride and provide an heir to the throne.'

They had been travelling along a main road, but now the taxi driver turned the car onto a gravel driveway that wound through a vast area of parkland. The frozen snow on the ground glittered in the bright glare of the street lamps, and the branches of the trees were spread like white lacy fingers against the night-dark sky. It was hard to believe that it was afternoon, Mina mused.

Her thoughts scattered as the royal palace came into view. With its white walls, tall turrets and arched windows, it looked like a fairy-tale castle, and the layer of powdery, glistening snow clinging to the roofs and spires reminded her of icing on top of a cake. The sight of guards in navy blue and gold uniforms standing in front of the palace gave her a jolt. For the first time it dawned on her that the man she had spent last night with, and who had made love to her with breathtaking passion, was actually a member of a royal dynasty.

The taxi driver dropped her at the public entrance to the palace and Mina joined the queue of people waiting to take a guided tour. An information leaflet explained that the public were allowed into the library and several reception rooms, which had been turned into a museum. The beautiful wood-panelled rooms filled with ancient tapestries and oil paintings were fascinating, but she was not in the mood for sightseeing.

She turned to the tour guide. 'Where can I see the prince?'

'You cannot see him—of course not.' The female guide looked shocked, but her expression lifted as she clearly thought that she had misunderstood. 'Do you mean you wish to buy a photograph of Prince Aksel? We sell souvenirs in the gift shop. The palace is about to close but you can visit the shop on your way out.'

The guide walked away, leaving Mina feeling a fool. Why had she thought that she would be able to stroll into the palace and bump into Storvhal's monarch? It was as likely as expecting to meet the Queen of England when Buckingham Palace was opened to the public in the summer. But the truth was she hadn't thought of anything past her urgency to find Aksel and convince him that she had not betrayed him to the press.

After learning from the taxi driver about Storvhal's royal family, and the unpopularity of Aksel's father, who had been known as the playboy prince, she could understand better why Aksel had reacted so angrily to the press allegations that they were having an affair.

The adrenaline that had been pumping through Mina's veins since she had arrived in Storvhal and mentally prepared herself for a showdown with Aksel drained away, and she felt exhausted—which was not surprising when she'd had very little sleep the previous night, she thought, flushing as erotic memories resurfaced. The knowledge that Aksel was somewhere in the vast palace but she could not meet him was bitterly frustrating.

She glanced out of the window and realised that she must be overlooking the grounds at the rear of the palace. A four-by-four was parked on the driveway and someone was about to climb into the driver's seat. The man was wearing a ski jacket; his hood slipped back, and Mina's heart missed a beat when she recognised the distinctive tiger stripes in his blond hair.

Aksel!

She tapped frantically on the window to gain his attention. He was going to drive away and there was nothing she could do to stop him! He did not look up, and she watched him take a mobile phone out of his jacket and walk back inside the palace.

Mina looked along the corridor and saw the guide shepherding the other people from the tour party into the gift shop. Walking as rapidly as she dared, she hurried past the shop and out of the palace before racing through the grounds. With every step she expected to be challenged by the palace guards, but no one seemed to have noticed her. When she reached the four-by-four she found the engine had been left running, but there was no sign of Aksel.

The freezing air made Mina's eyes sting, and she peered through the swirling snowflakes that had started to fall. She was likely to get frostbite if she stayed outside for much longer but she refused to give up her only opportunity to talk to Aksel. A few more minutes passed, and her toes and fingers became numb. There was nothing for it but to wait inside the vehicle, she decided as she opened the rear door and climbed inside.

The warmth of the interior of the four-by-four enveloped her. Gradually she stopped shivering, and as tiredness overwhelmed her she lay down on the seat and closed her eyes, promising herself that she would only rest them for a minute.

* * *

The snow was falling so thickly that the windscreen wipers could barely cope. Aksel knew that driving into the mountains in mid-October was a risk, but the weather reports had been clear, and he'd decided to visit the cabin for one last weekend before winter set in.

He guessed the blizzard had taken the forecasters by surprise. The road down in the valley was likely to be impassable already and there was no point turning round. Aksel was used to the harsh, fast-changing conditions of the Arctic landscape and wasn't worried that he would make it to the cabin, but he knew there was a chance he could be stranded there if the weather did not improve.

He probably should have listened to his chief advisor's plea to remain at the palace, he thought ruefully. But he had been in no mood to put up with Harald Petersen's pained expression as the chief advisor read the latest press revelations that Storvhal's ruling monarch was having a love affair with an English actress and apparently good-time girl, Mina Hart.

Love affair! Aksel gave a cynical laugh. Emotions had played no part in the night he had spent with Mina. If the press had accused him of having casual, meaningless sex with her it would have been closer to the truth. But he was meant to be above such behaviour, because, as Harald frequently reminded him, the population of Storvhal would not tolerate another playboy prince as his father had been.

Thank God he had managed to keep the story from his grandmother so far. Princess Eldrun's heart was weak and a rumour that her grandson might be following his father's reprobate lifestyle would be a devastating shock for her. Aksel's knuckles whitened on the steering wheel.

Mina's publicity stunt could have dire consequences for his grandmother's health.

A memory flashed into his mind of Mina's stricken face as he had walked away from her at the Globe Theatre earlier in the day. Damn it, he had overheard her admit that the rumours she was having an affair with him had earned her father's production of *Romeo and Juliet* extensive media coverage. So why did he still have a lingering doubt that he might have misjudged her?

Because he was a fool, that was why, he told himself angrily. He should despise Mina, but he could not stop thinking about her and remembering how she had felt in his arms, the softness of her skin when he had lowered his body onto hers. *Damn her*, he thought savagely, shifting position to try to ease the throb of his arousal.

A sudden movement in his rear-view mirror caught his attention. Something—a faceless figure—loomed up on the back seat of the four-by-four. Aksel's heart collided with his ribcage, and he swore, as shock and—hell, he wasn't ashamed to admit it—fear surged through him. His chief advisor's warnings that he should take more care of his personal safety jerked into his mind. But he refused to carry a weapon that had the potential to take a life. He had witnessed the utter finality of death when he had cradled his baby son's lifeless body in his arms. The experience had had a profound effect on him and made him appreciate the immeasurable value of life.

He only hoped that whoever had stowed away in his car valued *his* life. Most of the population of Storvhal supported his rule. However he could not ignore the fact that no leader or public figurehead was completely safe from the threat of assassination. *Was he going to feel a bullet in the back of his neck?*

The hell he was! His survival instinct kicked in and

he hit the brakes hard, causing the faceless figure to fall forwards. Adrenaline pumped through his veins as he leapt out of the truck and pulled open the rear door. The interior light automatically flicked on and Aksel stared in disbelief at the incongruous sight of a figure wearing a purple leopard-print coat with a hood trimmed with pink feathers.

'What in God's name…?' Conscious that the stow-away could have a weapon, Aksel grabbed hold of an arm, and with his other hand yanked the hood back to reveal a tumbling mass of silky auburn hair and a pair of deep green eyes.

'Mina?' His brain could not comprehend what his eyes were telling him. He was halfway up a glacier in the middle of a snowstorm and it was beyond belief that the woman who had haunted his thoughts all day was staring mutely at him.

'What are you doing? How did you get into my truck? *Hellvete!'* He lost his grip on his temper when she made no reply. The snow was swirling around him and he impatiently raked his damp hair off his brow and glared at her. 'What crazy game are you playing? Answer me, damn you. Why are you pretending to be deaf?'

'I'm not pretending.' At last she spoke in a tremulous voice that Aksel struggled to hear.

Mina stared at Aksel's furious face. She could tell he was shouting at her from the jerky way his lips moved, but she couldn't hear him. She could not hear anything. When she had woken, dazed and disorientated in the back of the four-by-four, it had taken her a few moments to work out why everything was silent. She had realised that her hearing-aid batteries had run down and remembered that she had fitted a new set at Aksel's hotel that morning, but the rechargeable batteries in her handbag had probably not been fully charged.

The faint gleam of the car's interior lamp cast shadows on Aksel's face and highlighted his sharp cheekbones and strong jaw. He was forbiddingly beautiful, and, despite the freezing wind whipping into the four-by-four, Mina felt a flood of warmth in the pit of her stomach.

She said shakily, 'I have a severe hearing impairment and rely on hearing aids to be able to hear.' She opened her hand and showed him the two tiny listening devices that she had removed from her ears. 'The batteries are dead, but I can lip-read if I watch your mouth when you speak.'

For one of only a handful of times in his life, Aksel had no idea what to say. 'Are you serious about being unable to hear, or are you playing some sort of sick joke?' he demanded.

'Of course I wouldn't joke about something like that,' Mina snapped. 'I've been deaf since I was a child. Most people don't know I can't hear because my hearing aids allow me to lead a normal life, and I'm good at hiding my disability from strangers,' she added with fierce pride.

'Last night we were as intimate as two people can get,' Aksel reminded her. 'I wouldn't call us strangers. Why didn't you tell me you are unable to hear?'

'I suppose for the same reason that you didn't tell me you are a prince.' Mina shrugged. 'I didn't feel ready to share personal confidences with you. And clearly we are still strangers, because otherwise you wouldn't have believed that I told the press about us.'

Aksel frowned. Snowdrifts were already forming around his legs, and more importantly around the wheels of the truck, and he knew he must keep the vehicle moving or risk becoming trapped on the exposed mountain road. But there were still a couple of questions he needed answered. 'Why the hell are you wearing a fancy-dress costume?'

Mina glanced ruefully at the horrendous purple coat. 'My friend lent me her coat because I only had a thin jacket. Kat has an…unusual fashion sense, but it was kind of her,' she said loyally.

'Do you mean to say that underneath that thing you're not wearing protective cold-weather clothing?'

'I didn't know I would need them when I got into your car at the palace. You had gone inside to talk on your phone and I decided to wait for you, but I fell asleep,' she explained when Aksel gave her a puzzled look.

That cleared up one mystery. 'I'm surprised you didn't bring your journalist friend with you,' he said bitterly.

'I'm not friendly with any journalists.'

'The man in the pub,' he reminded her.

She grimaced. 'I promise you Steve Garratt is no friend of mine.'

Aksel shook the snow out of his hair. He wished he could turn the truck around and drive Mina straight back to the airport, but the weather was worsening and his only option was to take her to the cabin.

'We'll have to save the rest of this discussion for later.' He turned away from her as he spoke. When she did not respond he realised that she had not heard him, and the only way they could communicate was for Mina to read his lips. Things were starting to fall into place—like the way she had focused intently on his face last night. He'd thought that she couldn't take her eyes off him because she found him attractive, but now he knew she had watched his lips when he spoke to disguise the fact that she was deaf.

She must have some guts to be so determined not

to allow her hearing impairment to affect her life, he thought, feeling a grudging admiration for her. He wondered if she felt vulnerable without her hearing aids. He couldn't imagine what it was like to live in a silent world, but he guessed it could be lonely being cut off from ordinary sounds that hearing people took for granted.

A muscle tightened in Aksel's jaw. He did not want to admire Mina, and he did not want to take her to the cabin. She was a dangerous threat to his peace of mind, especially when he could not forget the searing passion that had burned out of control between them last night. With a curse he slammed the rear door and climbed behind the wheel to drive the last part of the journey that could be made in the four-by-four.

'Where are we?' Mina asked as she climbed out of the truck and caught hold of Aksel's arm to make him turn around so that she could see his face. They had arrived at a building that had suddenly loomed out of the snow and seemed to be in the middle of nowhere. Aksel had driven the four-by-four inside the building, and the light from of the car's headlamps revealed that they were in some sort of warehouse. The place wasn't heated and Mina was already shivering from the bone-biting cold.

'This is as far as we can go by road. From here we'll be travelling on the snowmobile.' He pointed to a contraption that looked like a motorbike on skis.

Travelling to where? Mina wondered. She eyed the snowmobile nervously. 'You expect me to ride on that?'

'I didn't expect you to be here at all.' Aksel spoke carefully so that Mina could read his lips. The glitter in his ice-blue eyes warned her that he was furious with her. He strode over to a cupboard and pulled out several items of clothing, and then walked back to stand in front of her so that she could see his face. 'Luckily my sister keeps spare gear here for emergencies.'

Mina seized this tiny snippet of information about the man who had shared his body with her but nothing else. 'I didn't know you have a sister.'

'There are a lot of things you don't know about me.' He ignored her curiosity and handed her the clothes. 'Put a couple of sweatshirts on under the snowsuit. The more layers you wear, the warmer you'll be.'

Mina doubted she would ever feel warm again. She had to take her skirt off before she could step into the snowsuit and her numb fingers would not work properly. But at last she pulled her boots back on and Aksel handed her a crash helmet. He swung his leg over the saddle of the snowmobile and indicated that she should climb up behind him.

'What if I fall off?' she asked worriedly.

'Then you'll be left behind,' was his uncompromising reply, before he closed the visors on both their helmets and cut off communication between them.

Mina had never been so scared in her life, as Aksel drove the snowmobile across the icy wasteland that stretched endlessly in all directions. There was a grab-rail behind her seat, but she felt safer with her arms wrapped around his waist. At least if she fell off he would be aware of it and might stop.

It had stopped snowing, but the freezing air temperature even through the snowsuit made her blood feel as if it had frozen in her veins. The wind rushed past as the snowmobile picked up speed, and she squeezed her eyes shut and clung to Aksel. His muscular body was reassuringly strong and powerful, and an image flitted into Mina's mind of him naked; his golden-skinned chest crushing her breasts, and his massive arousal pushing between her thighs. Her fear faded and she put her trust in the giant Viking who was confidently steering the snow bike across the ice.

In the light from the snowmobile's headlamp the snow was brilliant white, and above them the vast black sky was crowded with more stars than Mina had known existed. The birch forest became sparser the higher into the mountains they went, and at last a log cabin with lights blazing in the windows came into view.

Mina was relieved to see a house, thinking that she would be able to charge her hearing-aid batteries. She always carried the charger with her but the device needed to be plugged into an electricity supply to work.

As Aksel helped her climb off the bike a strange-looking man stepped out of the shadows. He was wearing what looked like a traditional costume, with an animal hide draped around his shoulders. Mina watched him and Aksel talking and could tell that they were not speaking English or any other language she recognised.

'His name is Isku,' Aksel told her when the man got onto a sledge pulled by huskies and drove off into the night. Mina could feel the vibration of the dogs racing across the snow long after they had disappeared from sight. 'His people are called the Sami. They are reindeer herders and still live according to their ancient traditions. Isku's family are camping near here, and he came to the cabin to light the boiler and make a fire.'

Mina was thankful that Aksel hadn't planned to camp out in the sub-zero temperature. The log cabin looked well built to withstand the Arctic storms. Snow was piled high on the roof and a wisp of grey smoke curled up from the chimney. 'It's so pretty,' she murmured. 'It reminds me of the fairy-tale cottage of the Three Bears.'

Aksel unstrapped the bags from the back of the bike

and remembered to turn to her so that she could watch his mouth as he replied. 'There are no brown bears in Storvhal, and it is very rare that polar bears come this high into the mountains. Their territory is lower down near the coast. The largest predators you might see near the house are wolves.'

He noticed the fearful expression in her eyes as she hurried inside and thought it was probably a good thing she could not hear the howling of wolves close by.

Inside the cabin, a fire blazed in the hearth. Mina quickly started to overheat and had to strip out of the snowsuit and the layers of sweatshirts Aksel had lent her. Her face was flushed by the time she was down to her own shirt, and only then did she realise that she must have left her skirt in the four-by-four where she had got changed.

Aksel pulled off his boots and ski jacket and strode over to the drinks cabinet, where he sloshed neat spirit into a glass and gulped it down, savouring the fiery heat at the back of his throat. He glanced at Mina undressing in front of the fire and felt a tightening sensation in his groin. He recognised her shirt was the same one he had peeled from her body at the hotel in London the previous night. God knew where her skirt was, but he wished she would hurry up and put it on because the shirt only fell to her hips, leaving the creamy skin of her bare thighs above the lace band of her stockings exposed.

With her auburn hair tumbling around her shoulders, and her huge green eyes fixed on him, she was incredibly sensual, and Aksel wanted to forget that he was a prince and kiss her until she pleaded with him to pull her down onto the rug and strip off the remainder of her clothes.

He picked up a second glass and the bottle of liqueur

and walked over to join her in front of the fireplace. 'Here.' He half filled the glass and handed it to her.

Mina took a cautious sip of the straw-coloured liquid and choked. 'That's strong! What is it?'

'*Akevitt* is a traditional Scandinavian spirit. The Stor-vhalian version is flavoured with aniseed.'

A few sips of the fearsome drink would be likely to render her unconscious, Mina thought. She put the glass down on a table and took the battery charger out of her handbag.

'I need to plug this into an electrical socket to recharge the batteries for my hearing aids.'

Aksel frowned. 'There is no electricity at the cabin. The lamps are filled with oil, and the wood-burning stove heats the hot-water tank. The only modern convenience I keep here is a satellite phone so that my ministers can contact me if necessary. Don't you carry spare batteries for your hearing aids?'

'Both the sets I have with me are dead.' Mina had not anticipated being without her hearing aids. Her degree of hearing loss meant that she could hear certain sounds above a high decibel, but even if Aksel shouted at the top of his voice she would be unable to hear him. She chewed on her lower lip. 'I'm sorry I've spoiled your trip, but I'm going to have to ask you to take me back to civilisation.'

He shrugged. 'I can't take you anywhere. The heavy snowfall will have blocked the roads further down the valley, and it's snowing again.'

Aksel folded his arms across his chest and a nerve flickered in his jaw as he surveyed her half-undressed state. 'We could be trapped here for days,' he told her grimly.

CHAPTER SIX

MINA'S HEART SANK as she looked over to the window and saw the blizzard that was raging outside. Evidently they had reached the cabin just in time before the weather worsened.

Aksel slid his hand beneath her chin and tilted her face to his so that she could read his lips. 'Why did you come to Storvhal?'

Mina might not be able to hear the anger in his voice, but the rigid set of his jaw was an indication that his temper was on a tight leash. She had as much right to be angry about the photographs in the newspapers as him, she thought, her own temper flaring. His royal status had made them both a target for the paparazzi.

She focused on his question and decided to be honest. 'Before we left the hotel this morning you asked me to meet you in Paris.'

She paused, hoping that her voice did not sound too quiet or flat-toned. She felt self-conscious not being able to hear herself when she spoke, but speech therapy had taught her breathing techniques, and she took a steadying breath before continuing.

'You said that when we made love it had been perfect.' She stared into his eyes, daring him to deny it. 'But later, at the theatre, why did you walk away without listening to me?'

His eyes blazed. 'You tipped off the press that we spent the night together and used me for a publicity stunt. You know damn well the media hype that you are having an affair with a prince will raise your profile when you perform *Romeo and Juliet* in New York.'

Aksel's nostrils flared with the effort of controlling his anger. 'The journalist who was waiting for us outside the hotel this morning was the man I saw you looking at in the pub. He called out your name. You obviously know him so don't try to deny it.'

'His name is Steve Garratt.' Disdain for the journalist flickered across Mina's face. 'It's true that I recognised him when he came into the pub, but he's not a friend—in fact he's the reason I left early. I hate Garratt after he wrote a load of lies about me.'

She bit her lip. 'I know your PA has dug up all that regurgitated rubbish about my supposed affair with Dexter Price, but most of what has been written about me is untrue. I had no idea that Dexter was married or that his wife was ill. He had told me he was divorced and we grew close while we were working on a film in LA. But Steve Garratt accused me of having a torrid affair with him and made me out to be an unscrupulous marriage-wrecker.' Memories of how hurt and humiliated she had been left feeling by the journalist's assassination of her character, and by Dexter Price's refusal to defend her, churned inside Mina.

'No one ever listens to me,' she burst out. 'Not the press, or my father—or you. I may be deaf but that doesn't mean you can ignore me. I didn't tell *anyone* that you had invited me to your hotel. I didn't know when I met you that you are a prince.'

She wished her hearing aids were working. Standing close to Aksel and looking directly at his face so that she could read his lips created an intense atmosphere between them.

'You were just a man,' she said huskily, 'a handsome stranger. I couldn't take my eyes off you and I agreed to go to your hotel because you…overwhelmed me. Making love with you was the most beautiful experience I've ever had, and I…I thought it might have been special for you too—not just a one-night stand—because you asked me to spend a weekend in Paris with you.'

'It wasn't special.' Aksel ignored the stab of guilt he felt when he saw Mina's green eyes darken with hurt. He had been convinced that she had tipped off the press, but now he was beginning to wonder if he might have been wrong about her. Mina's feeling of disgust for the journalist who had taken photos of them outside the hotel had been evident on her expressive features. However, he reminded himself that she was a talented actress. And his instincts were not infallible. Once he had trusted Karena, he remembered grimly.

'Having sex with you was an enjoyable experience, but it was just sex,' he said bluntly, 'and I can't pretend that last night was anything more than a few hours of physical pleasure.'

It felt brutal to look into her eyes as he spoke such harsh words. Usually when he gave women the brush-off he avoided eye contact with them, he acknowledged with savage self-derision.

'Look…' He raked a hand through his hair, feeling unnerved by Mina's intent gaze. He felt as though she could see into his soul—and that was a dark place he never allowed anyone access to. He wanted to step away and put some space between them, but she needed to read his lips.

'I was carried away by the play. When I saw you on stage I was captivated by Juliet.' A nerve flickered in his jaw again. 'But Juliet isn't real—the woman I saw on stage was make-believe. It was my mistake to have forgotten that fact when we met in the pub.'

It was the only explanation Aksel could find for his behaviour that had been so out of character. In all the years he had been Storvhal's monarch he had never picked up a woman in a bar, never done anything to risk damaging his reputation as a responsible, moral prince who was the exact opposite of his father.

Helvete, he had even hidden his son's brief existence for the sake of the Crown. The secret gnawed like a cancer deep in Aksel's heart.

'I made love to Juliet,' he said, speaking carefully so that Mina would not mistake his words. 'For one night I forgot that I belong to an ancient royal dynasty. I was—as you said—just a man who desired a beautiful woman. But in the morning the fantasy ended. You are an actress, and I am a prince and ruler of my country. Our lives are set to follow different paths.'

Mina flinched at his bluntness. She had told herself she had come to Storvhal to clear her name and persuade Aksel that she had not told the press they had spent the night together. But in her heart she knew that her real reason for finding him was because she had felt a deep connection with him when they had made love, and she had been convinced that he had felt it too. His cold words seemed to disprove her theory.

'In that case why did you invite me to Paris?' she said stiffly.

'You looked upset when I told you that I was about to fly back to Storvhal. It seemed kinder to allow you to believe that I was interested in seeing you again, but we hadn't made a specific arrangement.'

Humiliation swept in a hot tide through Mina. Fool, she silently berated herself. She went cold when she remembered that Aksel had called her Juliet when he had kissed her. At the time she hadn't thought anything of it, but now she knew that he had been making love to a fantasy woman. He had been captivated by Juliet when he had watched her on stage, not by Mina Hart, the actress who played the role. According to Aksel, he hadn't felt any kind of connection to her. She had completely misread the situation.

Or had she?

Her mind flew back to the previous night, and the fierce glitter in Aksel's eyes just before he had climaxed powerfully inside her. For a few timeless moments when they had both hovered on the edge of heaven, she had sensed that their souls had reached out to each other and something indefinable and profound had passed between them.

Last night her hearing aids had been working. Could Aksel really have faked the raw emotion she had heard in the groan he'd made when he had come apart in her arms?

He lifted his glass to his lips and gulped down the fiery *akevitt* in a single swallow. For a split second, Mina saw him flick his gaze over her in a lightning sweep from her breasts down to her stocking tops, and she glimpsed a predatory hunger in his eyes before he glanced away.

Her heart thudded. Aksel might want to deny that he felt anything for her, but she had seen desire in his eyes. She couldn't shake off the feeling that when they had made love the previous night it *had* been special. She had not imagined his tenderness and she was convinced that they had shared more than a primitive physical act.

If he had spoken the truth when he'd stated that he'd just wanted sex with her, why hadn't he looked into her eyes as he had said it? And why was he still determined to avoid her gaze? Mina was adept at reading the subtle nuances of body language, and the tension she could feel emanating from Aksel suggested that he was not telling her the whole truth.

'So, you desired the fantasy Juliet, not Mina the real woman?' she demanded. When he did not look at her she put her hand on his jaw and felt the rough stubble scrape her palm as she turned his face towards her. His eyelashes swept down, but not before she had glimpsed something in his eyes that gave her courage. 'Prove it,' she said softly.

His dark blond brows drew together. 'What do you mean?'

'Kiss me and prove that I don't turn you on.'

'Don't be ridiculous.'

She stood up on tiptoe and brought her face so close to his that when he blinked she felt his eyelashes brush her skin. Being deprived of her hearing made her other senses more acute and she was aware of the unsteady rhythm of his heart as his breathing became shallow.

'What are you afraid of?' she said against his mouth. 'If I kiss you and you don't respond, then I'll know you're telling the truth and you don't want me.'

Are you crazy? taunted a voice inside her head. You won't dare do it! If he rejected her she would die of humiliation. But life had taught Mina that if you wanted something badly enough it was worth fighting for.

If she could only break through Aksel's icy detachment, she was convinced she would find the tender lover he had been last night. She hesitated with her lips centimetres from his and felt his warm breath whisper across her skin. He had tensed, but he hadn't pushed her away, and before she lost her nerve she closed the tiny gap between them and grazed her mouth over Aksel's.

He made no response, not even when she pressed her lips harder against his and traced the shape of his mouth with the tip of her tongue. Desperation gripped her and she began to wonder if last night really had been just a casual sexual encounter for him.

He stood unmoving, as unrelenting as rock, and in frustration she nipped his lower lip with her teeth. His chest lifted as he inhaled sharply, and Mina took advantage of his surprise to push her tongue into his mouth.

He curled his hands around her shoulders and tightened his grip until his fingers bit into her flesh. Mina tensed, expecting him to wrench his mouth free and cast her from him. But suddenly, unbelievably, he was kissing her back.

He moved his mouth over hers, tentatively at first— as if he was still fighting a battle with himself. Relief flooded through Mina and she pressed her body closer to him so that her breasts were crushed against the hard wall of his chest. And all the while she moved her lips over his with aching sensuality, teasing him, tempting him, until Aksel could withstand no more of the sweet torture.

A shudder ran through his huge frame. He loosened his grip on her shoulders and grabbed a fistful of her hair, holding her captive while he demonstrated his mastery and claimed control of the kiss.

It was no slow build-up of passion but a violent explosion that set them both on fire. Mina wondered if her bones would be crushed by Aksel's immense strength as he hauled her hard against him. But she did not care. His raw hunger made her melt into him as she responded to his demanding kisses with demands of her own. She curled her fingers into his hair and shaped his skull before tracing her fingertips over his sculpted face and the blond stubble covering his jaw.

He lifted her up and she wrapped her legs around his waist while he strode through the cabin and into the bedroom. Mina was vaguely aware of a fire burning in the hearth, and an oil lamp hanging on the wall cast a pool of golden light on the bed. The mattress dipped as Aksel laid her down and knelt over her. His eyes were no longer icy but blazed with desire that matched the molten heat coursing through Mina's veins.

She felt fiercely triumphant that her feminine instinct had been right and he wanted *her*. His excuse that he had desired the fantasy Juliet was patently untrue. The erratic thud of his heart gave him away, and his hands were unsteady as he tore open her shirt and pushed it over her shoulders. He slipped a hand beneath her back to unfasten her bra and tugged away the wisp of lace to lay bare her breasts. Mina watched streaks of dull colour flare on his sharp cheekbones, and, even before he had touched her breasts, her nipples tautened in response to the feral gleam in his eyes.

Aksel lifted his head and stared down at Mina. 'You are driving me insane, you green-eyed witch.'

She read his lips and smiled. 'Who am I?'

He frowned. 'You're Mina.'

'Not Juliet?'

Now he understood. 'You're a witch,' he repeated. She made him forget his royal status and his life of responsibility and duty. She made him forget everything but his urgent, scalding need that was unlike anything he'd ever felt for any other woman. He cupped her firm breasts in his hands and flicked his thumb pads across the puckered nipples, smiling when he heard her sharp intake of breath that told him her hunger was as acute as his.

Mina gave a choked cry as Aksel kissed her breasts, transferring his mouth from one nipple to the other and lashing the swollen peaks with his tongue until the pleasure was almost unbearable. She could feel his erection straining beneath his jeans and she fumbled with his zip, eager to take him inside her. There was something excitingly primitive about the way he jerked the denim over his hips; the fact that he was too impatient to possess her to undress properly.

She wrenched his shirt buttons open and spread the material so that she could run her hands through the wiry blond hairs that grew on his chest. He dragged her knickers down her legs, and then his big hand was between her thighs, spreading her wide, touching her where she ached to be touched.

Mina closed her eyes and fell into a dark, silent world where her other senses dominated. The feel of Aksel parting her and sliding a finger into her wetness was almost enough to make her come. She could smell his male scent; spicy aftershave mingled with the faint saltiness of sweaty and the indefinable fragrance of sexual arousal. When he moved his hand she arched her hips in mute supplication for him to push his finger deeper inside her.

It wasn't enough, not nearly enough. She curled her hand around his powerful erection and gave a little shiver of excitement when she remembered how he had filled her last night. She lifted her lashes and studied his chiselled features, and her heart stirred. He wasn't a stranger, she had known him for ever, and she wondered why she suddenly felt shy and nervous and excited all at the same time. She smiled, unaware that her eyes mirrored her confused feelings of hope and anticipation, but Aksel tensed, and silently cursed his stupidity.

Reality struck him forcibly. There were numerous reasons why he must not allow the situation to continue, but the most crucial was that he could not have unprotected sex with Mina. He never brought women to his private sanctuary and he did not keep condoms at the cabin. Perhaps Mina used a method of contraception, but years ago Karena had told him she was on the pill, and since then he had never trusted any woman. His gut ached with sexual frustration but, even though he was agonisingly tempted to plunge his throbbing erection between her soft thighs, he could not, would not, take the risk of making Mina pregnant.

A series of images flashed into his mind. He remembered looking into Finn's crib and pulling back the blanket that was half covering the baby's face. At first he had thought that his son was asleep. He'd looked so peaceful with his long eyelashes curling on his cheeks. The baby's skin was as flawless as fine porcelain—*but his little cheek had felt as cold as marble.*

Pain tore in Aksel's chest as he snatched a breath and forced air into his lungs that felt as though they had been crushed in a vice. There were other reasons why he should resist the siren call of Mina's body, not least the soft expression in her eyes that was a warning sign she hoped for something more from him than sex. He needed to make her understand that nothing was on offer. His emotions were as cold and empty as the Arctic tundra.

'Don't stop,' she murmured. Her words affected Aksel more than he cared to admit. He wondered if she could hear her own voice, or whether she was unaware of the husky pleading in her tone. He looked down at her slender body spread naked on his bed and could not bring himself to reject her when she was at her most vulnerable.

Helvete! How had he allowed things to get this far? He should have tried harder to resist her, but the sweet

sensuality of her kiss had driven him out of his mind.
She looped her arms around his neck and pulled his head
down, parting her lips in an invitation that Aksel found he
could not ignore. He slanted his mouth over hers, and desire ripped through him when he tasted her warm breath
in his mouth.

She twisted her hips restlessly, pushing her sex against
his hand. It would be cruel to deny her what she clearly
wanted, Aksel told himself. He could give her pleasure
even if he could give her nothing else.

The little moan she made when he slipped a second
finger inside her and moved his hand in a rhythmic dance
told him she was close to the edge. He forced himself to
ignore the burn of his own desire and concentrated on
Mina. Her head was thrown back on the pillows, her glorious hair spilling around her shoulders, and she closed
her eyes as tremors shook her body.

'Aksel…' Her keening cry tugged on his heart. He did
not understand why he wanted to gather her close and
rock her in his arms while the trembling in her limbs
gradually eased. The sight of tears sliding from beneath
her lashes filled him with self-loathing. She had flown all
the way to Storvhal to find him because—in her words—
she believed that last night had been special for both of
them. The brutal truth was going to hurt her feelings, he
acknowledged grimly as he withdrew from her.

Mina watched Aksel get up from the bed, and the
languorous feeling following her orgasm turned to excitement as she waited for him to strip off his jeans and
position himself over her. Despite the pleasure he had
just gifted her she was desperate to take his hard length
inside her. She did not recognise the wanton creature she
became with him. He had unlocked a deeply sensual side
to her nature that she had been unaware of, and she was

eager to make love with him fully and give him as much pleasure as he had given her.

But instead of removing the rest of his clothes he was pulling up the zip of his jeans. Her confusion grew when he walked over to the door. She sat up and pushed her hair out of her eyes. 'Aksel…what's wrong?'

He turned around so that she could see his face, and her heart plummeted at the coldness in his eyes. She watched his mouth form words that made no sense to her.

'This is wrong.' His eyes rested on her slender figure and rose-flushed face. 'You should not have come to Storvhal.'

Mina felt sick as the realisation sank in that he was rejecting her. 'Last night—' she began. But he cut her off.

'Last night was a mistake that I am not going to repeat.'

'Why?' Mina was unaware of the raw emotion in her voice, and Aksel schooled his features to hide the pang of guilt he felt.

She bit her lip. Her pride demanded that she should accept his rejection and try to salvage a little of her dignity, but she did not understand why he had suddenly backed off. 'Is it because I'm deaf? You desired me when you didn't know about my hearing loss,' she reminded him when he frowned. 'What am I supposed to blame for your sudden change of heart?'

'My heart was never involved,' he said bluntly. 'Learning of your hearing impairment is not the reason why I can't have sex with you again.'

'Then what is the reason?' The frustration Mina had felt as a child when she had first lost her hearing surged through her again now. She wished she could hear Aksel. It wasn't that she had a problem reading his lip, but not being able to hear his voice made her feel that there was a wide gulf between them.

'I can't have an affair with you. I am the Prince of Storvhal and my loyalty and duty must be to my country.'

Mina suddenly felt self-conscious that he was dressed and she was naked when she noticed his gaze linger on her breasts. She flushed as she glanced down at her swollen nipples—evidence that her body had still not come down from the sexual high he had taken her to—and tugged a sheet around her before she slid off the bed and walked towards him.

'I understand that you have many responsibilities.' She remembered the taxi driver saying that Aksel had needed to win the support of the Storvhalian people after his father had been an unpopular ruler. Aksel had admitted that, when they had made love last night, he had been able to briefly forget his royal status.

'You belong to an ancient royal dynasty, but surely the Storvhalian people accept that you are a man first, and a prince second?' she said softly.

She was shocked to see a flash of emotion in his eyes, but it disappeared before she could define it, and she wondered if she had imagined his expression of raw pain.

Aksel grimaced as he imagined how his grandmother would react to Mina's lack of understanding of his role as ruler of Storvhal. It was a role he had prepared for probably since he had taken his first steps. He remembered when he was a small boy, Princess Eldrun had insisted that he must not run through the palace but must walk sedately as befitted the future monarch. His whole life had been constrained by strict rules of protocol, and he had done his best to fulfil the expectations that his grandmother, his government ministers—the entire nation of Storvhal, it often felt like—had of him.

He had even kept secret his son's birth—and death.

He stared at Mina and hardened his heart against the

temptation of her beauty. 'I swore an oath promising my devotion to my country and my people. I will always be a prince first.'

'Do you place duty above everything because you feel you have to make up for the fact that your father wasn't a good monarch?'

He stiffened. 'How do you know anything about my father?'

She gave a wry smile. 'My father says that if you want to hear an honest opinion about politics or any other subject, talk to a taxi driver.'

The gentle expression in Mina's green eyes infuriated Aksel. She did not understand anything about his life. *The sacrifice he had made that would haunt him for ever.*

'Did the taxi driver you spoke to tell you that during my father's reign many of his own ministers supported a move to abolish the monarchy? There were incidents of civil unrest among the population and the House of Thoresen, who have ruled Storvhal for eight centuries, came close to being overthrown.

'My father betrayed Storvhal by selling off gold reserves and other valuable assets belonging to the country to fund his extravagant lifestyle. He was called the playboy prince for good reason and the Storvhalian population disliked that their ruler was setting a bad moral example.

'It has taken twelve years for me to win back the trust of my people.' Anger flashed in Aksel's eyes. 'But now, thanks to your wretched journalist friend and the photographs of me escorting an actress with a dubious reputation into my hotel, rumours abound that I lead a secret double life and I am a playboy like my father.'

Aksel knew as soon as he spoke that he was being unfair. The real blame lay with him. God knew what he had been thinking of when he had invited Mina to his hotel last night. The truth was he hadn't been thinking at all. He had been bewitched by a green-eyed sorceress and risked his reputation and the support of the Storvhalian people to satisfy his sexual desire for a woman whose own reputation, it turned out, was hardly without blemish.

Mina blanched as she read Aksel's lips. How dared he judge her based on what he had read about her in the newspapers? Good grief, she had only ever had one sexual relationship—two if she counted Aksel, she amended. But one night in his bed did not constitute a relationship—as he seemed determined to make clear. The unfairness brought tears to her eyes.

'At the risk of repeating myself, I didn't tell the press about us,' she said tautly. 'I discovered from bitter experience that the paparazzi prefer to print scandal and lies than the truth.'

Even with her talent for acting, could she really sound so convincing if she was lying? Aksel wondered. He had found the newspaper article about her affair with a married film director distasteful, but, hell, the paparazzi could make a vicar's tea party sound sordid.

Glimpsing the shimmer of her tears made him feel even more of a bastard than he'd felt when he had stopped making love to her. He wanted to look away before he drowned in her deep green eyes, but he forced himself to remain facing her so that she could watch his lips when he spoke.

'You should get some sleep. As soon as there's a break in the weather I want to get us off the mountain, and that might mean I'll have to wake you early in the morning. Put another log on the fire before you get into bed and you should be warm enough.'

'What about you?' Mina stopped him as he went to walk out of the room. 'Where are you going to sleep?'

'I'll make up a bed on the sofa in the living room.'

'I feel bad that I've taken your bed.' She hesitated, and glanced at the huge wooden-framed bed. 'It's a big bed and I don't mind sharing.'

'But I do.'

His glinting gaze made Mina feel sure he was mocking her. She flushed. 'Don't worry. I'd keep to my side of the mattress.'

He turned his head away, but not before her sharp eyes read the words on his lips that he had spoken to himself. 'I wish I could be certain that I could keep my hands off you, my green-eyed temptress.'

Mina felt confused as she watched him walk into the living room and pick up the bottle of fiery liqueur *akevitt* before he sprawled on the rug in front of the fire. She had not imagined the feral hunger in his eyes. But Aksel believed that he must put his duty to Storvhal above his personal desires. Perhaps that explained the aching loneliness she had glimpsed, before his lashes had swept down and hidden his expression, she mused as she climbed into the big bed and huddled beneath the covers.

CHAPTER SEVEN

THE FLAMES IN the hearth were leaping high into the chimney when Mina woke. The fire had burned down to embers during the night and she guessed that Aksel had thrown on more logs while she was sleeping. She slid out of bed and pulled back the curtains. It was not snowing at the moment, but the towering grey clouds looked ominous and Aksel's warning that they could be trapped at the cabin for days seemed entirely possible.

Although her watch showed that it was nine a.m. it was barely light. By the end of the month it would be polar night and the sun would not rise above the horizon until next year. The land was an Arctic wilderness: remote, beautiful and icy cold—a description that equally fitted the Prince of Storvhal, Mina thought ruefully.

A movement caught her attention, and she turned her head to see Aksel at the side of the house chopping logs with an axe. Despite the freezing temperature he was only dressed in jeans and a sweater. He paused for a moment to push his blond hair out of his eyes, and Mina's heart-rate quickened as she studied his powerful body. There was not an ounce of spare flesh on his lean hips, and his thigh muscles rippled beneath his jeans as he dropped the axe and gathered up an armful of logs.

Mina often rued her impulsive nature, but she could

not resist opening the window and scooping up a hand-ful of snow from the ledge. She took aim, and the snow-ball landed between Aksel's shoulder blades. He jerked upright, and she guessed he shouted something, but he was too far away for her to be able to read his lips. He must have heard her slam the window shut because he spun round and his startled expression brought a smile to her lips. It was heartening to know that he might be a prince but he was also a human being.

Having not brought any spare clothes with her, she had no alternative but to put on Aksel's shirt that he had taken off when he had started to make love to her the pre-vious night. The shirt came to midway down her thighs and, feeling reassured that she was at least half decently covered, she made a quick exploration of the cabin. She entered the large kitchen at the same moment that Aksel walked in through the back door, and stopped dead when she saw a snowball in his hands and a determined gleam in his eyes.

'No…!' She dodged too late and gave a yelp as the snowball landed in the centre of her chest. 'Don't you dare…!' Face alight with laughter, she backed away from him, her eyes widening when she saw he was holding a second snowball. She raced around the table but he caught her easily and grinned wickedly as he shoved snow down the front of her shirt.

'*Oh*…that's cold.' She gasped as the melting snow trickled down her breasts.

He slid his hand beneath her chin and tilted her face so that she could watch him speak. Amusement warmed his ice-blue eyes. 'You asked for it, angel.'

'That wasn't fair to bring snow into the house. Don't you know the rules of snowball fights?'

He shook his head. 'I've never had a snowball fight.'

'Never?' Mina stared out of the window at the snowy landscape. 'But you live in a land of snow and ice. When you were a child you must have had snowball fights with the other kids at school, and surely you built snowmen?'

'I didn't go to school, and I rarely played with other children.'

She could not hide her surprise. 'That's...sad. I know you are a prince, but in England the children of the royal family are educated at school. Didn't your parents think it was important for you to mix with other children of your own age?'

Aksel's smile faded at Mina's curiosity. 'My grandmother supervised my upbringing because my parents were busy with their own lives. I was taught by excellent tutors at the palace until I went to university when I was eighteen.'

The few years he had spent in England at Cambridge University had been the happiest of his life, Aksel thought to himself. He had enjoyed socialising with the other students who came from different backgrounds, and he had loved the sense of freedom and being able to lead a normal life away from the protocol of the palace. Even the press had left him alone, but that had all changed when his father had died and the new Prince of Storvhal had been thrust into the public spotlight.

Mina recalled something the taxi driver had told her. 'I heard that your mother is Russian, but the people of Storvhal didn't approve of your father's choice of bride.'

'Historically there was often tension between my country and Russia. Seventy years ago my grandfather signed a treaty with Norway, which means that the principality of Storvhal is protected by the Norwegian military.'

Aksel shrugged. 'It is true that my father's marriage

to my mother was not popular, particularly as my mother made it plain that she disliked Storvhal and preferred to be in Moscow. I grew up at the palace with my grandmother. My father spent most of his time with his many mistresses in the French Riviera, and I did not see either of my parents very often.'

Aksel's explanation that his grandmother had 'supervised' his upbringing gave Mina the impression that his childhood had been lacking love and affection. She pictured him as a solemn-faced little boy playing on his own in the vast royal palace.

'You said you have a sister.' She remembered he had mentioned a sibling.

'Linne is ten years younger than me, and she lived mainly with my mother. We were not close as children, although we have a good relationship now.'

'Does your sister live at the palace?'

'Sometimes, but at the moment she is on an Arctic research ship in Alaska. Linne is a glaciologist, which is the subject I studied at university before I had to return to Storvhal to rule the country.'

Although Mina could not hear Aksel's tone of voice, years of experience at lip-reading had given her a special understanding of body language and she glimpsed a hint of regret in his eyes. 'Do you wish you were a scientist rather than a prince?' she asked intuitively.

His expression became unreadable. 'It does not matter what I wish for. It was my destiny to be a prince and it is my duty to rule to the best of my ability.'

Mina nodded thoughtfully. 'I think you must have had a lonely childhood. I know what that feels like. My parents decided to send me to a mainstream school where I was the only deaf child, and I always felt apart from the other children because I was different. My sister was the only person who really understood how I struggled to fit in with my peers.' She gave a rueful smile. 'I don't know how I would have managed without Darcey. She was my best friend and my protector against the other kids who used to call me dumb because I was shy of speaking.'

Aksel gave her a puzzled look. 'In that case, why did you choose to become an actress?'

'All my family are actors. My father is often called the greatest Shakespearean actor of all times, but my mother is also amazingly talented. Performing in front of an audience is in my blood and I decided that I wasn't going to allow my loss of hearing to alter who I am or affect my choice of career.'

Mina sighed. 'I suppose I was determined to prove to my father that I could be a good actress despite being deaf. Dad was supportive, but I know he doubted that I would be able to go on the stage. I wanted to make him proud of me. But at the moment, he's furious,' she said ruefully, remembering Joshua Hart's explosive temper when she had met him at the Globe Theatre after she had spent the night with Aksel.

'Why is your father angry with you?' Why the hell did he care? Aksel asked himself impatiently. He told himself he did not want to hear about Mina's life, but he could not dismiss the image of her as a little girl, struggling to cope with her hearing impairment and feeling ostracised by the other pupils at school. He was glad her sister had stood up for her.

'Joshua was not impressed to see a photograph of me with a prince, and details about my supposed love-life, splashed across the front pages of the newspapers. I am his daughter and the lead actress in his production of *Romeo and Juliet,* and he feels that any sort of scandal

will reflect badly on the Hart family and on the play.'
She bit her lip. 'He accused me of turning Shakespeare
into a soap opera.'

Aksel frowned. 'Surely you told him it was not your
fault that you were snapped by the paparazzi?'

'Of course I did—but like you he didn't believe me,'
Mina said drily.

Aksel's jaw clenched. He felt an inexplicable anger
with Mina's father and wanted to confront Joshua Hart
and tell him that he should be supportive of his beautiful and talented daughter, who had faced huge challenges
after she had lost her hearing, with immense courage.

He stared at Mina and felt a fierce rush of desire at the
sight of her wet shirt—his shirt—clinging to her breasts.
The melting snowball had caused her nipples to stand
erect and he could see the hard tips and the dark pink
aureoles jutting beneath the fine cotton shirt.

Helvete! She had thrown what he had planned to be a
peaceful weekend into turmoil and the sooner he could
take her back down the mountain, the better for his peace
of mind.

'Linne left some spare clothes in the wardrobe. Help
yourself to what you need. There's plenty of hot water
if you want a shower, and food in the larder, if you're
hungry.' He grabbed his jacket. 'I'm going for a walk.'

'Do you think that's a good idea? It's snowing again.'

Aksel followed her gaze to the window and saw swirling white snowflakes falling from the sky. This was the
last time he would come to the cabin before winter set
in and he might not get another chance to visit his son's
grave. He could not explain to Mina that sometimes he
craved the solitude of the mountains.

'I won't be long,' he told her, and quickly turned away
from her haunting deep green gaze.

* * *

The pair of jeans and a thick woollen jumper belonging to
Aksel's sister that she found in the wardrobe fitted Mina
perfectly. With no hairdrier, she had to leave her hair to
dry into natural loose waves rather than the sleek style
she preferred. The only item of make-up she kept in her
handbag was a tube of lip gloss. She wondered ruefully
if Aksel liked the fresh-faced, girl-next-door look, and
reminded herself that it did not matter what she looked
like because he had made it quite clear that he regretted
sleeping with her and had no intention of doing so again.

Returning to the kitchen, she found rye bread, cheese
and ham in the larder. There was no electricity at the
cabin to power a fridge, but the walk-in larder was as
cold as a freezer. She could see no sign of Aksel when
she peered through the window that was half covered
by ice. His footprints had long since been obliterated by
the falling snow and in every direction stretched a bar-
ren, white wasteland.

It was more than two hours later when she spotted him
striding towards the cabin through snow that reached to
his mid-thighs. He stripped out of his snowsuit and boots
in the cloakroom and came into the kitchen shaking snow
out of his hair. Mina could not control her accelerated
heart-rate as she skimmed her eyes over his grey wool
sweater that clung to his broad shoulders and chest. His
rugged masculinity evoked a sharp tug of desire in the pit
of her stomach, but when she studied his face she almost
gasped out loud at the bleak expression in his eyes. She
wanted to ask him what was wrong—why did he look so
tormented? But before she could say anything, he walked
over to the larder and took out a bottle of *akevitt*, which
he opened, and poured a liberal amount of the straw-
coloured liqueur into a glass.

She glanced at the kettle on the gas stove. 'I was going to make coffee. Do you want some to warm you up?'

He dropped into a chair opposite her at the table so that she could see his face. His mouth curved into a cynical smile as he lifted his glass. 'This warms my blood better than coffee.'

Mina bit her lip. 'You were gone for a long time. I was starting to worry that something had happened to you.' When he raised his brows, she said quickly, 'You said there are wolves around here.'

'Wolves don't attack humans. In fact they very sensibly try to avoid them. I've been coming to the cabin since I was a teenager, and I know these mountains well.'

'Why do you come to such a remote place?'

He shrugged. 'It's the one place I can be alone, to think.'

'And drink.' Mina watched him take a long swig of the strong spirit, and glanced at the empty liqueur bottle on the draining board that he must have finished last night. 'Drinking alone is a dangerous habit.' She gave him a thoughtful look. 'What are you trying to forget?'

'Nothing.' He stood up abruptly and his chair fell backwards and clattered on the wooden floorboards. 'I come to the cabin for some peace and quiet, but clearly I'm not going to get either with you asking endless questions.'

As she watched him stride out of the room Mina wondered what raw nerve she had touched that had made him react so violently. Aksel gave the impression of being coldly unemotional, but beneath the surface he was a complex man, and she sensed that his emotions ran deep. Had something happened in his past that had caused him to withdraw into himself?

He strode back into the kitchen and leaned over her, capturing her chin in his hand and tilting her head up so she was forced to watch his mouth when he spoke. 'What makes you think you're a damn psychologist?'

'Actually, I have studied psychology, and I am a qualified drama therapist.'

Aksel stared into Mina's eyes and felt his anger drain out of him. She had come too close to the truth for comfort when she had suggested that he drank alcohol as a means of trying to block out the past. It wasn't that he wanted to forget Finn—never that. But sometimes the only way he could cope with the guilt that haunted him was to anaesthetise his pain with alcohol.

He frowned. 'What the hell is a drama therapist?'

'Drama therapy is a form of psychological therapy. Drama therapists use drama and theatre techniques to help clients with a wide range of emotional problems, from adults suffering from dementia through to children who have experienced psychological trauma.' Mina was unaware that her voice became increasingly enthusiastic as she explained about drama therapy, which was a subject close to her heart. 'In my role as a drama therapist, I use stories, role-play, improvisation and puppets—a whole range of artistic devices to enable children to explore difficult and painful life experiences.'

Aksel was curious, despite telling himself that he did not want to become involved with Mina. 'How do you combine being a drama therapist with your acting career?'

'I managed to fit acting work around my drama therapy training, but now that I am a fully qualified therapist I've been thinking about leaving acting to concentrate on a full-time career as a drama therapist.

'I love the stage. I'm a Hart and performing is in my blood. My father would be disappointed if I gave up acting,' Mina admitted. 'But I had been thinking for a while that I would like to do something more meaningful with my life. My sister Darcey trained as a speech therapist after seeing how vital speech therapy was for me when I became deaf. Being ill with meningitis when I was a child and losing my hearing was hugely traumatic. I feel that my experiences have given me an empathy with children who have suffered emotional and physical trauma.

'I didn't become an actress to be famous,' she told Aksel. 'I hate show business and the celebrity culture. When I made that film in America, and the media falsely accused me of having that affair, I saw a side to acting that I don't want to be a part of.

'The photos in the newspapers of me going into a hotel with you and leaving the next morning looking like I'd spent a wild night in your bed are the worst thing that could have happened as far as I'm concerned. The lies written about my relationship with Dexter Price have been reprinted and my reputation is in tatters.' She grimaced. 'You should have been honest when we met, and told me who you are. You might be a prince, but you're not my Prince Charming.'

Aksel's expression was thunderous, but he did not reply. Instead he grabbed the bottle of *akevitt* and walked out of the room, leaving Mina trembling inside and silently calling herself every kind of a fool, because while he had been leaning over her she had ached for him to cover her mouth with his and kiss her until the world went away.

By mid-afternoon the weak sun had slipped below the horizon once more and the snow clouds had been blown away to leave a clear, indigo-coloured sky. Aksel lit the oil lamps, and Mina was curled up in an armchair by the fire, reading. She had been surprised to find that many of the books in the book case were English.

'English is the second official language of Storvhal,' Aksel explained. 'When I became Prince I made it a law that schools must also teach children English. It is important for the population to retain a strong link to their culture, but Storvhal is a small country and we must be able to compete on world markets and communicate using a globally recognised language.'

He lowered his sketch pad where he had been idly drawing, and looked over at Mina. 'Why did your parents send you to a mainstream school?'

'I was eight when I lost my hearing and by that age I had learned speech and language. Mum and Dad were concerned that if I went to a specialist school for deaf children I might lose my verbal skills. But the hearing aids I wore then were not as good as the ones I have now, and I struggled—not so much with my school work, but I found it hard to be accepted by the other children.' She gave a wry smile. 'Luckily I learned to act, and I was good at pretending that I didn't care about being teased. Most people didn't realise that I could lip-read when they called me dumb or stupid.'

'You certainly proved your tormentors wrong by becoming a gifted actress.' Aksel frowned as he imagined the difficulties Mina had faced as a child—and perhaps still sometimes faced as an adult, he mused. She seemed to have no problem understanding him by reading his lips, but he wondered if she felt vulnerable without her hearing aids.

'I'd like to learn more about drama therapy,' he said. 'That type of specialised psychotherapy is not available in Storvhal, but I think it could help a group of children from a fishing village, whose fathers were all drowned when their boats sank during a storm at sea. Twenty families were affected, and the tragedy has touched everyone in the small village of Revika. The local school teachers and community leaders are doing what they can, but the children are devastated.'

'Such a terrible disaster is bound to have left the children deeply traumatised,' Mina murmured. 'Drama therapy could provide a way for the children to explore and express their feelings.'

She gave up trying to concentrate on her book. In truth she had spent more time secretly watching Aksel than reading. In the flickering firelight, his sculpted face was all angles and planes, and she longed to run her fingers through his golden hair.

She glanced at the sketch pad. 'What are you drawing?'

'You.' His answer surprised her.

'Can I see?'

He hesitated, and then shrugged and handed her the pad. Mina's eyes widened as she studied the skilful charcoal sketch of herself. 'You're very good at drawing. Did you study art?'

'Not formally. Drawing is a hobby I began as a child and I'm self-taught.'

Mina handed him back the sketch pad. 'You've made me prettier than I really am.'

'I disagree. I haven't been able to capture your beauty as accurately as I wish I could.'

Her heart leapt, but she firmly told herself she must have made a mistake when she'd read his lips, just as she must have mistaken the reflection of the firelight in his eyes for desire. The atmosphere between them pricked with an undercurrent of tension, and in an attempt to ignore it she turned her attention to a second sketch pad lying on the table.

'Do you mind if I have a look at your work?'

'Be my guest.'

The drawings were mainly done in charcoal or pencil and were predominantly of wildlife that she guessed Aksel had spotted in the mountains. There were several sketches of reindeer, as well as a lynx, an Arctic fox and some stunningly detailed drawings of wolves. The sketches were skilfully executed, but they were more than simply accurate representations of a subject; they had been drawn with real appreciation for wildlife and revealed a depth of emotion in Aksel that he kept hidden in all other aspects of his life.

He was an enigma, Mina thought with a sigh as she closed the sketch pad. She stood up and carried the pad over to Aksel to put back on the shelf, but as she handed it to him a loose page fell out onto the floor. She leaned down to pick it up, but he moved quickly and snatched up the drawing. However he had not been quick enough to prevent Mina from seeing the drawing of a baby. She guessed the infant was very young, perhaps only a few weeks old, she mused, thinking of her sister's twin boys when they had been newborns.

Her eyes flew to Aksel's face. She wanted to ask him about the drawing—a baby seemed an unusual subject for him to have sketched. But something in his expression made her hesitate. His granite-hard features showed no emotion but he seemed strangely tense, and for a second she glimpsed a look of utter bleakness in his eyes that caused her to take a sharp breath.

'Aksel…?' she said uncertainly.

'Leave it, Mina.'

She could not hear him but she sensed his tone had

been curt. He deliberately turned away from her as he slipped the drawing inside the cover of the sketch pad and placed the book on the shelf.

Her confusion grew when he turned off the oil lamps so that the room was dark, apart from the orange embers of the fire flickering in the hearth. Unable to see Aksel's face clearly to read his lips, Mina stiffened when he put a hand on her shoulder and steered her over to the window. But the sight that met her eyes was so spectacular that everything else flew from her mind.

She had heard about the natural phenomenon known as the aurora borealis but nothing had prepared her for the awe-inspiring light show that filled the sky. Swirling clouds of greens and pinks performed a magical dance. Mystical spirits, shimmering and ethereal, cast an eerie glow that illuminated the sky and reflected rainbow colours on the blanket of white snow beneath.

Mina vaguely recalled, from a geography lesson at school, that the aurora—sometimes called the Northern Lights—were caused by gas particles in the earth's atmosphere colliding, and the most stunning displays could only be seen at the north and south poles. But the reason why the aurora took place did not seem important. She was transfixed by the beauty of nature's incredible display and felt humbled and deeply moved that she was lucky enough to witness something so magnificent. As she stared up at the heavens the tension seeped from her body and she unconsciously leaned back against Aksel's chest.

Aksel drew a ragged breath as he struggled to impose his usual icy control over his emotions. Seeing the picture of Finn had been a shock and he'd felt winded, as though he had been punched in his gut. He hadn't known the drawing was tucked in the sketch pad. He must have put it there years ago, but he remembered sketching his son while the baby had been asleep in his crib.

His little boy had been so beautiful. Aksel took another harsh breath and felt an ache in the back of his throat as he watched the glorious light spectacle outside the window. He had seen the aurora many times but he never failed to be awed by its other-worldly beauty. It gave him some comfort to know that Finn was up here on the mountain. If there was a heaven, then this remote spot, with the aurora lighting up the sky, was surely the closest place to paradise.

He recalled the puzzled expression in Mina's eyes when she had seen the sketch. It had been obvious that she was curious about the identity of the baby. What shocked him was that for a crazy moment he had actually contemplated telling her about Finn.

He frowned. Why would he reveal his deepest secret to her when he was not certain that he could trust her? Why, after so many years of carrying his secret alone, did he long to unburden his soul to this woman? Perhaps it was because he recognised her compassion, he brooded. How many people would choose to give up a successful acting career to become a psychotherapist working with traumatised children?

But he doubted Mina would be sympathetic if he revealed the terrible thing he had done. For eight years he had hidden his son's birth from the Storvhalian people, his friends, and even from his grandmother. He had believed he was doing the best thing for the monarchy, but his guilt ate away at him. He did not deserve Mina's compassion, and he had not deserved her mind-blowing sensuality when they had made love.

His mind flew back to two nights ago, and the memory of her generosity and eagerness to please him caused subtle warmth to flow through his veins, melting the ice inside him. He became aware of her bottom pressing against his thighs and an image came into his mind of the peachy perfection of her bare buttocks. The warmth in his veins turned to searing heat and the throb of desire provided a temporary respite from the dull ache of grief in his heart.

In the darkened room he could see the profile of her lovely face and the slender column of her throat. Last night it had taken all his will power to walk away from her, but right now, when his emotions felt raw, it was becoming harder to remember why he must resist her.

He wanted to press his lips to her white neck, wanted it so badly that his fingers clenched and bit into her shoulder, causing her to make a startled protest. She turned her head towards him and her mouth was mere centimetres from his, offering an unbearable temptation. Surely there was no harm in kissing her? He felt a tremor run through her and knew she was waiting for him to claim her lips. He dipped his head lower so that his mouth almost grazed hers. One kiss was all he would take, he told himself.

One kiss would not be enough, a voice inside his head taunted. If he kissed her he would be bewitched by her sensual magic. But the reason he had fought his desire for her last night had not changed. He could not have unprotected sex with her and risk her conceiving his child. Nor would it be fair to allow her to think that he wanted a relationship with her. The brutal truth was that he wanted to lose himself in her softness and forget temporarily the past that haunted him.

Mina stumbled as Aksel snatched his hand from her shoulder. She did not know what had happened to make him move abruptly away from her when seconds earlier he had been about to kiss her. Feeling dazed by the sudden change in him, she watched him light an oil lamp. In the bright gleam it emitted his face was expressionless, his blue eyes as cold as the Arctic winter. He took a step closer to her—reluctantly, she sensed—so that she could read his lips.

'Go and put your snowsuit on,' he instructed. 'The sky is clear, which means we shouldn't get any more snow for a few hours, and I'm going to risk making a dash down the mountain.'

Aksel could not make it plainer that he did not want to spend any more time with her than was necessary. She could not cope with him blowing hot one minute and cold the next, Mina thought angrily. Coming to Storvhal had been an impulsive mistake, and the sooner she could fly home and forget she had ever met a prince, the better.

CHAPTER EIGHT

THE JOURNEY DOWN the mountain was thankfully uneventful. The snow that had fallen earlier in the day had frozen into an ice sheet, which reflected the brilliant gleam of the moon and the countless stars suspended in the dark-as-ink sky.

Halfway down, they swapped the snowmobile for the four-by-four. As Aksel had predicted, the snow was deep in the valley, but snow ploughs had cleared the roads and eventually they reached Storvhal's capital city Jonja and saw the tall white turrets of the royal palace rising out of the dense fog that blanketed the city.

Mina turned to him. 'Why have you brought me here? I thought you were taking me straight to the airport.'

Aksel was forced to stop the car in front of the ornate palace gates while they slowly swung open. He turned his head towards her so that she could watch his lips move. 'All flights are grounded due to freezing fog. You'll have to stay at the palace tonight.'

A bright light flared outside the window. 'What the hell...?' Aksel's jaw tightened when another flashbulb exploded and briefly filled the car with stark white light. 'I hadn't expected press photographers to be here,' he growled. The gates finally parted and he put his foot down on the accelerator and gunned into the palace grounds.

'You'd better prepare yourself for the reception committee,' he told her tersely as he parked by the front steps and the palace doors were opened from within.

'What do you mean?'

'You'll see.'

As Aksel escorted Mina into the palace she understood his curious comment. Despite it being late at night, a dizzying number of people were waiting in the vast entrance hall to greet the prince. Courtiers, palace guards and household staff dressed in their respective uniforms bowed as Aksel walked past. There were also several official-looking men wearing suits, and Mina recognised the young man with round glasses as Aksel's personal assistant, Benedict Lindburg. She knew there must be a buzz of conversation because she could see people's lips moving, but it was impossible for her to lip-read and keep track of what anyone was saying.

The crippling self-consciousness that Mina had felt as a child gripped her now. She hoped no one had spoken to her and thought she was being rude for ignoring them. Instinctively she kept close to Aksel and breathed a sigh of relief when he escorted her into a room that she guessed was his office and closed the door behind him so that they were alone.

Aksel's eyes narrowed on Mina's tense face. 'I did warn you,' he said, stepping closer to ensure that she could see his mouth moving. 'It must be difficult to lip-read when you are in a crowd. At least you can charge up your hearing-aid batteries while you are at the palace.'

'What do all those people want?'

He shrugged. 'There is always some matter or other that my government ministers believe requires my urgent attention.' His life was bound by duty, but for a few moments Aksel imagined what it would be like if he were not a prince and were free to live his life as he chose, free to make love to the woman whom he desired more than any other.

Daydreams were pointless, he reminded himself. 'The fog is forecast to clear by tomorrow afternoon and a member of my staff will drive you to the airport and book you onto a flight,' he told her abruptly. 'Whereabouts in London do you live?'

'Notting Hill—but I won't go back home until the paparazzi have grown bored of stalking my flat.'

Aksel frowned. 'Do you mean you were hounded by journalists?'

'My friend Kat saw a group of them outside my front door. She won't mind if I stay with her for a few days—and hopefully the furore about my alleged affair with a prince will die down soon.' She gave him a wry look. 'Anyway, it's not your problem, is it? You are protected from press intrusion in your grand palace.'

Although that was not absolutely true, Mina acknowledged as she remembered the press photographers who had been waiting at the palace gates. She wondered if Aksel resented living his life in the public eye, subjected to constant media scrutiny. In some ways this beautiful palace was his prison, she realised.

Aksel appeared tense. 'I'm sorry your life has been disrupted. I *should* have told you who I am when we first met.'

'Why didn't you?'

He hesitated. 'You might have thought I was lying to impress you and refused to have dinner with me.'

Mina stared at his mouth, feeling frustrated that she

could not hear him. 'Would you have cared if I had refused?'

His tugged his hand through his hair until it stood up in blond spikes. 'Yes.'

Her frustration boiled over. 'Then why did you leave me alone at the cabin? You let me think you didn't want me.' She bit her lip. The memory of Aksel's rejection felt like a knife wound in her heart. It had hurt far more than when she had discovered that Dexter had lied to her, she realised with a jolt of shock. How was that possible? She had been in love with Dex, but she certainly could not have fallen in love with Aksel after two days.

The glimmer of tears in Mina's eyes made Aksel's gut twist. 'My role as prince comes with expectations that would make it impossible for us to have a relationship,' he said roughly.

'That's another thing you forgot to mention when you took me to bed.'

'*Damn it*, Mina.' He caught hold of her as she turned away, and spun her round to face him. 'Damn it,' he growled as he pulled her into his arms and crushed her mouth beneath his. He couldn't fight the madness inside him, couldn't control his hunger, his intolerable need to possess her beautiful body and make her his as she had been two nights ago.

A knock on the door dragged Aksel back to reality. Reluctantly he lifted his mouth from Mina's and felt guilty when he stared into her stunned eyes. He couldn't blame her for looking confused, when he did not understand his own behaviour. His carefully organised life was spinning out of control and cracks were appearing in the ice wall he had built around his emotions.

He knew she could not have heard the knock on the door, but the interruption had reminded him that he had no right to kiss her. He dropped his arms to his sides. 'I'm needed,' he told her, before he strode across the room and yanked open the door. His mood was not improved by the sight of his chief advisor. 'Can't it wait, Harald?' he demanded curtly.

The elderly advisor frowned as he looked past Aksel and saw Mina's dishevelled hair and reddened lips. 'I'm afraid not, sir. I must talk to you urgently.'

Duty must take precedence over his personal life, Aksel reminded himself. However much he wanted to sweep Mina into his arms and carry her off to his bed, he would not allow desire to make a weak fool of him as it had his father.

He stepped back to allow his chief advisor into the room, and rang a bell to summon a member of the palace staff. When a butler arrived, Aksel said to Mina, 'Hans will show you to your room, and tomorrow he will escort you to the airport.'

It was impossible to believe that his cold eyes had blazed with desire when he had kissed her a few moments earlier, Mina thought. She sensed that his return to being a regal and remote prince had something to do with the presence of the grey-haired, grey-suited man who was regarding her with a disapproving expression.

She was not an actress for nothing, she reminded herself. Her pride insisted that she must hold onto her dignity and not allow Aksel to see that he had trampled on her heart.

She gave him a cool smile and felt a flicker of satisfaction when he frowned. 'Goodbye, Aksel.' She hesitated, and gave him a searching look. 'I hope one day you'll realise that you can't pay for your father's mistakes for ever. Even a prince has a right to find personal happiness.'

As Aksel watched Mina walk out of the room he was

tempted to go after her and kiss her until she lost her infuriating air of detachment and melted in his arms as she had before they had been interrupted by his chief advisor. He knew she was a talented actress—so who was the real Mina? Was she the woman who had kissed him passionately a few minutes ago, or the woman who had sauntered out of his office without a backwards glance?

'Sir?' Harald Petersen's voice dragged Aksel from his frustrated thoughts. 'Benedict Lindburg has informed me that members of the press were at the palace gates when you arrived and they may have seen that Miss Hart was with you.'

'Undoubtedly they saw her,' Aksel said grimly, recalling the glare of camera flashbulbs that had shone through the windscreen of the four-by-four.

The chief advisor cleared his throat. 'Then we have a problem, sir. The Storvhalian people might overlook your affair with an actress in London, but I fear they will be less accepting when it becomes public knowledge that you are entertaining your mistress at the palace as your father used to do. Some sections of the press have already made unfavourable comparisons between you and Prince Geir. The last thing we want is for you to be labelled a playboy prince.'

Harald Petersen sighed. 'You have proved yourself to be a good ruler these past twelve years, but the people want reassurance that the monarchy will continue. For that reason I urge you to consider taking a wife. There are a number of women from Storvhalian aristocratic families who would be suitable for the role. If you give the people a princess, with the expectation that there will soon be an heir to the throne, you are certain to increase support for the House of Thoresen and ensure the stability of the country.'

'What if I do not wish to get married?' Aksel said curtly.

His chief advisor looked shocked. 'It is your duty, sir.'

'Ah, yes, *duty.*' Aksel's jaw hardened. 'Don't you think I have sacrificed enough in the name of duty? For pity's sake,' he said savagely, 'I cannot speak my son's name in public, or celebrate his tragically short life.' He felt a sudden tightness in his throat and turned abruptly away from the older man. 'I cannot weep for Finn,' he muttered beneath his breath.

When he swung back to his advisor his hard-boned face showed no emotion. 'I will consider your suggestion, Harald,' he said coolly. 'You may leave me now.'

'What are we to do about Miss Hart?' Harald said worriedly.

'I'll think of something. Tell Benedict that I do not want to be disturbed for the rest of the evening.'

The following morning, Aksel stood in his office staring moodily out of the window at the snow-covered palace gardens. He tried to ignore the sudden acceleration of his heart-rate when there was a knock on the door and the butler ushered Mina into the room.

'Are your hearing aids working?' he asked as she focused her deep green gaze on his face.

'Yes, I can hear you.' She bit her bottom lip—something Aksel had noticed she did when she was feeling vulnerable. 'Why did you want to see me? I'm about to go to the airport.'

'There's been a change of plan,' he said abruptly. 'We need to talk.'

Mina suddenly realised that they were not alone. The elderly man she had seen the previous evening was in

Aksel's office and the censure in his cold stare made her flush.

'I don't believe we have anything more to say to one another,' she said bluntly.

The older man stepped towards her. 'Miss Hart, you clearly do not understand palace protocol. The prince wishes to talk to you, and you must listen.'

Aksel cursed beneath his breath. 'Mina, may I introduce the head of my council of government and chief advisor, Harald Petersen?' He glanced at the older man. 'Harald, I would like to speak to Miss Hart alone.

'Please forgive his brusqueness,' he said to Mina when the advisor had left the room. 'Harald is an ardent royalist who worked hard to help me restore support for the monarchy after my father's death. He is naturally concerned that I should not do anything which might earn the disapproval of the Storvhalian people.'

'He must have had a fit when he saw the photographs in the newspapers of you with an actress who the paparazzi labelled the Hollywood Harlot,' Mina said bleakly.

Aksel gave her a searching look. 'Why didn't you sue the newspapers for publishing lies about you?'

'I didn't have the kind of money needed to fight a legal battle with the press, and Dexter refused to deny that we were lovers because the scandal gave publicity to the film. I hoped that the story would be forgotten—and it was until I was photographed with a prince.

'What did you want to talk to me about?' Mina hadn't expected to see Aksel again and was struggling to hide her fierce awareness of him. It didn't help that he looked devastatingly sexy in a pale grey suit and navy-blue silk shirt. She longed to reach out and touch him.

Instead of responding to her question, he said roughly, 'You look beautiful. That dress suits you.'

'I feel awful for wearing your sister's clothes without her knowledge.' She glanced down at the cream cashmere dress that a maid had brought to her room that morning. 'The maid said that my skirt and blouse were being laundered, and I could borrow some clothes belonging to your sister. I'll return the dress and shoes as soon as I get back to London.'

'Don't worry about it. Linne is often sent samples from designers, but she rarely wears any of the clothes. Cocktail dresses aren't very useful on an Arctic research ship,' Aksel said drily.

He dragged his gaze from Mina's slender legs that were enhanced by three-inch stiletto-heel shoes. She had swept her long auburn hair into a loose knot on top of her head, with soft tendrils framing her face, and looked elegant and so breathtakingly sexy that Aksel was seriously tempted to lock his office door, sweep the pile of papers off his desk and make love to her on the polished rosewood surface.

He forced himself to concentrate on the reason he had called her to his office. 'You need to see this,' he said, handing her a newspaper.

Frowning, Mina took it from him and caught her breath when she saw the photograph on the front page of her and Aksel when they had arrived at the palace the previous evening. The photo of them sitting in the four-by-four showed them apparently staring into each other's eyes, but in fact she had been focused on his mouth because at the time her hearing aids hadn't been working and she had needed to read his lips.

Her frown deepened as she read the headline.

Royal Romance—has the Prince finally found love?

'I don't understand. I know there was speculation that we are having an affair, but why would the press suggest that our relationship is serious?'

'Because I brought you to the palace,' Aksel said tersely. 'You are the first woman I have ever invited here. The press don't usually camp outside the palace gates but I should have guessed they would want to follow up the story that we are having affair. If I had known the photographers were waiting when we came down from the mountains I would have arranged for you to spend the night at a hotel.'

It was what he *should* have done, Aksel acknowledged. But his conscience had refused to leave her at a hotel in a strange country when he knew how vulnerable she felt without her hearing aids.

Mina skimmed the paragraph beneath the headline. 'How did the journalist who wrote this know that I have recently qualified as a drama therapist?' Her eyes widened as she continued reading. 'It says here that you invited me to Storvhal so that I could help the children from the village of Revika whose fathers drowned when their fishing fleet was hit by a terrible storm.'

She lowered the newspaper and glared at Aksel. 'What's going on?'

'Damage limitation,' he said coolly. 'The palace press office released certain details about you, including that you are a drama therapist.

'I've explained that my father's reputation as a playboy prince made him deeply unpopular,' he continued, ignoring the stormy expression in Mina's eyes. 'I cannot risk people thinking that I am like him, and that you are my casual mistress. It will be better if the population believe that I am in a serious relationship with a compassionate drama therapist who wishes to help the children of Revika.'

Mina shook her head. 'I refuse to be part of any subterfuge. You'll have to give a statement to the press explaining that they have made a mistake and we are not in a relationship.'

'Unfortunately that is not an option when the photograph of us entering the palace together is a clear indication that we are lovers. Some of the papers have even gone so far as to suggest that the palace might soon announce a royal betrothal.'

Her jaw dropped. 'You mean…people believe we might get married? That's ridiculous.'

'As my chief advisor often reminds me—the country has long hoped that I will marry and provide an heir to the throne,' Aksel said drily.

'I thought you were expected to choose a Storvhalian bride?'

'I don't think the people would mind what nationality my wife is. It's true that my Russian mother was not popular, but she made it clear that she disliked Storvhal and had no time for the people she was supposed to rule with my father. Your offer to help Revika's children has gone down well in the press. The tragedy of the fishing-fleet disaster has aroused the sympathy of the whole nation and your desire to help the bereaved children appears to have captured the hearts of the Storvhalian people.'

'But I didn't offer to visit the children. You gave the press false information,' Mina said angrily. 'I mean, of course I would like to help them, but my flight to London leaves in an hour.'

'Your ticket has been cancelled. We will have to go along with the media story of a royal romance for a while,' Aksel said coolly. 'In a few weeks, when you go to New

York to perform on Broadway, we'll announce that sadly, due to the pressures of your acting career, we have decided to end our relationship.'

Mina sensed that the situation was spiralling out of her control. 'You've got it all worked out, haven't you?'

'I held an emergency meeting with my chief ministers this morning to discuss the best way to deal with the situation.'

'Had it occurred to you that I might not want to pretend to be in love with you?' she demanded coldly.

His eyes showed no emotion. 'Allowing people to think we are romantically involved could be beneficial to both of us. This afternoon we will visit the village of Revika to meet the children whose fathers were killed in the disaster. It will be a good PR exercise.'

Mina was shocked by his heartless suggestions. 'You can't use those poor children for a…a publicity stunt.'

'That isn't the only reason for the visit. I have spoken to the headmistress of the school in Revika. Ella Holmberg is enthusiastic about the idea of using drama therapy to help the bereaved children. She is concerned that without help to come to terms with their loss, they could suffer long-term emotional damage.'

'That's certainly true,' Mina admitted.

'It's also true that favourable publicity would improve your image and might make people forget the scandal surrounding your relationship with a married film director in America,' Aksel said smoothly.

'I'm not going to visit the children just to improve my image. That's a disgusting suggestion.' Mina marched over to the door. 'I'm sorry, but I'd prefer to stick to the original plan and leave Storvhal. I'm sure the press interest in us will eventually die down and I refuse to pretend that we are romantically involved. I can't bear to have my personal life made public again,' she said huskily.

'What about the fishermen's children?' Aksel's voice stopped her as she was about to walk out of his office. 'They have been desperately affected by the tragedy. I thought you said you had trained as a drama therapist because losing your hearing when you were a child gave you a special empathy with traumatised children? You told me you wanted to do something meaningful with your life—and this is your chance.' He crossed the room and stood in front of her, tilting her chin so that he could look into her eyes. 'I am asking you to come to Revika for the children's sake.'

His words tugged on Mina's conscience. She felt torn between wanting to leave Aksel before she got hurt, and sympathy for the children whose lives had been shattered by the loss of their fathers. It was possible that they might benefit from drama therapy and it would be selfish of her to refuse Aksel's request to visit the children with him.

She looked away from him and her heart thudded beneath her ribs as she made a decision that she hoped she would not regret. 'I'll come with you today to make an assessment of how best to help the children. But it's likely they will need a programme of drama therapy lasting for several months.'

Aksel gave a satisfied nod. 'There is one other thing. My grandmother has asked to meet you.' Sensing Mina's surprise, he explained. 'When Princess Eldrun saw the photograph of us in today's newspapers she was dismayed because the picture reminded her of how my father had been a playboy during his reign and an unpopular monarch. My grandmother is old and frail, and to avoid upsetting her I reassured her that we are in a serious relationship.'

'I can't believe you did that!' Mina's temper flared. 'It seems awful to lie to your grandmother, even to protect her from being upset. I've told you I don't feel comfortable with the idea of fooling people, and I can't pretend to your grandmother that I'm in love with you.'

'No?' He moved before she guessed his intention and shot his arm around her waist as he lowered his head to capture her mouth. Mina stiffened, determined not to respond to him, but her treacherous body melted as he deepened the kiss and it became flagrantly erotic and utterly irresistible. With a low groan she parted her lips beneath his, but when she slid her arms around his neck he broke the kiss and stepped back from her.

'That was a pretty convincing performance,' he drawled. 'I have no doubt my grandmother will believe that you are smitten with me.'

She blushed and clenched her hand by her side, fighting a strong urge to slap the mocking smile from his face. 'You were very convincing yourself.' She was shocked to see colour rising on his cheeks. The flash of fire in his eyes told her that he was not as immune to her as he wanted her to believe, and she was certain he could not have faked the raw passion in his kiss.

'Perhaps we won't have to lie?' she murmured.

His eyes narrowed. 'What do you mean?'

She looked at him intently and noted that he dropped his gaze from hers. 'Who's to say that a relationship won't develop between us while we are pretending to be in love?'

'I say,' Aksel told her harshly. 'It won't happen, Mina, so don't waste your time looking for something that will never exist.' He breathed in the light floral scent of her perfume and felt his gut twist. 'I'm different from other people. I don't feel the same emotions.'

'Is it because you're a prince that you think you should put duty before your personal feelings—or is there another reason why you suppress your emotions?' she asked intuitively.

The image of Finn's tiny face flashed into Aksel's mind. The memory of his son evoked a familiar ache in his chest. He equated love with loss and pain and he did not want to experience any of those feelings again.

'I don't have any emotions to suppress,' he told Mina brusquely. 'I'm empty inside and the truth is I don't want to change.'

CHAPTER NINE

SHE MUST HAVE been mad to have agreed to Aksel's crazy plan to pretend that their relationship was serious, Mina thought for the hundredth time. The only reason she had done so was because she wanted the chance to try with drama therapy to help the bereaved children from the fishing village, she reminded herself.

They were on their way to Revika and the car was crossing a bridge that spanned a wide stretch of sea between the mainland and an island where the fishing village was situated. Although it was early afternoon the sun was already sinking behind the mountains and the sky was streaked with hues of gold and pink that made the highest peaks look as though they were on fire.

But the stunning views out of the window did not lessen Mina's awareness of Aksel's firm thigh pressed up against her. The scent of his aftershave evoked memories of him making love to her, when she had breathed in the intoxicating male fragrance of his naked body. It was a relief when they arrived in the fishing village, but her relief was short-lived when she saw the hordes of press photographers and television crews waiting outside the community hall to snap pictures of the prince and the woman who they speculated might become his princess.

As they stepped out of the car Aksel slid his arm

around her waist. For a moment she was glad of his moral support but she quickly realised that his actions were for the benefit of the press. When he looked deeply into her eyes she knew it was just an act, and as soon as they walked into the community hall she pulled away from him, silently calling herself a fool for wishing that his tender smile had been real.

They were greeted by the headmistress of the school where most of the children affected by the tragedy were pupils. 'The children are pleased that you have come to spend time with them again,' Ella Holmberg said to Aksel. 'They look forward to your visits.' Noticing Mina's look of surprise, she explained, 'Prince Aksel has come to Revika every week since the fishing fleet was destroyed in the storm. Many of the children whose fathers drowned are suffering from nightmares and struggling to cope with their grief. I haven't mentioned that you are a therapist,' she told Mina. 'I've simply said that you are a friend of Prince Aksel.'

The first thing that struck Mina as she walked into the community hall was the silence. There were more than thirty children present, and many of the fishermen's widows. Their sadness was tangible and would take months and years to heal, but Mina hoped that drama therapy might help the children to voice their feelings.

To her amazement, the minute Aksel stepped into the room and greeted the children he changed from the cold and remote prince she had seen at the palace and revealed a gentler side to his nature that reminded her of the man she had met in London. In order to assess the best way to help the children, Mina knew she must first win their trust, and she was pleasantly surprised when Aksel joined in the games she organised.

By the end of the afternoon the hall was no longer silent

but filled with the sound of chattering voices, and even tentative laughter. Mina sat on the floor with the children grouped around her. 'In the next game, we are going to pretend that we are actors on a stage,' she told them. 'Instead of speaking, we need to show the audience what emotions we are feeling. For instance, how would we show that we are happy?'

'We would laugh, and dance,' suggested a little girl.

'Okay, let me see you being happy.' Mina gave the children a few minutes of acting time. 'How would we show that we are feeling angry?'

'We would have a grumpy face,' said a boy, 'and stamp our feet.'

The mood in the hall changed subtly as the children expressed anger. Many of them stamped loudly on the wooden floor and the sound was deafening, but Mina encouraged them to continue. 'It's okay to be angry,' she told them. 'Sometimes we lock our feelings inside us instead of letting those feelings out.'

On the other side of the room, Aksel felt a peculiar tightness in his throat as he listened to Mina talking to the children. She seemed to understand the helpless fury that was part of grief, just as he understood what it felt like to lock emotions deep inside. He found her depth of compassion touching, but it was part of her job, he told himself.

At the end of the session the headmistress came over to speak to Mina. 'The children are having fun for the first time since the tragedy. You've achieved so much with them after just one visit.'

'I would love to spend more time with them,' Mina said softly. 'I believe that drama therapy sessions over a few months would be very beneficial in helping to unlock their emotions.'

She glanced across the room at Aksel and wondered what feelings he kept hidden behind his enigmatic façade. He was chatting to a widow of one of the fishermen. The woman was cradling a tiny baby and she held the infant out to Aksel. To Mina's shock, he seemed for a split second to recoil from the baby. His face twisted in an expression of intense pain and although she had no idea why he had reacted so strangely she instinctively wanted to help him and hurried across the room to stand beside him.

'What a beautiful baby,' she said to the child's mother. The baby was dressed in blue. 'Would you mind if I held your son?'

The woman smiled and placed the baby in Mina's arms. She was conscious that Aksel released his breath on a ragged sigh, and, shooting him a glance, she noticed beads of sweat on his brow. She supposed that the prospect of holding a tiny baby would be nerve-racking for a man who had no experience of children—but his extreme reaction puzzled her.

The moment passed, Aksel turned to talk to another parent and Mina handed the baby back to his mother and walked back to rejoin Ella Holmberg, but she was still curious about why Aksel had seemed almost afraid to hold the baby.

Ella followed Mina's gaze to him. 'The prince is gorgeous, isn't he? Plenty of women would like to catch him, but until you came along he seemed to be a confirmed bachelor. It was rumoured that he was in love with a Russian woman years ago, but I assume that he was advised against marrying her. Prince Aksel's mother was Russian, and she was as unpopular with the Storvhalian people as Aksel's father.'

Mina's stomach lurched at the idea that Aksel had loved a woman but had been unable to marry her. Had he come to the Globe Theatre in London to see three performances of *Romeo and Juliet* because the story about the young lovers whose families disapproved of their union had deep personal meaning for him? She wondered if he was still in love with the woman from his past. Was that why he had never married?

'That seemed to go well,' Aksel said to Mina later, when they were waiting in the lobby for the car to collect them. 'You made a breakthrough with the children today.' His expression tightened. 'Watching you with them was really quite touching,' he drawled. 'You seemed to empathise with them, but I suppose that was part of your training to be a drama therapist.'

Aksel was struggling to contain the raw emotions that he had kept buried for the past eight years. Shockingly, he found himself wanting to tell Mina about Finn. But how could he trust her? He was still undecided about whether she had tipped off the press that she had slept with him at his hotel in London. *Helvete*, it was possible she had betrayed him just as his mother and Karena had done, he reminded himself angrily.

He looked into her deep green eyes and the ache in his chest intensified. 'Who is the real Mina Hart?' he asked her savagely. 'You acted like you cared about the children, but maybe your kindness this afternoon *was* all an act? After all, why should you care about them? You have a talent for making people believe in you, and today you played the role of compassionate therapist brilliantly. The journalist who was reporting on your visit is convinced that you are a modern-day Mother Teresa.'

For a few seconds Mina was too stunned to speak. 'Of course, I *wasn't* acting. Why shouldn't I care about the children? Anyone with a shred of humanity would want to help them deal with their terrible loss.' Her temper simmered at Aksel's unjust accusation. 'How dare you suggest that I was playing to the press? You're the one who thinks your damn image is so important.'

Tears stung her eyes and she dashed them away impatiently with the back of her hand. 'The person you saw today is the real Mina Hart. But who are you, Aksel? I don't mean the prince—I'm curious about the real flesh-and-blood man. Why do you hide your emotions from everyone? And what the hell happened when you were invited to hold the baby? There was a look on your face—' She broke off when his jaw tensed. 'That little baby was so sweet, but you looked horrified at the prospect of holding him. Don't you want a child one day?' She stared at his rigid face, wondering if she had pushed him too far, but she was desperate to unlock his secrets. 'How do you feel about fatherhood?'

'It is my duty to provide an heir to the throne,' he said stiffly.

'Oh, for heaven's sake!' She did not try to hide her exasperation. 'You can't bring a child into the world simply because you need an heir. I'm curious to know if you would like to have a child.'

He swung away from her as if he could not bear to look at her. *'Damn your accursed curiosity!'* he said angrily.

Mina swallowed. She had glimpsed the tormented expression in his eyes that she had seen at the cabin when she had asked him about the drawing of the baby that had fallen out of his sketch book. 'Aksel...what's wrong?' she said softly. She put her hand on his arm, but he shrugged her off.

Aksel closed his eyes and pictured Finn's angelic face on that fateful morning. How could the loss of his son hurt so much after all this time? he wondered bleakly.

He lifted his lashes and met Mina's startled gaze. 'If you want the truth, I find the idea of having a child unbearable.'

Unbearable! It was a strange word for him to have used. Mina wanted to ask him what he meant, but he strode across the lobby and opened the door.

'The car is here,' he said harshly.

He said nothing more on the journey back to Jonja and his body language warned Mina not to ask him any further questions. It was a relief when they arrived at the palace and she could escape the prickling atmosphere inside the car.

As they walked into the palace Aksel was met by several of his government ministers all requesting his urgent attention. On his way into his office he glanced back over his shoulder at Mina.

'I'm going to be busy for the rest of the afternoon. This evening we will attend a charity dinner, which has been organised by Storvhal's top businesses to raise funds for the families in Revika affected by the tragedy.'

'I don't want to go.' A note of panic crept into Mina's voice. 'I can't spend an evening in the full glare of the public and the press pretending that we are a blissfully happy couple.' She hated knowing that they would be fooling people with their so-called romance.

'Tickets for the event sold out when it was announced that you will be attending with me,' he told her. 'You can't disappoint the guests who have donated a lot of money to the disaster fund to meet you.'

Frustration surged through her. 'That's blatant emotional blackmail…' Her voice trailed away helplessly as he disappeared into his office. Benedict Lindburg, Aksel's personal assistant, noticed Mina's stricken expression.

'It's easy to understand why he's known by his staff as the Ice Prince, isn't it?' he murmured.

'That's the problem—I don't think anyone does understand him.'

The PA looked at her curiously. 'Do *you*?'

'No.' Mina bit her lip. 'But I wish I did,' she said huskily.

Half an hour before they were due to leave for the charity dinner, Mina was a mass of nerves at the prospect of facing the press who Aksel had warned her would be present. Earlier, she had decided to tell him that she would not continue with the pretence that she might be his future princess. But she had changed her mind after she had met his grandmother.

Despite being ninety and in poor health, Princess Eldrun was still a formidable lady. She had studied Mina with surprisingly shrewd eyes, before inviting her to sit down on one of the uncomfortable hard-backed chairs in the princess's suite of rooms at the palace.

'My grandson informs me that you are a therapist helping the bereaved children from the fishing community whose fathers drowned.'

'I hope, through drama therapy, to be able to help the children express their emotions and deal with their grief.'

The princess pursed her lips. 'I believe too much emphasis is put on emotions nowadays. I come from an era when it was frowned upon to speak about personal matters. Unfortunately my son Geir's private life was anything but private and his indiscretions were public knowledge. I was determined that my grandson would not follow in his father's footsteps. I taught Aksel that, for a prince, duty and responsibility are more important than personal feelings.'

'What about love?' Mina asked, picturing Aksel as a little boy growing up with his austere grandmother. 'Isn't that important too?'

Princess Eldrun gave her a haughty stare. 'Falling in love is a luxury that is not usually afforded to the descendants of the Royal House of Thoresen.' She looked over at Aksel, who was standing by the window. 'However, my grandson has informed me that he loves you.'

Mina quickly quashed the little flutter inside her, reminding herself that Aksel was pretending to be in love with her so that his grandmother did not think he was turning into a playboy like his father.

'And are you in love with Aksel?' the elderly dowager asked imperiously.

Mina hesitated. She could not bring herself to lie to the princess, but she realised with a jolt of shock that she did not have to. Like Juliet, she had fallen in love at first sight. She glanced at Aksel and her heart lurched when she found him watching her. His hard features were expressionless, but for a second she glimpsed something in his eyes that she could not define. Telling herself that it must have just been a trick of the light, she smiled at his grandmother.

'Yes, I love him,' she replied, praying that the princess believed her and Aksel did not.

Now, as she prepared to spend the evening pretending that she and Aksel were involved in a royal romance, Mina's heart felt heavy with the knowledge that, for her, it was not a charade. What if he guessed her true feelings and felt sorry for her? The thought was too much for her pride to bear. Tonight she was going to give the performance of a lifetime, she told her reflection. Somehow she must convince the press and the Storvhalian people that she was in love with the prince, and at the same time show Aksel that she understood they were playing a game, and that when she smiled at him it was for the cameras and he meant nothing to her.

A knock on the door made her jump, and her breath left her in a rush when she opened it and met Aksel's ice-blue gaze. His superbly tailored black dinner suit was a perfect foil for his blond hair. He combined effortless elegance with a potent masculinity that evoked an ache of sexual longing in the pit of Mina's stomach. That feeling intensified when he swept his eyes over her, from her hair tied in a chignon, down to the figure-hugging evening gown that a maid had delivered to her room.

'I'm glad the dress fits you,' he said brusquely.

Desperate to break her intense awareness of him, she said brightly, 'It's lucky that I'm the same dress size as your sister. I assume the dress belongs to her?'

Aksel did not enlighten her that he had ordered the jade-coloured silk evening gown from Storvhal's top fashion-design house to match the colour of Mina's eyes. 'I've brought you something to wear with it,' he said instead, taking a slim velvet box from his pocket.

Mina gasped when he opened the lid to reveal an exquisite diamond and emerald necklace.

'People believe that our relationship is serious and will expect you to wear jewels from the royal collection,' he told her when he saw her doubtful expression.

She caught her lower lip with her teeth as she turned around, and a little shiver ran through her when his hands brushed her bare shoulders as he fastened the necklace around her throat. Her eyes met his in the mirror and her panicky feeling returned.

'I'm not sure I can do this—face the press and all the guests at the party.' She fiddled with her hearing aids.

'When I'm in a crowd and lots of people are talking I sometimes feel disorientated.'

'I will be by your side for the whole evening,' Aksel assured her. Mina's vulnerability about her hearing impairment was at odds with the public image she projected of a confident, articulate young woman. Once again he found himself wondering—who was the real Mina Hart? She looked stunning in the low-cut evening gown and he wished they were back at the London hotel and he could forget that he was a prince and spend the evening making love to her.

As ever, duty took precedence over his personal desires, but he could not resist pressing his lips against hers in a hard, unsatisfactorily brief kiss that drew a startled gasp from her and did not go any way towards assuaging the fire in his belly.

'Don't bother,' he told her as she went to reapply a coat of lip gloss to her lips. 'You look convincingly love-struck for your audience.'

For a second her eyes darkened with hurt, but she shrugged and picked up her purse. 'Let's get on with the performance,' she said coolly, and swept regally out of the door.

The fund-raising dinner was being held at the most exclusive hotel in Jonja. The limousine drew up outside the front entrance and Mina was almost blinded by the glare of flashbulbs as dozens of press photographers surged forwards, all trying to capture pictures of the woman who had captured the heart of the prince.

A large crowd of people had gathered in the street, curious to catch a glimpse of their possible future princess. 'Are you ready?' Aksel frowned as he glanced at her tense face. She took a deep breath, and he noticed that her hand shook slightly as she checked that her hearing aids were in place. Her nervousness surprised him. After all, she was a professional actor and was used to being the focus of attention.

A cheer went up from the crowd when the chauffeur opened the car door and Aksel emerged and turned to offer his hand to Mina as she stepped onto the pavement. For a second she seemed to hesitate, as if she was steeling herself, but then she flashed him a bright smile that somehow failed to reach her eyes.

'Wave,' he murmured as they walked up the steps of the hotel.

Feeling a fraud, Mina lifted her hand and waved, and the crowd gave another loud cheer. 'I can't believe so many people have come out on a freezing night,' she muttered. 'Clearly your subjects are keen for their prince to marry, but it feels wrong to be tricking people into thinking I might be your future bride when we both know that I'll be leaving Storvhal soon and we will never see each other again.'

There was no chance for Aksel to reply as they entered the hotel and were greeted by the head of the fund-raising committee, but during the five-course dinner he could not dismiss Mina's comment. He glanced at her sitting beside him. She was playing the part of his possible future fiancée so well that everyone in the room was convinced she would be Storvhal's new princess. *Helvete*, every time she leaned close to him and gave him a sensual smile that heated his blood he had to remind himself that she was pretending to be in love with him. Her performance was faultless, yet he was becoming increasingly certain that it *was* a performance and the woman on show tonight was not the real Mina Hart.

'Can you explain how drama therapy could help the

children who have been affected by the fishing-fleet disaster?' one of the guests sitting at the table asked Mina.

'When we experience a traumatic event such as a bereavement we can feel overwhelmed by our emotions and try to block them out. But when we watch a film or play, or read a book, we are able to feel strong emotions because we are emotionally distanced from the story.' She leaned forwards, and her voice rang with sincerity. For the first time all evening Aksel sensed that the real Mina was speaking. 'Drama provides a safety net where we can explore strong emotions,' she continued. 'As a drama therapist I hope to use drama in a therapeutic way and help the children of Revika to make sense of the terrible tragedy that has touched their lives.'

A nerve flickered in Aksel's jaw. How could he have doubted her compassion? he wondered. Her determination to try to help the bereaved children shone in her eyes. There was no reason for her to take an interest in a remote fishing village, but it was clear that the plight of the children who had lost their fathers affected her deeply. It was impossible that Mina was faking the emotion he could hear in her voice. It struck him forcibly that she was honest and trustworthy, but his view of all women had been warped by the fact that his mother and Karena had betrayed him. He had believed that Mina had betrayed him and spoken to the press in London, but as he looked at her lovely face he saw that she was beautiful inside, and he knew he had misjudged her.

The rest of the evening was purgatory for Aksel. For a man who had shut off his emotions, the acrid jealousy scalding his insides as he watched Mina expertly work the room and charm the guests was an unwelcome shock. With superhuman effort he forced himself to concentrate on his conversation with a company director who had donated a substantial sum of money to the Revika disaster fund for the privilege of sitting at the prince's table, but Aksel's gaze was drawn to the dance floor where Mina was dancing with Benedict Lindburg.

His personal assistant was simply doing his job, Aksel reminded himself. Benedict understood that protocol demanded the prince must mingle with the guests and make polite conversation, but Mina had looked wistful as she watched some of the guests dancing, and Ben had smoothly stepped in and asked her if she would like to dance.

Aksel frowned as he watched Benedict place his hand on Mina's waist to guide her around the dance floor. In normal circumstances he liked Ben, but right now Aksel was seriously tempted to connect his fist with the younger man's face. The circumstances were anything but normal, he acknowledged grimly. Since he had met Mina his well-ordered life had been spinning out of control.

His mind replayed the scene earlier today when he had taken her to meet his grandmother. He had been fully aware that Mina had not meant it when she had told Princess Eldrun she loved him. But hearing her say the words had evoked a yearning inside him. It was ironic that in his entire life only two women had ever told him they loved him—and they had both been lying. Karena had deliberately fooled him into believing she cared for him, while Mina had gone along with the pretence of the royal romance at his request.

He scanned the dance floor, hoping to catch her eye, but she wasn't looking at him because she was too busy laughing with Ben.

'Excuse me,' Aksel said firmly to the company director before he strode across the dance floor.

'Sir?' Benedict immediately released Mina and stepped back so that Aksel could take his place. The PA could not hide his surprise. 'Sir, the head of the National Bank of Storvhal is waiting to speak to you.'

'Invite him to dinner at the palace next week,' Aksel growled.

He stared into Mina's green eyes and felt a primitive surge of possessiveness as he swept her into his arms. Desire heated his blood when she melted against him. He did not know if her soft smile was real or part of the pretence that they were romantically involved. The lines were blurring and the only thing he was certain of was that he had never ached for any woman the way he ached to make love to Mina.

'Ben,' he called after his PA. 'Send for the car. Miss Hart and I are leaving the party early.'

'But…' Benedict met the prince's hard stare and decided not to protest. 'Right away, sir.'

'Aksel, is something wrong?' Mina's stiletto heels tapped on the marble floor as she followed Aksel into the palace and tried to keep up with his long stride. He did not answer her as he mounted the stairs at a pace that left her breathless. At the top of the staircase he caught hold of her arm and swept her along the corridor, past her bedroom and into the royal bedchamber.

Mina had never been into his suite of rooms before and her eyes were instantly drawn to the enormous four-poster bed covered in ornate gold silk drapes. The royal coat of arms hung above the bed, and all around the walls were portraits of previous princes of Storvhal. From the moment Aksel opened his eyes every morning and looked at his illustrious ancestors he must be reminded that the weight of responsibility for ruling Storvhal sat on his shoulders, she thought wryly.

She was shocked by the fierce glitter in his eyes as he tugged his tie loose and ran his hand through his hair. As far as she could tell the charity dinner had gone well, but Aksel was clearly wound up about something.

'What's the matter?' she said softly.

'I'll tell you what's the matter!' He crossed the room in two strides and halted in front of her. *'You!'* The word exploded from him.

Mina stared at him in confusion. 'What have I done?'

'I don't know.' Aksel seized her shoulders and stared down at her, a nerve jumping in his jaw. 'I don't know what you have done to me,' he said roughly. 'You've bewitched me with your big green eyes and made me feel things that I didn't know I was capable of feeling—things I sure as hell don't want to feel.'

He was on a knife-edge, Mina realised. She did not pretend to understand the violent emotions she sensed were churning inside him, but her tender heart longed to ease his torment and, with no other thought in her mind, she cupped his stubble-rough jaw in her hands and pulled his head down so that she could place her mouth over his.

He groaned and clamped his arms around her, pulling her hard against him so that she felt his powerful erection nudge her thigh.

'Desire was my father's downfall. I vowed that I would never be weak like him and allow my need for a woman to make a fool of me.' He slid his hand down to her bottom and spread his fingers over her silk dress. 'But I need you, Mina.' There was anger in his voice, frustration with himself. 'I want you more than I knew it was possible to want a woman.'

CHAPTER TEN

A SHUDDER RACKED Aksel's body. He could not control his hunger for Mina and it scared him because he had always believed he was stronger than his father.

He needed to make her understand how it was for him. That all he wanted was her body and nothing else—not her beautiful smile, or the tender expression he glimpsed in her eyes sometimes, and not her compassionate heart—he definitely did not want her heart.

'You are not your father, Aksel,' she said gently. 'The people of Storvhal admire and respect you. They think you are a good monarch—as I do. But I want to know the man, not the prince. I want you to make love to me,' she whispered against his mouth, and her husky plea destroyed the last dregs of Aksel's resolve.

Wordlessly he spun her round and ran the zip of her dress down her spine. The strapless silk gown slithered to the floor. She wasn't wearing a bra and Aksel's breath hissed between his teeth as he turned her back to face him and feasted his hungry gaze on her firm breasts and dusky pink nipples that were already puckering in anticipation of his touch.

'You are exquisite,' he said hoarsely. 'At the dinner tonight I was imagining you like this—naked except for the diamonds and emeralds glittering against your creamy skin. But the truth is you don't need any adornment, angel. You're beautiful inside and out, and I...' his voice shook '...I want to hold you in my arms and make you mine.'

The flames leaping in the hearth were reflected in his eyes, turning ice to fire. 'Will you give yourself to me, Mina?'

Her soft smile stole his breath. 'I have always been yours.' She lifted her hands and unfastened the necklace, dropping the glittering gems onto the bedside table at the same time as she stepped out of the silk dress that was pooled at her feet. 'I don't need diamonds or expensive gowns. I just need you, Aksel.'

He reached for her then and drew her against him, threading his fingers into her hair as he claimed her mouth. His kiss was everything she had hoped for, everything she had dreamed of since the night at the hotel in London. They had been strangers then, but now her body recognised his, and anticipation licked through her veins as he stripped out of his clothes. In the firelight he was a powerful, golden-skinned Viking, so hugely aroused that the thought of him driving his swollen shaft inside her made Mina feel weak with desire.

He laid her on the bed and removed the final fragile barrier of her underwear before he knelt above her and bent his head to kiss her mouth, her throat and the slopes of her breasts. The husky sound she made when he flicked his tongue across her nipples made Aksel's gut twist with desire and a curious tenderness that he had never felt before. Satisfying his own needs took second place to wanting to give her pleasure.

He moved lower down her body, trailing his lips across her stomach and the soft skin of her inner thighs before he gently parted her with his fingers and pressed his mouth to her feminine heart to bestow an intensely intimate caress that drew a gasp of startled delight from Mina.

Aksel was taking her closer and closer to ecstasy, but as Mina twisted her hips beneath the relentless onslaught of his tongue she wanted to give him the same mind-blowing pleasure he was giving her. She wanted to crack his iron control and show him that making love was about two people giving themselves totally and utterly to each other.

He moved over her, but instead of allowing him to penetrate her she pushed him onto his back and smiled at his obvious surprise. 'It's my turn to give, and your turn to take,' she told him softly, before she wriggled down the bed, following the fuzz of blond hairs that adorned his stomach and thighs with her mouth.

'Mina…' Aksel tensed when he realised her intention and curled his fingers into her hair to draw her head away from his throbbing arousal. But he was too late, she was already leaning over him, and the feel of her drawing him into the moist cavern of her mouth dragged a harsh groan from his throat. The pleasure was beyond anything he had ever known. He had never allowed any women to caress him with such devastating intimacy, and he had always held part of himself back because he could not bear to be weak like his father. The Prince of Storvhal must never lose control.

But his body did not care that he was a prince who had been schooled since childhood to shoulder his royal responsibilities. His body shook uncontrollably as Mina ran her tongue over the sensitive tip of his erection. He gripped the sheet beneath him and gritted his teeth as he fought against the tide that threatened to overwhelm him.

'Enough, angel,' he muttered, tugging her hair until she lifted her head. His hand shook as he donned a protective sheath. His usual finesse had deserted him and he dragged her beneath him, his shoulder muscles bunching as he held himself above her. He watched her green eyes darken as he pushed her legs wide to receive him, and at the moment he entered her and their two bodies became one she smiled and whispered his name, and Aksel was aware of an ache inside him that even the exquisite pleasure of sexual release could not assuage.

As Aksel drove into her with strong, demanding strokes Mina knew that her body had been made for him. She arched her hips to meet each devastating thrust, until she was teetering on the edge, and her muscles clenched in wave after rapturous wave of pleasure. At the moment she climaxed Aksel gave a husky groan and buried his face in the pillows while shudders wracked his big frame.

His few seconds of vulnerability touched Mina's heart. Her passion was spent and in its sweet aftermath she felt a fierce tenderness as she cupped his face in her hands and gently kissed his mouth.

'I don't believe you are empty inside,' she whispered.

He rolled away from her and stared up at the ornate bed drapes decorated with the royal coat of arms.

'Don't look for things in me that aren't there,' Aksel warned. 'I made love to you selfishly for my own pleasure and to satisfy my needs.'

Mina shook her head. 'That isn't true, although I think you want it to be the truth,' she said intuitively. 'I think something happened that made you lock your emotions inside you.' She hesitated. 'Are you still in love with the woman in Russia who you had hoped to marry?'

'Karena?' He gave a harsh laugh, 'God, no—my youthful infatuation with her ended when I discovered the truth about her. How do you know about Karena, anyway?'

'I don't know much. Ella Holmberg told me you had been in love with a Russian woman but couldn't marry her because the Storvhalian people would not have approved.'

Aksel sat up and raked a hand through his hair. Mina missed the warmth of his body and sensed that he was drawing away from her mentally as well as physically. She was convinced that the key to unlocking him was in his past.

Wrapping the silk sheet around her, she moved across the bed so that she could see his face. She was still wearing her hearing aids, but earlier, concentrating on numerous conversations with guests at the party had been tiring, and she found it easier to read his lips.

'What did you mean when you said you discovered the truth about Karena?' she asked curiously

For a moment she thought he wasn't going to answer, but then he exhaled heavily.

'You cannot underestimate how badly my father damaged the monarchy during his reign. As you know, it wasn't just his many affairs that caused unrest.

'My father married my mother because her family owned a mining company which had discovered huge gold reserves in Storvhal's mountains,' Aksel explained. 'Instead of sharing the discovery with his government ministers, my father made a secret deal, which allowed the Russian company to extract the gold in return for a cut of the profits. He abused his position as ruling monarch and when the Storvhalian people found out that he was stripping the country's assets they were naturally horrified.

'I did not know the full extent of my father's treachery until after his death. My mother had inherited the mining company and she hoped to win my support to continue extracting the gold. I was in a difficult position. My mother was disliked in Storvhal, and by my grandmother, but she was still my mother. I often visited her at her home in Russia, and that's where I met Karena.'

He gave a cynical laugh. 'I was a young man burdened by the responsibilities of being a prince and perhaps it was no surprise that I fell madly in love with the beautiful Russian model my mother introduced me to. It was certainly what my mother had intended,' he said harshly. 'She hoped that if I married Karena it would strengthen my ties with Russia.

'But my grandmother and Harald Petersen were afraid that the Storvhalian people would not accept another Russian princess and tried to dissuade me from marrying Karena. Harald went as far as to have Karena spied on by government agents. I did not approve of his methods,' Aksel said grimly. 'But it soon became clear that Karena had duped me and pretended to be in love with me because my mother had sold her the idea that if I married her she would enjoy a life of wealth and glamour as a princess.'

'You were betrayed by Karena and your mother,' Mina said softly. 'You were hurt by the two women you loved and it's no wonder you shut off your emotions.' Aksel must have yearned for love when he had been a child growing up at the palace with his strict grandmother, she mused. She did not think Princess Eldrun had been unkind, but she had told Mina that she had taught her grandson to put his duties as a prince before his personal feelings.

His hard face showed no emotion and she despaired that she would ever reach the man behind the mask. 'After you had learned the truth about Karena, did you end your relationship with her?'

He nodded. 'I returned to Storvhal and did not expect to see her again.'

Aksel stared into Mina's deep green eyes and wondered what the hell was happening to him. He *never* talked about his past, but it was as if floodgates in his mind had burst open, and he wanted, needed, to let the secrets he had kept hidden for so long spill out of him.

'Eight months after I broke up with Karena I went to see her in Russia.'

Mina looked at him intently. 'Were you still in love with her?'

'No.' Aksel's chest felt as if it were being crushed in a vice. He drew a shuddering breath and dropped his head into his hands. 'Karena had contacted me out of the blue to tell me she had given birth to my child. She told me I had a son.'

'A son...!' Mina could hear the shock in her voice. 'You have a child? Where is he?' Her heart hammered against her ribs as she tried to absorb Aksel's startling revelation. 'Does he live with Karena in Russia?'

Aksel lifted his head from his hands, and Mina caught her breath at the expression of raw pain in his eyes. 'Finn is on the mountains, beneath the stars,' he said huskily. 'I took him to the Sami reindeer-herders because they are the most trustworthy people I know. They buried him according to their traditions, and they tend to his grave when I can't get up to the cabin.'

'His grave...' Mina swallowed hard. 'Oh, Aksel, I'm so sorry.' Driven by an instinctive need to comfort him, she put her arms around his broad shoulders and hugged him fiercely. A memory flashed into her mind. 'The sketch of the baby at the cabin, that was a picture of Finn, wasn't it?' she said softly. 'What happened to him?'

'There is no medical explanation of why Finn died.

He was a victim of sudden infant death syndrome—sometimes known as cot death.' Aksel took a deep breath and inhaled Mina's delicate perfume. There was something touchingly protective about the way she had her arms wrapped around him and it was not difficult to tell her the secrets he had never told anyone else.

'I'll start at the beginning,' he said gruffly. 'When I broke up with Karena I discovered that she had been cheating on me with a Russian businessman. She assumed the baby she was carrying was his, but when the child was born her boyfriend insisted on a DNA test, which proved he wasn't the father. Karena knew the only other person it could be was me, and another DNA test showed that the baby was mine.

'But even without the test I would have recognised that Finn was my son.' Aksel's face softened. 'He was so beautiful, Mina. I'd never seen such a tiny human being. He was perfect, and when I held him in my arms I promised him I would be the best father that any little boy could have.'

Tears clogged Mina's throat at the thought of Aksel, whose own father had more or less abandoned him when he had been a child, promising to be a good father to his baby son. 'You loved Finn?' she said gently.

'More than I have ever loved anyone.' Aksel's voice cracked with emotion. 'I asked Karena to marry me. She was the mother of my child,' he said when Mina looked shocked. 'I knew the marriage might not be popular in Storvhal, but Finn was my son. More importantly, I hoped we could put aside our differences for the sake of our son and give him a happy childhood. Karena agreed because she liked the idea of being a princess, but she wasn't interested in Finn. She had kept her pregnancy a secret in case it harmed her modelling career, and once the baby

was born she went to nightclubs and parties every night.'
Aksel's expression hardened. 'One night she wanted to go
out as usual and was annoyed because it was the nanny's
night off. I was leading a double life, spending the week
in Storvhal carrying out my royal duties and returning
to Russia to see Finn at weekends. I was tired that night,
but I was still happy to look after my son. But he was
restless and cried constantly. In desperation I moved his
crib into my bedroom and when he finally settled I must
have fallen into a deep sleep.

'The next morning I was surprised that Finn hadn't
woken for his next feed and I checked the crib.' Aksel's
throat felt as if it had been scraped with sandpaper. 'At
first I thought he was asleep. But he was paler than normal, and when I touched his cheek it was cold.' His throat
moved convulsively. 'That was when I realised that I had
lost my precious boy.'

Mina blinked back her tears. She had heard pain in
Aksel's voice but his face revealed no emotion. 'Have
you ever cried for Finn?' she whispered.

His expression did not change. 'Princes don't cry.'

'Did your grandmother teach you that?'

He shrugged. 'I blame myself for Finn's death,' he
said harshly.

'*Why?* You've told me that there is often no medical
explanation for sudden infant death syndrome.'

'If I hadn't been tired and slept so deeply I might have
realised something was wrong and been able to save him.'

Mina held him tighter and rocked him as if she were
comforting a child. 'I don't believe there was anything
you could have done. Finn's death was a terrible tragedy. But because you feel guilty I bet you haven't talked
about what happened, not even to your close friends or
your grandmother.'

'No one apart from Karena, my chief advisor and the Sami herders knows about Finn. You are the only person I've told.'

'You mean…?' She broke off and stared at him. 'Don't the people of Storvhal know that you had a son?'

'Harald Petersen thought if news got out that I had fathered an illegitimate child it would prove to the Storvhalian people that I was an immoral and degenerate prince like my father. There had already been one civil uprising in the country, and to maintain peace and order I agreed with Harald to keep Finn's brief life a secret. It suited Karena because she went back to her Russian oligarch who didn't want to be reminded that she'd had a child with another man.'

Mina cupped his face in her hands and looked into his eyes. 'Oh, Aksel, don't you see? You feel empty inside because you have never been able to grieve openly for Finn. You've carried the secret that you had a son who died, and it's not surprising you blocked out your emotions that were too painful to cope with.' She hesitated. 'I want to help you to deal with the painful experiences in your past. There are various kinds of psychotherapy—'

'I don't need therapy,' he interrupted her. 'I realise you mean well, Mina, but no amount of talking about the past can change what happened or bring my son back.'

'No, but it might help you in the future to love again like you loved Finn.'

'I don't want to love. I managed for most of my life without it.' He moved suddenly, taking her by surprise as he pushed her flat on her back and rolled on top of her so that his muscular body pressed her into the mattress.

'It's a fallacy that sex can only be good if emotions are involved. I can't pretend to feel emotions that don't exist for me, but I can give you pleasure when I make love to you.'

He lowered his head and captured her mouth in a hungry kiss that rekindled the fire in Mina's belly.

'This is what I want from you, angel,' Aksel said roughly. 'Your beautiful body and your sweet sensuality, that makes my gut ache.'

Mina's breathing quickened as he ripped the sheet away from her and, after sheathing himself, ran his hand possessively down her body to push her thighs apart. His erection pressed against her moist opening and her muscles quivered as he eased forwards until he was inside her.

She wondered how he would react if she told him she loved him. With horror, probably, she thought sadly. Aksel did not trust emotions and believed he was better off without love, which meant that her feelings for him must remain a secret.

Mina was not surprised when she woke up and found herself alone in Aksel's bed, but her heart sank when she turned her head and saw he had gone. She had hoped that the night of the charity dinner the week before, when the prince had so uncharacteristically opened up to her, would be the start of a new chapter in their relationship. She had hoped that Aksel was beginning to let her into his heart, but he had got up before she had opened her eyes every morning of the past week. She sighed as she looked at the empty space on the pillow beside her.

When they made love every night it was more than just good sex. Much more. He was a demanding and passionate lover, but he was tender and gentle too, and made love to her with such exquisite care that her eyes would fill with tears and he would kiss them from her cheeks and hold her so close to his heart that she felt its erratic beat thudding through his big chest. The Viking prince had a softer side to him, but in the morning she sensed that he regretted what he regarded as his weakness and resented her for undermining his iron self-control.

The situation could not continue, she acknowledged. Every day she remained in Storvhal she became more deeply immersed in the pretence that she was romantically involved with Aksel, furthering the media speculation that a royal betrothal was imminent. The press interest was so frenzied that she'd had to stop going to the village of Revika to visit the children affected by the fishing-fleet disaster, and instead the families came to the palace so that she could continue the drama therapy sessions.

The drama sessions with the children had cemented her decision to retire from acting and become a full-time drama therapist. She hoped it would even be possible for her to work with the children of Revika again after she had finished performing in *Romeo and Juliet* in New York. But first she would have to break the news to her father of her decision to leave his theatre company.

Mina sighed. Joshua was immensely proud of the Hart acting dynasty and he had been disappointed when his older daughter Darcey had turned her back on a promising stage career to train as a speech therapist. Darcey handled their temperamental, perfectionist father better than she did, Mina acknowledged. Looking back at her childhood, she realised that she had always tried to win Joshua's approval because after she had lost her hearing she'd been afraid he would love her less than her brother and sisters. She had spent her life trying to please him, and, if she was honest with herself, she dreaded Joshua being disappointed with her when she told him she was going to leave acting.

It was amazing how parents could influence their children even when they were adults, she mused. Aksel believed he must repair the damage his father had caused to the monarchy of Storvhal, and in his efforts to prove that he was not a playboy like Prince Geir he carried the tragic secret that he had fathered a son who had died as a baby. He had been unable to mourn for Finn and his grief was frozen inside him. Mina had hoped that, having confided in her once, Aksel would feel that he could talk to her about the past, but he had never mentioned his son again and any attempts she made to bring up the subject were met with an icy rebuttal.

The sound of the coffee percolator from the next room told her that Aksel must still be in the royal suite. Usually he ate breakfast early and had already left for a meeting with his government ministers by the time she got up. Hoping to catch him before he left, Mina jumped out of bed and did not bother to pull on her robe before she opened the door between the bedroom and adjoining sitting room.

He was seated at the table, a coffee cup in one hand and a newspaper in the other. He was suave and sophisticated in his impeccably tailored suit, and with his hair swept back from his brow to reveal his chiselled features he looked remote and unapproachable—very different from the sexy Viking who had made love to her with such breathtaking dedication last night, Mina thought ruefully.

She suddenly realised that Aksel was not alone and his chief advisor was in the room. To her astonishment Harald Petersen dropped onto one knee when he saw her and said in a distinctly shaken voice, 'Madam.'

As the elderly advisor stood up and walked out of the suite she glanced at Aksel for an explanation. 'What was all that about?' Her eyes widened when she saw that the front page of the newspaper had three photographs of her wearing different wedding dresses. Closer scrutiny revealed that a photo of her head had been superimposed on the pictures of the dresses, and the accompanying article discussed what style of wedding dress the Prince of Storvhal's bride might wear if there was a royal wedding.

Mina dropped the newspaper onto the table. 'Aksel, this has got to stop,' she said firmly. 'The press are convinced that we are going to get married, and we must end the pretence of our romance. It isn't fair to mislead the Storvhalian people or your grandmother any longer.'

'I agree.' He stood up and walked over to the window to watch the snow that was drifting down silently from a steel-grey sky.

'Well…good.' Mina had not expected him to agree so readily. Perhaps he had grown tired of her and was looking for an excuse for her to leave Storvhal, she thought bleakly. Her stomach hollowed with the thought that there really was no reason for her to stay. She was staring heartbreak in the face and she was scared that all the acting skills in the world would not be enough to get her through saying goodbye to Aksel without making a complete fool of herself.

'It's time to end the pretence,' Aksel murmured as if he was speaking to himself. He swung round to face her, and his mouth twisted in a strange expression as he ran his eyes over her auburn hair tumbling around her bare shoulders and the skimpy slip of peach satin that purported to be a nightgown.

Desire ripped through him, and for a few crazy seconds he almost gave in to the temptation to carry Mina back to bed and make love to her as he longed to do every morning when he woke and watched her sleeping beside him. All week he had managed to resist, reminding himself that it was his duty to be available to his ministers during working hours. He would not be held to ransom by his desire for Mina, Aksel vowed. He would not allow his weakness for a woman to deter him from his responsibilities as monarch as his father had done.

'The reason Harald knelt before you is because, by tradition, only the wife or intended bride of the prince can sleep in the royal bedchamber,' he told her.

Mina paled as his words sank in. 'We can't allow your chief minister to think I am going to be your bride. I have to leave Storvhal.' She could not hide the tremor in her voice. 'I've received a message from my father to say that *Romeo and Juliet* will open on Broadway a week early, and rehearsals are to begin in New York next week. It's the ideal opportunity to make a statement to the press that the pressure of my career has led to us deciding to end our romance.'

Aksel's brooding silence played with Mina's nerves. 'There is an alternative,' he said at last.

She shrugged helplessly. 'I can't see one.'

'We could make the story of our royal romance real—and get married.'

She fiddled with her hearing aids, convinced she had misheard him. 'Did you say...?'

He walked towards her, his face revealing no expression, while Mina was sure he must notice the pulse of tension beating on her temple.

'Will you marry me, Mina?'

Her surge of joy was swiftly extinguished by a dousing of reality. Aksel hadn't smiled, and surely a man hoping to persuade a woman to marry him would smile?

'Why?' she asked cautiously.

He shrugged. 'There are a number of reasons why I believe we could have a successful marriage. It is evident from the press reports that you are popular with Stor-vhalian people. They admire your work with the children in Revika. I also think you would like to continue to help the children,' he said intuitively. 'You could combine being a princess with a career as a drama therapist, and I believe you could be happy living in Storvhal.' He glanced away, almost as if he wanted to avoid making eye contact with her. 'It is also true that I have shared things with you about myself that I have not told anyone else,' he said curtly.

He meant his baby son. Mina's heart clenched and she reached up and touched his cheek to turn his face towards her. 'I swear I will never tell anyone about Finn...but I truly believe you should tell the Storvhalian people about him. I don't think they would judge you or compare you in any way to your father. You are a good prince, and everyone knows it. You need to be able to grieve properly for your son and lay the past to rest, and only then can your life move forwards.'

Something flared in his eyes, and Mina held her breath, willing his icy control to melt. But then his lashes swept down and his expression was guarded when he looked at her again.

'You haven't given me an answer.'

'My answer is no,' she said gently, ignoring the voice inside her head that was clamouring to accept his offer. He had said he believed they could have a successful marriage and perhaps that meant he was willing to build on their relationship, but it wasn't enough for her. 'You listed several reasons why we should get married, but you didn't mention the *only* reason why I would agree to be your wife.'

He watched her broodingly but made no attempt to close the physical space between them. Mina told herself she was relieved, knowing that if he pulled her into his arms and kissed her she would find it impossible to resist him. But perversely, part of her wished he would take advantage of the sexual chemistry they both felt. When he made love to her she could pretend that he cared for her. But there must be no more pretence, she told herself firmly.

'Is it so important that you hear me say I love you?' he demanded tautly. 'Would your answer be different if I uttered three meaningless words?'

His cynicism killed the last of Mina's hope. With a flash of insight she realised that if she married him she would for ever be trying to please him and earn his love, as she had done with her father throughout her childhood. She remembered how desperately she had sought Joshua's praise, and how a careless criticism from him had crushed her spirit. She deserved better than to spend her life scrutinising every word and action of Aksel's in the vain hope that he might one day reveal he had fallen in love with her.

'I would only want you to say those words if they *weren't* meaningless,' she told him honestly. She walked towards the bedroom. Her heart felt as if it were being ripped from her chest but her pride refused to let her break down in front of him. 'If you'll excuse me, I need to pack and phone the airport to book a flight home.'

CHAPTER ELEVEN

BENEDICT LINDBURG ENTERED the prince's office and found Aksel standing by the fireplace, staring at the flames leaping in the hearth. 'I've arranged the press conference as you requested, sir.'

'Thank you, Ben.' Aksel's stern features lightened briefly with a ghost of a smile. 'I'll be with you in a moment.'

The PA departed, leaving the prince alone with his chief advisor. 'You mean to go ahead and make a statement, then?' Harald said tensely. 'For the good of the country and the monarchy I urge you to reconsider, sir.'

Aksel shook his head. The people of Storvhal have the right to know the truth, and my son deserves to have his short life made public. Mina's words flashed into his mind. *You need to be able to grieve properly for your son.*

'I intend to commission a memorial for Finn, which will be placed in the palace gardens.' So often he had imagined his son running across the lawn in summertime and playing hide-and-seek in the arboretum. The gardens were open to the public, and he wanted visitors to pause for a moment and think of a baby boy whose time on earth had been cut tragically short.

The conference room was packed with journalists who were clearly curious to learn why they had been called to the palace. Aksel strode onto the dais, and as he looked around at the sea of faces and camera lenses he had never felt so alone in his life. His throat ached with the effort of holding back his emotions as he prepared to tell the world about Finn. He opened his mouth to speak, but no words emerged.

Dear God! He lifted his gaze to a ceremonial sword belonging to one of his ancestors, which was hanging on the wall. The ornate handle was decorated with precious jewels including a stunning green emerald that glittered more brightly than the other gems. Aksel thought of Mina's dark green eyes and a sense of calm came over him. She'd been right when she had said he could not look to the future until he had dealt with his past. Until he'd met her, he had not cared what the future held, but now he no longer wanted to be trapped in the darkness.

He took a deep breath and looked around at the journalists. 'Eight years ago, I had a son, but he died when he was six weeks and four days old. His name was Finn… and I loved him.'

Yellow taxis were bumper to bumper all the way along Forty-Second Street, and car horns blared as Mina darted through the traffic. She stumbled onto the pavement and collided with a mountain of a man who put his arms out to catch her.

'After watching you cross the road with complete disregard for your safety, I think I'd better warn your understudy that there is a very good chance she will be playing the role of Juliet when the play opens tomorrow night.'

Mina looked up at her father. 'I've got things on my mind, and I wasn't concentrating,' she admitted.

'I've noticed,' Joshua said drily. 'You've seemed distracted during rehearsals. But I suppose it's to be expected that you're nervous about making your debut on Broadway.'

Of course her father would assume that the only thing she could be thinking about was the play, Mina thought as she followed Joshua into the theatre. He strode into his office without giving her another glance and she sensed that he had already forgotten about her. His criticism hurt, especially as she had tried hard during rehearsals to hide her misery. It seemed that she could never please her father, she thought bitterly. He hadn't commented when she had told him she was giving up acting to pursue a career as a drama therapist, but she sensed he was disappointed with her.

Joshua looked surprised when she followed him into his office. 'As a matter of fact, I'm not worried about the first night,' she told him. Her frustration bubbled over. 'Can't you see I'm upset?' Heartbroken was nearer to the truth, she acknowledged bleakly. 'You must have seen the media reports that my relationship with Prince Aksel is over.' She bit her lip. 'I understand how important the theatre is to you, but sometimes, Dad, I wonder if you care about me at all.'

Joshua's bushy eyebrows knitted together. 'Of course I care about you,' he said gruffly.

'Do you?' Mina hugged her arms around her body. She could tell her father was shocked by her outburst, but this conversation was long overdue. 'Ever since I lost my hearing I've felt that you pushed me away,' she said huskily. 'It seems like nothing I do is good enough for you.' She swallowed. 'When I became deaf, I was scared that you didn't love me as much as Darcey and Vicky and Tom. You are proud of your other children, but you've never once told me that you are proud of me.'

Joshua did not respond. Mina was sure he would insist

that he had not treated her differently from her brother and sisters, but to her shock he sank down onto a chair and sighed heavily. 'I didn't mean to make you feel that I loved you less than the others, but I...well, the truth is...' For a moment Joshua Hart, the great Shakespearean actor, struggled to speak. 'I have always felt guilty that you lost your hearing, and I thought you must blame me.'

'Why would I blame you?' she asked, stunned by her father's confession. 'It wasn't your fault that I had meningitis.'

'Don't you remember I was looking after you the night you became ill because your mother was performing in a play?' Joshua said. 'You were running a slight temperature, and I gave you some medication and intended to check on you later, but I became immersed in learning my lines. By the time your mother came home and checked on you, she realised that you were seriously ill and called an ambulance.

'If it wasn't for your mother's quick actions, you could have died,' he said thickly. 'If I had called a doctor sooner, you might not have lost your hearing. I watched you struggle to cope with your deafness and I felt eaten up with guilt and sadness that I had let you down. The specialist said that we should treat you the same as we had when you could hear and not make an issue out of your hearing impairment, but when you cried because you had been teased by the other children at school it broke my heart. I think I distanced myself from you so that you did not have to cope with my emotions on top of everything else, but I didn't realise that you thought I loved you less than your siblings.'

Mina brushed a tear from her cheek. She was astounded by her father's revelation. 'I never blamed you, Dad. I was just unlucky to fall ill, and I don't suppose the outcome would have been any different if you had called a doctor earlier. Meningitis is a horrible illness that can develop very quickly. I had no idea that you felt guilty. I thought you didn't love me because I am deaf.'

'I'm sorry I didn't show how incredibly proud I am of you,' Joshua said deeply. 'You are a brilliant actress, and I know you will be a wonderful drama therapist.' He stood up and opened his arms, and Mina flew across the room and hugged him.

'Oh, Dad, I wish I had told you how I felt years ago.' She had been afraid that her father would admit he did not love her, Mina realised. Her fear of rejection and her father's feeling of guilt had created a tension between them, but she hoped that from now on they would be more open with each other.

'What happened between you and your prince?' Joshua asked. 'He has been in the news again today. Haven't you seen the headlines?' He picked up the newspaper from his desk and handed it to Mina.

Her heart missed a beat as she stared at the picture of Aksel on the front page. He looked as handsome and remote as he had done the last time she had seen him, when she had turned down his marriage proposal and he had walked out of the royal suite without saying another word.

Benedict had accompanied her to the airport. The usually chatty PA had been strangely subdued and had called to her as she was about to walk through to the departure lounge. 'I was hoping that you might be able to understand him,' he said accusingly.

Mina had struggled to speak through her tears. 'Look after him, Ben,' she'd choked, and hurried off before she changed her mind and asked him to drive her back to the palace.

The newspaper headline proclaimed: *'Prince Faces Further Heartbreak!'*

Mina quickly read the paragraphs beneath Aksel's photo.

> *Prince Aksel of Storvhal has made the shocking revelation that he fathered a child eight years ago. Tragically his son died when he was six weeks old. The announcement has caused a storm of public interest in Storvhal and comes a few days after the announcement that his relationship with English actress Mina Hart has ended.*
>
> *The Prince issued a statement saying he was deeply saddened by the break-up and took full responsibility for Miss Hart's decision not to marry him. He went on to say he would always regret that he could not be the man Miss Hart deserved.*

'Why did you decide not to marry him?' Joshua Hart said gently. 'Don't you love him?'

'I love Aksel with all my heart, and that's why I turned him down.' Her voice shook. 'He doesn't love me, you see.'

Her father studied the newspaper article. 'Are you sure he doesn't? It seems to me that he has laid his heart on the line. Why would Aksel think that he can't be the man you deserve?'

'I didn't know he felt like that,' Mina whispered. She looked at the photograph of Aksel being mobbed by journalists who were no doubt demanding to know more about the child he had fathered. His hard-boned face showed no emotion, but there was a bleak expression in his eyes that tore on Mina's heart. He must find talking about his son desperately painful, especially as he was facing the press alone.

He had been alone all his life, she thought sadly. Brought up by his grandmother who had taught him to put duty before personal happiness, he had been rejected by both his parents and Karena, the woman he had fallen in love with soon after he had been thrust into the role of Prince of Storvhal and a life of responsibility.

It was little wonder that Aksel found it hard to open up and talk about his feelings. Perhaps he did not love her, but she hadn't stayed in Storvhal and asked him outright how he felt about her because she had been afraid that he might reject her, just as she had been afraid to confront her father and risk Joshua's rejection.

Swallowing the tears that threatened to choke her, she turned to her father. 'I've been such a coward. I have to go to Storvhal right away.' She looked at Joshua uncertainly. 'But what about the opening night of the play?'

He squeezed her arm. 'I'd better go and tell your understudy to prepare for the biggest role of her life,' he murmured.

The tall white turrets of the royal palace were barely visible through the snow storm. Winter was tightening its grip on Storvhal and by early afternoon the daylight was already fading, yet Mina found the dramatic landscape of snow and ice strangely beautiful. The car drove past a park, and the sight of children building a snowman was a poignant reminder that even as a young prince Aksel had not been free to enjoy simple childhood pleasures and he had never played in the snow or built a snowman.

Benedict Lindburg met her in the palace entrance hall. 'The prince is in his office. I didn't tell him you were coming,' he told Mina.

Taking a deep breath, she opened the office door. Aksel was sitting behind his desk and had a pile of paperwork in front of him. The light from the lamp highlighted his sharp cheekbones and the hard planes of his face. He looked thinner, she noted, and her heart ached for him.

He frowned as he glanced across the room to see who had walked in without knocking. When he saw Mina his shoulders tensed and his expression became shuttered.

'Mina! I assumed you were in New York preparing for the opening performance of *Romeo and Juliet* this evening.' Although his tone was coolly detached his ice-blue eyes watched her guardedly. He picked up a pencil from the desk and unconsciously twirled it between his finger and thumb. 'Why are you here?'

As she walked towards his desk she hoped he could not tell that her heart was banging against her ribs. But then she reminded herself that she was through with being a coward and hiding how she felt.

'My father has released me from my contract with his theatre company and I've handed the role of Juliet over to another actress.'

Aksel looked shocked. 'Why would you turn down the chance to star on Broadway? Surely it's the opportunity of a lifetime that every actor aspires to?'

'I have different aspirations,' she said steadily. 'I hope to make a career as a drama therapist, but more importantly, I've changed my mind about marrying you—and if your offer is still open I would like to be your wife.'

The pencil between his fingers snapped in half and the lead tip flew across the desk.

'Why the change of heart?' he demanded. 'I thought you needed to hear a declaration of my feelings before you would accept my proposal.' Aksel's jaw tensed. 'I have to warn you that my feelings haven't changed.'

For a second her courage nearly deserted her, but for some reason she remembered the snowman in the park and her resolve strengthened.

'Nor have mine,' she said huskily. 'I fell in love with you the moment we met.'

'Mina, don't!' He jerked to his feet and strode around the desk. 'I don't want you to say things like that.' He raked his hair back from his brow and she noticed that his hand shook. The tiny indication that he felt vulnerable moved Mina unbearably.

'That's too bad, because I refuse to keep quiet about my feelings for you any longer.' She lifted her hand to his jaw and felt the familiar abrasion of blond stubble against her palm. 'I love you, Aksel. I know you can't say the words, and maybe you never will, but I don't believe you are empty inside. You were hurt, and you're still hurting now, especially since you have spoken publicly about your son.

'I can't imagine how painful it must have been for you to lose Finn,' she said gently. 'I hope that being able to talk about him will help to heal the pain in your heart, and I want to be beside you, to support you and to love you with all my heart.'

For a moment he gave no reaction. His skin was drawn so tightly across his cheekbones that his face looked like a mask, but as she stared at the rigid line of his jaw Mina suddenly realised that he was far from calm and in control of his emotions. His eyes glittered fiercely, and she froze as she watched a tear cling to his lashes and slide down his cheek. 'Aksel—don't,' she whispered, shaken by the raw pain she saw in his eyes.

'Oh, God!—Mina.' His arms closed around her and

held her so tightly that the air was forced from her lungs. 'I love you so much it terrifies me.'

His voice was ragged and she could hardly hear him, but she watched his lips move and her heart felt as though it were about to explode.

'I couldn't bear to lose you. It would be like losing Finn all over again,' he said hoarsely. 'I convinced myself that I would be better off not to love you. I thought that if I denied how I felt about you the feelings would go away.' He rubbed his cheek against hers, and Mina felt a trickle of moisture on his skin.

'I didn't want to love you,' he whispered. 'But when you left I felt like someone had cut my heart out, and I had to face the truth—that I will love you until I die, and without you my life is empty and meaningless.'

He drew back a fraction and looked down at her. 'I planned to wait until *Romeo and Juliet* had finished its run on Broadway, and then come and find you and try to persuade you to give me another chance.' He brushed away the tears on her cheeks with his thumb pads. 'Does the thought of me loving you make you cry, angel?'

'Yes, because I know how hard it is for you to speak about your feelings,' she said softly. 'You were taught to put your duties as a prince before your personal happiness.'

'The night in London and the time we spent together when you came to Storvhal were the happiest times of my life. I have never met anyone as caring and compassionate as you, but I told myself I could not trust you because it made it easier to deny my feelings for you.' Aksel's throat moved convulsively. 'You were right when you guessed that I had buried my grief about Finn, but you gave me the guts to face up to the past and tell the Storvhalian people about my son as I should have done years ago.'

He dropped his arms from her and walked around his desk to take something out of a drawer. Mina caught her breath when he came back and opened the small box in his hand. The solitaire diamond ring glistened like a tear drop, like the bright stars that watched over the mountain where his baby son rested.

'Will you marry me, my love, and be my princess? Will you walk with me all the days of our lives and lie with me all the nights, so that I can love you and cherish you with all my heart for ever?'

She gave an inarticulate cry and flung her arms around his neck. 'Yes—oh, yes—on one condition.'

Aksel searched her face and felt that he could drown in her deep green eyes. 'What condition, angel?'

'That, as soon as our children are old enough, we will teach them to build a snowman.'

He understood, and he smiled as he slid the diamond onto her finger. 'We'll also tell them how much we love them every day. Out of curiosity, how many children were you thinking we should have?'

'Four or five—I'd like a big family.'

'In that case—' he swept her into his arms and carried her out of his office, heading purposefully towards the stairs that led to the royal bedchamber '—we'd better start practising making all those babies.'

Aksel glanced over the bannister at his PA, who was hovering in the hall. 'Ben, I'd like you to draft an announcement of the imminent marriage of the Prince of Storvhal to Miss Mina Hart, who is the love of his life.'

Benedict Lindburg bowed and surreptitiously punched the air. 'I'll do it immediately, sir.'

On Christmas Eve the bells of Jonja's cathedral rang out in joyful celebration of the marriage of the Prince of

Storvhal and his beautiful bride. Despite the freezing temperature, a vast crowd lined the streets to watch the candle-lit procession of the prince and princess as they travelled by horse-drawn carriage to the palace where they hosted a feast for five hundred guests, before they left by helicopter for a secret honeymoon destination.

Mina wore her white velvet wedding dress for the short flight to the cabin in the mountains. She carried a bouquet of white roses and dark green ivy, and wore a wreath of white rosebuds in her hair.

'Have I told you how beautiful you look, my princess?' Aksel murmured as he lifted her into his arms and carried her into the cabin. 'You took my breath away when you stood beside me at the altar and we made our vows.'

'To love and to cherish, till death do us part,' Mina said softly. 'I meant the words with all my heart, and I will love you for ever.'

Aksel kissed her tenderly, but as always their passion quickly built and he strode into the bedroom and laid her on the bed. 'You could have chosen to spend our honeymoon at a luxury hotel anywhere in the world,' he said as he stripped out of his suit and began to unlace the front of Mina's dress. 'Why did you want to come here to this remote place?'

'It's the one place where we can be completely alone.' Mina caught her breath as he tugged the bodice of her wedding gown down and knelt over her to anoint her dusky pink nipples with his lips.

He smiled. 'Just the two of us—what could be more perfect?'

'Well…' She took his hand and placed it on her stomach. 'Actually—there's three of us.'

She held her breath as emotion blazed in his eyes, sadness for the child he had lost that turned to fierce joy as the meaning of her words sank in.

'Oh, my love.' Aksel's voice cracked as he bent his head and kissed her still-flat stomach where his child lay. 'As I said—what could be more perfect?'

* * * * *

THE PRINCE WHO
CHARMED HER

BY
FIONA McARTHUR

A mother to five sons, **Fiona McArthur** is an Australian midwife who loves to write. Medical Romance gives Fiona the scope to write about all the wonderful aspects of adventure, romance, medicine and midwifery that she feels so passionate about—as well as an excuse to travel! Now that her boys are older, Fiona and her husband, Ian, are off to meet new people, see new places and have wonderful adventures. Fiona's website is at www.fionamcarthur.com.

Dedicated to my prince, Ian. xxx

CHAPTER ONE

DR KIKI FENDER gazed across the blue of the Mediterranean to distant houses that clung like pastel limpets onto the cliffs of Italy and breathed in the beauty of the day.

It wasn't something she'd done when she'd first boarded the ship, but it was easier now as she listened to the delight of the newly embarked passengers.

These first few hours sailing along the Italian coast was her favourite time. But duty called so she brushed the hair out of her eyes and turned towards the hospital below. Four months of shipboard life had brought the purpose back into her life and she was so grateful for that.

Her smile slipped when she remembered it was only five days until the date she'd so looked forward to would be behind her, and then it would get even easier.

One deck down, Prince Stefano Adolphi Phillipe Augustus Mykonides tried not to think of the worst-case scenario as he rolled the unconscious wife of his brother into the recovery position. With immense relief he noted the blue of her lips improve slightly as her airway cleared.

He'd hoped Theros could stay out of trouble this week, on his wife's birthday holiday, but it seemed it wasn't so. With a sigh, the eldest son of Prince Paulo of Aspelicus, a tiny but wealthy principality in the Mediterranean Sea, knew it was his fault his brother had done something else stupid.

When he looked up at Theros his brother was as helpless as ever, his handsome face twisted in distress. 'Get the ship's hospital on the phone. Tell them it's an emergency,' Stefano said.

Theros's mouth worked silently, like a child's, and he looked shocked and incredulous as his wife began to turn blue again.

Stefano lowered his voice to a stern order. 'Now! Tell them it's a reaction to latex. To bring adrenalin.' He said the words slowly and enunciated clearly.

Theros blinked and stumbled to his feet as Stefano began to strip Marla of her skintight rubber playsuit, cursing under his breath as her breathing became even more laboured, but thankful that at least Theros had had the good sense to call him in time.

His concern lay in removing the offending clothing as fast as possible—before his sister-in-law stopped breathing. Not an easy job—which he gathered should have been half the fun. What he would have given for a scalpel...

Ten doors away Dr Kiki Fender jogged down the hallway to the largest suites, running over in her head what she knew about latex allergies. In truth Kiki was the on-call doctor for crew—not passengers—and she hoped her boss would follow quickly in case the patient was *in extremis*.

She'd hate to lose a patient on departure day, and royalty at that—very poor form. Terrible luck that Will had been on a cabin visit when the call had come in, so she was it till he came. She didn't even bother to try and imagine where this latex exposure had come from.

She'd tossed the usual personal protection gloves out from the emergency pack and donned latex-free ones, reminding herself they should use them in the whole medical centre in this current climate of escalating allergies, and had packed extra adrenalin ampoules. She carried in her hand the Epi-pen which made administration much quicker in such emergencies.

She prayed the patient's airways wouldn't have closed completely by the time her boss arrived with the rest of the equipment.

When the door opened she barely glanced at the distressed man in black shiny underwear and glanced ahead to the woman on the floor. Another man was bent over her as he struggled to extricate her legs from skintight latex leggings.

There was something oddly familiar about the shape of his head, but the woman was already unconscious and her skin was blotched with a paling red rash.

Kiki spoke to the dark hair of the man kneeling on the carpet as she bent down beside him. 'Is she breathing?'

'Just.'

Kiki glanced at the man's face and recognition slapped into her like one of the ocean white caps outside the window.

What the hell was Stefano Mykonides doing on her ship? *Lock that away, quick-smart,* she chastised herself, and quickly pinched the woman's leg to inject the adrenalin. Her eyes skimmed the almost naked woman for tiny rapid rises of her chest, aware that the movements would tell if the medication was helping. Most times with this type of shock recovery was dramatic, because the drug turned off the body's flooding allergic response like a tap.

But a tiny section of her brain was still suggesting that the Stefano she'd known was the last person who needed a threesome with a dolly bird in latex to fill his day.

She heard her boss and the nurse arrive with the emergency stretcher as Stefano leaned towards her.

'Of course I expect you to remain discreet about this event.'

She could see the pulse beating in his strong neck and a part of her responded involuntarily—and that increased her dislike. She met his eyes and tried with only some success to keep the contempt from her face. So typical. The woman was fighting for her life but it was all about how important the good name of the Mykonides family was.

She could say a few things about his good name. Instead she nodded at her patient. 'Of course, Your Highness.'

Stefano turned back to extricating Marla's foot. He was in shock—much like poor Marla without the benefit of the drug's reversal. Kiki Fender was *here* and to see her like this... As a saviour to his family, dynamic, confident of her skills as he'd known she would be. But it was not these things he remembered the most. Nor the woman who looked at him with distaste and called him Your Highness.

Before he could think what to say Marla groaned

and stirred, and his sigh of relief escaped silently as Kiki leant over and spoke near her ear.

'You're okay. Take it easy.' She looked at him and silently mouthed, *name*?

'Marla,' he said quietly, just as thankfully the last of the trouser leg came free over her foot with an elastic snapping noise. He slid the rubber suit under the seat of the lounge chair out of sight as more medical staff approached.

Kiki saw him do it and rolled her eyes at his priorities as she turned back to her patient. 'I'm going to put another needle—a cannula —in your arm and tape it there, Marla, as a precaution, but I think you're improving every second.'

The cannula slid in easily. Always a relief.

'Like I said, this is only a precaution,' she said to the dazed woman, 'in case you need further medication or intravenous fluids.' But within herself, Kiki thought the response appeared adequate from the initial dose— often the way—and it seemed the crisis was over.

She felt the trolley being manoeuvred in beside her and Stefano stood up.

He said, 'Please take my towelling robe,' and handed it to Kiki to cover the patient with.

Her nod of appreciation wasn't only for the gown for Marla, but because with him gone there seemed so much more air around the patient—and herself—more distance. Funny, that, and funny that she wasn't in the mood for laughing.

She had always had a respiratory awareness of him—like her own damned anaphylaxis—but she'd thought herself desensitised against that response after what she'd been through. Later, on her own, she would worry about that.

'Hi, Will.' Kiki glanced at the senior ship's doctor as he knelt down beside her. 'This is Marla. Severe reaction to latex. We've removed the causative agent.' She flicked an ironic glance at Stefano before she turned back to her boss.

Dr Wilhelm Hobson leaned over and took the woman's wrist to feel her pulse. 'You've given adrenalin?'

'Two minutes ago.' Kiki finished taping the intravenous cannula in place.

Marla groaned and opened her eyes more positively. 'Where am I?'

'It's okay, Marla. You're in your cabin. Just close your eyes and rest. You'll feel better soon.' She rested her hand over Marla's in sympathy. She and Wilhelm looked at the welts on her arms that seemed to be fading before their eyes. 'Good response, as you see.'

Will nodded, then wrote the pulse-rate, dose and time down on his scribe sheet while Kiki took the blood pressure cuff from the nurse and wrapped it around Marla's arm. As expected, the pressure was very low.

'In shock.' The nurse nodded as she adhered cardiac dots to the patient's skin and the sound of a racing heartbeat permeated the room. They began to assemble an intravenous line to increase the pressure in Marla's blood vessels with an extra fluid bolus.

Confident now that their patient was stable, Will stood up and faced the two men in the room. *This'll be good,* Kiki thought, and though she didn't look away from her patient her ears were tuned for their explanation.

'And who is responsible for this woman?' Wilhelm's

tone was deadly serious. But then he was serious most of the time.

Stefano had watched Marla wake up with relief and now he refocused on the room. Kiki, down on the floor with Marla, ignored him—as she should. He glanced at the man in charge—a stocky blond-headed man with a South African accent and air of command. A ship this size would need a competent senior. One who knew how to be discreet.

Then he looked to Theros. His brother stood, twisting his hands across his body, suddenly aware that he looked strange in those ridiculous shorts. His mouth worked but, as usual in times of stress, nothing came out.

Stefano sighed and stepped forward. Of course he was responsible. He had been since the moment of Theros's accident all those years ago. It did not occur to *him* to feel vulnerable, dressed only in swim-trunks, and he glanced coolly at the medic. 'I am.'

Kiki flinched when she heard Stefano's voice and realised she'd hoped otherwise. It shouldn't have mattered. Didn't matter. She'd always expected him to be more than he really was. A prince who lied and made promises he didn't keep.

She didn't wait to hear the rest. 'Okay, Ginger,' she said to the nurse. 'Let's help Marla up onto the trolley and we'll take her down to the hospital for observation.'

Fifteen minutes later Stefano paced in front of the window in his brother's suite. 'Please get rid of those ridiculous shorts,' he said. Stefano moved very slowly, with rigid control, frustrated at his brother's propensity for disaster and his own for not preventing it—and at the fruitless urge to ask why he had to deal with this. He knew why.

At seven Stefano had pulled Theros from a deep ocean pool on their island and saved his life with a boy's rough and ready resuscitation. Unfortunately Theros had been left with an injury to part of his brain from its time without oxygen. After that Stefano's young brother had not been the most sensible of boys, and later had become a handsome and lovable but childish man.

But that had not stopped Theros from diving into mischief and danger whenever he could, and as often as he was able Stefano would be the one to rescue him.

'Trouble. It will find you in the dark. Or in this case broad daylight. Is sex so tedious with your wife that you must risk her life with latex?'

Theros wrung his hands. 'No. *No*. One of her friends gave the suits to us for her birthday… We were playing. Laughing. Suddenly she could not breathe. I did not know Marla was allergic to rubber.'

'Latex.' Stefano squeezed the skin under his nose with his fingers in a pincer grip to stop himself from losing patience. He never lost patience with Theros. His father had been right to say that if only he, Stefano, had been faster at getting help perhaps his brother's brain would not have been damaged.

It was a legacy of guilt he could not shake. The job of protecting the family and Theros from ridicule had fallen to Stefano, and he had protected his brother well for many years—because he'd been willing to take up the mantle and carry it regardless of the impact on his own life.

His foray into medicine—the vocation that should

have been Theros's—had stemmed from that guilt, from his father's distress and disappointment, and from his own lack of ability to prevent such a sequela for his brother. Even at such a young age he had vowed if such a situation ever arose again he would know what to do. Unexpectedly, medicine had also provided a true vocation, and something that soothed his soul.

His father, Crown Prince Paulo III of Aspelicus, had hired a sensible woman to supervise Theros while Stefano had been away at a medical symposium in Australia earlier that year, and to everyone's surprise his simple little brother had found true love.

At his father's urgent request Stefano had rushed home from the arms of Dr Kiki Fender—but too late.

Theros had already eloped. Then Stefano himself had been involved in a serious motor vehicle accident, and during his slow recovery months had passed.

To his unexpected relief Theros's sensible wife had proved helpful in steering Theros on a more stable path, but even the most sensible could make an unfortunate mistake. So any notion of Stefano being released from his duty of care was a misconception. Theros would always need him, and he could offer no life to a vibrant and intelligent woman like Kiki, who was not accustomed to the strictures of royal duty.

In the harsh light of reality he knew that as heir to the throne he should let go of what had passed between he and Dr Fender in Australia. That was for the best.

But it seemed she had not forgiven him for his failure to return.

Theros coughed and Stefano returned to the present. His brother still waited for reassurance.

He took his fingers from his face and stared at Theros so he could be sure he was listening. Perhaps even absorbing the gravity of the situation.

'Marla could have died. Almost did.' He paused, let that settle in. 'One of you must carry an injection, similar to that which the doctor had, in case she is exposed to this product again accidentally.' He stared hard. 'You are her husband and it is your duty to keep her safe. Do you understand?'

'Yes, Stefano.' Theros chewed his lip. 'The doctor said she would be all right, though? They'll let her out of the hospital this afternoon?'

Not surprisingly, Theros had an irrational fear of hospitals—which hadn't been helped when Stefano had nearly died.

Stefano saw that fear, and his irritation with his brother seeped further away. His voice gentled. 'For the moment the danger is gone. Yes.'

Theros climbed into his swim-trunks and sadly handed Stefano his latex briefs. 'And she will be fine tomorrow, won't she? We're going to Naples to climb Vesuvius. You're coming with us.'

'My leg is a little painful.' Why must his brother love adventures that required exposure to the public? It would be so much easier on the island of Aspelicus, their island home off mainland Greece, and he had so many things that required his attention there. But his father had asked him to watch over them on this short cruise that Theros had promised his wife.

Ashore, his man could be with them. And while they were touring it would be a good time for him, Stefano, to reacquaint himself with Dr Fender.

After finding Kiki where he least expected her, he

had pressing matters to attend to. First an apology for his non-return. Past ghosts to lay.

The problem was that the woman he'd left behind in Australia had stayed like a halo around his heart. He, of all people, knew it wasn't sensible to desire a woman who did not understand or deserve the ways of royal commitment. As heir, in his country's crises *he* was the one who was called.

But still he smarted from the thinly veiled contempt in her sea-blue eyes, because he remembered the warmly passionate, fun-loving side of sweet Kiki.

The gods must be laughing at this insult to his pride. If they had been destined to meet again this was not how he would have orchestrated the moment.

Less than an hour ago—still achingly beautiful, yet transformed—she'd hated him.

She'd always been confident, sassy, and so different from the women he was usually introduced to. Of course he'd been recklessly drawn to the young doctor during his Sydney study tour to promote groundbreaking surgery at his small hospital. What a week *that* had been.

He would admit he had not behaved thoughtfully during their intense time together. Neither of them had. Everything had progressed far too quickly. They'd immersed themselves in each other for a torrid affair of incredible closeness, tucked away from the world in her tiny flat when they weren't at the hospital.

Until another crisis created by the man in front of him had required his immediate presence on Aspelicus and he had left her bed and flown out that same night.

He had spent the last few months recovering from his own accident—months of rehabilitation after he'd almost lost his leg. He'd barely been able to look at himself in the mirror, let alone consider showing himself to a woman.

But that excuse had gone now and his treatment of Kiki Fender had recently made him feel ashamed. It was another burden of guilt he found he could not move on from, because it had taken him almost five months before he was able to rule his own life again. A loss of control he never wanted to experience again.

By the time he had begun to search for her, at least to attempt an explanation, she'd been untraceable.

At first he had tried the hospital in Sydney, then her home phone, mail to her old lodgings. He did not know her friends or family. She had disappeared without a trace. Ironically to this very ship.

Tomorrow he would finish this and then fulfil his destiny for his country. Seek her forgiveness, allow himself to let go, and move on to secure the succession.

But for the moment his man-boy brother needed reassurance. Theros was playing with the legs of the latex suit he'd found under the chair and Stefano reached out and took them from him gently. 'Manos will drive you to Vesuvius.'

'Oh, good. And Marla will come.'

Theros looked childishly happy and Stefano supposed it was good that *someone* was pleased.

Later that afternoon, in the ship's medical centre ten floors below the royal suite, Dr Hobson was ready to discharge Marla.

'You can go back to your suite.' Kiki helped her sit up. 'Your observations are fine, and will stay that way if you stay away from latex.'

Poor Marla blushed again. 'No more birthday gifts that almost end it all!'

'It was just bad luck.' There was a lot of that around at the moment. Kiki grimaced with her. 'Allergies can be to anything. It could have been peanuts.'

Marla smiled. 'I'm supposed to be the sensible one. But thanks for that.'

'Hey, it was your birthday.' Kiki grinned back. 'At least now you know latex sets up a reaction in your body and you can make sure that if you ever go into hospital the staff keep you latex-free.'

The young woman nodded and stared down at the little Epi-pen in her hand.

'And be careful with that.' Kiki smiled. 'You can get into trouble if you inject it in the wrong place.'

Maria nodded.

'True,' Will said helpfully. 'I saw a man once who injected it into his thumb trying to work the plunger. It's a powerful drug and it shuts down the peripheral blood flow. His thumb fell off with gangrene.'

Kiki's eyes widened as she helped Marla up. 'Imagine what a disgruntled wife could do?'

The senior medic held out his hands in horror. 'That's true. Don't go there.'

Kiki shook her head in amusement, because Wilhelm's seriousness always cracked her up. 'Is he scaring you, Marla?'

'Only because of my husband.' The girl laughed and shook her head. 'I will not let Theros near it. I truly can be sensible.'

'Not too sensible.' Kiki smiled. 'Still have a great birthday. It's such a shame this has marred your holiday.'

Kiki couldn't help but think that Marla wasn't the

only one whose voyage had been affected. And this week of all weeks, when her emotions were already on a rollercoaster. Bummer. Bummer. *Bummer.*

Usually fair-minded, Kiki guessed she owed Stefano an apology—but it wasn't going to happen. She still didn't get why he was on his brother's holiday as his minder—on *her* ship—and was finding it hard to forget that somewhere above her head was the man she'd accepted she'd never see again.

She glanced at the ceiling above her head. Up there, larger than life and twice as disconcerting—because she might not have agreed to dress in latex for him, like Marla had for Theros, but she'd been just as weak, losing her common sense in the sensual haze they'd created together.

And as for her less than flattering thoughts of him earlier—well, he could jump off the owner's suite balcony before she'd apologise.

Ginger's offer to escort Marla to the suite was jumped on with enthusiasm. No way was Kiki going back up there. Because during the long weeks while she'd waited for his promised return, during the phone calls when she'd tried to contact him after she'd discovered she was pregnant, it had been too shameful.

There had been an unexpected lowness of her spirits when he hadn't called, and she'd been so sick and weak, barely able to function in early pregnancy, that she hadn't been able to motivate herself to do anything more about it.

By the time the first trimester had been over and she'd begun to feel more like herself again Kiki had accepted that Stefano wasn't coming back. He had clearly decided his royal status meant she wasn't good enough for him to follow up. Well, she and her baby didn't need him. All her life she'd been independent—the youngest sister to three brilliant sisters who didn't need her, with her doctor parents who were busy. The only person she'd felt connected to had been her big brother Nick. And briefly Stefano. But soon she'd have her baby and they would be a team. She couldn't wait.

But at eighteen weeks, when she'd already begun to create a nursery of tiny clothes and softest wraps, the pains had come and suddenly her baby was gone. Soon her baby's due date would pass and she would finally be able to move on. She'd promised herself.

The best thing she'd done was to come here to heal and move on to a new life.

Wilhelm wandered back into the main office. 'Marla seems very sweet.'

'She does.' Kiki blinked and came back to the present.

'Embarrassing for our royal guests, though.'

'Mortifying.' Kiki raised a smile. 'I bet her brother-in-law hated that!'

Even in the brief time they'd been together Stefano's avoidance of the whole topic of his royalty and his absolute hatred of the press had been obvious. At the time it had seemed sensible—she knew little of the life of a minor royal, which was the impression of himself he'd left her with. Not that she'd even thought about it much when they were together. As a man he'd been able to help her forget the world.

She dragged her mind back to Marla and Theros. 'It's Marla's birthday. They've been married less than a year. And Theros wanted to holiday on a cruise ship instead of their island like most of the family do.'

Will shrugged. 'So why is his brother here? Heir to the throne and all that. A bit high-powered for a minder, don't you think.'

Kiki tried for a careless shrug. 'Family name is very important to everyone, so I imagine in a royal family it would be more so.' She wasn't sure who she was trying to convince—Will or herself. 'Apparently Marla's husband has bad luck with the press.'

'Bad luck, eh?' Will raised his brows as he waved Ginger off duty on her return and shut the clinic door.

Kiki picked up her bag, but he put his hand up to stop her.

'One sec.'

She paused, looked back, and her stomach sank. She'd been afraid of this.

Will scratched his head. 'So what's going on between you two?'

'Which two?' She'd hoped nothing had been noticed. Nothing had been said. She hadn't even looked at Stefano as they'd wheeled Marla out.

Will waited patiently and Kiki felt the blush heat her cheeks. The silence stretched and she didn't like silence. That was her only excuse for being unable to extricate herself. 'You mean me and Theros's brother? Nothing.' How the heck had Wilhelm sensed that? 'I don't know what you mean.'

She switched off a computer she'd thankfully missed at shut-down. An excuse to turn away.

But the flood of memories she'd been holding back all day rose like a wave in her throat. Such rotten timing. She concentrated on her feet, firmly planted on the deck. She was *not* going under. Control re-established, she turned back to Will, who tilted his head and went on.

'Come on. I may be a bit oblivious sometimes, but the air was thick between you two and the guy was watching your neck like Dracula on a diet. Nick didn't mention you knew any royalty?'

Because she'd told no one about her stupidity—not even her closest sibling, and definitely not any of her sisters. 'Nick has nothing to do with this.' Because her brother Nick would be out for Stefano's blood if he knew what the Prince had done to his little sister. 'Stefano is a surgical consultant I worked with him briefly in Sydney during my last rotation.'

'You worked with a *prince*?'

Will looked even more interested, not less, and Kiki could feel the walls of the little clinic begin to close in on her. She didn't want to think about that time with Stefano, let alone talk about it, but her South African colleague could miss the obvious sometimes.

He proved it. 'So what happened?'

'That's all there is.' To her horror her eyes filled with tears. Not because of Stefano, but at the thought of the sadness that had been building for this past week.

'Hey. I've upset you.' Will shook his head. 'Sorry. I just want you to know I'm here to listen if you need an ear.' He raised his hands in defence. 'I promised Nick I'd look out for you.'

Don't mention this to Nick. But if she said it out loud it would be the first thing he'd do. 'I'm a big girl, Will. I don't want to talk about it. Don't need to talk about it.'

Even she could hear the over-reaction. She sighed. Too vehement.

She turned away to wipe at the tear that had slid

out against her will. 'Sorry—water under the bridge, that's all.'

'Well, if he gives you a hard time just let me know,' Will said gruffly, and she nodded and fled.

CHAPTER TWO

WHEN KIKI FINALLY fell asleep that night her dreams were filled with the sensation of being lost and alone, and always in the distance was Stefano, turned the other way and choosing not to see her.

When she woke she had tears on her cheeks, and despite the sun streaming in she was so exhausted she wanted to roll over and bury her head. Her shift didn't start until eleven but she wouldn't get back to sleep.

Through the open window she could hear the mooring crew as they secured the ship to the wharf in Naples, and she lay on her bunk and felt the ship creak and strain against its ropes.

And that made her think of yesterday's latex session gone wrong.

Unwillingly, she felt her lips curve—which wasn't a bad thing considering the night—and she knew at some stage she would have to share the story—names changed to protect the innocent—with her closest sibling. Nick would certainly enjoy the sense of the ridiculous.

She still didn't get why Stefano was on his brother's holiday.

From the brief mention Stefano had made of Aspelicus, Kiki gathered the island, once home to an ancient Greek school of physicians, a splinter school similar to the one on the more southern island of Asclepius, was a beautiful cliff-edged principality, with a harbour originally on the trade routes as a safe haven.

She'd spent hours online and discovered it had grown more Italian and French since its Greek heritage, and that its royal family were far more famous than she'd realised.

She'd been a fool. Of *course* Stefano had not returned for a brief fling he'd once had in the Antipodes.

His family had developed a stronghold in spices and teas from China, and the tiny monarchy had become incredibly wealthy. Now it was thriving on the sale of gourmet olive oil from the trees that dotted the hills, its cash flow supplemented by high-roller casinos and its own world-famous horse race along the lines of neighbouring Monaco's, which had its Grand Prix, and a borrowed idea from its neighbour to become a tax haven for residents.

On the other side of the island a sprawling low-rise hospital had gained international recognition for reconstructive surgery, with Stefano as its director.

The royal family could be traced back a thousand years, but somewhere each generation held a physician who had been available for the poorer people, as well as those who could pay.

It had all sounded incredibly romantic even from the few facts Stefano had shared with her.

She had waited for him to return.

But he hadn't.

She could remember as if it were yesterday when she'd

applied for the job on the *Sea Goddess*, her brother's old ship.

Kiki had always idolised her gorgeous, crazy show-man of a big brother—the only one of her high-achieving siblings who understood her.

She never had found out what had precipitated Nick's escape from reality but for herself it was wanting something totally different from the empty nurs-ery she'd created for a child that would never come.

She'd never shared her loss with anyone. She hadn't been able to share with the absent Stefano, and she'd thought an ordinary cruise ship the last place she would find him and reopen wounds.

Unlike her older sisters, Nick had seen she wasn't herself and cheered her on. So she'd started on the hospitality side of the ship, which had forced her to return to her usual outgoing self, the person she'd lost for a while, and she'd even started to forgive the male of the species, to laugh with Nick's friend Miko and the waiters.

Until she'd begun to miss medicine.

When the opportunity had come she'd switched roles, and the last three months had been good under Wilhelm's guidance in the ship's hospital.

It had all been fine—*until now*.

Maybe it was time to find her real calling. Hiding from the world had proved fruitless. But why couldn't this have happened next week, when she just knew she'd be stronger? She sighed.

Stefano was here and there was nothing she could do about that. It was time to move on. She'd go and see Will and ask how hard it would be for her to be replaced.

With that thought crystallising in her mind, Kiki rose from her bed and walked to the window with new purpose.

She'd put her notice in and leave as soon as they found someone to take her place.

There were still the next four nights to get through, but she'd manage that if she had a plan. She'd foolishly succumbed to ridiculous attraction last time he'd entered her orbit and that would not happen again.

Stefano woke with purpose. Today he would deal with what he should have dealt with months ago. Laying this admittedly delectable ghost was well overdue.

He'd discovered the opening times of the ship's hospital and by the time Theros and Marla had left for their day-trip the clinic was almost due to close, which suited him perfectly.

He descended the stairs almost at a jog—foolish when his hip would kill him later, and he reminded himself it was not fitting to appear too eager.

The nurse greeted him with a smile. She was the same one he'd seen yesterday, and he inclined his head at the obvious approval he read in her face. She was a handsome woman, of the type he'd used to dally with a lifetime ago, but, like a stamp on the front page of his passport, no matter where he was, Kiki had dampened any desire on his part to consort with other women.

'I wish to see Dr Fender. I am Stefano Mykonides.'

'Of course, Your Highness, I know who you are.' She smiled at him coyly, fiddled excitedly with her collar, and blushed.

Stefano smiled back blandly, curbed his impatience as the woman went on.

'But Dr Fender isn't on duty until later this morning.'

A door across the waiting room opened and the senior doctor ushered his patient out.

As the young boy and his mother walked past them the nurse said, 'Perhaps Dr Hobson?'

'No.' Stefano inclined his head at the doctor, but before he could leave Hobson crossed the room and held out his hand. They shook hands briefly.

'Ah, Your Highness. Good morning.' He turned to the nurse. 'Can you run those blood samples up to the courier, please?'

He turned back to Stefano. 'I hope all is well with your sister-in-law this morning?'

Stefano tried not to show his irritation, but he was trapped. And where was his quarry if not here? 'Yes. Thank you.' He was over discussing Theros's disasters.

Hobson glanced at his watch. 'How can we help you?'

Stefano picked up nuances and wondered why this man felt Kiki needed protection. From him. 'I had hoped to thank Dr Fender personally, for her timely assistance yesterday. I did not have the opportunity at the time, of course.'

'Of course.'

Hobson smiled non-committally and Stefano felt like gritting his teeth.

'I could convey your appreciation?'

Very pointed, Stefano thought, but he held his temper. 'Thank you, but I wish to do so myself. I will return at another time.'

Hobson didn't shift. 'I'll let her know.'

Stefano could see that the good doctor was in protection mode. He wondered just what kind of personal relationship he had with Kiki and had to admit he disliked the idea very strongly. His hand tightened on the room card in his pocket. The card bent. Disliked very strongly. He examined the doctor more closely. He was a well-muscled man, almost as tall as himself, and no doubt attractive to women.

He tested the water. 'Or I could surprise her.'

Hobson's smile appeared frozen on his face. 'I think she has had enough surprises.'

Stefano had to give the man respect. Loyalty was a good thing, and despite his own misgivings he could not grudge Kiki her friend's championship. Though his cousin, who owed Stefano many favours, *did* own this shipping line.

His fingers loosened. *Relax. Let it go.* He, too, cared that Kiki was not upset. 'It is not my intention to distress her.'

Hobson met his gaze head-on. 'Good.'

Enough. His day had soured and the pain in his hip from his reckless descent down the stairs was annoying him. 'And good day to you, Dr Hobson.'

Stefano pressed the button for the lift with remarkable restraint, not stupid enough to brave an ascent of twelve floors despite his sudden frustrated desire for explosive energy. The lift doors opened and, as if conjured, Kiki stood waiting to alight.

'Just the person.' Wonderful how good humour could be instantly restored. 'One moment, please, Dr Fender.' He could not believe his good luck—finally—and gestured for her to wait. With a relief he was careful not to show he stepped in beside her as she hesitated.

Kiki couldn't believe her bad luck. So close to being safe. 'What if I was on my way to work?'

He shrugged those shoulders that still made her weak at the knees. Damn him. It was so hard to not to stare and just remember.

'I have been told you are not working for a few hours.'

His voice always had made her mouth dry, and now was no exception. What was the scientific reason for that? She searched a little desperately for distraction as she watched him press the lift button for the sixteenth floor.

Of course he had looked for her in the hospital. If only she hadn't run down for a quick chat with Will.

The doors began to close and for a moment she did consider diving out before the doors shut, like some female secret agent with a barrel roll in her repertoire—but she'd just look awkward, and probably get sandwiched by the doors.

Or, a hundred times worse, he'd put out his hand and touch her, and she wanted to avoid that at all costs. That was what had happened the first time. He'd laid his hand on her arm to help her from the car and she'd woken up in bed with him. And stayed there for a week.

That left the smart mouth as her only defence. 'So where are we going?' As if she didn't know.

He didn't reply, and she remembered that. The frustrating habits of a man used to answering questions he felt inclined to and ignoring the rest. A prince with his own agenda unless it was for his family. Lucky him.

She stared straight ahead at the doors of the lift as if they'd magically open and she could float out to safety somewhere in the stairwell. She could feel his eyes on her.

'Why are you on this ship anyway, Your Highness?'

She heard him sigh. 'Do you call me that to annoy me?'

Now she glanced at him. Sugared her voice. 'Is it working?'

He looked at her from under his own raised brows, and then in the ultimate retaliation he smiled. Blinded, she felt it rip open the wound she'd healed so diligently over the last months aboard ship. *Blast, blast and double blast.* She needed to get away.

She'd fallen in lust with him the first time she'd seen him. Only lust. Love wouldn't have ended as it had.

Stefano had smiled at her then, as if they shared a secret, when she'd been late for her last surgical day in the operating theatres because of car trouble. He'd been a guest consultant of her boss, and should have chastised her like all the other consultants would have done, but instead he'd shown her surgical techniques she'd never thought to witness.

Later, he'd bought her coffee, plied her with cake to replace her missed breakfast, and invited her to ride home with him at the end of the day. When his hand had touched hers she'd been stunned like a landed fish, all big glassy eyes and floppy with desire.

And she knew where that had led.

The flicker of the number lights speeding upwards brought her back to the present and her sense of impending danger grew exponentially. This wasn't sensible. Or safe. Though she wasn't sure who she was more afraid of. Him or herself.

'I don't want to go anywhere with you.'

She thought for a moment she'd actually hurt him. There was just a flicker behind his eyes... But that was a joke. Instead he sighed as if she were a troublesome child, or probably just a troublesome subject.

'I will not keep you long.'

'Well, I know *that*.'

This time he did flinch. She saw it. Good, he felt guilty—even though he didn't know how guilty he *should* feel. But she was tired of scoring points or second-guessing his intentions. She just wanted to forget she'd seen him again and re-grow the scar tissue so she could complete her healing.

When the lift stopped she planted her feet more solidly on the spot. He waited for her to pass him and when she didn't lifted his hand to direct her. She stepped out of his way and back against the wall so fast his hand fell.

'No.' She licked dry lips. 'Goodbye, Prince Stefano. Have a good life.'

There. She'd said it. What she hadn't had a chance to say nine months ago. Now it was done. Finished.

Except he didn't get out, and the silence lengthened.

Without direction from them the lift doors shut and the chamber began its descent to another level.

His voice was mild. Slightly amused. 'So, are we to ride up and down in the lift all day until you wish to get out?'

She stepped further to the left of him. 'Leave me alone, Stefano.'

He didn't lift his hand again, but his voice reached out to her. She tried to imagine a soft ball of cotton wool jamming her ears to mute the sound—it didn't work.

'Is a few minutes of your time so much to ask? A chance to apologise, explain a little, and then we may part as friends—or less, if that is what you wish.'

She didn't know how much more of this power struggle she could take before those damn tears she could feel prickling behind her eyes made their escape.

She could get out on another floor, stride away, and then spend the day dreading what could be over in a few minutes if she just faced it. Over and done with. Great theory, but what if it wasn't? She still wasn't sure who she trusted least.

The silence lengthened. The lift stopped and began to go down further. 'For goodness' sake. Must you get your own way in everything?' She stepped forward and stabbed the light for the sixteenth floor. The little button rattled with the force. 'Get it over with.' The lift whooshed upwards again.

Stefano winced. This was not how he had expected it would turn out. A polite thank-you, a question as to whether she was well, an apology because he had had to leave so abruptly the last time they'd been together, and—most importantly—he would see that he was not as attracted to the flesh and blood woman as his imagination had assured him. Then he could move on to his duty.

In fact, to his discomfort, the desire for Kiki back in his arms, and most assuredly in his bed, was growing stronger by the second.

Perhaps he should have stepped out of the lift on his own after all. But how was that going to help his predicament?

The lift doors opened again and he extended his arm against the doors to hold them. 'After you.'

'Are you? Not again, I hope,' she muttered, and he had to bite back the smile.

This was the woman who had captured his attention over that long-ago week. With her tiny rebellions that always startled him out of his self-assurance, the rapier wit that amused him with its irreverence, the unpredictability of Kiki with the crazy name and so alluring body.

He was in trouble. But, then again, so was she.

CHAPTER THREE

KIKI PRECEDED HIM into the suite and glanced around. Very grand. Split level. She hadn't noticed much yesterday—too many other things had been going on. Like a woman critical with shock. Like Stefano reappearing beside her. Like a hundred memories she didn't want to remember.

She kept her back to him. 'Must be cosy, sharing with a married couple.'

'Their suite is very similar. Next door.' Kiki could hear the smile in his voice. The lock clicked. 'This is mine.'

Why did she feel there was emphasis on 'mine'? She squared her shoulders and faced him. Why did he have to look so damned amazing. 'So let's have our little conversation and then I'd like to leave.'

He ignored that. The ignoring thing again. He prowled over to the drinks cabinet. Turned to face her and asked mildly, as if they did this every day, 'Would you like something to drink?'

No, but she wouldn't mind something in her hand she could fiddle with—or throw in defence.

Kiki circled the plush sofa and sat on an upright armchair. 'Thank you. Soda water.'

He smiled. 'You were always so confident.'

She ground her teeth. 'Until I met you and thought the sun shone out of your tailbone.'

Of course he ignored that too. 'You always had fire when roused.' They both heard the echo of a similar word. Was that *a*roused?

He held out her drink and she took it carefully, so as not to touch his hand. Again his gaze met hers and she looked away. Knew his gaze never left her face. She could tell even with her fierce concentration on her glass.

His voice drifted over her like a wraith, encircling her, pulling tighter. 'But still there is more. Yesterday you were incredibly efficient. Practised. Calm. Capable. All things I knew you would be.'

She didn't want to hear this. She wanted out. 'Why don't you cut to the chase, Stefano? Why are you here on this ship?' And, more to the point, 'Why am I here in your suite?'

He stepped closer. 'The truth?'

She shrugged, trying hard to disguise the fact she was getting more spooked by the minute. 'Novel idea, I know.'

He came to stand in front of her chair. 'I could not forget you.'

'Spare me.' *Please don't say that,* she pleaded mentally. 'It took you nine months to figure that out?' She winced. Unobtrusively she eased back in the seat to create a little more space. Now she could inhale his aftershave, just a wisp, and it was true: the sense of smell was the one true memory.

He looked down. Apparently sincere. 'I did search for you.'

'Then you're not very good at it, are you?' She'd still been in the same flat for the next five months. Waiting. Hoping he'd at least call back. Until she'd woke up to reality. 'Tell me. When did this fictitious search occur?'

Thankfully he stepped across to the window that looked out from the stern of the ship and she could breathe again.

The glorious picture window framed the blue of the ocean, the trail of the wash from their ship, and the haze of land off to the east. And the outline of Stefano's magnificent frame.

'It was many months before I could begin. Only now, through chance,' he added more thoughtfully, 'or fate, have I found your whereabouts...'

He'd waited *months*! Not in a hurry to find her, then. Four weeks after he'd left she'd discovered she was pregnant. Another fourteen weeks and she'd been desperate for him to call so she could share her confusion, share her joy at the promise of finally feeling as if she belonged to someone, share her fears and hopes with the father of her child. Instead she had been completely alone.

But not as alone as she'd been when her baby had slipped away one silent night. The doctor had said her baby had a cardiac malfunction, a missing part so the growth could not progress, and she had accepted that—with grief, like the lacking in the relationship it had come from. The grief had been worse because in the beginning she had been ambivalent about its coming. Had thought more of the complications than of her own child until it had been too late for fierce regrets.

And the due date was next week.

The ever-present ache squeezed in her heart. It was

time to go before her control let her down. 'Great. Thanks for that.' She stood, glanced at him up and down. 'You look well. Don't seem to be pining. I think you'll survive.'

He stepped back into her comfort zone. 'Is Hobson your lover?'

They were standing chest to chest, a pulsing fission of air between then, and she almost missed the question.

What? Where did this guy get off? But stoking up her anger was a good idea. Much better than sadness. Anger made her feel less trapped. Less baited by his need for control at this moment. Less weak.

Flippantly, with an airy wave of her hand, she said, 'He's one of them.'

The flare in his eyes stunned her.

'Then his position has become vacant.'

She blinked. 'Don't be ridiculous.' She sat down again in shock. Any other man and she'd think he was joking. 'You can't do that.' Wrong thing to say. She knew it as soon as it was out of her mouth.

He didn't even have to say it out loud. Of *course* he could do it. The power of the Mykonides in the Mediterranean had never been in doubt.

Her turn to back-pedal. She'd suspected he had this side, had just never been shown it before. 'Of course Will's not my lover.'

Stefano cursed his temper, something he usually had an iron control over, and wheeled away to look over the sea again. The sea was unpredictable today, like his feelings for Kiki, and just as dangerous. More bad behaviour on his part. But despite that he felt his shoulders relax a little. He had not believed Hobson was her lover, but the concept had been gnawing at him since his visit to the ship's hospital this morning.

So what else had she said that was not true. 'Is there a man in your life at the moment?' He could feel the beast within him stir at the thought, and it didn't escape his notice that he had no right to ask such a thing.

She opened her eyes wide. 'Is there a man in yours?'

Little witch. 'Why are you baiting me?'

She glared back at him. 'Because apologies and good wishes haven't appeared on the menu and that was what I was promised.'

She had a point. And again he was behaving badly. Why did this happen with the woman he wanted to liaise honourably with?

He paced and came to stop in front of her. 'I sincerely apologise for leaving without explaining my reasons.'

She nodded. 'And the phone calls you didn't return?'

Those he could not remember? 'I did not get them.'

'Perhaps not.' Her tone said she didn't care any more and she put her glass down. 'I accept your apology. Thank you for my drink.' It was untouched.

So that was that. The degree of disappointment seemed out of proportion to what he'd expected. The wall between them was too great for them to part amicably but his expectations had been optimistic. At least he knew where he stood. It was time to move on. To duty.

She stood again. 'Goodbye, Stefano.'

But as she passed him his hand reached out of its own volition and captured her wrist. Her skin was soft and supple and so fragile. She froze and lifted her eyes to him. Limpid pools. He'd forgotten how her emotions

changed their colour from brilliant blue to dark violet
when she was aroused. Or angry. Which was it?

His thumb stroked the pulse on the underside of her
wrist. 'Dine with me. Tonight.'

'No.' She tugged in slow motion, as if already unsure if she wanted release or not.

'Tomorrow?' He stared into deepening violet and
between them the fire flickered and stirred and the
wraith encircled them both.

'I'm working.' Almost a whisper.

He stroked her wrist again. 'Then it must be tonight.'

Huskily, With another brush of her tongue over her
lips, she said 'What part of no don't you understand?'

But for Kiki it was too late. Too, too late. He'd
touched her.

His hand held her wrist, his skin was on hers, and
the two receptors were communicating, entwining in
their own matrix of reality. The warmth crept up her
body, wrapped around her in tendrils of mist, and in
slow motion he drew her forward. Subconsciously she
swayed like a reed towards him.

His other hand came up and tenderly brushed the
hair out of her eyes. 'You have grown even more beautiful.'

With worship his fingers slid across her cheek and
along her jaw as his mouth came down, and she could
do nothing but turn her face into his palm and then
upwards. To wait.

As he had with their first kiss he took her breath, inhaled her soul as she did his, and the sometimes comi-
cal, sometimes cruel world disappeared.

Her hands crept up around his neck and his hands
slid down, until he cupped her buttocks and pulled her

in hard against him. With the taste of his lips on hers, she could feel all of him, rock-solid against her, familiar, and then his mouth recaptured hers in the way only Stefano's could.

She moaned against his lips, her mind blank in the thick sensuality only he could create. She forgot all her intentions, all her reservations, and when he lifted her shirt, swept it over her head, sighed at her lace-covered breasts, she gazed up in a sensual mist of buried memories at the man she'd dreamt about last night.

He carried her across the room and she hooked her legs around his hips. Her mouth was on his, starving for the fuel of life she'd missed, as they went up the stairs to the loft bedroom in a haze of heat and hunger and primitive surrender.

The fog parted briefly as he lay her down, stripped off his own shirt. She could see the muscled perfection of his chest, the fine sprinkling of dark hairs and the nipples erect with his desire. Quickly he protected them both. And before her brain could function sensibly he was beside her, stroking, murmuring his delight, kissing her mouth as if he would never stop, and she was lost again despite the insistent whisper that warned she would taste remorse later.

She felt a long ridge of unfamiliar scarring on his thigh, a myriad of smaller ones, and her hand stilled. But he swept her up again before she could investigate further and the moment was lost in the maelstrom.

Stefano felt the swell in his chest, the furnace of desire for this slip of a woman who, until he touched her, could hold her own. Then she was his. He sensed it. Tasted the victory he hadn't known he burned for until it was upon him.

Clothes had fallen away, skin melted into skin, and heat seared between them as they reacquainted, shifted, joined. Together they cried out, until the sound died in the little death and she lay beneath him, limp and spent in his arms.

Then he moved again, slowly, savouring every tiny moment, every gentle trail across pearl-coloured skin, every cupping of mounds and exploration of hollows. And always he returned to her mouth, her honeyed mouth that he could never have enough of, until the beat grew faster, the hunger more desperate, the climax more shattering, and again they collapsed.

Replete for now, in awe, still confused by the speed and urgency that had carried them both, he lay back with his arm under her, hugged her close, smiling and sated.

For the moment.

Until the drop of a tear landed on his bicep.

'You are crying?' Stefano felt the dagger of shame and turned to see her face. Kiss her hand. 'I have hurt you. God, no. I am a beast.'

Kiki was in shock. She'd done it again. One touch and she'd lost all will. How could that be? She was no young and foolish teenager, swept off her feet by a handsome man. She knew what he could do. Had wept buckets at his hands before. If she didn't get out now she would lose what shreds of self-respect she could gather from the clothes strewn around the floor.

'I have lint in my eye. It's okay.' She eased out from under his hand and inched to the edge of the bed.

He sat up, the sheet falling from his chest, his hand out. 'Let me help you.'

'No.' It was sharp and panicked, and she tried again in a calmer voice. 'No. Thank you. One moment.'

A plan. She had no plan except to escape. Not to let him touch her again. Her feet touched the floor and she scooped up her underwear on her way down to the bathroom, padding down the stairs in bare feet to where her shirt lay at the bottom of the steps like an abandoned child. She scooped it up. Hopped on one leg as she slipped on her panties.

God. What had she done? How had it happened? At least he had used protection—but then they had done that last time. She would get a morning-after pill. Make sure.

All stupid thoughts when really she should be worried about escape and remaining undetected by a ship full of people who knew her. She opened and closed the bathroom door noisily, yet didn't go in. Instead she hurriedly pulled on her bra and her shirt and slipped out through the door as soon as she was dressed.

Outside she pulled on her sandals and smoothed her clothes. To top everything off if somebody saw her leave the suite of a passenger her job would go. And she was due at work in an hour.

On the crew level she passed Miko, her friend from her first early days on the ship, when she'd been more than a little lost. He was another of her brother's confidants, and the restaurant manager on the *Sea Goddess*.

She ran her fingers through her hair. *Nooooo*, she must look a sight. Miko raised his eyebrows, smiled sardonically, and walked on without saying a word. Did she look like a woman who had just left a man's bed? Kiki hurried to her cabin in the crew's quarters and as she went she groaned.

* * *

Stefano groaned too.

She'd gone. He knew it. And now, instead of finding resolution, they were in deeper trouble than before. What the hell had happened? He pushed the heel of his hand back into his forehead. *Idiot!*

It had been like this the first time he saw her. She'd arrived breathless, like a beautiful, vibrantly exotic bird, grabbing his attention so that he'd barely been able to concentrate on surgical technique. Her fierce intelligence had shone joyfully out of the most beautiful eyes in the operating theatre, like the Mediterranean Sea at sunrise, and he'd been lost.

His time with Kiki in Australia had blurred into a golden haze of laughter and loving and lust, and even his responsibility to Aspelicus had faded for a brief while.

When duty had called he'd fully intended going back to reassess it all properly—discover where it led. He had thought it would be a matter of days before his return, but first there had been the accident, then the months of rehabilitation, when the chance of losing the use of his leg had hung in the balance. It had all kept him away. As if the gods had intended they should both suffer for too perfect a match.

By then she'd disappeared. And more crises had arrived. Slowly his mind had been torn from her as well—except for that tiny halo in his heart.

But it was bad that he had hurt her. Profoundly. He could see that now, and deeply he regretted it. The trouble was that it seemed if he had an opportunity to hold her again he had no choice but to take it. Hold her. Lose himself. This had to stop. This was not healthy.

Not wholesome. Because the way he felt at this moment he would destroy them both before he could stop the way he wanted her.

The next morning, as the ship moored at Civitavecchia for Rome, the clinic was quiet.

'You okay?' Will looked at Kiki with concern.

She forced a smile. 'I must have eaten something that disagreed with me.'

Like a morning-after pill that sat on her stomach like a rock. She couldn't rid her mind of the distant warning that this had been the only chance she'd had to carry Stefano's child again. She hated that thought.

'Take the day off sick. I've got nothing planned. We'll manage.'

'No. I'll be better with something in my stomach, perhaps. It's fine. I'll stay.'

'Why?' Will gently propelled her out into the empty waiting room and towards the door. 'Go. Lie down. Read a book. You're allowed five sick days a year and you haven't had one.'

She didn't want to go back to her cabin to beat herself up. To go over in her mind relentlessly how she'd allowed herself to be seduced, had reciprocated in the seduction. It was an even tougher pill to swallow.

But she did feel miserable—and not just mentally.

'Okay. But I'll swap a day. I'll do one for you next week.' She looked at Will's concerned face and felt bad, but relieved. 'Thanks. I'll see you tomorrow.'

'Do you want me to get them to send up some food?'

'You're a sweetie.' She offered a wan smile. 'No. I'll wander. See if anything looks appealing.'

At least she needn't worry about running into Stefano in the public dining rooms. Far too plebeian for a prince. Though, to give him his due, he just avoided public places himself—he had no grudge against them.

Stefano had never played on his royal privileges or his power with her.

Except yesterday, when he'd thought she was sleeping with Will.

That had shocked her. There had been real possessiveness in that threat, and she didn't understand why.

If he'd wanted her, truly wanted her, then surely he would have moved heaven and earth to get back to her. How hard was it to pick up a phone? E-mail? Even a stamped addressed envelope would have been nice.

That was the crux of everything. She hadn't meant enough for him to follow through and say he wasn't coming back. Though, looking at what had happened between them yesterday, maybe he'd just expected to drop in every couple of months or so and be back in her bed.

She groaned and climbed the stairs to her room. As expected, when she got there it closed in around her.

Nope. She couldn't stay here.

Swiftly she shed her white uniform and stood in front of her small wardrobe. Brightly printed sundresses made her want to shade her eyes, and she winced her way along the rack until she came to black. Perfect. It suited her mood. Suited her intentions if the absolute worst happened and she came across him.

CHAPTER FOUR

STEFANO HAD LEARNED from last time. When he telephoned the hospital, as expected, the nurse answered.

'No, Dr Fender is not working today. In fact she has just left to get something to eat.'

She thought perhaps in the main dining area.

Stefano had not been through the main entertainment and restaurant areas. Apart from an early-morning swim in the lap pool just before Marla's unfortunate medical crisis, he'd avoided the other passengers. A discreet perusal of the common areas would not hurt him.

Kiki looked at the array of food, grimaced, and chose a banana. She knew they were good for hangovers and, while she hadn't had any alcohol, the Stefano hangover left her all kinds of miserable. Her belly rolled and she glanced at her watch. Not time yet for her next antiemetic. That was the problem with morning-after pills. The nausea that accompanied them was pervasive.

As she wandered back out to the pool area a redheaded pre-teenage boy scooted past, almost knocked her down, slowed, and called sorry over his shoulder. He spied his brother, obviously a twin because they looked so similar, closing in, and put on speed again.

To have that much energy... 'Hey, slow down,' Kiki called after him.

Just then his brother slid into sight, didn't make the corner, lost purchase as he rounded a post at speed, and before Kiki could tell him to slow down it was too late!

The second boy's feet flew from under him and, unable to save himself, he slammed his head of red hair into the steel pole.

Kiki stood, stunned, then her mind clicked into gear. She took two quick strides and fell to her knees to bend over him, but the boy had clearly been unconscious before he hit the ground.

Kiki hailed a passing waiter who'd missed the action and sent him off speedily to summon further medical aid. Apart from him there were very few people near her.

Until the last passenger she wanted to see appeared and strode over.

For the boy's sake she was glad. For herself less so. She ignored the surge of nausea as Stefano approached, and forestalled any comment other than on the present. 'Did you see him hit?'

Stefano nodded. 'If he has not fractured his skull he is very lucky. I will take the neck as we roll.'

Stefano placed his hands either side in case of spinal injury, and together they turned him carefully onto his side to keep his airway clear.

Just then his brother reappeared around Stefano's shoulder, his freckled face screwed up with fright. 'Is he okay?'

Kiki recognised him with relief. 'What's your name?'

'Mikey.'

'And your brother's name, Mikey? And the number of the cabin your family's in?'

The terrified boy stuttered out that his name was Chris, and the number, and Kiki repeated it to make sure she had it right.

'Okay. Go get your parents. I'm a doctor. Your brother hit his head and knocked himself out. We'll take him down to the ship's hospital as soon as the stretcher gets here and we'll meet you down there with them.' The frightened boy nodded and sped off. 'Slowly!' Kiki cautioned him, and she saw him reduce his pace to a jog.

Stefano's mind rolled back the years to a moment he'd never forget. A time when he too had been terrified at his brother's lack of response. The feeling of being powerless to prevent an accident, to prevent disaster. His father's constant reminder that *he* had been the responsible one weighed heavily even now. It was no wonder he needed to feel in control as a man. But he could feel that control slip away now, as this boy sank deeper into unconsciousness.

Kiki must have seen the sadness in his eyes, because she paled and he recognised the moment when she too felt the presence of impending disaster.

'You think he's critical?' she asked quietly.

'Theros was like that as a boy. Always rushing.'

She frowned, missing the context—for which he was glad. No doubt she was impatient with his latex-loving sibling right now.

She shook her head and concentrated on the boy. 'I heard the impact. Horrible. Wilhelm should be here with a stretcher ASAP, but he'll need to be shipped out.'

'I agree.' Stefano lifted the boy's eyelids one at a

time to see his pupils and frowned. 'If we are that lucky.'

Will and Ginger arrived and Stefano helped them ease on a spinal collar and slide the boy onto the stretcher on a spine board. Within minutes they were all crammed in the lift on their way to the hospital, and Stefano could feel his own heart-rate increase as he watched tiny ominous changes in the boy. A flicker of a tremor in one finger. The shudder of an indrawn laboured breath. Nobody spoke as the doors shut and they all watched their patient.

He saw Hobson look at Kiki. 'He'll need to be shipped out immediately.'

Stefano checked the pupils again. 'There may not be time. Already one pupil is dilating.'

Will shuddered. 'So fast?'

'It happens.' He glanced up at him. 'Do you have the equipment for burr holes here?'

'Craniotomy? I guess so.' Will looked at Ginger, who nodded. 'But I've never done it. Cranial surgery's not a common thing on cruise liners. We should chopper him out from the wharf. Faster than an ambulance.'

Stefano shook his head. 'The preferred option is retrieval, but I do not like the look of this. It should be considered just in case.' They all knew even that took time.

'Kiki says you're a surgeon. If it's burr holes will you stay? Supervise?' Will asked.

Stefano nodded. He could not leave and never know.

'Of course.' Then he saw the limbs on one side of the boy begin to tremble, faintly at first, and then with greater intensity as he began to convulse. Stefano helped Hobson hold him desperately to keep his cervical spine stable until the seizure ended.

Chris's breathing slowed, stuttered, and the boy's condition deteriorated further even in the short time it took to descend to the hospital. Stefano's heart sank. To them all Chris's prognosis had begun to look horrifyingly bleak.

Kiki fought back the horrible feeling they would be too late and helped Ginger steer the trolley from the lift as soon as the fit ceased. That was when she realised the boy's parents had arrived before them.

Stefano hadn't seen them. 'The fits will get worse as the pressure builds.'

'What will get worse?'

A bluff redheaded man hurried across to them with his worried wife and Mikey in tow. Kiki gently guided them aside as the others pushed through to the hospital.

'Hello, I'm Dr Fender.' She took the man's hand. 'Is Chris your son?'

Worried grey eyes met hers. 'Yes. Mikey said he hit his head.'

Kiki nodded. 'It was a very nasty fall. I saw it. Dr Hobson and Dr Mykonides are going to examine him now. While they're doing that we need to know if Chris has any other illnesses, or allergies that we should know of. Has he ever had any operations?'

The father looked at his wife and she shook her head, fear huge in her eyes as she realised the gravity of Chris's accident. 'Is he going to be all right?'

Kiki could only pray. 'I'm sorry, I can't answer that. He's very ill. He may have fractured his skull and torn a vessel inside his head. It looks as though he is building a collection of blood that is pressing on his brain.

Our first preference is to fly him out by helicopter from the wharf because his condition is so critical.'

She looked at them, deeply sympathetic, but sensible to the fact they needed to know what was going on.

'As soon as the doctors have examined Chris we'll know if we have time to transfer him. Dr Mykonides is a passenger, but also a very experienced surgeon. He will know what is best.' Chris's mother began to weep silently and Kiki drew them into the waiting room. 'I'll send the nurse out to see if she can get you something while I find out what going on.'

'Thank you, Doctor.' The boy's father drew his wife and son under the shelter of his arms and Kiki felt the tears sting her eyes.

'I'll be as quick as I can.'

The father's voice followed her. 'Take all the time you need. We'll wait.'

She nodded, left and prayed as she hurried into join the others. Surely Chris would recover. She knew how she'd felt the pain of grief when she'd lost her tiny baby, but couldn't imagine the worry *they* must be feeling.

Wilhelm had booked the retrieval team but they would be thirty minutes before arrival at the earliest.

'We'll lose him if we wait.' Stefano examined the depressed skull fracture on the rapid X-ray they'd taken while Kiki read out the boy's blood pressure and pulse. He shook his head. 'I give fifteen before brain damage is irreversible,' Stefano confided in Kiki quietly.

Kiki agreed. 'Systolic blood pressure's rising, widening of pulse pressure, and his pulse is slowing.'

The pressure inside the head was compressing

Chris's brain down towards the base of his skull. At some point it would do irreversible damage.

Will nodded. 'Let's do it.'

Kiki looked at Wilhelm. 'I'll talk to the parents, get consent, while you and Stefano get scrubbed. The nurse can get him set up in the suture room. We can make this happen fast.'

Chris's parents stood up quickly when Kiki hurried into the waiting room.

'A helicopter's on its way but Chris has pressure from the blood building very quickly on his brain. Already his blood pressure is high and his pulse has slowed right down. Dr Hobson and the surgeon, Dr Mykonides, agree it is imperative to operate now to relieve that pressure. I'm sorry to have to tell you there is a real risk Chris might not survive his arrival at the hospital if we don't do something now.'

Chris's mother put her hand over her mouth and hugged her husband, and Kiki saw the lump shift in his father's throat as he gathered his wife in. 'Then do it.'

Kiki passed them the consent form, and the father signed quickly. 'They're setting him up now. The object is to make small round holes in Chris's skull to let the pressure out and repair the bleeding artery before the brain is damaged. It's an emergency lifesaving procedure. We may be too late. Do you understand?'

'Just save him. And afterwards?'

'A medical team will arrive to stabilise him and transfer him to a hospital neurological ward.' She squeezed the mother's shoulder. 'Do you have any other questions?'

The father looked at his wife and other son. 'Not now. He's in your hands. Hurry.'

Kiki nodded and did just that.

By the time she was back in the tiny operating theatre Chris's skull had been shaved on the side of the fracture and draped to create a sterile field. Will and Stefano were preparing the area with an antiseptic solution.

'Consent signed. They'll ask questions later. Please go ahead.'

The ventilator machine was breathing for him, but no anaesthetic had been used because the boy was deeply unconscious. It would be Kiki's task to monitor that and Stefano handed Will a syringe of local anaesthetic for the skin incision just in case.

Will hesitated and Stefano waved him on. 'Let's go. Inject the site. Make a three-centimetre incision through the skin. Separate the fascia.'

Will did so and the boy didn't move. His breathing sounded mechanically in the room and Kiki was glad they'd had time to intubate, because at least they could keep him going until the pressure on his breathing centre was released.

She'd never seen the operation before, and Stefano kept a commentary going as Will performed the surgery.

'Control the bleeding with the diathermy. Use the retractors now.' They could all see Will's hands shaking but Stefano's voice was rock-solid. 'Exactly. Yes. Now drill the hole with the hand drill two centimetres above and behind the orbital process of the frontal bone.'

Will's hands shook more, and Stefano leaned across and steadied him.

'This is good. You will be an old hand soon.' He glanced at Kiki. 'How's our boy going?'

'Holding his own, just. Pulse now forty. BP one fifty on forty.'

'We have a minute or two at the most. Faster drilling.'

Stefano's eyes looked even grimmer and Kiki wondered if he was frustrated by Will's nerves. She couldn't tell, and wondered if he might throw legality to the wind and take over.

Will continued with the procedure.

'Watch for the release of pressure.' Just as the words left Stefano's mouth a thin, powerful stream of blood shot upwards high off the table from the collection in Chris's head.

Will jumped back as it slowed to an oozing trickle and Stefano murmured, 'Good. Pressure is released.'

Will shuddered. 'No wonder his observations were going off.'

'Speed is essential. Now we find the bleeder.' Stefano pointed with tiny mosquito forceps. 'There it is. Tie it off.'

Will leaned in. Tying off vessels was something he was good at.

'Good. Now bandage for transfer.'

Half an hour later the emergency team loaded an almost stable Chris into the helicopter.

Stefano walked across to where the other boy watched the transfer of his brother. His red hair stood on end from his agonised raking and fat tears rolled down his freckled face. He knew the turmoil ahead and Stefano's heart ached for him.

Mikey looked up. 'It's my fault. I shouldn't have teased him. He wouldn't have been so angry.'

Stefano put his hand on the boy's shoulder, squeezed the bony ridge as Mikey dashed his hand across his eyes. 'It is hard to watch. Especially for you as a twin.'

Stefano sighed as he fought back his own images. He couldn't bear the thought that this boy would go through the remorse he had.

'My brother was sick like yours once. And I tell you it is *not* your fault your brother hit his head. Boys run and chase, and things happen we have no control over. It could have been you that fell and he would not have been able to stop it happening.'

Mikey looked away from Chris to the man beside him and he did not look so woebegone. 'You think?'

He knew. 'You did everything right by getting your parents to the hospital. We might not have saved your brother without them being there so quickly.'

Mikey sniffed and rubbed his nose with the back of his hand. 'I ran. I did what the doctor asked me to do.'

Stefano nodded and patted the boy's shoulder again before he lifted his hand. 'You did well. Your brother is strong and he has you.'

They watched the helicopter pilot start the rotors and soon it was in the air. Chris parents came across to shake Wilhelm's hand and thank Kiki and Stefano, and then with Mikey they climbed into a waiting taxi that would take them to the hospital.

Will turned to Stefano and nodded. 'Thank you.' He sighed ruefully. 'Though I wish you could have done it.'

Stefano smiled grimly. 'No. It is better to have the experience. One day another boy may need your skills, and doing it yourself can never be replaced by watching. There were only seconds between the same result for you or I.'

Will nodded again and glanced at the ship that shadowed them on the wharf. 'I need to report to the Captain.' He glanced at Kiki, and then Stefano, but held his tongue. 'See you later.'

Kiki felt as if she'd been run over by steamroller now the tension had been relieved by Chris's transfer, and suddenly it didn't matter that Stefano was the only one left beside her.

She saw him in a different light. She'd watched him go out and talk to Mikey and hadn't been able to help overhearing some of his words.

Today Stefano had been kind, thoughtful, and a steady teacher. As much as she hated to admit it, he'd seemed like the man she'd fallen for. He'd been great with Will. And he obviously cared about the trauma to both boys.

So what had happened to them? Her and Stefano? Nine months ago? Didn't she deserve the same consideration that he now gave to an unknown family?

It didn't make sense that he'd stepped out of character and left her with no further contact after the week they'd had without a good reason.

Was there more she didn't know?

'Perhaps we should talk?'

Stefano smiled ruefully and she felt the mirror of her own response. 'Somewhere public?'

'Lord, yes.' No way was she going anywhere near his bedroom.

CHAPTER FIVE

STEFANO STEERED KIKI to the rooftop coffee shop and chose a corner table behind an exuberant fake palm. Kiki didn't mind because she was feeling particularly pale and not very interesting as nausea elbowed its way back into her consciousness now she had time to think about herself.

Stefano frowned as he noticed her pallor. 'Do you wish for something to eat?'

Kiki's stomach rolled and she winced. 'No, thank you. Just black tea.'

'You are unwell?'

He leaned towards her and again she recognised the tang of his cologne. This time, unfortunately, it wasn't her stomach that reacted. Something much more visceral stood up and waved.

She leaned back. 'Something I ate.'

'Strangely, my appetite for food is also absent.' His eyes darkened and she hated that—because she could feel herself weaken...and waken.

There was that damned glint in his eyes that she couldn't help but smile at. 'Stop it.'

He shrugged those shoulders and she looked away.

He said, 'So, I admit it is good to see you, Kiki.'

She wasn't falling into that one. 'No comment.'

His brows went up teasingly. 'So comment on something else.'

Umm. Something safe. 'Do you think Chris will be okay?'

He shrugged, not with unconcern—she could see that—but with a glimmer of hope despite the contrariness of life. 'I will keep in contact by phone, but I think the surgery should have done the job before damage, and his vitals maintained perfusion. Tomorrow will give a good indication.'

She'd known that. But still it was good to hear the hope in his voice. A silence fell. She could feel his eyes on her.

'I think there is more you wish to discuss with me.'

Well, he was right there. She should get it out and finished with. Dispel the questions that were beginning to eat at her all over again. She drew a deep breath and looked back at him. 'Why didn't you contact me after you left so hurriedly?'

The waitress arrived, took their order, smiled and batted her eyelashes at Stefano. He allowed her to walk away, and when she was out of earshot he leaned forward and said the last thing she'd expected.

'I was in an accident. Unconscious and then physically disabled.'

He had her full attention as she searched his face. Now she could see them. Tiny lines that hadn't been there before, a few strands of silver through his black hair at the side of his face. She had a sudden memory of that ridge of scar on his hip she'd fleetingly discovered yesterday. Her fingers fidgeted with the salt shaker, tensed, ached to reach across and touch his hand in sympathy. But luckily she wasn't that stupid.

She let go of the shaker and retreated her hand to the edge of the cloth. 'What kind of accident?'

'Motor vehicle. I spent several months in hospital. By the time I was discharged and could begin to sort what needed to be sorted you were gone.'

He laid his hand palm up on the table, as if to signal he knew she wanted to comfort him with touch. Like a coward she shifted her hand into her lap, and his fingers closed over themselves emptily as he sat back.

When she didn't say anything he said, 'By the time I could look, I could not find you. I thought perhaps you wished it that way.'

He watched her face and she saw the moment he understood that she had, actually. By then.

So would she tell him about her own little visit to hospital? No. She couldn't go there now. It was all too painfully close.

'I was on ship. Had my own family stuff happening. My brother got married. I made friends here.'

He sat back further, as if to illustrate the distance between them now. 'Life went on?'

She nodded, as if everything was sweetness and light. Not the way she was feeling. 'As it does.'

'But now we meet again.'

His voice dropped like that cloak around her shoulders and she mentally shook herself at the spell he could weave just by words and cadence and his very presence.

Harden up, she reminded herself, and sat straighter in the chair. 'Life is still going to go on, Stefano. You'll get off the ship. I'll sail away.'

He leaned forward. 'It does not have to be that way.'

'Yes, it does.'

She wasn't stupid. She'd learnt her lesson. Yes, he'd been sick for a couple of months, but that had been months ago. No contact after that because she didn't count enough. Well, she deserved better than that.

'Because we're from two very different worlds.'

It would always be that way, which was why she wasn't going to put her heart out there to be stamped on again. Or be seduced into his bed for the next few convenient days.

Now his voice was more formal and his expression more difficult to read. 'So are you always going to be a ship's doctor?'

But she didn't need to read him. She just needed to get out of here. 'No. I'm ready to move on.' Now. Literally. She glanced at him. 'Funny how I feel so unsettled today,' she said dryly.

'And where would you move on to?'

She shrugged. This whole scenario was surreal. They were like two acquaintances, chatting over a cup of tea. 'Maybe I'll go for experience. There's always the other extreme to this—foreign aid medicine. My brother's wife worked in a tent city in the Sudan. Or I could move into family medicine with Nick and his wife back in Australia.'

He nodded. 'It is very beautiful there.'

'They're having twins.' She shut her mouth with a snap as hurt from the past rose in her chest.

Her eyes prickled. She did not want to talk about expected newborns with Stefano.

She looked away hurriedly, in case he saw something in her face, then went on brightly as she drained her tea. 'Or I could go back to Sydney to another hospital. The family home's still there.'

'I see you have put some thought into this.' He looked pensive.

She didn't like to tell him it was only since yesterday. His fault. All she had to do was resign.

The nausea rose unexpectedly and she stood up. 'I'm sorry. I have to go.'

He rose also, his forehead creased with concern. 'Let me see you to your cabin safely.'

She could almost smile at that. 'I'm in the crew section. Out of bounds for passengers. So you see...' she leant on the table and pushed herself away from him '...I will be safe.'

Stefano watched her hurry away. Was she really nauseated? She looked pale—or was she upset? Did she hate him that much? All questions he would like an answer to, he mulled as he walked back to his suite. There was more going on than she had explained, he was certain of it, because deep in his gut he knew she was hurting—and he had caused it.

It seemed it was his lot in life to hurt the people he loved. But how to ensure she would at least talk to him?

Perhaps it was time to take the Captain up on his offer to inspect the bridge.

Will sent Ginger to check on her around four. 'Will wants to know if you're up for dinner in the officers' mess tonight. Captain's request.'

Kiki sighed. 'Bloody Stefano.' She didn't think she'd said it out loud but apparently she had.

Ginger looked suitably shocked. 'Kiki! I haven't been here long but I've never heard you swear.'

Stefano hadn't been here then. 'Sorry, Ginger. But stick around for the next three days and you might hear more.' *Oooohhh,* she'd kill him.

Ginger sighed dreamily. 'He must really like you.'

Yeah, right. 'He liked me before. For a week.' Indiscreet. She shouldn't have said that. But she guessed most people could tell they knew each other a little. Even Wilhelm had noticed. 'Stefano's bored and he thinks he can amuse himself before he disappears back to his little island.'

Ginger laughed. 'You can't really call Aspelicus a little island. It's got mountains, and flat lands—and casinos, even. And it has this massive village on the side of the volcano, a gorgeous palace, and a fab hospital.' She rolled her eyes in ecstasy. 'It's the most amazing place.'

Kiki had to laugh. 'You've obviously been there?'

'Last year. I was knocking around with the in crowd with my on-again off-again boyfriend—gossip columnist, long story—and we ended up there for the Prince's Cup.'

'A horse race?'

Ginger nodded nostalgically. 'Magical horse race they do there every year along this spit of sand at the edge of the island. Raises squillions for the hospital. And there's balls and cocktails and champagne lunches. I swear I put on ten pounds over five days.'

Ginger grinned.

'Anyway, Stefano looked pretty amazing as the host. So I guess I have a soft spot and can't get over the fact you don't want to play with him.'

Kiki rolled her shoulders and rubbed the wooden

block full of tension that was her neck. 'Because after the fun and games I'm left picking up the pieces.'

'He really hurt you.' Ginger must have heard the truth because her expression changed to one of sympathy. 'I'm sorry. Want me to tell Wilhelm you're not up to dinner?'

Kiki knew she'd have to go. 'It was a request from the Captain. I can't decline just because I want to avoid his guest.'

Ginger was still new. 'Why not?'

You just didn't do it. 'Because Stefano will blow it all out of proportion, I'll find myself in sick bay, and Will doesn't deserve the hassle.' She sighed. 'What time?'

'Seven.' Ginger twisted her hands. 'The nurses have been invited as well. Umm…do you think you could introduce me to that dishy Miko if you get a chance?'

Her friend Miko, who smiled as if he knew more than Kiki was saying. 'He's a heartbreaker.'

Ginger shrugged. 'I need someone to take my thoughts away from my ex. I'm not here for marriage. And I heard he was fun.'

Kiki grinned. 'He's fun, all right.'

When Stefano saw Kiki enter with Hobson the rest of the room faded. He thought she looked less pale than earlier, which was what he'd wanted to see. Or that was what he told himself.

'Ah, the medical staff are here.' The Captain smiled. 'But of course you have shared high drama with them already. Dr Hobson tells me your advice was invaluable.'

Through his contacts Stefano had been updated

hourly on Chris's condition and the boy was improving steadily. 'Dr Hobson and Dr Fender were instrumental in saving that boy's life. And the nurses, of course. You have a brilliant medical team on your ship, Captain.'

The Captain visibly preened. 'I'm glad to hear it.'

'Of course Dr Fender and I are old friends.' His companion straightened with interest and Stefano chose his words carefully. 'We met during a consultancy I held in Sydney last year. I fear she is concerned someone might think she's consorting unprofessionally with a passenger if she's seen too much with me.'

The Captain was eager to dispel such a thought. 'Not at all. Fraternisation does not apply with previous acquaintances.'

'I thought not,' Stefano said smoothly, 'but of course I'm glad to hear you say so.'

'No problem.' The Captain stepped forward to meet Wilhelm and Kiki as a waiter circled with a tray of champagne.

Kiki knew the Captain and Stefano were looking her way and were talking about her. Her ears were practically on fire.

'Soda for me,' Kiki said, and took the glass with a thank-you nod at the waiter as Stefano and the Captain approached. She should have asked for something with a kick. She plastered a smile on her face.

'Prince Stefano has been singing your praises, Kiki. All of the medical team, in fact.'

Kiki could play that game. Nice and impersonal. 'We were lucky to have such a surgeon to consult with, sir.'

'Prince Stefano tells me the boy is improving consistently. There is real hope he will make a full recovery. And no threat of the parents suing my ship.'

She didn't care if Stefano saw how much that news improved her evening. It was worth coming just for the information. 'That is wonderful news about Chris, sir. And of course your ship.'

The impulse to share her joy with Stefano meant she couldn't avoid looking at him any longer. Of course he was watching her when she did sneak a glance.

She searched manfully for a topic to deflect the pink that was rising in her cheeks. 'Your brother and his wife are not here, Your Highness?'

She saw his brows lower at her mode of address. 'Theros and Marla are watching the show tonight.'

The Captain nodded eagerly. 'The show is excellent. Of course the crew's pageant will be on in two nights. You must not miss it, Prince Stefano. Kiki and Miko dance.' The Captain sighed nostalgically, glanced around and gestured the restaurant manager over. 'They tango brilliantly.'

Kiki distracted herself by watching Miko cross the room. All the women smiled as he joked and nodded, more of celebrity than the actual Prince. Kiki couldn't help her smile. He was such a hoot.

'Sir.' Miko saluted and the Captain introduced Stefano.

'I think you have not met our royal guest—Prince Stefano of Aspelicus.'

Miko made a very creditable bow and Stefano nodded his head.

Oblivious, the Captain went on. 'I was just saying how much I enjoy watching the crew pageant and especially your dances.'

Miko gallantly turned to Kiki. 'It is all because of my beautiful partner. She is a feather.' He lifted Kiki's fingers to kiss her hand with consummate grace. 'You look ravishing as always, Dr Fender.'

Kiki grinned and pulled her hand away. Something made her glance at Stefano, who had narrowed his eyes at the interloper. All trace of good humour had disappeared from his face and she remembered the way he'd reacted to her quip about Will.

Kiki decided discretion was the better part of valour. 'I have someone who wants to meet you, Miko. Excuse me, Captain, Prince Stefano.' And she drew the playful restaurateur away before more damage could be done.

'Ho-ho, if looks could kill,' Miko whispered teasingly in her ear.

Kiki relaxed against him. 'You are a menace.'

Miko's voice dropped even lower. 'And you have been sleeping with the Prince.'

'Stop it.'

He shrugged. 'You have known him before, perhaps? He is very jealous.'

Jealous, or a dog in the manger? 'That's his problem.'

'And mine if he thinks you care for me.' But Miko laughed. He wasn't stupid. 'And also a problem for you too.' He shrugged as they moved out of sight. 'So why do you fight this great attraction?'

Survival. 'Because we are from different worlds and he has hurt me before.'

'And Nick knows of this?'

Kiki felt like stamping her feet. 'Why does everyone think my brother has to know about my life?'

Miko shrugged. 'Because he will kill us if anything happens to you. So it is purely selfish on my part.'

She had to laugh. 'You are so shallow.'

'That is true. But it's also true that is what you love about me. Come. Introduce me to this woman who wishes to meet me and I will let you go back to your brooding Prince.'

Kiki poked him. 'I'm sticking with you and I'm going to spoil your chances of seduction.' Kiki stopped when she found the nurse. 'Ginger, I'd like you to meet my friend Miko. I'm sure you've seen him around.'

Miko bowed. 'It is a great pleasure to meet you, Ginger. I believe this is your first cruise with us?' Miko lowered his head over Ginger's fingers and while his vision was obstructed Ginger winked her thanks.

The Second Officer approached and as Miko straightened he glanced at Kiki and grinned. 'Kiki? You are leaving us? I fear the Captain has placed you at his table.'

Next to Stefano.

The men stood as she approached and Stefano frowned away the waiter who'd moved to hold her chair.

As she slid into her seat she murmured, 'Seated by a prince. I am lucky,' and sat demurely with her hands in her lap. Stefano settled in next to her.

'Behave or I will not sit next to you.'

'You arranged it.'

'True. Because I can.' He changed the subject. 'I realise we have not danced.'

What had brought that on? Dog in the manger? 'Apparently you have to go out in public to do that.'

He sat back in his chair and regarded her. 'Not always, but *touché*. Of course I am happy to meet your conditions.' He gestured with his hand. 'After this, perhaps?'

Not likely. 'I'm afraid not.'

Silkily he said in her ear. 'And why are you afraid?'

Thankfully the entree arrived at the same time and she didn't have to answer. She turned to the person on her right.

Stefano was not altogether displeased. So she was afraid of her own response in his arms? A healthy respect for the severity of their fierce attraction was wise. Not fear of him, but of herself, for he had never sought to inspire anything but lust in Kiki's beautiful breast.

Stefano hid his smile and turned to the lady on his left.

The Captain's wife was Sicilian and had visited Aspelicus before. She was very pleased to be seated next to the Crown Prince. Stefano knew it would amuse Kiki to see him cornered, so he paid such flattering attention to the good lady he doubted he would be allowed to eat in his suite again.

Thankfully the Captain's wife enjoyed her food, and when the main course arrived he could turn to his other companion.

'The Captain tells me you are off duty tomorrow when we dock. I will be flying out to Aspelicus for the day on a matter of state that will not take long. Perhaps this could be a chance for you to see my homeland.'

Before she could decline he went on.

'We would have time to visit my facial reconstruction clinic before we leave. It has facets of treatment that may interest you.'

She shouldn't be tempted, but his genuine passion for his work was clearly evident and it called to the vocation in herself. 'How far is Aspelicus that you can fly to do business and come back?'

He clicked his fingers. 'A mere hour's fight.'

The Captain's wife leaned across. 'You should go, dear. It's fabulous. And the Prince will look after you.'

Kiki muttered under her breath. 'That's what I'm afraid of.'

CHAPTER SIX

THE NEXT MORNING, as the ship docked in Livorno, after a night of mental flogging because she'd weakened, Kiki had to school the shock from her face when Stefano arrived at the gangway to disembark.

Dressed in a designer suit as black as his hair, with his royal chain of office flashing gold and precious stones in the sunlight, he looked nothing like the man she could lose herself in.

Her first taste of royal bling and she had to admit he wore it well. Too well.

The passengers leaning over the ship's verandas seemed impressed too, if the flashing of cameras was anything to go by.

His man opened the door of the official car and gathered her in. It was a discreet luxury sedan, so hopefully people wouldn't gawk and point at them as they drove along. She slid across the seat, suddenly glad she'd worn her best trousers and a camisole with a jacket, because even though she was off the ship it looked as if this was a day when she'd need everything she had to keep her head above the water line.

'I'm sorry to have kept you waiting.' Stefano slid in next to her, and despite the gap between them on the seat she could feel the shimmering energy field as he settled.

'You made quite an entrance.'

He narrowed his eyes at her as if perplexed. 'How so?'

And didn't she wish she hadn't started *that* conversation? 'You look very princely.'

'At the risk of being simplistic, it is my job.'

Well, she'd asked for that. But he looked so overpoweringly regal she was feeling threatened by her own insignificance. Not something she'd ever felt before. And what would it be like when they arrived at the palace, where he held considerable power?

Just the thought of feeling inferior made her spine stiffen. 'You said you have matters of state to deal with? What will I do while you attend to those?'

His gaze softened as if he sensed how unsure she was about their arrival. 'I had thought Elise, my housekeeper, could show you over the palace if you would like. She will no doubt burn your ears with her historical fervour. Elise is very proud of the island's heritage.'

So she was to be diverted to the housekeeper. That should keep her out of the way. 'She sounds interesting.'

He didn't turn to face her. 'She is, but if you are not in the mood for a history lesson you could relax in the library and browse. We have an extensive collection of original books collected by my mother.'

'Both options sound appealing.' But the history more so. She could sit in libraries any day.

Now he turned to her. Searched her face. 'I should not be long. It is a matter of signing papers that should have been ready a week ago, and the settlement of a matter which has caused my father some concern for too long. Hence my decision to be done with it today.'

The car drove onto the tarmac of the airport and eased smoothly to a stop.

Stefano glanced out of the window. 'I hope helicopters do not worry you?'

'Not that I've noticed in the past.' *Never been in one.* She was quite pleased with her nonchalant tone, but seriously, how many people chose helicopters as their basic transport?

She'd been psyching herself for a sleek little Learjet at worst, but there was not much she could do about their mode of travel now.

'I'll be fine.' Though it looked more like a large bumble bee than an aircraft.

To top it off Stefano had climbed into the pilot's seat and the lump in her throat tightened. His man opened the rear door. 'I'll sit in the back, shall I?' she murmured to herself, and allowed him to bow her into the helicopter with its royal insignia, her reluctance disguised because she'd always prided herself on her sense of adventure.

This definitely rated as an adventure. She'd bet there were hundreds of girls who would have changed places with her, and she wondered again why Stefano had manoeuvred her into accompanying him on this excursion.

As soon as the pre-flight check was complete Stefano turned and assured himself that she was strapped in before he started the engine.

As the roar grew louder the little cabin began to shake and she resurrected the deep breathing exercises she'd learnt long ago during her obstetric term. Calmness at take-off seemed a great idea.

In through the nose all the way down to the base of her lungs, hold for three, and ease out through the mouth before breathing in again. She didn't care that the breaths seemed loud in her ears and that Stefano's man must be looking at her strangely.

Thankfully after six inhalations the flutter in her chest began to ease, and when she opened her eyes that were three feet above the ground and going up fast.

Everything happened very quickly after that as they rose and turned and soared away from the helipad towards the Mediterranean Sea. The shimmer of the waves below made her squint and reach for her sunglasses in her bag, and away to her left the hull of their ship overshadowed the docks.

Islands dotted the horizon in tiny volcanic outcrops, some with soaring peaks and others quite low to the water. After nearly an hour, during which she'd begun to enjoy the bird's eye view over the waves. she realised they were approaching a larger island, shaped almost like a whale, with the hump of a volcano in the middle and three separate areas of inhabitation. A long beach on one side edged a magnificent horse racing track, and she guessed that was where all Ginger's action had happened.

They approached the soaring volcanic cliffs and flew towards a turreted castle perched in a position impossible to assail without permission. As she looked down at a ribbon of winding road that circled the cliffs she guessed that was the way to the gate. And when she saw the even tinier toy cars that clung to it she wondered if that was where Stefano had had his accident.

To the left were rolling hills with what looked like miles of olive trees and scattered small villages, and on the other side of the island it seemed there was a small city she barely saw before the sight was cut off as they approached the castle.

Her stomach rose and fell as they landed on a brightly painted H on the castle forecourt with a tiny bump, and then Stefano had lifted his headphones and turned back to her with the flash of a white smile. A man who enjoyed his time at the controls. Why would that surprise her?

The door beside her opened and she fumbled to release her seat belt as fresh mountain air rushed into the little helicopter. Her companion was already out, and Stefano had waved away the person in front of him and waited with hand outstretched to help her from the cabin.

'Welcome to Aspelicus, Dr Fender,' he said formally, but the twinkle in his eye showed he was pleased to be able to share this moment with her.

She had no choice but to lay her hand in his, and of course when his hand closed around hers she couldn't help the smile she returned. She really needed to learn to avoid physical contact with this man.

'Thank you, Your Highness.' She gathered her own control and looked around. 'Your castle is very beautiful.' The words replayed in her head. Even the conversation was surreal.

'I think so.' He turned to a tall grey-haired woman who had crossed to his side. Her eyes were warm and kind and she obviously adored Stefano. 'Elise, this is Dr Fender. Please care for her this morning, until I can return.'

'Certainly, Your Highness.' She inclined her head, obviously happy to do whatever he wished.

Stefano nodded and strode off towards another stair-way, surrounded by suited figures, before Kiki realised he was going away.

So much for goodbye, Kiki thought. A bit abrupt in the leave-taking department, to her mind, but maybe she was being childish to expect anything else.

Elise waved her hand gracefully towards the main sweeping castle steps. 'This way, Dr Fender.'

Feeling a little like an unwanted package, Kiki lifted her chin. 'Please, call me Kiki.' She smiled at the older woman. 'And may I call you Elise?'

'Certainly. Welcome to Aspelicus.'

They turned and began to climb the wide stone steps. Sections of the stone had been worn away by feet over the centuries.

Kiki glanced around. Everywhere the castle was me-ticulously maintained, from its flowerbeds to lichen-free stone. 'The castle looks old but very beautiful.'

'Some form of the castle has perched here for over a thousand years, and thankfully all generations have continued to treat it with respect and care so that it re-mains as strong today as it has ever been.'

Elise glanced around and Kiki had no doubt that any fault found would be swiftly acted upon.

'And has Prince Stefano's family always been the ruling family?' She couldn't believe she was talking about the man whose bed she'd left only yesterday. At that thought the heat rushed to her cheeks, and she stopped to examine a particularly ugly gargoyle and breathe back control.

Elise's voice drifted over her shoulder as she, too, paused. 'Indeed. Which is rare. They have been fortunate in that their sons have been most virile and capable of siring many lines.'

With a pang of loss, Kiki knew she could believe that.

'Now, with Prince Theros happily married, there is even more surety of the line continuing. And I'm sure Prince Stefano will marry before the year is out.'

Kiki frowned at that little pearl of information. 'Do you mean he *has* to marry?'

Elise inclined her head. 'It is by royal decree that the heir to the throne must marry by the time he turns forty.'

So Stefano must be thirty-nine. Ten years older than her. She hadn't realised there was such a gap, but then when had they sat and discussed mundane matters like his needing to be married by the time he was forty and only having a year to do it? Instead they'd made love. Often.

Her mind darted like the birds swooping outside the windows and she had to remind herself to be in the moment. It wasn't every day she had a private tour of a palace. So she tried to concentrate as they walked through into a vaulted main entry with impressive tiling in glorious Italian marble that seemed to shimmer with light. Their footsteps echoed away to the gold-trimmed ceiling that soared to a huge dome adorned with age-darkened seascapes in turbulent oils.

During the next hour Elise opened doors to lush apartments filled with gilt furniture and more framed artwork. Some of the paintings were so huge they covered entire walls, while the floors glowed with the subtlety of magnificently woven rugs from the Orient.

The throne room proved the most regal, with red

silk walls, two huge portraits of a man and a woman, and an extremely ostentatious fireplace that seemed to be made out of solid gold adorned with the royal crest.

'This is where the current Prince, Paulo III, was married. That is the late Princess Tatiana.' Elise sighed. 'She was a wonderful woman.'

Kiki looked at Stefano's mother and saw her regal son in the same hooded yet beautiful grey eyes. 'And very lovely. Everything is magnificent.'

Elise nodded and led her back to the main hall. 'It is a mission I take on gladly to keep it this way. But these formal areas are not the most comfortable to sit in. These are state apartments, for formal gatherings and the hosting of foreign dignitaries.' She gestured to a side stairway. 'If you would like to follow me we will go through to the family apartments, where it is easier to relax. Perhaps a cup of tea would refresh you?'

'Thank you. Lovely.' An overused word, but Kiki couldn't help feeling a little overwhelmed.

The idea that Stefano had been so comfortable in her little two-room flat seemed ludicrous and hard to imagine. No wonder he sat blasé amongst the furnishings on board the ship. It was nothing compared to his home. And yet when they'd been alone together she'd known there was nowhere else he'd wanted to be than with her.

'The upkeep must be horrendous?'

Elise frowned. 'It is a duty and a privilege.'

Oops. Of course it was. That's what royal families and their subjects did.

They went through a set of large stained glass doors and suddenly the light and warmth of a much less formal area lay before them.

'Oh, this is gorgeous.' Kiki could see a conservatory to the side, overflowing with lush green plants, and to the left a sunken lounge with a handful of plush cushioned lounges and chairs. There were flowers everywhere, and even the artwork was modernistic and lighter, but no less magnificent.

'The late Princess, Prince Stefano's mother, refurnished this.'

'She had lovely taste.'

Elise sighed with pleasure. 'Our tiny country is fortunate that its ruling family is wise in the ways of fashion and finance.'

Kiki glanced around. *They'd have to be.* 'Very wise.'

'Yes. The family fortune has built since not long after the Doges of Venice began amassing their own fortunes. Before the family became the Aspelican monarchy one distant uncle was even friends with the famous Venetian Marco Polo, and the island became an outpost on the routes of trade and gathered the riches of silk and spices.'

Elise waved at a wall full of glorious pottery from all over the world.

'But since early Greek times always the family has held physicians. The Crown was bestowed on the first Prince of Aspelicus because he saved the eldest son of the Italian King during a fever that all had thought would carry him off.'

Elise really did love her history, Kiki thought with a smile, and encouraged the woman to go on.

'In every generation one of the family becomes a physician, and I understand Prince Stefano will be showing you his hospital this afternoon.'

'He did mention that.'

'Prince Stefano does great work.'

There was an extra thread of emotion in her voice that had Kiki turning back to look at the woman.

'Personally for you?'

'My son. After many miscarriages I bore a live child, but he was born with a lip and pallet deformity. Prince Stefano reconstructed his face.' The woman's face seemed to glow. 'It is a miracle.'

Many miscarriages. Kiki could only imagine the pain. 'That's wonderful, Elise.'

The woman nodded eagerly. 'And his work is not confined to those who know the family. He will repair any child, and do what he can for the damage that affects peoples' lives. He is a great man.'

No wonder Stefano had wanted her exposed to Elise. The woman hero-worshipped him. Kiki would hold judgement until this afternoon, but it seemed Stefano had had many reasons apart from his accident for not contacting her when she'd needed him.

There was so much to learn about him and yet so little time. And he had shared barely anything with her of his life here. She wondered if her exposure to Elise was the most he could do to open up.

By the time they had drunk their tea and eaten the tiny pomegranate cakes a maid had brought the glass doors opened and Stefano strode in. Suddenly the huge apartment seemed smaller.

'Ah, here you are, and I see you've had tea.'

Elise jumped up, wreathed in smiles. 'And cake. Will you join us, Highness?'

He'd changed into less formal dark trousers and an open-necked shirt so she could hopefully assume his royal duties were over.

'No. Thank you.' He glanced at his watch and then at Kiki. 'I hate to rush you, but flights are easier to and from the island the earlier in the day we travel. Air currents become stronger as we go into late afternoon. Are you happy if we leave for the hospital soon?'

Rough air currents on the way home? Excellent. 'Of course.' She tried to sound upbeat. 'Are we flying?'

'No.' He smiled as if he knew it was an act. 'We will be driving across as I wish to give you a brief glimpse of the scenery on the island. But we must get back to the ship as promised.'

Their trip to the other side of the island started with a winding descent from the castle—an exercise in S bends with the cliffs falling away to the side and the sea below. Not dissimilar from being in a helicopter, really.

Stefano drove a little convertible with total disregard for the precipice, and despite a few gasps on the whole Kiki knew she was safe. Strange.

'I hope this isn't where you had your accident?'

He laughed. 'Nothing so impressive. I hit a cow on the way to the hospital.'

At the bottom of their descent they drove parallel to the beach, and Stefano pointed out the famous race track where the Prince's Cup would be held the following week. She remembered what Ginger had said. 'A nurse on the ship says you have quite a social event with your race.'

He smiled. 'It is popular with the sophisticated traveller and with philanthropists, and we raise more than enough money to cover the hospital's costs for that year as well as for several health research projects. Last year we raised money for a gynaecological wing which opens in a few days.'

'So it's not just a party?' She liked that.

He shook his head. Twice. 'It is a week of tedious social engagements which I would prefer not to have to attend, but the good it achieves makes me appreciate the generosity of those who come.'

'Poor sad Prince. So you don't have any fun?'

He flashed a grin at her. 'Sometimes. The race is fun. If you would consider joining me I think I could have more fun?'

She'd bet he would. 'While you make a fortune?'

'That too.'

Not a sensible idea. 'Sorry. I'm a working girl.'

He flashed another grin at her. 'I thought you might say that.'

There was something in his voice that made her frown, but just then they rounded a bend and turned away from the sea. Now they drove through rolling vistas of olive groves with grey-green leaves that glittered like stars in the sunlight and stretched away to the base of the mountain and a third of the way up its sides.

'We grow only three varieties of olive here and Aspelicus is famous for the gourmet oil it produces. One of my ancestors proclaimed that every family must plant three olive trees a year. We have many thousands of them now.'

'So when do you pick the olives?'

'We harvest in November. It is all done by hand.' She raised her eyebrows, and he laughed. 'I admit. Not *my* hand.'

'But it doesn't hurt to have the Royal Seal on the bottle?'

He grinned. 'Not at all.'

The largest village, though really it seemed almost

like a city, was clustered above the last of the olives and clung to the southern side of the mountain, its red-tiled houses and larger official buildings secured to the rock with Aspelican determination.

She could see the spires of several large churches, and the main belltower of a cathedral soared above the rooftops.

'I love the narrow stone streets. I'll bet the roads are cobbled and cool in the summer up there.'

He glanced where she pointed. 'If you come back I will show you. It is serene and very special. Most families go back hundreds of years.'

'And yours a thousand?' She was teasing him, but she was beginning to see that he had a heritage he was responsible for.

He tapped his forehead. 'Elise has been giving lessons again.'

As if he hadn't known she would. 'Wasn't that the idea?'

He shrugged innocently, and she had to smile when he said, 'I wouldn't dream of boring you.'

'You knew you wouldn't.'

The rapport between them was undeniable, and Kiki could easily have pretended he'd never been away. There was danger in that. Real danger. Because it wasn't true. He *had* gone away, and left her to face the worst time in her life alone. The sparkle seemed to drain from the day.

'Why am I here, Stefano?'

Stefano sighed. He could not but be aware that there was a distance between them that might never be breached, and still he was not sure how to repair the damage. All he knew was that he wanted back his rapport with Kiki. That after months of feeling flat suddenly he was alive again.

'When I saw you I had an idea.' He shrugged and the movement tightened his hands on the wheel. 'A thought to show you my work. Perhaps for you to consider a change in your medical direction. Even to consider coming here and working with me for a time.'

She shouldn't have been surprised. He'd already said they should spend more time together. So he'd been plotting to entice her to his island with the carrot of working with him in surgery...

Unfortunately the idea was attractive, because the tiny fragment of surgery she'd seen him perform in Sydney had been incredible. And she knew he was a good teacher. Further evidence had been in his direction of Wilhelm only yesterday.

To have the opportunity to watch and learn from such a surgeon would be the dream of many a young doctor looking to expand her skills.

But those other doctors wouldn't be as fatally attracted to Stefano as she'd been once before, and she didn't trust him. She knew, fatalistically, that if she moved here and spent time with Stefano he would ensure she become more than an associate. She would become the Prince's temporary mistress.

She must have been silent for an extended time, because the car slowed and she could feel his gaze on her.

'Do not concern yourself. This discussion is for another day. Enjoy the moment without strain. Let me show you first. Not obliged or pressured to consider anything you do not wish to do. It is my foolish pride that wants to show you my work.'

He shrugged. 'Of course I do not like the idea of

you going off to live your life without the chance of at least sharing my own dreams with you.'

Life. Dreams. Chance. All dangerous words for Kiki. Empty words. What was he trying to do?

'Why me?' And how was she going to quiet her unsettled thoughts now that he had spoken?

His attention returned to the road. 'Why anything?'

He was giving nothing else away.

Their snaked their way up a final hill and against the backdrop of more marching rows of olives a modern building sprawled elegantly over several acres, two-storeyed, and painted olive-green to blend into the countryside.

The closer they drove the more attractive it became. Now Kiki could see vine-covered verandas running around both floors, and the windows winked with white wooden shutters latched back against the olive walls.

'It's so pretty.' Gorgeous, really.

'My mother's design.' Pride was unmistakable in the gesture of his hand and in his voice.

'You miss her?'

'Very much.' He kept his eyes on the road. 'She was the voice of reason and the one who did not hesitate to laugh at me if I became too serious. Perhaps that is why I find you a breath of fresh air.' He looked away. 'But then she could forgive me if I made a mistake.'

He looked thoughtful for a moment, shrugged and went on.

'She could not change my father, for he was trained differently, but she influenced me greatly with her humanity and sense of fairness.'

This unexpected insight into Stefano as a very young man touched her deeply. 'When did she die?'

He hesitated, as if it was physically difficult to talk about himself. 'When I was a teenager. An unexpected aneurism. Before I began medical school.'

So he had lost his mother around the same age as she had. She knew that feeling. The devastation, the aching void in the family, the feeling of betrayal at being left an orphan. 'I lost both my parents in a car accident.'

He looked at her. 'I am sorry. I did not ask enough about you in Sydney.'

She grimaced to herself. 'No, you didn't. But I understand your loss.' And there had been little time between work and bed for conversation. 'I had my sisters and Nick to look after me.' To look after the nuisance youngest sister. Though to be fair Nick had never treated her like that.

'But it is not the same, eh?'

'No.'

But this was not what she needed to think about as her baby's birthday came closer, and she pulled her mind away from the fact that she'd finally felt complete at the thought of being a mother. That too she had lost. As she would Stefano when the time came— a huge reason not to risk losing her heart to this man again. She was sick of loss.

But Stefano's past? It was the last thing Kiki had expected. A royal tragedy—the loss of a mother he adored. Kiki began to wonder about the man who ruled this little principality—Stefano's father. A man who didn't forgive easily. Who'd been brought up differently from someone with a sense of humour, perhaps?

It made her wonder what sort of life it had been for

the young Stefano and his brother after their mother died. How had his father reacted to her death? How had these events moulded the man she'd thought she'd known?

But they had arrived.

CHAPTER SEVEN

STEFANO STOPPED THE car and vaulted over his door to come round to hers. Flamboyantly he opened it and held out his hand. 'Come. Let me show you my work.'

Kiki looked at his fingers, outstretched, waiting, and handed him her handbag. Especially vulnerable after the recent disclosures, now was not the time to ler herself hold his hand. But scrambling from a low-slung sports car was a little more difficult than climbing down from the helicopter. She achieved it, although not with elegance, and eventually stood beside him. It would have been easier to take his hand. She ignored the tilt to his mouth and allowed him to lead the way.

The foyer of the hospital was bright and airy, with serene watercolour seascapes and lush potted greenery. The receptionist appeared and bowed, and Kiki was reminded that this man was accorded deference. But not from her. He seemed to cope with that remarkably well, really.

They were met by an auburn-haired woman with bright green spectacles perched on a snub nose. She had a stethoscope poking from the pocket of her white coat. 'Your Highness. Welcome.'

'Ah, Dr Herore, I hope you are well?'

'Yes, thank you.'

He gestured to Kiki, who stood quietly by his side. 'This is Dr Fender.'

Kiki and the young doctor shook hands, and she could tell the woman was wildly curious about her, in a nice way, and that made it easy to smile.

Stefano strode forward and they hurried to catch up. His whole demeanour had changed again and it was easy to see he loved his work. 'How are my patients today?'

'Jerome has been very silly and picked at his stitches. He will not listen to me, but perhaps now you are here…'

'We will start there.' He turned to Kiki. 'Jerome is five.' He slanted a glance at her. 'An orphan, caught in a bomb blast. I have been reconstructing his face and chest. He has been very brave but is quite the mischief.'

They walked the length of the corridor and turned into another wing. The wooden floors glowed with the deep red of cedar and Kiki wondered where they'd sourced these building materials on an island this size. It was a warm alternative to the marble everywhere else.

In the children's ward teddy bears, bright red cars and happy circus animals adorned the walls. With his back to them, a little boy was hunched over a red fire engine. By the set of his shoulders he wasn't happy.

Stefano stopped and tilted his head at the solemn figure. 'Jerome, what is this I hear?'

The child turned and even in the shadows his surly face lit up when he saw Stefano. But the ravages of war were still apparent in the criss-cross of tiny sutures that mapped his mouth and neck as he jumped to his feet and limped towards them in his striped pyjamas.

'Papa,' he lisped in broken English, and Dr Herore bent down and hushed him.

'You must not call His Highness this.'

'All is well, Dr Herore. Until he finds his new family I may be his papa. And how are you, my son? What is this I hear of scratching sutures?'

The little boy hung his head and Stefano tilted his chin with one gentle finger.

'No more of this. My good work and that of Dr Herore needs to be carefully nurtured. Like the plant you care for me. How *is* my plant?'

The boy looked up with worship and reached for Stefano's hand. 'See the plant,' he said, and Stefano allowed himself to be dragged towards the window. 'It goes well, and when it is strong I too will be strong.'

'This I believe—and see how pretty it is?' They both gazed at the robust olive seedling in a red pot. 'I wish this for you, too, so you must promise not to scratch your sutures.'

'I will not.'

'Good. Now, climb to your bed and I will wash my hands. This is my friend Kiki. She is a doctor too, and I would like to lift the bandages on your chest and show her how well you are healing. If that is all right with you?'

'Okay.' It seemed nothing could faze his good humour now that his hero was here.

Kiki could barely restrain her smile. There was so much pleasure to be had from their conversation, but even in short acquaintance she could tell Jerome was far too serious to laugh at. She had not expected Stefano's rapport with children. But then he had been good with Mikey too. It made her wonder why he had left having a family so late when he would obviously be a splendid father. The smile slipped from her face and she glanced away from the little boy.

'Perhaps we will be able to leave the bandages down today and the dressing will not annoy you so much?' Stefano looked at Dr Herore.

She crossed her fingers and said softly while the boy's back was turned, 'It would help. He has been very patient, but the bandage is chafing him and he will not let us touch it.'

When Stefano had donned the gloves that Dr Herore had laid open a nurse wheeled in a trolley with dressing equipment.

Stefano spoke to Kiki but his words were for Jerome even though he didn't look at the boy. 'It makes me sad when Jerome does not let my fellow doctors and nurses look at his wound, because when I telephone for his progress they cannot tell me.'

Jerome shifted guiltily on the bed, but Stefano continued to gaze steadily at Kiki.

'He has been brave and strong since he came here. Now we have repaired his face and neck and used skin grafts for his chest he will be as other boys his age when we have finished.'

'Except I will have learnt your English.' The boy held his head still as he spoke.

'It is not *my* English. We speak it here so that all you children may grow up with two languages at least. Now is the perfect time to learn.'

Jerome shrugged. 'I do not mind.'

Luckily Kiki's giggle drew a smile from the boy and not a frown.

'She's nice, your friend.'

'I think so.' Stefano was engrossed in lifting the edges of the thick dressing carefully. The little boy's fingers clenched on the sheet but he didn't move.

Kiki stepped closer and slid her fingers across the sheet next to his.

Jerome looked up with gritted teeth and tentatively reached out and held onto her fingers as if to draw strength. Kiki's eyes stung as she studied the brave little face and saw his sheer determination to be good. When she glanced up she saw Stefano had stopped his easing of the bandages and was watching her.

'Did I not say he was brave? But we will count to five—' he wagged his fingers at Jerome '—in English, before we start so that he can be brave again.'

Gradually the extent of the chest wound was exposed, and Kiki had to fight not to dig her own nails into the sheet. Everywhere across the boy's sunken chest tiny sutures trailed over the livid skin like rows of tiny ants, pulling together what must have been an almost mortal wound.

'Ah. It heals well. Your big heart is safe again.' The wound was clean and dry, and the graft site looked well fixed. 'Dr Herore will check the donor site later today, when you have had a break from people disturbing your wounds but you are on the mend, my brave friend.'

When it was done Jerome let go of Kiki's fingers as if he'd never needed them and turned his worshipping eyes to his hero. 'That is good.' Then he broke into Lebanese.

To her surprise Stefano answered him fluently and the conversation flowed over her head.

While Stefano spoke with Jerome, Kiki was drawn to a cot in the corner of the room, where a dark-haired little girl with a bandaged hand heavily disguised by white crêpe sat quietly. The little girl turned big, mournful eyes to Kiki and did not return Kiki's tentative smile.

'And what is your name, little one?'

Dr Herore spoke from behind her shoulder. 'Her name is Sheba and she is from the nearest village. Her mother comes daily. Sheba's fingers were almost amputated in an accident, Prince Stefano has managed to reattach, and we have great hopes she will regain full use.'

'She seems heavily bandaged.'

'This one we cannot stop from pulling at her wound, so it needs to be well out of her way. We are still worried it may become infected.'

Just then a small-boned woman came into the room. Until she turned sideways to curtsey to Stefano Kiki didn't realise she was heavily pregnant.

'Ah, here comes mama now. *Bongiorno*, Rosa.'

The woman was panting a little as she arrived, and Kiki wondered if she was in some pain. Her face seemed especially strained, even though she smiled at Dr Herore.

'*Ciao*, Dr Herore. How is my little Sheba today?'

They all looked at the little girl standing on tiptoes in her cot, reaching out for her mother, and such was the anguish on her little face Kiki could barely watch.

'She misses you badly.'

'*Si.*' Rosa brushed away her own tears, heaved the

little girl into her arms to comfort her and was almost strangled by the tightness of her daughter's grip.

Dr Herore dropped a hand on Rosa's shoulder. 'A few more days, until the risk of infection is gone, and she will be able to go home.'

'I know. She is so lucky to come here. And soon my new baby will be born and Sheba will be home.'

Stefano crossed the room and joined the conversation. 'Take care, Rosa. You are rushing too much at the end of your pregnancy. You must be well for this little one too.'

'Yes, Your Highness.' Rosa looked totally overwhelmed by Stefano and Kiki glanced at him, confused by the many facets of this man she had thought special but still a man.

The silence became a little awkward and Stefano settled it for everyone. 'Time passes.'

Though Kiki felt he was very aware he was disturbing the mother's time. He nodded kindly, brushed the shiny hair of little Sheba, and placed his hand on Kiki's arm.

'Come, before we leave I will show you the viewing window into our theatres. I am very proud of them.'

As they left Kiki glanced back at the children, at the warmth they all showed towards Stefano. As the distance increased she could just make out the mother and child locked in an embrace.

'How did Sheba hurt her hand?'

'A dog attacked her—thus the risk of infection has been very great. She has many intermittent antibiotics so she cannot go home yet, which is hard. Her mother will not miss a day and walks four miles to see her.'

'Can't you send a car to bring her?'

He smiled at her censure. Shook his head at the idea of doing so. 'I offered and she declined. I will get Dr Herore to ask again. But I must be careful of the old ways of the village.'

'The children love you.'

He shook his head. 'They are away from their families. It is easy to grow attached to an adult they think will keep them safe.'

She didn't think that was it at all.

They left the children's ward behind and turned another corner to climb a tiny spiral staircase with intricate ironwork. The steps were narrow, and looked incredibly old and frail for a new building.

Stefano saw her hesitate. 'As you see, these stairs have been restored. They are safe.'

'Okay. I believe you.' She was beginning to understand that Stefano took his responsibilities very seriously. And he didn't know he should have felt responsible for *her*.

He ran his fingers up the iron handrail and there was something so gentle and reverent in the way he touched the cold steel she couldn't help the memory of other times when she had watched his hands—on her…

When he spoke she almost stumbled, jerked from the past, and he put out his hand to steady her.

Luckily it was only for a moment, and his conversation remained on the steps. 'They are from a section of the castle that crumbled in a landslide and had become dangerous. I had them transplanted to this spot. They are beautiful, are they not?'

She ran her hand gently over the balustrade. 'I've always wanted a spiral staircase.'

He smiled down at her. 'Come work for me and I could call it the Kiki Stairwell.'

So now he would name a staircase after her? Tempting, but... 'You never give up. I'm sure the others who spend so much time here would not be happy with such favour.'

He shrugged. 'It is my hospital. I do as I wish.'

That was the man she knew was under there. 'How disagreeable.'

He stiffened, searched her expression, and then relaxed at the amusement on Kiki's face. 'Perhaps, sometimes, I am. Even need to be.' It was a fact—not an apology.

They reached the top of the stairs and turned onto a landing with windows on both sides of a narrow corridor. The outward-facing window opened over the roof and the lawns, and the inward-facing windows gave a superb view of a pristine operating theatre. Even from here Kiki could tell Stefano had every latest device for his patients, for comfort, and for the surgeon's expertise.

She couldn't help but imagine working there. Working with him. 'Wow. It's fabulous.'

Stefano looked quietly pleased by her response. 'I knew you would appreciate the promise of facilities like these.' He turned and his face grew more serious. 'Even in the few days I saw you at your work in Sydney, barely trained in operating theatre techniques, you had the potential to be a great surgeon. Yet I find you on a pleasure ship?'

'And you.' She was flippant. 'Ironic isn't it?' *Don't spoil the day*, she thought. But they'd always be skirting the edge of this discussion.

'So why did this irony occur?' Stefano watched her. He could see she would choose not to enlighten him and he stamped back his impatience.

She shrugged. 'Things happen. Life throws you something you don't expect and your path changes.'

He wished she would tell him something he didn't know. 'And what changed *your* path, Kiki. Or who?'

She turned her back. Stepped closer to the next window. 'So, tell me about the type of operations you have here. Is this the only OR you have?'

'*Bah!* You are like a clam.' She was the most frustrating woman. He would never have believed it before.

She shrugged. 'And you are used to getting your own way. Not this time.'

He looked at her. Her back was towards him. None of his people would have dared to turn their backs on him. It did not seem at all difficult for Kiki to do so. But he would not have her different. He revelled in the difference.

'So we continue the dance.' *Bah* again.

Then he shrugged and went on as if the conversation had never happened. He saw the slight loosening of her shoulders. So she was more tense than she appeared. He would watch for that sign again.

'Operating theatres. We have two others—though one is really only used in emergencies.'

She turned to face him. 'What emergencies do you have?'

'Most often the sudden influx of more than one patient. It is word of mouth. I have a representative in most medical facilities in trouble spots where children are at risk. They contact my team and when information is gathered they can phone me any time. We discuss if the child or children will be strong enough to withstand the journey. To remove a child from all they know is no light matter.'

She could certainly see that. 'Of course not. So who brings them?'

Good. She was deeply interested. He relaxed a little as he let her into his world. The memories of many retrievals coloured his response.

'I have a team who fly in and out when we hear of a case that would benefit greatly from our intervention. There is also a political team who work with governments and organise extradition, and a medical team that goes in on the ground to source the patient from whatever hospital they are in and stabilise for transport.'

'Sounds efficient.'

They were paid to be efficient. 'Most times. Before they retrieve, my political team endeavours to trace parents and relatives, if we can find them alive, so they know the child has survived and is being cared for. We always leave a point of contact.'

He watched her lean her nose against the glass, and not for the first time today he wanted to turn her cheek his way and kiss those stubborn lips of hers.

'Your organisation sounds amazing, but still, a medical crisis for a child... Losing their families... The children must be terrified.'

'I am very aware of that.' Something crossed his face that made her look more closely at him, but he turned away and took a step closer to the viewing window, so that all she could see was his profile. *Back off, I'm royalty*, was stamped all over it.

It was his turn to use the window to escape. 'As you

see, the other theatres are along here—but perhaps we should go. It is getting late.'

She'd said something to upset him. The mood had changed, and it seemed there was nothing she could do about that now, as he marched her along corridors towards the entrance. In the distance she could see the children's ward, and she wished she could revisit again just for a short time.

But he had moved on more than physically. 'I have asked the helicopter to meet us here. We'll fly back to the palace for lunch—there is a group of people I must meet with—then leave for the ship straight after.'

As they took off and soared across the tops of the olive groves it seemed surreal that her pilot was a prince, and she was the reason they were flying across these paddocks. How did she feel about that? Honoured? Chuffed? Excited? Certainly not oblivious.

Well, she wouldn't be human if she didn't feel a little bit special. But it was only one day. She'd just have to be careful to protect herself, because her senses were going into overload with all this care he was taking of her.

She'd enjoyed morning tea in the intimacy of the family apartments, and she hoped, if she was lucky, lunch would be similar, only with Stefano present.

How wrong could she be?

Lunch was served in the formal section of the palace, and she could barely see him at the head of the table, let alone need to worry about accidentally touching him. It seemed her escort—what a joke—was in great demand, judging by the procession of dignitaries that kept interrupting any attempt on his part to address his food.

There'd been a brief flurry of attention when everyone in the room had looked at her as she had been introduced to his father—a shorter version of Stefano, with bushy white eyebrows and scarily piercing blue eyes—and her composure had taken a beating as the older man had stared right through her.

Stefano had moved her on and then handed her over to Elise again, so she'd felt transformed back into parcel mode, and the island's hero had disappeared even faster than before. She'd begun to have an inkling as to how busy his life was when he was home and just what might have happened to thoughts of her when he went away.

But that still hadn't prepared her for lunch.

To say the lunch was formal was an extreme understatement.

She'd half expected a servant to bring in a whole pig, complete with apple in mouth, but they didn't. Not that they didn't have the silver serving dishes and a multitude of crystal glasses down pat. And this was *lunch*. About as intimate as a hotdog at a football game.

The woman beside her constantly complained about how far down the table she was while the tall, good-looking man on her other side quivered with mischief. There was something about him that reminded her of Miko, the charmer of the ship. There was no decision on who she'd rather talk to.

She held out her hand. 'My name is Kiki Fender. A pleasure to meet you.'

He took her hand in his with studied gallantry. '*Bon-*

giorno, signorina. Franco Tollini.' Of course he raised it to his lips instead of shaking it.

His kiss lingered on her fingers. Kiki kept her grin behind her lips but unfortunately for the first time since she'd sat down managed to catch Stefano's eye. How amusing—for her, at least. The Prince seemed less than happy. She turned back to her companion, who had no intention of letting this opportunity go by.

Franco reluctantly gave back her hand. 'I am part of the Prince's team. We transfer the children home to their parents when they are well enough to return.'

'So do you have a medical background, as well, Franco?'

'*Si.* Dr Tollini.' He shrugged with self-deprecation. 'I am a specialist in rehabilitation, but since coming here I have been performing some surgery.'

'Ah. The hospital. You obviously enjoy your work.'

He smiled, and thankfully Kiki could see it wasn't just in appreciation of her. He did love his work.

'The children are incredible. And it is my job to take them back to their families after they heal and help them settle.'

She couldn't help but think of Jerome. 'What if their parents are not there?'

His dark eyes flashed with fervour. 'Then they are adopted into families that will take very good care of them. Our mission is not to lose them entirely. We ensure their schoolwork is well catered for, and more often than not they will have better learning when they return, with opportunities for further study provided if they wish.'

Why hadn't she heard more about this place? 'It seems a fabulous cause.'

Earnestness shone from Franco's eyes. 'Prince Stefano is a great humanitarian and a great surgeon.'

Another fan. She was surrounded by them. 'I have heard the Prince is also a good teacher.'

'Spare my blushes, Kiki.'

They both looked up as Stefano sat elegantly down on her other side, like an unhurried lion settling to watch his prey. Goodness knew what he'd done with the person who'd been there a moment ago, Kiki thought, and had a sudden vision of the woman being thrown into a dungeon by Stefano merely because he'd wanted her seat.

'Hello there, Franco.'

'Your Highness.' Strangely, with Stefano now beside her, Franco seemed to shrink and become a little less boldly defined. Again Kiki realised the Stefano she'd thought she'd known was a totally different person when in his own pride. There was that lion analogy again. She could almost see his aura of power, which grew more apparent despite the gentleness of his tone.

Stefano went on conversationally. 'I've just been showing Dr Fender over the hospital.'

Franco looked at her, and then at the Prince. He swallowed. 'I was just telling...' he paused nervously '...Dr Fender, about our work. She has not had a chance to mention she knows you or that she's seen the hospital.'

'How remiss of her.'

Kiki had had enough of this. She turned to Stefano. 'And how unfortunate that you interrupted our conversation.'

His eyes flared but his voice remained even. 'My apologies. But the helicopter awaits and we must return—or should we be delayed until tomorrow?' He let the question hang.

Kiki blinked, decided she needed to be on the ship, and pushed back her chair. One of the waiters nearly broke his leg, trying to get to her to help, but he was still too slow for Stefano. The Prince assisted her sardonically.

The sooner she left here and returned to the real world, the sooner her head could try to sort out the hundreds of different messages she was getting today.

'Goodbye, Franco. Nice meeting you.' Deliberately she held out her hand, quite sure Franco wouldn't kiss it this time, with Stefano watching.

She was right.

Franco also stood. 'Goodbye, Dr Fender.' He bowed deeply. 'Your Highness.'

'You were really obnoxious.'

Stefano nodded and smiled as the dignitaries bowed as they departed. He ignored the hiss from Kiki beside him and kept her hand firmly in his. To hell with what the gossips said.

It had been a very unusual day. He supposed he should really try and curb his desire to run through any man who spoke to Kiki, let alone those who actually kissed her hand, but he wasn't sure it was worth the effort.

He was beginning to understand the pirate tendencies of his ancestors when they'd captured women and dragged them off. His mother would have been horrified. Then he smiled and remembered something she had once said to him about his father's courtship.

Perhaps his mama would not have been so horrified after all.

When they reached the helicopter he waved the pilot into the front with his man and climbed into the back with Kiki.

When she said, 'I think I'll sit in the front...' he laughed out loud and helped her fasten her seat belt.

When he looked again at her face she was shaking her head. The struggle on her face suddenly gave way and she smiled too.

They grinned at each other, and his relief was a warning about how much this woman's good opinion mattered to him. That and having his arms around her. He'd been fantasising about that all day. Not his usual *modus operandi*. It would be better if he kept Kiki in his bed—that way she would not mess with his head, just his skin. Even at this brief thought his body stirred.

But his prestige would suffer if others heard the way she spoke to him. He really needed to do something about that, but he wasn't sure what. He had a feeling that a direct order would give her the excuse to walk away.

She straightened her face and pretended to frown at him. 'I'm not happy with you.'

He inclined his head and threw caution to the wind rushing by outside the helicopter. 'And there are things I need to discuss about *your* behaviour. Perhaps we could examine this over dinner. Privately. Say seven? My suite.'

'Six-thirty, if you don't mind. I work tomorrow. And the restaurant will be fine.'

Kiki wondered if she'd gone too far. She'd been very surprised when Stefano had decided against piloting their way back to the ship, and disappointed she wasn't going to have the cooling-off period she needed to recover from his grabbing her hand like that and marching her onto the helicopter.

It had certainly surprised a few people—not least her.

The problem was as soon as he'd touched her she'd been captive, and it had nothing to do with force. She glanced down at her fingers in her lap. She wouldn't have been surprised if her hand glowed like one of those luminous fish in the deepest depths of the ocean they were flying over right now. It felt irradiated with his touch, still warm from his warmth, and she was still subdued by the leashed power she had felt.

She wriggled her fingers until his hand came in over hers and stilled them. She glanced up and saw the devilish gleam in his eyes grow. *He knew.* Her face flamed and she pulled her hand away.

Stefano smiled. 'You may choose the restaurant this time.' He turned to look out of the window.

They landed back at the airport without too many of the bumpy updrafts Stefano had mentioned. There were a few minutes' delay while they waited for the pilot to give them the all-clear to alight, and then their transfer by car back to the wharf beside the ship took no time.

Kiki could feel herself tense as she waited for the vehicle to stop. Suddenly everything was awkward, overwhelming—the gulf between them, the hundreds of different examples of how Stefano's life and upbringing were so different from hers. She was a fool to think anything could come of falling in love with this man. She should never have agreed to dine with him.

'Thank you, Your Highness, for an interesting day. Excuse me if I rush off. I must check in with my colleagues.'

He leaned towards her and spoke over the noise of the ship's loudspeakers. 'Liar.'

She forgot her recent revelation and glared back at him. 'Bully.'

His eyebrows rose. 'Two hours' time.'

Thankfully someone opened her door to help her out and she could escape.

For the next two hours Kiki felt as if a huge clock was ticking inside her head. Each tick was louder than the previous one as the hands crept closer to six-thirty. With an hour to go she'd tried and discarded a hundred excuses, each lamer than the last, and in desperation taken herself down to the sick bay to see what was going on there. Nothing. The place was locked and empty.

She declined to ride back up in the lift. It was the hour for pre-dinner drinks, and well-dressed men and women would be crowding the lifts for the next few hours, so she trod the stairs, hoping the exercise might burn off some of the nervous energy she seemed over-endowed with.

Nothing for it but to get dressed and get it over with. The problem was she still didn't know what she wanted.

If she was honest with herself there were many reasons why she would love to go to Aspelicus and work. Not the least that it was time to leave the ship, stretch her brain, learn new skills. But was it time to risk her heart again? And why this week, of all weeks, when her guard was down from a countdown she'd been dreading? Could she keep the distance she knew she'd need when she was feeling so fragile?

CHAPTER EIGHT

WHEN KIKI ARRIVED for dinner, she'd chosen black. The demure effect of her high collar was lost by the keyhole yoke neckline which allowed a glimpse of the swelling valley between her breasts.

Stefano rose smoothly, as did his libido, and one glance at the *maître d'* was enough to keep the man away from her chair.

'You look stunning.' He leaned over her shoulder as she was seated. Along with the subtle scent of spring flowers he always associated with Kiki the view was even more incredible from this angle.

He returned to his seat and looked across at her with a lightness of spirits he wasn't used to.

As he glanced down at the menu he wondered how she did it—lifted him from being immersed in business, too involved in matters of state, too focussed on his patients. She made him remember he was truly a man who deserved a life that was not always lived for others. It was this quality that so intrigued him, tantalised his consciousness, because *with* her he felt unlike he did at any time without her.

They had two days left —not enough to throw caution to the winds, but enough to convince her she needed to join his team. And then he could see if they had a future. Already it was at that stage.

When they had both ordered, and the champagne had been poured, he raised his glass. 'To an interesting day together.'

She bit back a laugh. *Interesting* didn't nearly describe it. 'Great word-choice.' He did make her laugh. *'Salute.'*

He leaned forward. 'So, what did you think of my hospital.'

Kiki felt her shoulders relax a little. He'd started with an easy one. Thank goodness.

She'd spent the last half an hour shoring up her defences. She needed a protective barrier around herself just in case he brought up the fact that she was like soft soap in his hands as soon as he touched her.

The easy stuff first.

'Your hospital is amazing. I love your work and the miracles you create.' *And I see you love children.* But she didn't say it. Couldn't say it. She just felt the gaping hole and smoothed it over before it could cloud her mind.

He smiled, and her heart ached while she smiled back. It wasn't fair. Why had she crossed paths with a man it would be so hard to forget?

He leaned towards her. His intense gaze captured her as easily as if he'd caught her physically, yet her fingers were tucked safely in her lap.

'And if I offered you a position there? On a surgical term, learning what I could teach you? Would you be interested?'

'Is that what you are offering?' Because she knew

without a doubt that if she became his mistress again she would lose herself. One day she would regret it.

And she worked hard, believed in the good she could do, and deserved more self-respect than choosing that life for herself.

'It is a job offer. Yes. I believe so.'

'Do you?' She shook her head. 'If it was a stand-alone package, just that position, it would be hard to refuse.' These were dangerous waters and she saw the flare of triumph in his eyes. *Not so fast, buddy.*

She read his fierce intelligence, searching between her words, sifting for weakness, assessing his own strengths.

He took a sip from his glass and set it down. 'And what did you think of the palace?'

The palace. She thought of his father's cold eyes. The long formal rooms. Her own feeling of insignificance and his vast importance. Not a comfortable place. 'Your palace is very beautiful.' Now to the more difficult part. 'But I wouldn't want to live there.'

'So where *would* you live?'

'In the village. A walk across the fields would be a delight after a hard day in the OR. I could practise my Italian, or French, or whatever language it is they speak up there.'

'Italian.' He sat back with a smile. 'So you have at least thought about the position?'

'And its disadvantages.' She didn't delude herself that he would marry her, or even that she wanted to be a princess, watching her husband from the other end of a long, table of dignified guests. But that was far fetched.

He frowned. 'Disadvantages? I see none.'

The entrées arrived. As they ate she changed the

subject. 'Elise said you operated on her son? Was the defect a difficult one?'

'Yes. Full thickness and requiring several operations.'

He explained in detail and drew on the table with his finger, outlining the sections that had required repair. Again he made it easy for her to understand why and how.

She would learn so much, the voice inside her insisted.

'His mother is pleased with his recovery,' she said.

'Elise has had a hard life. She would have loved more children. Though with her husband passed away that will not be possible unless she remarries.'

'I can't imagine her leaving her position. She admires you very much.'

'She has worked for our family since she was a girl. For the last few years she's been my housekeeper and she expects perfection for me.'

Now, *that* brought up an interesting topic. 'She said you must marry before you are forty. Are you feeling the pressure?' Did she really want to know this? In case he thought she was putting herself forward, she hurriedly added, 'I'm sure there are dozens of perfect future princesses out there for you.'

'A few.'

He was watching her and she didn't know where to look. 'So what happens if you don't?'

He shrugged. 'I forfeit my royal inheritance.'

She frowned. He didn't seem too perturbed. 'Might it be hard to live as a subject again?'

He shrugged again. 'I make my own fortune. I spend it on the hospital. I would have more than enough to live on, and I would still be a prince. I could not leave my country for personal satisfaction.'

Her stomach sank and her appetite drifted away. 'So you will marry?'

'Yes.' He smiled, but there was no humour in his eyes. 'My father has several women he approves of.'

She knew one his dad wasn't so keen on. 'Congratulations.'

'Are not in order yet.' He glanced at her plate, seeing the signs that she had eaten all she wanted. 'Dessert?'

'No, thank you.' She folded her napkin and placed it on her side plate.

He lifted the bottle. 'More wine?'

She shook her head and took another sip of the mineral water she'd changed to before the main course.

'Good.' He signalled the waiter. 'Then if you have eaten enough perhaps we could go somewhere more private to finish this discussion?'

Kiki glanced around. The atmosphere was elegant, non-intrusive and discreet. Above all—safe. 'I think not. I'm very happy with the company we are in.'

If he was disappointed he didn't show it. He just waved the waiter away again, as if it was of no matter, then was straight back to the hunt. 'So, what is it you'd want from me if you took this position?'

He had brass, asking that. 'I could ask you the same question.'

'Ladies first.' He gestured with his hand.

'I think not.' She lifted her chin.

'So stubborn.' He glanced away and then back, and she couldn't read the expression on his face. 'So determined not to show me the respect I am used to.'

He was right, but she didn't think she could change.

'I do not intend to offend you. I respect you, but I will not give in to your need for control all the time.' *Because I would lose respect for myself.* And in the end that was all she would have left. *Herself.*

'Well, let me see.' He ran his eyes lingeringly over what he could see of her and smiled. 'The idea of working with you, watching your surgical skills grow, feeding your desire to repair intricately and restore function, to watch you blossom into the surgeon I know you could be—that is enticing.'

Kiki could admit the concept was very attractive. 'And for me also.'

His voice wrapped around her. 'As well, I wish to show you the beauty of my homeland with its depths that you can only begin to imagine. Celebrations like the Prince's Cup, the galas held after the harvest season, the saints' days and the markets...'

He opened his hands and she couldn't help but be enthralled with his passion for his island.

'In my palace are long tunnels from the castle to the sea, works of art nobody views, buildings so old and manuscripts so holy and so fragile even the Pope agrees we do not move them.'

She did appreciate his deep pride, and the responsibility he took with his position, and she was not immune to the honour he spoke of bestowing on her. 'That would be wonderful.'

'And...' He left it hanging.

'Is there more?'

Of course there was more that he wanted. And that was what she was so afraid of.

'Yes. Then there is the heart of it.'

His eyes darkened and his voice took on a quality that made the gooseflesh rise on her arms.

'Then there is the woman who makes me understand the baser instincts of a bygone age. Who makes me re-member I am a man not to be trifled with. A woman I burn to protect and long to conquer. I want the lot—and I don't want you staying half an hour from my bed in the village.'

She shivered. It was there. Plain speaking, as she'd asked. There was no doubting his intent—nor the fact that every nerve in her body leaned towards him as he said it. She'd asked for honesty and got it. With a vengeance.

He shrugged his shoulders, as if he'd been discussing the weather. 'But I understand your dilemma.'

Holy Dooley—what could she say to that? 'I don't think you do.'

He tilted his head. 'So tell me.'

Where to start? With her mind blown by the fantasy he had conjured she was starting from way behind. 'I appreciate your honesty…' *Sort of.* She paused. 'And I will try to reply with my own.'

'See…' He smiled and looked at her as if she was a wonder of the world. 'This is why you hold me.'

She shook her head, not willing to be diverted from saying her piece while she had some structure in her head. 'Strictly business. My own residence away, from the castle—preferably in the village, if possible—and set work hours.'

He shook his head. 'I do not find that possible. A single woman living in the village would be prey to gossip and perhaps even harassment.'

He shook his head again, but she ignored him with

a smile. 'The harassment I'm worried about lives in the castle.'

He stared her down, dark eyes full of wicked amusement. 'It is not me you are afraid of, Dr Fender. It is your own base instincts and the fact that we spontaneously combust when we are alone.'

Didn't she know that? 'Exactly. But I did not interrupt you—perhaps you could show me the same courtesy?'

He straightened, only half joking when he said, 'You are speaking to a *prince*.'

But she wouldn't be shut down. Not now. Not by him when so much was at stake. 'And that's why you like me.'

It was Stefano's turn to laugh. 'So what am I to do? See you through the day, toss in my lonely bed at night, only to be exposed to your unreachable womanly wiles again the next day? I think not.'

She spread her hands, borrowing his favourite mannerism. '*Impasse*. Your choice.'

He sat back further and a slow smile crossed his face. 'I will sleep on it. Though I will not sleep.'

She gathered her purse. 'Well, I have to sleep because I have work in the morning. Which reminds me—if you meet my requirements, I would need to give two weeks' notice.'

He glanced away. 'I will see that the cruise line does not suffer, if you leave with me it will be when the cruise ends in two days.'

By the time Kiki made it back to her cabin her knees were shaking. What had she talked herself into? When she'd left this same cabin two hours ago it had never been going to happen and now, after one meal with him, she was negotiating contracts. *Crazy, foolish woman.* She needed serious advice.

She didn't know who to turn to. Now would be the perfect time to talk to Nick, but her brother had his own life, and anyway they were at sea so her mobile wouldn't work. She couldn't talk to Ginger because of the risk of her capturing the scoop of the week for her ex-boyfriend's gossip column, and Wilhelm, while a great boss, just wouldn't understand.

But when she went to work the next morning, as the ship docked in Monte Carlo, everyone already knew. Because Prince Stefano Mykonides had put in her notice for her and a replacement doctor was arriving tomorrow, when the ship returned to Livorno. So, not only would tomorrow be the day before the one she was dreading for emotional reasons, now she would be out of work and out of her home.

Ginger's eyes were wide with a grudging respect for Kiki's new notoriety, which didn't help at all.

She looked at Wilhelm and her stomach sank at the worried expression on his face. She couldn't believe Stefano had been so arrogantly sure of her decision—plus so high-handed that he didn't think there would be repercussions.

It was a classic example of his privileged lack of thought. How could he not realise this would send her back the other way?

'It's not true,' she said, conveniently forgetting that she had already decided to finish work on the ship regardless of Stefano's offer.

Wilhelm patted her on the back. 'Well, the new guy's

coming and your resignation papers have been drawn up without the need for any notice.'

She looked for inspiration or explanation but there was none on Wilhelm's face. 'How could he *do* that?'

Wilhelm shrugged again and rubbed his hands together awkwardly. 'Easily, apparently. It's by order of the cruise line's owner.'

Kiki stared at him and through him, trying to see an answer. 'Can I reverse it?'

Wilhelm sighed. 'Apparently not. I already asked, because I figured it was something like that.'

She could feel incredulous anger building. 'Well, thank you for that.' She could not believe this was happening. At least Will had had some faith in her. 'Of course I wouldn't resign without telling you. I can't believe he's done this. Is he insane?'

Wilhelm rubbed the underside of his jaw. 'No. Just used to power. Owed favours by the owner.'

She needed to get out of this small room before she exploded. This couldn't be happening. 'I'll be right back.'

'You want me to come looking for you if you aren't?' Wilhelm was beginning to get the idea that this man played hard.

She was about to say yes, then thought about the repercussions that didn't just involve her. 'No. I can handle it. You stay out of the firing line. He has just bought more trouble than he knows.'

Kiki fumed all the way up in the elevator. Halfway she briefly wondered if perhaps she should have taken the stairs, to at least try and calm down and heighten the chances that she would act rationally when she arrived.

That thought was vetoed.

As each floor flashed by on the control panel of the lift she couldn't remember ever being this incensed, but the annoyingly persistent voice in her mind was suggesting again that this headlong course of action might not be the wisest one.

Well, to hell with that. He deserved a blast. A quick in and out might not save her job on the ship, but it was going to make her feel a whole lot better.

When the suite door opened she let him have it. 'How dare you—?'

Wrong man. Blast!

She scanned past the shoulders of the bristling man in front of her and spied her prey at the windows of the suite. She took a step, but came up against the surprisingly solid bulk of Stefan's manservant.

'Let her in, Manos.' Stefano's voice was even. 'Then leave.'

Which only served to incense her more.

She threw daggers at him as she waited for the hulk to get out of the way. 'You might want to keep him around for protection.'

'I think not.'

The man hesitated as Kiki swept past, but Stefano waved him on and the door shut silently after him. When she glanced behind her he'd gone. Kiki kept walking until she was a hand's breadth away from him and glared into his face.

'I've upset you.' Stefano watched her with a wariness born of unfamiliarity with this kind of scenario.

'Brilliant deduction, Sherlock.'

He blinked.

'As I was saying—how *dare* you hand in my resignation without my permission?'

He stepped to the side and picked up a half-filled glass of juice. 'Don't you think you are overreacting?'

His voice was mild, but the thread of sudden amusement in it was a torch to Kiki's anger.

'Not yet, I'm not.' There was probably steam coming out of her ears—not that he'd notice.

Unperturbed, he shrugged. 'I saw you were worried about giving the correct amount of notice.' He crossed the room and sat down on the lounge, crossed his legs and looked at enquiringly. 'My cousin owes me favours. I have merely taken the matter out of your hands.'

She spun and stormed across the room until she stood over him. 'Well, I want it back in my hands. And I'm giving you a straight refusal on the offer of a position while I'm at it.'

He remained impassive. 'Don't be foolish. What will you do for a job?'

She lifted her head. 'I have plenty of options.'

That wiped the smile from his face. 'I'm sure you have.'

'What's that supposed to mean?'

He put the glass down and she could tell his temper had slipped a little.

'Whatever you wish.' He rose and took a step towards her, his eyes drilling into her.

Alarm bells started to ring. She needed to get her piece said and go. 'Well, know this, Prince Stefano Mykonides. I'm leaving this ship tomorrow, and I'm *not* going to Aspelicus.'

Then she spun on her heel and got out of there while she still had her clothes on.

The door closed and Stefano stared at it. He should have caught her before she left, because the sex would have been explosively incredible. But in fact he had been in the wrong. Out of line. And to take advantage of her emotion would have made him more culpable, not less.

She was totally correct. He had no right to assume control. *Yet.* Difficult to remember when all his life decisions had needed to be made and he'd gone with them. Most times he chose the correct path. With Kiki it had been one false step after another.

Now he needed to win back her good graces. Because she *was* coming to Aspelicus.

Late that afternoon Stefano waited around the corner beside the lifts. He knew she would be out soon. He could imagine the headlines: *Prince Waits to Pounce on Innocent Doctor!*

The door opened and she walked across the foyer from the hospital to the elevator with a nurse, who pressed the button for the lift.

Kiki's hands were full. At least she hadn't tossed his flowers out, or left them in the waiting room.

It was a two-fold ploy on his part—to apologise in public with flowers, knowing if he made the bunch large enough she would have to take the lift to get them to her room. His plan to throw himself at her mercy would not work if he had to follow her up the stairs.

Amazing how devious he could be when he had to.

He waited until the lift doors began to close and then strode across the distance between them.

'Hold the lift, please.'

He pressed the button for good measure, in case she was quick enough to realise it was him.

He slipped in between them as the doors shut. 'I'm very sorry.'

'You can't buy me with flowers.' Kiki pushed the bouquet towards him but he was way ahead of her.

He took them and handed them straight to Ginger. 'Would you be so good as to hold these?'

Then he turned back to Kiki and lifted her hands in his, squeezed and kissed her fingers.

'Forgive me.'

Her hands and her eyes were cold. 'Done. Now leave me alone.'

The lift slowed. His plan had not met his expectations. Again. Why did that happen with this woman?

'It was a misjudgement on my part. I have withdrawn your resignation.' He hadn't, but he could do it very quickly if need be. He'd hoped for some response, but again she just looked at him coolly and that surprised him.

'I'm sure you haven't.'

How did she know that?

'But don't bother. If the cruise company can do that without my knowledge I don't want to work for them. And if you think you can control my life I certainly don't want to work for *you*. Not everything is under your control, Your Highness.'

The lift stopped.

He watched from the back of the lift as she stepped out, and as she walked away he heard her say, 'I'll see you at the show. Please keep the flowers, Ginger.'

CHAPTER NINE

MONACO WAS A great place to buy a sexy catsuit—even in a thirty-minute dash by tender after work.

The salesgirl had assured her it was latex-free—Kiki didn't want to brush up against Marla and start that whole scenario again—and the blatant sexual statement that she could wear what she wanted, in front of whoever she wanted, would annoy Stefano. She hoped. It was her last chance to do so.

An hour ago it had seemed like a brilliant idea.

The final night crew's pageant always proved popular with the passengers because it was more personal to cheer for their favourite crew member, waiter or cabin person while watching them perform on stage.

Kiki had been dancing at the pageant with Miko for almost four months, so there was little practice needed for their tango session. And this was the last night to end all last nights.

Tonight the theme was the *Lion King*, but any type of animal was acceptable. The skintight silver suit dipped low at the front and, with a sheepdog's tenacity, rounded her breasts up and pointed them in the right direction without the benefit of padding. She hoped it wasn't cold in the auditorium.

Now she was dressed it looked so much worse under fluorescent light, and Kiki laughed with a trace of hysteria. All in all, the suit left nothing to the imagination, she thought as she stared at herself. Maybe she couldn't do this?

But this was her last night aboard. Kiki gulped one last time at herself in the mirror, then stepped out into the corridor.

The first man who saw her whistled.

It was lucky she trusted Miko to look after her, because this suit was designed to say one thing. *Come hither.*

Her shoes clacked down the hallway and she wondered why the heck she hadn't brought a coat. But it was too late now. Maybe it hadn't been such a good idea after all to flaunt herself, but it had seemed the most efficient way of annoying her nemesis for the last time.

Ginger had somehow discovered that Stefano would be in the Captain's box in the auditorium, so he would have a good view of what he couldn't have. That thought straightened her spine.

Unfortunately, once backstage, Kiki had a hard time fielding the ribald comments because Milo had been held up with a disaster in the restaurant. Finally she dragged Wilhelm to stand beside her so he could glower at anyone who dared to raise an eyebrow.

'Not so sure brother Nick would like this outfit, Kiki,' Wilhelm said in his measured way as he looked anywhere but at her.

Kiki felt as if she should pat his arm to comfort him. 'I'm a big girl, Will.'

'I hadn't realised quite how big,' he said, with a rare attempt at humour.

'Wilhelm. Don't you start.'

Thankfully Miko arrived, all suave black panther, and took one appreciative look at her, bowed and kissed her fingers.

'I see we will be dancing for effect, my sweet. I will step up to that challenge.'

This was followed by a ludicrously wicked wink that had Kiki smiling again.

'Well, you only just made it.'

'Such is the drama of my position.' He squeezed her hand, noticed the chill of it, and rubbed her fingers between his own. 'Enjoy your last night. Be Catwoman for me. Hopefully I will not wake up in a dungeon tomorrow.'

Kiki's nervousness receded. Miko always made her feel better. Like a favourite cousin. Funny how she'd never fancied him and yet he was a delight.

'I promise we will have fun.'

She'd never see these people again, would never do anything like this again. She might as well give it everything she had.

She lifted her head and plastered on a smile.

Their turn. The red light came on.

How appropriate for her costume, she thought sardonically as Miko straightened and she put her hand on his arm.

He patted her shaking fingers. 'Good girl. Let's do it.'

Stefano conversed pleasantly with the Captain's wife. It was what he'd been trained to do. He'd promised to attend but he wished the night over, so he could return to his real world and decide on his next strategy for seducing Dr Fender.

His brother and sister-in-law were in very good spirits and had enjoyed their short holiday, and they had all survived without any further dire embarrassments.

The music changed to the unmistakable beat of the tango, and Stefano, like every other male in the auditorium, drew in his breath and held it when Kiki stalked onto the stage.

He heard Theros say, 'Is that the doctor?' but his eyes never moved.

Her ridiculous tail twitched, seductively sinuous and provocative, and the lights caught the skintight shimmer of her perfectly luscious body. Her breasts gleamed high and proud, shimmering with stardust. Stefano's mouth dried.

Mesmerised, he followed every sway and bend, each drift and spin. The woman in silver was heating his blood to boiling point, and never had he wanted her more.

Then he realised every man in the room had their eyes glued on his woman and wanted her too.

The flash of a camera from behind him made him grit his teeth, and he resisted the almost uncontrollable urge to reach back, grab the offending instrument and smash it into a million non-recording pieces. Instead he clenched his hands in his pockets and remembered to breathe, letting the air out slowly and with intent. He repeated the process, as if he would feel better soon. Unfortunately he didn't.

While he could almost admire the grace and precision of the dance, admire the rapport and impeccable timing between male and female, he would have given the crown jewels for it to end. He wanted her covered from head to foot at this moment, as his anger built, preferably bound and in the back of his helicopter heading for home.

How could she flaunt herself so?

As soon as the dance finished, to the most enthusiastic applause of the night, the rest of the cast came on for the final joint farewell and she flaunted herself all over again.

Stefano gritted his teeth as the crew sang their way through the final number. There was thunderous applause and he wondered grimly how much of it was for his little Dr Fender.

Finally he could excuse himself, and with Olympian control he strode to the stage door just as she stepped out in a group.

Thankfully someone had given her a coat. She was laughing as he approached, and that incensed him more, but he was no fool.

Miko was the first to notice his approach. 'Here comes retribution.'

He said it quietly in Kiki's ear but she heard and turned, plastered a smile on her face. 'Did you enjoy the show, Your Highness?'

'Most illuminating.' He smiled at the crowd, moved in next to Kiki, and laced his fingers through hers in a statement nobody could doubt. 'What a naughty suit.'

He stroked her palm with his thumb and her legs almost buckled.

This was not what she'd expected. Battle-ready, Kiki was confused by his soft tone, by the damned weakness she always had when he touched her, and the come down from the adrenalin of the dance. And that thumb, insistently vibrating at the core of her, in tendrils of heat from her palm, was blurring her mind so she couldn't think at all.

Still he hadn't looked at her.

'If you would all excuse us for just a few moments? I'd like to speak to Kiki. We'll catch up.'

She had to hand it to him. He'd asked nicely, but the projection that instant obedience was expected was miraculous—though Miko looked more than a little worried as she handed him back his coat.

How the heck did Stefano do that?

Maybe he didn't even care that she appeared almost naked in some lights. She sneaked a look at his face, saw his eyes and the penny dropped. Might be a good time to run after her friends...

Black pupils filled with sparks and his hand tightened on hers. 'I won't take up much of your time.'

If she could disentangle her hand she'd be able to think.

More people tumbled from the stage entrance and another camera flashed. Stefano swore softly—the first time she'd ever heard him swear—and let go of her hand to remove his jacket.

Kiki's mind began to clear the second they disconnected. She only had these few moments until he put his coat around her shoulders. The reality of the danger switched on like a light in her befuddled brain.

They were on the lowest level open to passengers, one below the gangplank, and there was no way he could get her to his suite unless she got into a lift. So she should be safe if she didn't.

'No lift!' At least she managed to get that out before he captured her hand again.

He nodded. Directed her to the stairs—innocuous enough. Almost as if he knew, his thumb circled her palm again, and her will weakened as a brief lull in the flow of passengers gave them a moment of privacy in the bend of the stairs.

He leaned her back against the wall, captured her chin and kissed her—not with force, he even started gently, though she could feel the tightly leashed control, the simmering emotion as he seduced her with implacable intent. He kissed her thoroughly until she could barely stand, would have followed him blindly over the edge of the ship into the water below.

Then he drew her up to the next level and into a packed but serendipitously waiting lift. It was as if even fate was against her. The whole time his fingers were linked through hers.

Her head began to insist she took note. She looked around and whispered, 'I said no lift.' She tugged on her hand but he didn't let go.

He whispered back. 'If that is the worst I do then you will be lucky.'

The idea was scarily attractive.

'Could you let go of my hand, please?' She said it a little too loudly but it had the desired effect. Everyone turned to look at them and Stefano dropped her fingers like a hot potato. 'Could someone press five, please?'

Her ears burned from the attention but to hell with it. She wasn't going to be monster'd by a royal bully even if she had pulled his tail deliberately. There was very real danger here—and not all of it was coming from him.

The lift stopped on her floor and she alighted without obstruction from Stefano. As the doors shut she refused to look back and took off, with her own tail in her hand, as fast as she could towards the crew's quarters.

The ship docked in Livorno at five a.m. Kiki woke after a restless night with her pillow screwed in a ball under her neck, her sheets twisted and creased and her body aching as if she'd done ten rounds in a boxing match. But worse was the mental exhaustion from duelling with Stefano in her dreams all night.

She crawled into the shower with a whimper, infinitely glad she didn't share her cabin with anyone else.

It was both an anticlimax and a blessing that she wouldn't see Stefano Mykonides and his entourage leave the ship. Because despite her resistance he had invaded her heart again, and now she'd have to re-banish him.

Today was going to be almost as big as tomorrow. She had to say goodbye to colleagues who had been her friends, and she needed to find somewhere to stay tonight with all her luggage.

Then she needed to start forgetting the last week and sorting out a plan of action for work.

When she walked into the medical centre Wilhelm was talking to Ginger, and judging by the amount of gesticulating going on there was a problem.

'You guys okay?'

Ginger had tears streaming down her pale cheeks, Wilhelm was red-faced and angry, and both of them looked at her in varying degrees of distress when she arrived. Kiki felt her stomach sink.

'Tell her.' Wilhelm vibrated with emotion.

Ginger twisted hands that trembled as she turned

to Kiki, but no words came out except a whisper that trailed off. 'I'm sorry...'

Kiki was liking this less by the minute. 'Sorry for what, Ginger?'

Wilhelm couldn't stand it any longer. 'She's sorry she e-mailed your story and a photo to her sleazy gossip columnist ex-boyfriend. You and the Prince will be splashed across every newspaper and magazine that can manage to change their lead article in Italy today.'

Kiki felt the cold seep into her bones. 'What story?'

'That you had an affair with Prince Stefano. That you flew to his island the day before yesterday.' Wilhelm dropped his voice and his eyes, unable to look at her while he broke the worst news. 'And that he didn't come to you when you lost his baby earlier this year.'

Kiki felt sick. And faint. And incredulously angry. 'How did you know about my pregnancy?'

Ginger looked as if she was going to be sick. 'My ex-boyfriend did some digging.'

Kiki's mouth opened and shut several times before words came out. 'And you sent my private life to a newspaper?' She looked at Wilhelm. 'And you knew?'

'No.' He shook his head vehemently. 'Ginger came and told me what she'd done this morning.'

Kiki could barely follow it. All she knew was that the whole sordidly tragic story, the pain and anguish she'd suffered alone, was now up for discussion by any busybody who fancied reading about her. Incomprehensible.

'How could you do that? Why would you do that?'

'I'm so sorry.' Ginger sobbed the words out. 'Last night I'd had too many drinks. Didn't think it through. Josh rang me. Asked for help. He said he was suicidal and he needed one good story to keep his job. I panicked. I love him, and I was scared he'd do it. So I gave him the best story I could find.'

'Mine?'

Ginger swallowed and then nodded. 'Yours. But I didn't know about the baby.'

Kiki sank back into a chair in the waiting room and shook her head, unable to comprehend just how public this was. That everyone would know a secret she'd kept hidden from everyone…most of all Stefano.

'Are you sure they'll publish it? The Mykonides family have a lot of power.' Didn't she know that? With the thought came the first hint of light. 'Of course they won't let them publish, and I'm not interesting enough to write about if his name isn't there.'

Wilhelm spun the computer screen around to show her. 'It's online already.'

That was when she saw the explicit glory of her catsuit, in full colour, and Stefano holding her hand. She looked like a call girl.

'That picture…' She put her head in her hands. 'My family don't know about the baby.' She looked at Wilhelm, but all his sympathy wasn't going to help her now. 'Nick doesn't know, or my sisters.'

He sighed. 'Then you'd better ring him.'

'I can't.' She shook her head. 'I can't think.' An image of Stefano flew into her mind and she groaned. 'Stefano… His family… He hates the press.'

Running the gauntlet of the ship as she said goodbye was nothing compared to the reception the Italian newspaper journalists had planned for her when she stepped onto the wharf.

The flash of cameras and the surge of the bodies that crowded round her stole the breath from her lungs and she felt herself sway with the onslaught.

A car screeched to a halt.

'Enough!'

One voice, a whiplash of command, and four body-guards, hastily shielding a central figure. The crowd parted and fell silent in shock as Stefano strode forward, dropped his arm protectively around her shoulders and swept her back to his car. Her luggage was quickly packed into a second car by Stefano's man-servant.

As she slid along the back seat the flash as the first photographer recovered ignited others, and the din returned full force as Stefano slid in behind her.

The door shut and both vehicles pulled away. The guards followed behind as Kiki huddled in the corner of the seat, shaking, tears thick in her throat as she tried to regain her composure in a world that had suddenly gone mad.

She supposed she should be thankful he'd come, but she had no idea what to say to him. Where to start. What he thought. Her head still spun from the ramifications of such a private airing of her deepest pain. Many women had suffered such a loss but it hurt even more to expose it publicly. Not just the memory of the physical, the cramps and the loss of control, but emotionally it had been traumatic. And now the world was privy to that pain.

Stefano could barely see straight, barely think as he struggled with a feeling of betrayal greater than anything he had ever experienced before. This did not happen to him. He was careful. In control. Master of his own fate and no one else's—because his goal in life was never to be responsible for someone else's downfall again.

But control had been taken from him. This news had been waiting for him as soon as he woke.

His office had gone into disaster mode. His security staff had arranged a different departure point for himself, Theros and Marla from the ship, to avoid the inevitable press, and he had seen them to the airport and discreet safety. But he'd had to return for Kiki, though he wondered bitterly if she deserved it.

All this because he had terminated her employment. It was a smallness he hadn't expected. Fool that he was. He had been told many times, and even in the last few days by his father, that he should stay within the circle of people who understood the rules. And he had defended her.

Now all the world knew she had been pregnant. *His* child. Even when he had been in hospital she would have been able to reach him. His child had died at the time when he too had almost died. Another painful situation out of his control.

His anger bubbled and boiled. Or had it really been his child? Had there been any child at all?

He sifted through what he knew, what had been written, and tried to discern what was truth and what was fiction even as she who had caused this furore shivered beside him. He would find out. He would keep her close until this all died down and she could not spread more lies about him.

The hardest part was the fact that he had always been the one to protect his family from his brother's many scrapes. His way for making up the past, perhaps. By being the son his father wanted and Theros could not be.

Because of *him*.

But this—this was all his doing, and the woman beside him. They had brought shame to the royal house. Now he needed to be strong. Not weak. He repeated it in his mind. *Show strength not weakness.* The plan of action he had decided on was not the answer, but perhaps it would buy him time and stop the damage to his family until the truth could be ascertained.

Kiki could feel tension vibrating from the man beside her, emanating in waves, like a radioactive leak from a damaged core. Well, she guessed she had pierced his protective shell with the last news he'd expected.

Stefano's voice, coldly formal, as if he were talking to a bare acquaintance he disliked intensely, made Kiki feel even more alone.

'It seems you must come to Aspelicus after all. You will be safe there until all this dies down. The rest we will discuss later, when I can be sure I will not do something I regret.'

That stiffened her spine. As if *she* didn't have regrets. As if *she* had orchestrated the most public airing of her grief. Grief he hadn't even been there to share.

'Oh, it's all about *you*? Typical.'

He shot her a look of loathing and she returned it with interest. 'I am not informed. Yet you tell a newspaper.'

So that was what he thought. Again, typical.

'You think I would share my pain so publicly?' She turned her head and stared at the swiftly passing streets. 'You really don't know me at all, do you?'

She couldn't believe he thought that. But then again why wouldn't he? It was all about him.

Now she was on her way to Aspelicus and too emotionally drained to fight it. Not what she would have believed possible less than twelve hours ago. The way she felt at this moment he could drop her off on the moon and she wouldn't care. In another world she would be waiting with bated breath for her labour to start. For her baby to be born. Instead she was the instigator of an injustice to him.

She just wanted to hide. And cry. But she wouldn't give him the satisfaction. Instead she stared unseeingly out of the window as they turned into the airport and drove onto the tarmac.

Before they got out he had one last thing to say. 'Your pregnancy. Was it really my child?'

Kiki turned her head and stared at this man she'd thought she knew, looked at him with such disgust he flinched.

At last he had the grace to say, 'I apologise.'

But it was too late. Of course he would think that. How could she have ever thought she loved him?

'Too damn late. It will never be unsaid.'

His implacable face stared at her. 'So when were you going to tell me you were pregnant?'

She could do cold. She should be able to, because she felt as if her heart had frozen over like those lakes in Switzerland she'd always wanted to see. Never more than at this moment.

'When you came back. But you didn't. So I tried to phone. But even then I didn't get the chance.'

Her car door was opened from the outside and the helicopter looked almost reassuringly familiar. It was funny how things could change in so short a time, and she was glad when he handed her coldly into the rear of the aircraft and climbed into the pilot's seat himself. At least she wouldn't have to sit next to his smouldering disapproval for the next hour.

Their ascent and the flight were a blur as her mind fought the paralysis this morning had left her with. It seemed only a short time later that they were landing on the forecourt of the palace, and she lifted listless eyes to the gathering that waited for them.

Stefano opened her door and shielded her from the waiting throng. 'For the moment, of necessity and to save face for my family, we are engaged. Perhaps some of the damage can be repaired. The engagement can be terminated when enough time has passed.'

His statement hit her like a blow to the chest. This day just kept getting worse.

'I'm not pretending any such thing.'

She would not be the outsider again, like during her whole childhood. She wanted to fit. To be loved, not tolerated. To be the centre of someone's universe, not a distant moon floating in his orbit until he was ready to evict her from his gravitational pull.

'It is not pretence.' He pulled a box from his pocket and lifted her unresisting hand, slid on the heavy stone. The ring hung like a shackle from her finger, a monstrous square-cut diamond, mocking her newly engaged status. 'It is temporary.'

'That's all right, then.' A semi-hysterical laugh slipped out. 'I'm used to temporary.'

His hand tightened on hers. 'Can you not see you have done enough damage?'

She felt so tired. What about the damage to *her*?

This time when he took her hand no sparks flew. Their misery separated them completely and she should be grateful for that. What did she expect? That he would take her in his arms and weep with her, say he was sorry he hadn't been there for her? Unlikely. But it would have been nice.

He turned inscrutably to introduce her to those who waited.

She didn't understand any of this. How could a fake engagement help this situation? It would have to end some time. But she tried to smile as she mumbled, 'Hello.' Then she was towed across the forecourt to a line of servants, where another flurry of introductions was performed until finally it was over.

The wall between them must be visible to all who watched, but no doubt the loyalty of his people would colour it differently.

Once inside the palace Stefano dropped her hand and strode ahead, so she followed him up the inner staircase to the family apartments, more unhappy with every step.

They even passed the stained glass doors without opening them—so much for her favourite place—and climbed another staircase to a redwood landing.

He gestured her through some white doors and followed her in. 'These were my mother's rooms. It will be expected that you stay here. There is a turret if you wish for a quiet place to sit until I return. A place to gather your thoughts.'

He was just going to leave her here? Alone?

His face softened a fraction and she thought he was going to say something less harsh, but in the end he shook his head. 'This whole thing is a fiasco. I must see my father.'

And then he was gone.

CHAPTER TEN

MORE OF A tragedy than a fiasco.

Kiki stood, shivering, in the vast apartment with several doors that were closed, like strangers shutting her out. She didn't know what to think or do. She hadn't felt this numb and directionless since that night when her baby had left her.

Stefano strode away, but in the back of his mind was the picture of Kiki's white face and how small she'd looked alone in his mother's rooms. But he had to harden his heart to that because his weakness with this woman had caused all this. He must put aside the guilt that whispered to him that in truth he had not tried hard enough to touch base with a woman who had given him everything he had asked for.

And this new pain—this gnawing emptiness he had never experienced before—could it be the loss of something he had not thought would affect him so powerfully? But over it all was the disgust that he had let his family down again. That he could not forgive. He wasn't even sure where to start to repair the damage.

Kiki had fallen asleep on the sofa, and when she woke Stefano was back, sitting opposite, watching her with an unreadable expression on his aristocratic face.

She sat up, ran her hand through her hair and tried to straighten her clothes unobtrusively. Hard to gather her composure when he continued to stare.

'Do you feel better?' Not friendly, but at least the freezing tone of his voice had risen a few degrees.

She blinked and sat up straighter. 'That depends. Was it all a bad dream?'

He shook his head. 'It is still a bad dream.'

She sighed. 'Then I don't feel better.'

He almost smiled. 'So, I must apologise for assuming you told the papers.'

That was one bright moment in a bad day. 'You believe me?'

He had the grace to look away. 'I have the truth from your doctor friend, Hobson, who has been concerned for your safety.'

She sighed. 'Of course you didn't believe me.' She looked around then, hoping for a glass of water or a cup of tea. Anything for her dry throat. She saw the ring lying on the table where she'd taken it off. 'How long do I have to stay here?'

He too looked at the ring and his eyes narrowed. 'Is the apartment as well as the ring not to your liking?'

She shrugged. 'I haven't seen the rooms. And you haven't answered my question. In fact you've said precious little, and I've had just about enough of being kept in the dark.'

He said implacably, 'You must stay until I say you may go.'

She shook her head and stood up. 'That doesn't work for me.'

It was his turn to sigh. 'Again we are at loggerheads. And if I were to ask what *will* work for you?'

'I need to find a job.' She glared at him. 'Thanks to

you. Find a place to live. Leave this fiasco behind and get on with my life.'

He lifted his hand. Gestured to the room. 'All these things you can do on Aspelicus.'

She shook her head. 'I'm not staying in the palace.'

He shrugged. 'For the moment needs must. But in a few weeks perhaps you could move to the village through the week and stay in the castle during the weekends.'

As she lifted her head to dispute that he went on.

'You will be undisturbed in these apartments, of course, but for the next two weeks at the very least we must be seen together.'

She didn't understand. How could it help her, being here? She didn't want to be reminded every day that he hated her. 'Why perpetuate a myth that will be found out in the end?'

He stood and walked to the window. 'Because my father is old-fashioned. Because he and my people wish desperately for my heir and they are greatly distressed to think I would leave the woman who carried my child alone. The loss of that dream and the blow to my esteem has created a furore. If they think I am engaged to you then not all is lost.'

'Your father hated me from first sight. Let alone now.' The way Prince Paulo had stared her up and down the first time they met had promised little rapport.

'You imagine things. My father is very focussed on the good name of Aspelicus. He believes I should marry a woman of similar social standing, but this is my decision.'

'And mine. And I'm not marrying you.'

'But you will remain engaged to me for the time being, because you owe me that.'

Kiki felt as though her head was going to explode. 'I owe you nothing.'

But he was not having any of it. 'Is two weeks too much to ask? For the damage that has been done?'

She could feel the trap closing. 'Can't we just be seen together at the hospital? I can work with that.'

'In due course.' He stood up. 'For now, there will be a formal reception this evening. You are guest of honour. At seven I will come for you. The timing is poor, with the Prince's Cup next week and all the functions that require my presence.' He looked at her with a cynical smile. 'And now *your* presence too.'

She was sick of it all but too exhausted to fight. What did it matter? She looked down at her crumpled clothes. 'I'm going to look fabulous for the event.'

He stood. 'One of our local designers will take care of everything. She has several outfits she wishes to show you. Please try for a demure neckline.'

Her eyes glittered. 'Shame it isn't fancy dress. She might have a habit and I could go as a nun.'

'You look good in black.' His tone was less than flattering.

'With a wimple? So would you.'

He turned and left and Kiki stared at the closed door. What was she going to do? She had no idea how to survive what he was asking. Especially the way she felt at this moment.

And the wall around him was so thick she couldn't see the man she had once thought she loved. How had this happened? She was alone, held on an island where the ruling family decided whether she could go or stay.

No allies except her family, and she didn't want to involve them until she could see her way out.

Before she could think of anything else there was a knock on the door and a maid brought in some tea and a cake.

Kiki decided the world might look less disastrous if she at least drank something.

By the time she'd finished her tea the designer had arrived and they discussed Kiki's fashion needs for the next two weeks.

It seemed there were mammoth requirements for the Prince's Cup. Shoes and handbags had been chosen, undergarments arrayed.

Of course Stefano hadn't mentioned the beauty technician who arrived to manicure, pedicure and mini-facial her before the hairstylist arrived...

It was perhaps fortunate that Kiki felt like a rag doll, able to be pulled this way and that, because her brain was whirring like a machine as she realised that she was truly officially engaged to a prince—albeit short-term—even if the world thought she had trapped him into it. And she would be expected to know what to do.

For the moment, she let them have their way. Perhaps externally she would look the part, and it required no mental energy from her.

To her surprise, all the attendants seemed genuinely glad to be of service to her, and she wondered why Stefano's subjects didn't hate her for putting him through the gossip mill.

But it seemed that despite what he had said to Kiki personally Stefano had cast her as the victim, not the offender. Shame he didn't believe it himself, because that shift would make this whole scenario so much easier to bear.

She didn't know if she could do this without his support. Her emotions were shot, and she had been getting more fragile every day—until here she was, on the eve of the day she had dreaded for months.

Never would she have believed it would be overshadowed by something else.

Even some direction on what she should do or say would be helpful in her current fragile state. How dared he not see how lost she was and how in need of support from him, no matter how pressing the affairs of state?

The only other person who might possibly be able to help her was Elise, but the housekeeper had been conspicuous by her absence and, given her extreme loyalty to Stefano, that was not surprising.

Just disappointing, because Elise was the one woman in the palace who would know what was going on. And maybe even understand how Kiki couldn't possibly be responsible for airing something so privately tragic. Elise might just understand because she too had lost her dreams of children.

At one o'clock the attendants had gone. A maid knocked and delivered a small salad and a roll for lunch, and a pot of coffee. Desperately Kiki stopped her as she was about to disappear.

'The housekeeper—Elise. Is she here today?'

'Of course, Dr Fender. Mrs Prost lives in the palace and is on duty whenever Prince Stefano is at home.'

She should have known. No surprises there. *That's how he'd like me,* Kiki thought cynically, *on duty whenever he wants.*

She nodded. 'Lovely. Then could you ask if she has a moment? I would like to see her, please.'

'Of course, Doctor.' The maid curtsied and slipped out through the door.

When Elise arrived, not many minutes later, Kiki wasn't even sure what she was going to say to the housekeeper. One glance at her impassive face showed Elise was withholding her own opinion.

Kiki needed this woman as her ally—she had to have at least one in the castle—and nothing but the truth was going to secure that.

'Please sit down, Elise.'

The woman perched uneasily on the edge of a chair. 'I hope everything is to your satisfaction, Dr Fender?'

The lines were drawn, then. 'I thought we were on a first-name basis?'

'That was before you became engaged to Prince Stefano. It would not be proper now.'

Kiki sighed. 'Fine. I need you to understand that I would never ask you to do anything that would harm Prince Stefano or the royal house of Mykonides.'

The woman's eyes flashed. 'And I would rather die.'

'I had already guessed that.' Kiki smiled. 'It is good to have that said.' She folded her hands in her lap. 'But I also need you to understand that I had nothing to do with publishing or giving the information that was printed by that newspaper.'

'So His Highness has said.'

She wasn't getting anywhere. The woman still distrusted her, and how could she blame her? 'Elise. I met Prince Stefano and we were very drawn to each other. As a woman who has lost her own children surely you can see that a mother would not share her grief with the world as has happened to me?'

Elise stilled, stared at her, and finally nodded.

Kiki felt the first glimpse of hope she'd felt all day and went on.

'I believe the Prince is a good man and is distressed by the news. Did you know I tried to contact him? I had no idea his royal duties were so arduous, or that his recent accident was the reason he didn't answer me.' She saw the moment Elise understood and finally sighed with relief. 'There is still a chemistry that neither of us thinks sensible. Now this has happened, and for the moment at least I must stay here. Behave as his betrothed. I don't want to let him down again. But I need help.'

Was that an imperceptible relaxing of her face? Was she imagining just a little more warmth in the woman's eyes?

'I see.' Elise looked away to the tall windows for a moment and then looked back. 'And I am sorry for your loss.' She nodded. 'Yes. You will need help. I will help.' She added primly, 'Also, I can say there has been a retraction in the paper, stating the fact that His Highness was gravely injured at the time of your miscarriage, and that he found you only a few days ago. Things do not look so bad when the true facts come to light. Legal action has commenced.'

Kiki could almost spare a thought for Ginger and her boyfriend. Almost.

Elise stood up. 'I can see that it will help if you sail smoothly through the next two weeks.' She paused at the door. 'I will return with your itinerary and discuss what is required of you.'

* * *

For Kiki, at least, things improved after that. Elise's support, once offered, was beyond generous. By the time Stefano came to escort his new fiancée to dinner she knew the correct curtsies, the names of the five most important people she would meet, and the itinerary for the evening. Even the menu.

It felt good to have a little more control.

And Elise's final suggestion had come in words from her late princess—'God rest her soul.'

She'd told her, 'See only one person or the occasion will overwhelm you. Look, speak and smile at one person and you will be in control of the room.'

Kiki nodded. Sound advice and she'd certainly try. Because it seemed that no help would come from the man who had let her down when she most needed him. *Again.*

Kiki wore a classic black floor-length gown, with just enough cleavage to say, *so this is why the man is smitten.* Her dark hair had been artfully piled on top of her head, and with her faultless make-up her composure appeared complete. Too complete. Because she felt like a figurine in a wax museum—incredibly lifelike but numb to sensation. But she would get through this without his help.

Stefano didn't know what to expect when he reached the door to his mother's rooms. He hoped Kiki was still not slouched in the chair.

When he opened the door, for the first time in his life Prince Stefano Mykonides felt intimidated.

She looked at him with such indifference his blood chilled.

'I am ready, Your Highness.'

His Dr Fender looked like a film star.

The besieged and crushed victim whom he'd rescued from the press had been replaced by a self-assured young woman waiting calmly and coldly to take his arm.

He glanced around the apartment as if to see the other person he'd expected. This woman did not look out of place. The room could have been designed for she who consistently stunned him when he least expected it.

The grandmother clock in the corner chimed and he was jolted back into reality. Now was not the time to mull over questions that required thoughtful answers.

'Of course. Let us go.'

She put her hand on his arm without hesitation as he led the way and her fingers did not waver. It was his turn to feel the wall between them.

All rose as they entered. Kiki smiled slightly and nodded—not effusively, but that was good. She curtsied to his father with such gracefulness that even the women of the court smiled and Stefano felt his chest swell just a little with pride. This morning he would never have dreamed that she would carry this off so magnificently. This morning there had been no pride to be had.

'She has presence,' his father grunted for his ears alone. 'But it remains to be seen if you have ruined someone else's life by your reckless actions.'

Stefano felt familiar guilt chill the pleasure he had gained in the moment and he glanced at Kiki. Something in her expression made him wonder if she'd overheard. He could only hope not.

When he seated her beside him she answered his questions, but there was still the distance that had been there since he'd collected her. A gulf so wide he could see no way of bridging it. He assured himself that was good.

She seemed to prefer to converse quietly with the Mayor, on her right at the table, and yet he, the more practised statesman, was too much aware of her. Probably just the upheavals of the day.

The evening continued to unnerve him. He had been prepared to protect her, gloss over the mistakes she wouldn't see, but she required no help.

Kiki nodded and smiled and held her composure with concentration. If she excluded the grandeur of the surroundings and the glitter of the people and concentrated on one person at a time she found her advice held good.

Especially if she blocked Stefano out.

Just in that first moment before they'd left, when he'd entered her rooms to escort her, he'd looked so tall and forbidding in black tails and the royal sash, with jewelled medals flashing, she'd mentally faltered.

But only for a moment, before she'd stoked up her anger. She'd concentrated on the person, searched behind the regalia and remembered the man who had left her without support and now expected her to fail in such unfamiliar and challenging surroundings.

That had been inexcusable, and the reminder had protected her from any connection that would discomfort her—until she'd heard that muttered judgement from Prince Paulo.

It had been a glimpse into Stefano's life and what he dealt with every day. She remembered his comment that his mother had been the lighter-natured of the two. She could see that now, and despite herself felt herself soften and sympathise with Stefano.

She glanced across to the old Prince and unexpectedly caught his eye. She glared at him, glad the engagement was a farce, because she didn't need a person like that permanently in her life. He blinked. Grumpy old man. She turned away.

If tonight's disapproval had been there all Stefano's life no wonder he could become tense with pressure.

She could sense him beside her now. Feel the awareness that seemed to inhabit the space between them even when they were not conversing. But she couldn't afford to lay her hand on his arm and express the sympathy she wanted to because she needed to stay focussed until she could return to the safety of her room. But perhaps she understood him a little more.

Luckily the gentleman beside her could converse easily, with little prompting from her. The Mayor of Aspelicus was one of the five Elise had mentioned, so she knew his role in the business, and that his son was in charge of festivities for the Prince's Cup. He did seem delighted with her knowledge and her appreciation of his heavy civil duties, and mentally she thanked Elise for her tutelage.

Eventually the older gentleman excused himself to answer a question from another table companion and Kiki had to turn back to Stefano.

He raised his brows. 'And how is my old friend Bruno Valinari?'

Kiki smiled, because in a lesser man he would have sounded almost petulant. 'He is well. And proud of his son—as he should be. And how is your dinner and your evening, Your Highness?'

His mouth came down level with her cheek and she tried not to inhale the subtle tang of his aftershave, because it floated too many memories for a state function. Tried not to look at the strong cheekbones and carved mouth as he drew closer.

'I am wondering if there is to be any attention from my fiancée.'

Subtly she drew back further. 'You'll survive without my attention.' She raised her brows. 'As I did without yours today.' She met his eyes. 'Did it occur to you I could have done with a little guidance from you?'

'My apologies. My duties constrained me.' His glance travelled over her. 'Though I see no lack in your instruction.'

'Gee, thanks.' She could play that game. 'How unusual for you *not* to see something.'

His eyes gleamed. 'So the cat has claws.'

Kiki sat straighter in her chair and even leaned a little to the right to increase the distance between them. She kept the smile on her face but there was none in her voice. 'I'm not duelling with you at this table.'

Actually, when it came down to it, she couldn't. She didn't have the headspace.

She glanced around for a friendly face and Marla waved her fingers discreetly from across the table. Kiki realised she did have another ally in the palace. When people began to circulate, perhaps she could excuse herself and cross over to Marla. The chance to seek out her supposed future sister-in-law would help enormously.

She changed the subject. 'I see Theros and Marla are here. They look happy.'

Stefano turned to look at his brother and his face became more guarded. 'Yes. It is good to see him not as restless as usual.'

That seemed a strange thing to say. 'So he is normally restless?'

He glanced around to see if anyone had overheard. 'That also is not for this table.'

No-go zones made life even more difficult, but what did she expect when in truth she knew little about his family? 'In that case it's your turn to start a conversation or I'll go back to Bruno.'

He smiled and inclined his head, and the appreciation in his eyes made the heat rise in her own face. She jammed the rising weakness back into its box.

'You look beautiful. And confident. I applaud you.'

Maybe he should go back to mocking her, because compliments played havoc with that very composure. 'Thank you.' She glanced at his father, who watched them both from under fierce white brows, and then back at Stefano. 'It could just be confidence from designer clothes and my own stylist.'

'Perhaps. Perhaps not. We shall see. Tomorrow you must meet the people. Two more critical children have flown in for surgery and I must go to the hospital. As soon as they are stabilised I will be in surgery.'

She wanted to ask more but he went on.

'Unfortunately the new wing—funded by last year's Prince's Cup—is to be opened. Now I cannot be there and my father's advisors have requested you attend with him.' He mocked her. 'Are you free?'

As if she had so much to do. And what if she said no? But just the idea of getting away from the palace made her feel better. She thought of the hospital and her spirits lifted. 'Of course. And could I visit the children as well?'

His eyes shuttered. 'I doubt there will be time.' He shrugged. 'You will be busy with your duties. It is only to be a short visit.'

The flattening of her spirits at his refusal did more to unnerve her than anything the glittering room could achieve. That he could so nonchalantly ignore the fact that to visit the children would give her pleasure seemed so out of character for the man she'd thought he was. It hurt anew.

Someone spoke to him from his left and she sank back in the seat. Sank back, not relaxed back, because foolishly she looked along the row of guests, most of whom glanced her way every few seconds, and knew this wasn't her natural habitat. She'd never get used to it—didn't want to get used to it, because in fact she disliked the grandeur, the formality, the opulence of it all intensely. At this moment she also disliked Stefano intensely, and this was where Stefano belonged. Not her.

When she glanced down to the end of the table a man smiled at her and she realised it was Dr Franco Tollini from the other day. She raised her brows and smiled and let her gaze drift away. Complications were too hard. Her head was above water—just—and she wanted to keep it that way.

She lifted her spoon and tasted the dessert but she didn't want it. Too much food.

How did Stefano keep so fit? He was all lean muscle and power…and perhaps she shouldn't let her thoughts drift there while she was being watched by a hundred eyes. Thankfully, Bruno turned to her and asked a question before she lost herself in remembering just how weak she was when he held her in his arms and how she had arrived at this moment.

Finally the long dinner was over. Nobody circulated, and Kiki had never felt more trapped. They bade good-night to the Crown Prince, who glanced over them both coldly, and then to Kiki's relief they bumped into Marla and Theros. Stefano seemed reluctant to chat, but Kiki made a point of asking Marla how she was.

Before she could answer her husband chimed in with, 'Catwoman. Meow.'

Theros grinned at her and Kiki blushed. Stefano stepped in and took his brother's arm, steered him away. Kiki wasn't sure what had happened.

She looked at Marla, who smiled apologetically. 'I'm well.' She glanced at her husband and lowered her voice. 'He's an absolute darling but he has no social skills.'

It seemed a strange thing to say about a prince, but Marla went on warmly.

'What about you? I thought you were so brave, coming tonight.'

That made her laugh for the first time of the night. 'I didn't have much choice.'

Before she could enlarge on that Stefano returned with a subdued Theros, and Marla whispered, 'Let's catch up tomorrow,' before she caught her husband's hand and led him away.

Something wasn't right, and Kiki frowned after them, but all she could think was that perhaps the younger prince had had too much to drink.

CHAPTER ELEVEN

STEFANO STEERED HER in the other direction. 'Come. It is late and we both have a big day tomorrow.'

His hand was on her arm again, and she didn't know how much more of this hot and cold treatment she could take. Her physical awareness of him beside her only made her more cross. Judging by the way his hand came over hers on his arm, he might have picked up on the vibe that she was about to shake him off.

Stefano meant to leave her at the door and stride away. Because if he didn't there was a risk he would sweep her into his arms and forget everything. But he wasn't that man.

That man who had temporarily ignored the responsibilities of his station.

That one lapse.

Once in his life he had allowed his heart to rule his head and look what had happened. But he could not rid himself of the look of hurt in Kiki's eyes and his own heart ached in a way he had never felt before.

When he let her go to open the doors to her suite Kiki paused as he looked down at her. She stared at him, as if trying to see beneath his skin, and the mo-

ment stilled. The ever-present sounds of the grandmother clock faded and their eyes met and held.

Here they were, and for the first time that evening
Kiki had time to feel like putting her head in her hands
to mourn what they had lost.

How had they found themselves at such loggerheads? How had she ended up here, 'temporarily engaged' to the man she had tragically made a child with?

What series of events, trends of fate and plain bad
luck had mocked them both and put such obstacles in
the way of a woman and a man who were attracted?

'What happened to us, Stefano?' Kiki asked carefully.

Again he let her down. Just compressed his lips and
shuttered his eyes.

'Almost everything. We must try to make the best
of this disastrous situation while I deal with it.'

Her temper flared. 'I am not a "disastrous situation". I am a respected medical practitioner who has
been kidnapped.'

She saw him glance around to check they were alone
before he steered her through into the rooms, closed
the doors and stood with his back to them. 'Please try
and remember what happens when people overhear
things they shouldn't.'

She was sick of worrying about what others thought.
'Why do you think you can shut me out? Why do you
need to control everything? Do you think it actually
changes fate? Life is learning to live with what happens.'

One of them needed to be honest.

She gestured to the room. 'Everything is different
here. *You're* different. Especially now I've seen a small

part of what your lifestyle entails and how it changes you.' She stepped up to him and he watched her with very little expression on his face. She wished he would react at least. 'This control freak is not the man I fell in love with.'

He blinked when she said she'd loved him.

'I need control.'

The words seemed almost torn from him and she stopped, arrested by the expression on his face.

Some nuance captured her attention, cut through her distress, sharpened her instincts. 'Why do you need control?'

He stepped away from the door, walked past her towards the settee she'd slept on earlier.

'How do you find my brother?'

She frowned. That was random. She almost said, *I'd look for Marla*, but she didn't want to talk about Theros. 'He seems nice.' She thought for a moment, and then a suspicion began to form in her mind. Something Marla had said. And Stefano had said Theros was restless. 'Is there something wrong with Theros?'

He sighed. 'You know Mikey's brother—Chris—he woke up. He'll be fine.'

Another random comment. Or was it?

'I'm glad.' She sat down beside him as he stared straight ahead. She waited.

Finally he began to speak. 'There was an accident when we were children. Theros almost drowned in an ocean pool. I managed to resuscitate him but not fast enough. He is a child in a man's body because of me.'

She lowered her voice. It all began to make sense. Guilt. Shame. Loss of control. 'How old were you?'

'Eight.' Still he stared straight ahead, and somehow

she knew he had never spoken about this to anyone. She couldn't understand how he had kept it from being common knowledge.

'Eight years old?' Her stomach dropped and she wanted to take his head in her hands and kiss him for the years of pain and self-flagellation she could now see he had been determined to endure. Had probably been *encouraged* to endure, if she'd read his father right. But she needed to speak carefully if he was ever to have peace. 'And you resuscitated your drowned brother?'

He flexed his shoulders. 'Not quickly enough to prevent damage.'

She said, 'You resuscitated your drowned brother, by yourself, so that he breathed again?'

'Yes.'

She saw him blink. Consider. Finally use his powerful brain to think about himself. He closed his eyes.

She persisted. 'Would you have blamed Mikey if he had done the same?'

His eyes flew open and he sat straighter. 'Of course not.'

She stared at him, but he refused to meet her determined gaze with his own. She lowered her voice but knew he heard every word. 'Then perhaps it is time to forgive yourself.'

Finally he looked at her. 'I fear I am destined to hurt the ones I love.'

She nodded and took his hand, stroked the strong fingers that had held her through memorable nights, felt his pain and rested his fingers against her heart. She understood him so much more.

'And that is the dilemma. Perhaps it's time to let go that which can't be changed. Perhaps consider that happiness doesn't need perfection. Theros seems very happy.'

Stefano looked down at the slender fingers that stroked his and felt the weight of the years grow imperceptibly lighter. Just a little. He thought about his brother. Smiled at the thought. 'He *is* happy when he isn't in trouble with me.' He could acknowledge that if he allowed himself to consider it.

She put his hand back down and moved hers away. 'Then let it go. You can't control everything.'

How did she do that? Suggest gently and steer him towards peace when he'd carried guilt like a blanket made of lead around his shoulders for as long as he could remember?

The grandmother clock began to chime and neither of them spoke as the toll rang out until midnight was proclaimed.

Suddenly Kiki realised the day she had dreaded was here. But, despite his presence, Stefano wasn't with her for that.

She stood up. God, she was so tired. And there was so much to think about. Tonight she was going to try and do the same thing she'd told Stefano to do, because she'd promised herself that when this day came she would let go.

'Please leave. I'm tired and I can't think any more.'

She knew he could sense her withdrawal, so she was surprised when he asked, 'What if I don't want to go?'

She turned her back on him, because she didn't have the reserves to fight. 'I can't help that,' she said. And she walked away.

After an emotional discussion with her pillow Kiki slept fitfully. She was woken by Elise with coffee and croissants and a warning that soon the stylist would arrive to prepare her for a day of official functions.

Every time her mind wandered to the significance of the date she pushed it away.

The really bad news came with her breakfast. She must travel with Crown Prince Paulo in the official convoy.

She sipped her tea pensively. What the heck could she talk about? Or maybe you didn't talk to the Crown Prince—though an hour of disapproving silence would be like water torture.

By the time she was handed into the official car she was feeling more sure than ever that she wasn't cut out for this life. And the royal scrutiny was such that she couldn't tell if he was satisfied with her appearance or not.

'Good morning, Dr Fender.'

'Good morning, Prince Paulo.' She slid into the car past the footman holding the door.

'Did you sleep well?'

Apparently he did talk, and Kiki felt herself relax slightly. She usually did after a big cry. 'It was a different sleep than on the ship.'

'Of course.'

He transferred his attention to the cobbled streets of the castle forecourt as they began their journey and Kiki sighed. That was that, then.

How had she ended up in a royal car with an autocratic old despot?

'If you don't mind me asking, why am I with you today, Prince Paulo?'

The Prince turned back to her. 'Because Stefano is not. Too often he neglects his royal duties for his passion with surgery.' He glanced back out of the window. 'And see where that gets him.'

Kiki's sense of fairness disputed that. Couldn't he see the good Stefano did? The depth of care and kindness his son showed his patients was admirable, even if that kindness didn't extend to *her* at the present time.

Kiki narrowed her eyes on the back of the Prince's head. 'Your son saves lives. Has there not been a physician in your family since the first Mykonides?'

That turned his head. Now he was every inch the monarch. His bristled white brows soared, his eyes narrowed, and in that moment she saw the dark eyes of his son at their most arctic.

'Who are you to presume to tell me my own history?'

But strangely Kiki wasn't afraid or uncomfortable. It was as if a calm voice whispered in her ear to let him bluster.

She should say *she* was the woman pretending to be engaged to his son to help the family's good name. But she didn't need this man as her enemy.

'My apologies, Your Highness.'

But they both knew she wasn't cowed by him, and she wondered if she could detect just a glimpse of approval in his eyes.

In a more conciliatory tone she went on, 'I'm saying his skills as a surgeon are a gift.'

The Prince shrugged and allowed himself to stop pretending he was enraged. 'So they say.' He turned to look out of the window and she heard him mutter, 'He should be more of a prince.'

Kiki turned to her own window as they began their

spiral descent of the mountain. 'He could hardly be more.'

She heard the indrawn breath of the old man but she couldn't regret it. What could he do? Put her out of the car. Well, she was happy with that idea.

'So you champion a man who leaves you pregnant in another country?'

It seemed the old man had rallied.

They faced each other like circling dogs.

'Circumstances were not kind to us.'

'If he has any of me in him he will not be kind to you either.' He glared at her, and then slowly his gaze softened. 'You remind me of someone I knew long ago. She too was fearless.' He laughed without amusement. 'And stubborn. This may not turn out badly yet.'

Kiki had nothing to say to that. Now she felt less sure of herself, and wondered what had possessed her to take him on.

The drive through the olive groves passed silently and Kiki chewed on her lip as she worried what would be asked of her today.

Finally the Prince roused himself. 'I think you should address the women. The patronesses. It is a gynaecological ward we are opening. Thank them for their donations which have helped create the facility and they will be happy.'

Her worst nightmare. What should she say? 'Surely they would prefer your address to mine?'

'Ha! You are a woman.' He turned away. 'I have decided.'

Typical. Like father, like son, she thought with an unhappy sigh.

* * *

As Kiki came to the end of her speech—more of a lecture on meeting health needs as all women deserved—than an informal thank-you, and Prince Paulo seemed happy enough. It had proved less of a trial than she had anticipated. But it had been stressful, and underneath she seethed.

She'd had an epiphany. Here she was for these women, and today of all days Stefano, of course, was not here for *her*.

Kiki estimated there were about fifty well-dressed women, most of them around her age. With women's health so important she'd spoken from the heart, because that way at least she could be happy with what she said.

Until she asked for questions and of course the most difficult one surfaced.

Kiki looked at the woman and something warned her. Despite her designer clothes, her coiffed hair, she had sad, sad eyes, and Kiki knew this woman struggled in a dark place too.

The woman moistened her lips and Kiki leaned forward slightly to hear. 'Are you afraid of miscarrying again?'

Kiki sighed and nodded. 'But as a doctor I remind myself that one miscarriage, or even two miscarriages, does not mean I am more at risk. Yes, it crosses my mind, but I have to trust in the future.'

The woman smiled gently, closed her eyes and nodded. Then she whispered, 'I lost my baby last month.'

Kiki felt her eyes sting and stepped down off the little podium. The others parted to let her through, and the two women embraced. Quietly, but unashamedly, so it carried to everyone in the room, Kiki said, 'My baby would have been due today.'

When they drew apart and smiled mistily at each other Kiki knew she had found a friend, and for the first time she thought perhaps there *were* things she could achieve here if she and Stefano ever worked it out. But at this moment that seemed very unlikely. And the waste made her angrier.

Out of the corner of her eye she saw Prince Paulo gesture to the Mayor to conclude the event, and she mentally prepared herself for the trip back with the Prince.

Bruno directed her to the podium again and then turned to the audience. 'Thank you so much, Dr Fender, for your sincerity. We are all deeply appreciative of your presence today.'

Kiki stepped back, the crowd began to disperse, and she gathered her emotions and control. Just.

Until she saw Stefano arrive and cross to his father. She narrowed her eyes. Typical. *Great timing,* she thought, *when it's too late to support me, but in time to judge me.* Her anger stepped up another notch. Of all days she had had to do this and he didn't even know.

Stefano spoke briefly to his father and she saw Prince Paulo pat his son's shoulder in an unusual gesture of affection. He nodded in her direction, and with his entourage cordially turned away.

Stefano crossed to her side. He seemed bemused. 'My father said you did well. That the women liked you. Congratulations.'

Something snapped inside her. 'Gee, thanks.' She saw he didn't miss the sarcasm and was glad. How dared he? She 'did well'? So magnanimous of him.

Was she supposed to be thrilled at his approval? And what if she hadn't done well? Would he have been here to support her?

His gaze narrowed. 'You're angry? With me?'

'Do you know what I told them?'

He shook his head warily, and she could feel emotion bubbling when she wanted to be ice-cold. Angry tears stung her eyes and she turned away from him, because the words wouldn't come. She wanted them to spill out, hurt him as they hurt her, but she couldn't make her mouth work.

He followed her as she walked blindly along the corridor back towards the entrance, and once he steered her gently when she would have taken a wrong turn.

Stefano didn't know what to do. He could see that Kiki seethed with emotion. Had he pushed her too far by expecting her to do this today? But he'd had to operate. He reminded himself that she hadn't been trained for these occasions as he had, and yet every time he asked something of her she responded magnificently. But at what cost?

She swept out of the hospital and he kept pace, nodding at those he passed as if it was his decision to continue this headlong race she had begun. She stopped at his car and spun to face him. The look in her eyes made him step back.

'Do you know what you asked of me today?'

He didn't want to know right here, right now, because it was not going to be pretty. He opened her door. 'Please, first sit.'

She opened and shut her mouth, and with relief he saw she would do as he asked. When he slid behind the wheel her emotion was like a wall between them and he put up his hand as if to touch it.

'Can I ask you to wait a few more minutes? For the privacy you deserve, not for me. I wish to give you my undivided attention.'

Again she nodded, and he started the car and drove along the road until he came to a lay-by that overlooked the olive groves. He turned the engine off and faced her.

Finally the words spilled like bullets, and he winced. 'Since yesterday morning my life has not been my own.' She drew a breath. 'You have accused me of many things, all of them incorrect, and you have constantly thrown me into situations that were beyond my control.'

He knew it was true. Last night, when he'd finally stopped thinking about himself, he had begun to realise just what he had put her through. And yet still she had been there for him. The more he had considered it the more he'd been able to see how he had failed her.

He deserved every accusation for the mistakes he'd made. For the need he couldn't let go of to maintain control over his life. He wanted to say he was sorry for whatever he'd done, to hold her, comfort her. But the wall between them kept him back.

'Can you tell me what happened in there?'

She jabbed her finger towards his head. 'Can *you* tell me what happens in *there*? In your closely guarded mind that simply refuses to open to me. To trust.' She shook her head with frustration. 'You expect so little from me…'

'No.'

'Yes,' Kiki insisted. 'You would rather think I am a woman who will fail you than a woman who can succeed. I can succeed at anything.' She looked at him sadly. 'And I can succeed without you, Stefano.'

'You have more than proved that.' And then he looked at her. 'Not once have you failed me. It is the other way round.'

'I know. Why is that?'

He had no answer. He watched her shudder against the door as she leaned as far away as possible from him. His hand clenched uselessly, because he couldn't mistake her aversion to any movement towards her on his part.

She stared out through the front windshield. 'Today I was there for those women in a way you have never been for me. And it came home to me just how much you have let me down. The waste when we could have been so good. And, yes, it makes me very angry.'

She pointed an accusing finger at him.

'I gave more than I thought I would have to. Again without your support. In the last few days I have been forced to publicly expose my pain again and again— and you know what? I can't do it any more.'

She was right, and he hastened to reassure her. 'I won't ask it of you.'

She turned towards him and he saw the tears in her eyes, could feel her hurt in his own chest. She finally lifted her chin. As always, her strength astounded him.

He could hear the control she clung to in her voice. 'You've missed the whole point of what I needed from you. Especially today.'

The words captured him. Something in her voice… 'Why today?'

She didn't answer that right away, and he almost missed the significance—again.

'Because it's heartbreaking to lose a baby. And today should have been about life. Not loss.'

'Today?' The full import of what she was saying finally seeped into his consciousness along with the anguish in her voice.

He read the confirmation on Kiki's face and realised he truly did deserve to lose not only his child but this woman. And just when he'd come to understand how much he needed her in his life.

That he didn't ever want to lose her.

Couldn't lose her.

He was so afraid he had finally completely driven her away?

Stefano knew it was time to battle his own demons. To risk everything. Because if he didn't he would lose the best thing that had ever happened to him. He reached for her, and to his shuddering relief this time she didn't pull away.

He slid his finger under her chin and gently turned her to him, so he could cradle her face in his hands, stare into her beautiful eyes. 'I am so sorry.'

He saw the reflection of his own sense of loss for what they'd had between them and ached to ease her pain.

'I am sorry,' he said again, and sighed. Why did he always do and say the wrong thing around this woman? 'What I have done to you is unforgivable.' He reflected over the last twenty-four hours and winced. His voice was bitter at his own stupidity. 'My bullying and my anger at the public scrutiny didn't take into account the cost to you.'

Mental screenshots flickered past like a horror film—the way he had dragged her to the palace, thrust his mother's ring on her finger, installed her in his mother's isolated rooms with barely an explanation. Left her alone to suffer while he'd worried more about others.

To make matters a hundred times worse he had then forced her to attend a ceremonial function that very night—most probably because he had truly expected her to fail. Then he would have been able to tell himself it would never work.

How could she ever love the monster he had become?

He heard the rasp as she drew in her breath. Watched her blink away the tears that glittered on her lashes as she raised her head.

He had lost her.

'I was a monster to you.'

'Yes, you were.' But then she hugged him. 'All that and more.' She shifted her head back a little, so she could focus. 'Why?'

He had nothing left to give her but the truth. 'Because I was afraid.'

'Of me?'

'Of course of you.' He ran his hands through his hair. 'Of losing control of my life.'

She shook her head. He could see she didn't understand that he knew she was already gone. That he knew he'd knew left his run too late.

She said again. 'What are you talking about?'

'Already I have hurt you in so many ways because of my fears. I will take you back to the mainland this afternoon.'

'You still don't get it. I don't want to go. You've been horrible, but I'll survive.'

His hand lifted and one finger stroked her silken cheek. 'Of course you will survive. You are magnificent. Last night you rose and faced them all as if you had been born to stand head and shoulders above the world.' He was so proud of her, and ashamed of being the man who had subjected her to that. 'No thanks to me.'

She went on in the same hard little voice. 'And today I was there for those women in a way you have never been for me. It came home to me just how much you have let me down. And, yes, it makes me very angry.'

Her lips tilted, teased him, and his fear eased a little that she could still smile his way.

'Some things I *can* thank you for. You rescued me from the press at the dock.'

'Pah.' He snapped his fingers. 'That is nothing. I should not have left you. Well before that I was not there when you needed me the most.'

Stefano leant across and gathered her in next to him, felt her slight weight against him and wanted to protect her from the world. It had taken him too long to realise that was his mission.

'You are here now,' she said.

He drew her even closer. 'Is it true that our baby was to have been born today?'

She nodded her head against him. Whispered, 'Yes,' and his heart contracted.

He moistened his lips, prayed she would hear the truth in his words, and finally said what he should have said when he'd first found out that they had made a baby together. 'I am so sorry I was not there with you when our child slipped away from us.'

Her eyes shadowed as she returned to her most painful memory, allowed him to see through a small window to how it had been. She acknowledged his right to see, and he realised that was the greatest gift she had given him yet.

'It was night and I was alone.' Kiki pressed her lips together to stop their wobble.

He closed his eyes and breathed deeply, more ashamed than he had ever been in all his life. 'My poor, poor love. I wish I could have held you and shared your grief. I should have been there. Let me share it now.' He squeezed her to him as he felt the dampness of his own eyes. 'Please.'

Kiki turned her face into his chest and he stroked her hair as she remembered that night in the hospital. Her tiny, solitary room, dark and metallic, the loneliest place in the world when the pains had increased. Within minutes the bleeding had been so great that by the time a nurse arrived and rushed her off to Theatre her life had almost drained away.

She whispered into the silence between them, in a tiny sports car pulled over at the side of the road, on an island in the Mediterranean Sea with her prince beside her.

'I knew that when I woke up from the anaesthetic it would be gone. Not just our baby, but any link to you.'

And then the tears came, great gulping sobs, and the tearing of her heart that she could finally share with Stefano as she was wrapped in the very arms she'd needed so badly that night so many lonely nights ago. And at last, after far too long, the final healing could begin.

Stefano held her tightly against him, gathering her shudders of grief as he gathered her closer, inhaling the scent of her hair, stroking her over and over again with all the tenderness he had in him. He had never felt as close to anyone in his whole life as he did to this woman at this moment. Had never allowed himself to do so in case he lost himself. But now he wanted to be lost.

Lost with her.

Random flashes of his past with Kiki rolled through his mind.

The first time he'd seen her, like a ray of sunshine in his day, radiant, confident, joyous. A heroine on her quest to help mankind.

The first time he'd held her hand and sensed there was something between them that defied description yet was instantly recognisable—something he would never forget despite all the obstacles fate had thrown up against them.

And that magical week when she had opened her home, her arms and her heart just for him. Stefano the man—not Stefano the Prince. Even when he'd been away, recovering, she'd been like a shadow behind him that refused to be forgotten.

He would make it up to her. He would make it all up to her. He just hoped she felt the same about him, because now that he had her back in his arms he didn't think he could let her go. Ever.

Slowly her weeping turned to hiccups and her flood of tears to a trickle. He mopped her face and hugged her again and kissed her damp mouth gently. He wanted to repeat his apology, but he was afraid she would weep all over again.

But Kiki was made of sterner stuff than that. One last sniff, the hijacking of his handkerchief, and she wiped her eyes and blew her nose resolutely. 'I'm sorry.

That was torrential. Thank you for letting me soak your shirt.'

The knot in his stomach loosened. 'You are very welcome.'

She sniffed again and smiled, with a tiny wobble still in evidence. 'Thank you, anyway. I think I needed that.'

He watched the old Kiki emerge and sat back on his side of the car with bemusement and wonder. Relief expanded in his chest as he realised she had already begun to forgive him. Now all he had to do was forgive himself.

Kiki screwed up the handkerchief after one last trumpeting blow. If he still fancied her after this then there was hope for them yet. But that thought and all it involved was terrifying.

'Thank you for listening, and for being here now.' She glanced around at the grove of olives across the road. 'But perhaps we should talk of something else.'

He didn't move.

'Or head back to the castle?'

The way his gaze moved across her face made her cheeks burn. His grey eyes were softer than she'd ever seen them, and he kissed her fingers and brushed her cheek with a gesture. More heat to her red face, and she looked away, embarrassed, suddenly remembering again that this man was a prince and she'd sobbed all over him.

'How was I so fortunate as to find you?' He shook his head in wonder, and as if unable to help himself reached and took her hand.

They both gazed down at the ring he'd insisted she wear. The huge square diamond flashed with reflected light even when there didn't seem to be any beams to catch. It wasn't hers. Not really.

He leaned forward and spoke very slowly and gently. 'So, my question is this. To the world we are already engaged. But the man who demanded this did not deserve you.'

He stroked the ring on her finger and drew it off. To her dismay, she felt bereft. So this was where they faced the truth. She drew in a breath and steadied herself for the end.

He raised her hand to his lips and caressed her knuckles with his mouth. 'May I start again?'

She blinked, not sure what he meant. A crazy, stuttering hope like a flame caught in a cross breeze tossed her into confusion. Start again? With what?

Stefano searched her face, saw her turmoil, and knew it was time to be brave as this woman had been brave. To lose himself for ever and hand her the power to destroy his world if she willed it. He'd never thought he would see this moment.

He drew a deeper breath. 'Do you know that I love you?'

Her eyes flared and she opened her beautiful mouth and closed it. Then finally she said, 'No.'

His tension increased as she shook her head. How to convince her? 'I love you and wish to spend my life with you. To respect and honour you. But only if this is what you want too.'

He saw the fear, understood she had glimpsed what that would mean and seen not all of it was good. None knew more than he that he asked for an enormous commitment. 'Will you share my life with me as my princess. Do me the honour of being my wife? Wear this ring always?'

She looked down at the ring in his hand. Remembered the weight of it. Could she? Rules and etiquette… Royal crises and functions… Their work at the hospital would keep them busy enough. She thought of the women, of the first of many friends she could make, of those she could help.

Then Kiki imagined a life never seeing Stefano again, losing her dream of dark-haired arrogant little boys like Stefano and tiny little girls in pink tulle, and there was no contest. She would not be alone. She would have Stefano the person. Not the heir to the throne. Just her gorgeous man. Stefano.

She leaned across and kissed him softly on the lips. 'I love you. Will always love you. And that's enough for me.'

He slid the ring back on her finger with immense satisfaction. 'Then that is a yes.'

CHAPTER TWELVE

KIKI'S BROTHER NICK and her sister-in-law had arrived to save her. Instead they accepted an invitation to the Prince's Cup.

This year, when the glitterati arrived on the Friday night before the race, a huge stage had been set in the centre of the racetrack with the sea as its background and festooned with a thousand lights.

There was to be a magnificent celebration for the engagement of Prince Stefano Mykonides and his bride-to-be Dr Kristina Karine Fender and the whole island was invited.

Open-sided marquees were provided for the guests to wander through, eat and drink, barbecue steaks, and strange Australian damper, while they listened to music from among the world's greatest musicians—including Kiki's favourite Australian band, flown over at the last minute.

As a gift and gesture of acknowledgment Stefano had set up a huge screen—a never-ending light show depicting the glory of his betrothed's homeland. From harbour to Outback, it showed soaring scenery, a bird's-eye view circumnavigating the whole coastline and across the continent. From Barrier Reef, to Uluru, the screen breathed life into a continent thousands of miles away, so that his people understood that he was a part of that world as his bride was now a part of theirs.

And through it all Kiki and Stefano walked among the people, shaking hands, smiling at each other and at the world. For Kiki, the magnitude of the spectacle had started as a challenge—but then she'd met people she knew: Dr Herore and her husband. Rosa's family plus Sheba and the new baby. Elise had brought her son, and to Kiki's surprise, Jerome. Stefano had whispered that Elise had asked for his thoughts on adoption.

She began to enjoy meeting the hundreds of people they spoke to, all eager to wish them well and ask about the wedding.

Kiki's brother Nick and his very pregnant wife, Tara, shook their heads repeatedly at his little sister's surprise rise to fame.

Wilhelm and Miko from the ship were there, and audaciously, Miko kissed Kiki's hand right in front of her fiancée. Kiki laughed and Stefano growled goodnaturedly about it being his last chance to do so.

But finally, well after midnight, it was over, and Stefano kissed her as soon as they were through the door of their apartments.

'I have been waiting to do this all night.'

It felt so good to have his arms around her and feel the world just disappear.

She sighed happily as she lay back in his arms. 'When I marry you will the wedding be big?'

He laughed ruefully. 'Bigger than you can imagine. It will be a marathon. But at the end we will have each other.'

She leaned across and kissed him softly on the lips. 'Then that's enough for me.'

EPILOGUE

Six months later, in the red silk-lined formal throne room of the palace, arranged in front of the huge gold fireplace and the soaring portraits of the current ruler and his late princess, in the presence of Prince Paulo, Prince Theros and his wife Princess Marla, a dozen dignitaries, and the bride's four siblings and their partners, a civil ceremony of marriage was carried out by His Excellency the Mayor, Bruno Valinari.

Kiki, dressed in coral-coloured Dior, sat straight-backed, her hands folded demurely in her lap, as she listened to the long legal discourse required before Stefano could legally make her his princess.

Finally the moment came, and without hesitation his voice decreed his intention. 'I pledge my life and legally bind myself to Kristina Karine Fender. My Princess.' And then softly, with joy and belief as he met her eyes, 'My Kiki.'

The Mayor said, 'For ever?'

'I do.'

Her eyes stung, but she knew she couldn't cry. She wondered if princesses were allowed to cry. She'd meant to ask Elise.

Then it was her turn, and she listened, minute after

minute, to the legal jargon mixed with advice in the way of royal wedding ceremonies for the last five hundred years on this sovereign island discovered by pirates and ruled by physicians.

The longer the discourse went on the more nervous she became. Her heart began to pound. She would miss her cue, would stumble, would open her mouth and no sound would come out.

Suddenly she became conscious that tomorrow, in the cathedral, it would be a thousand times worse, with millions upon millions of television viewers. What if her words got stuck?

The Mayor's words seemed to join together in her ears, so she couldn't tell where one began and the other ended, and the lump in her throat grew so large she could barely breathe. Her mouth dried and she began to shake as a surge of adrenalin coursed through her body and made her want to stand up and run.

Finally she understood those movies where the bride bolted…

Then gradually, as if directed by a hand other than her own, she lifted her eyes to the portrait of Stefano's mother, which seemed to glow above the gold fireplace. The beautiful woman there smiled down at her.

My love to you both. The words were as clear as if she were sitting beside the mother-in-law she would never meet. *See only one person or the occasion will overwhelm you.*

Finally Kiki felt the knot that had tied her tongue ease and drift away as if it had never been. *Look, speak and smile at one person and you will be in control of the room.* Kiki sighed and closed her eyes.

When she opened them, the room had narrowed to

the one person who mattered the most—the man she loved with all her heart and who would stand beside her anywhere. Joined to Stefano, she would never be afraid again.

All nervousness fled.

Finally the moment came, and she was so very ready. 'I pledge my life to you, Stefano Adolphi Phillipe Augustus Mykonides.' She smiled. 'My Stefano.'

The Mayor said, 'For ever?'

'I do.'

And they were wed.

When they stepped out onto the balcony of the palace the square below it was filled with Stefano's people— her people now—and the roar of the crowd swelled like the roar of a train, building in intensity and promising to carry her into a new life and new experiences.

Stefano turned her to him and she lifted her face for their first kiss as man and wife. As his lips touched hers the roar of the crowd doubled until they broke apart and smiled at their world.

On the morning of their cathedral wedding Stefano and Kiki lay entwined, heavily asleep, smiles on their faces and hands clasped.

Elise didn't want to wake them, so she sent Jerome in.

'Wake up!'

The young boy had a part to play today and he wanted to get started.

Four hours later in the bride's chambers it was time to leave for the cathedral. It was good to have Nick's hand to stop her trembling, but Kiki could see that today it seemed her big brother was the more nervous one.

Nick had told her that yesterday he'd thought she would faint from fright. He had been worried his little sister had chosen far too public a road for herself. But today she was a new woman, and she could see the look of love and awe on his face and it gave her even more confidence.

Her dress had been created by the principal of a famous Parisian couture house, with lace inserts from its high neck to under her bodice, and sewn with a thousand crystals and the fall of a thousand pearls. The train had her six attendants scurrying, and made Nick shake his head in male confusion.

And the veil… A thousand hours of stitching and twenty yards long, it was so thin and insubstantial it was like looking through a cobweb.

Nick scratched his chin. 'I have no idea how they're going to get this dress into the car.'

Kiki shrugged and twitched her sleeve straight. 'Don't worry. They'll have an expert do it. And it's a very long car.' Already she had learnt.

Her brother raised his brows, threw back his head and laughed.

'What?'

She did not want to be fashionably late. She couldn't wait to see Stefano.

Nick glanced at the open door held by a liveried footman and then back at his radiant sister. 'You've changed.'

She lifted her head. 'I've accepted and I'm blessed.'

She would take everything in her stride. One thing at a time. Because at the end of the day would be Stefano.

'I'm Stefano's wife. I'm going to be a very good one. And I'm not going to worry about the small stuff unless I have to.'

They did get the dress into the Rolls Royce. Just. With a hundred perfect folds so that it would leave the car as beautiful as it had gone in.

The streets were lined with flag-waving residents as Kiki and Nick drove slowly towards the cathedral. They passed huge screens set up on walls to televise the wedding to those outside. In the two cars behind, her six attendants followed: her own three sisters, Nick's wife Tara, two small royal flower girls and one little page boy, smiling so hard the scars on his face shone white in the sunlight.

Jerome's was the face of joy projected around the world which encompassed the celebration for the people in the streets. Finally their favourite prince had wed. They loved their new princess, and they were all invited.

Stefano arrived at the cathedral first, and the crowd roared their approval that he had shunned protocol and chosen to arrive first and wait for his commoner wife. He turned, waved, and entered the building.

Theros accompanied him nervously down the long red carpet to the marble altar at the front. Every red velvet seat was taken. Every foot of space was jammed with bodies and cameras.

Theros kept patting his pocket, where the rings sat. He and Marla had eloped to avoid this very spectacle. This was frighteningly huge.

Nervous of crowds, and frightened of the cathedral,

he was diffident about following his brother, but his own bride had been so sure he could do it and he was determined he would.

Stefano recognised his brother's distress. 'Thank you for standing by me, Theros.' He looked around and spoke quietly, so the microphones wouldn't pick it up. 'I wanted to marry here. Mama is here, and I want her to meet my new princess.'

Then the music started, played by the minstrels in the gallery on golden horns: a serenade on the bride's arrival. Stefano felt his heart trip. So much he had asked of a woman not born to this, and to every new challenge she had risen, teaching him so much about true inner strength. So brave was his bride, and he could not wait for her to stand here beside him and before God.

Then she was at the door, on the arm of his new brother-in-law.

She was a vision. An angel in white with her head high. Through the fine mist of her veil her eyes were searching, finding his, and the music swelled. But it was no match for the swelling in his heart as the woman of his dreams walked slowly towards him. Everything else faded. There was just this woman, fearlessly announcing to the world that she would love him for ever.

As he would love her.

* * * * *

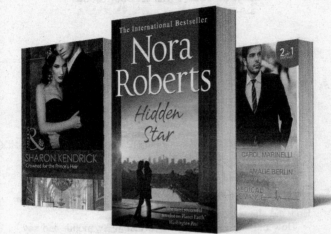

MILLS & BOON®

Congratulations
Carol Marinelli
on your 100th Mills & Boon book!

Read on for an exclusive extract

How did she walk away? Lydia wondered.

How did she go over and kiss that sulky mouth and say goodbye when really she wanted to climb back into bed?

But rather than reveal her thoughts she flicked that internal default switch which had been permanently set to 'polite'.

'Thank you so much for last night.'

'I haven't finished being your tour guide yet.'

He stretched out his arm and held out his hand but Lydia didn't go over. She did not want to let in hope, so she just stood there as Raul spoke.

'It would be remiss of me to let you go home without seeing Venice as it should be seen.'

'Venice?'

'I'm heading there today. Why don't you come with me? Fly home tomorrow instead.'

There was another night between now and then, and Lydia knew that even while he offered her an extension he made it clear there was a cut-off.

Time added on for good behaviour.

And Raul's version of 'good behaviour' was that there would

be no tears or drama as she walked away. Lydia knew that. If she were to accept his offer then she had to remember that.

'I'd like that.' The calm of her voice belied the trembling she felt inside. 'It sounds wonderful.'

'Only if you're sure?' Raul added.

'Of course.'

But how could she be sure of anything now she had set foot in Raul's world?

He made her dizzy.

Disorientated.

Not just her head, but every cell in her body seemed to be spinning as he hauled himself from the bed and unlike Lydia, with her sheet-covered dash to the bathroom, his body was hers to view.

And that blasted default switch was stuck, because Lydia did the right thing and averted her eyes.

Yet he didn't walk past. Instead Raul walked right over to her and stood in front of her.

She could feel the heat—not just from his naked body but her own—and it felt as if her dress might disintegrate.

He put his fingers on her chin, tilted her head so that she met his eyes, and it killed that he did not kiss her, nor drag her back to his bed. Instead he checked again. 'Are you sure?'

'Of course,' Lydia said, and tried to make light of it. 'I never say no to a free trip.'

It was a joke but it put her in an unflattering light. She was about to correct herself, to say that it hadn't come out as she had meant, but then she saw his slight smile and it spelt approval.

A gold-digger he could handle, Lydia realised.

Her emerging feelings for him—perhaps not.

At every turn her world changed, and she fought for a semblance of control. Fought to convince not just Raul but herself that she could handle this.

Don't miss
THE INNOCENT'S SECRET BABY
by Carol Marinelli
OUT NOW

BUY YOUR COPY TODAY
www.millsandboon.co.uk